WAR CRIMINALS

BOOK THREE OF THE BASTARD LEGION

GAVIN G. SMITH

To Phill, Abi, Merrill & Maisie

This edition first published in Great Britain in 2019 by Gollancz

First published in Great Britain in 2018 by Gollancz
an imprint of the Orion Publishing Group Ltd
Carmelite House, 50 Victoria Embankment
London EC4Y 0DZ

An Hachette UK Company

1 3 5 7 9 10 8 6 4 2

Copyright © Gavin G. Smith 2018

A CIP catalogue record for this book
is available from the British Library.

ISBN (Paperback) 978 1 473 21729 4
ISBN (eBook) 978 1 473 21730 0

Typeset by Deltatype Ltd, Birkenhead, Merseyside

Printed in Great Britain by Clays Ltd, Elcograf S.p.A.

www.gavingsmith.com
www.gollancz.co.uk

WAR CRIMINALS

BOOK THREE OF THE BASTARD LEGION

CHAPTER 1

Miska drifted through the humid air. She was rendered almost invisible by the reactive camouflage of both the stealth chute and her own ghillie suit. The air reeked of the wet, perfumed rot that suffused the moon. Epsilon Eridani B was visible in the night sky overhead, the streaked bands of cloud glowing red from the reflected light of the system's main sequence star. Miska could make out the vast mega storms that wrapped themselves around the gas giant. The planet was just a little larger than Jupiter. The moon's position was such that the huge chunks of ice and rock that formed Epsilon Eridani B's rings were clearly visible in the night sky. Miska suspected that if she knew where to look then Waterloo Station would just be another star, albeit a large and fast-moving one.

Triple S's big mistake had been the deforestation of the rear echelon areas of New Ephesus that they controlled. The rest of the conflict was being fought under the cover of the thick foliage of the monstrous, skyscraper-sized trees that covered much of the surface of the jungle moon. Miska was learning that Stirling

1

Security Solutions' biggest weakness was their over-confidence. No, not over-confidence, arrogance. The military contractors had assumed that the mech base was too far behind their lines to be at risk. Miska intended to prove them wrong.

She dropped through the muggy night air towards one of the mech cradles. The thirty-foot-tall, roughly humanoid armoured fighting vehicle was upright and surrounded by a scaffolding structure. Both the cradle and the mech itself had been raised on hydraulics from the bed of the heavy-duty low loader truck parked directly behind the mech. There were eight of the low loaders and mech cradles, in two rows of four, but only seven of the Martian Military Industries Medusa-class mechs. Miska suspected that the missing eighth was in the concrete hangar at the end of the two rows, presumably undergoing maintenance or being refitted. That complicated things slightly.

Beyond the hangar were two large Harpy-class heavy lift drop shuttles. The armoured behemoths, their huge engines mounted in two domed nacelles, were designed to carry mechs. The two rows of mechs were facing each other. It was sloppy. They should have been facing the perimeter. Not that the base was unprotected. Vehicle-mounted multi-role missile launchers and trailer-mounted point defence systems spotted the perimeter at regular intervals.

Miska checked the Internal Visual Display superimposed over her vision. Her IVD overlaid the position of each of the thirty-six men of her Sneaky Bastards platoon. The perimeter wasn't fenced but it was mined. Raff, her CIA handler, had provided a schematic of the mines. There was a further complication in that motion detectors covered the area of the mine-field. There was only one real way to defeat motion detectors and that was to move very, very slowly. To that end the Sneaky

Bastard platoon was formed of burglars, sneak thieves and other criminals who had demonstrated nerves of steel and a great deal of patience. All of them picked from the six-thousand-strong penal legion she had formed out of the inmates on board the prison barge the *Hangman's Daughter*.

The Sneaky Bastards had spent hours negotiating the minefield under the cover of their reactive camouflage ghillie suits. The whole thing had taken so long that all of them wore adult diapers. The minefield's schematics would appear in the Sneaky Bastards' own IVDs, or the head-up displays on their helmets' goggles, and they were running a simple algorithm that told them if they were moving fast enough to risk discovery by the motion detectors. The algorithm erred heavily on the side of caution. Even so it must have been nerve-wracking as hell, which was borne out by the biometric data she was receiving from her soldiers. She guessed those that weren't showing an elevated heartbeat and respiration were the clinical psychopaths in the platoon.

Sneaking in through the minefield wasn't something that Miska had the patience for. Lack of patience was one of the reasons she'd never wanted to be a sniper. That and the diapers. She had jumped from one of the Pegasus assault shuttles some distance away and glided silently into the base.

The mech's armoured head and the top of the cradle were less than twenty feet below her now. She could see a guard standing on the highest level next to the Medusa's head. He wore full combat armour, an inertial suit with hard plate over the top and a high-threat helmet, but his carbine was slung. Even from above Miska could tell by his body language that he was bored and oblivious. Miska drew the SIG Sauer GP-992 from the drop holster on her thigh. The power of her gauss pistol was dialled down so the rounds would be silent. That meant they didn't have the velocity to go through the guard's armour, which in turn meant that she only had the tiny target of the guard's unprotected face and currently she was looking at the top of his very protected head. She had to time this just right.

'Hey,' she said quietly. Her feet were level with his head. He looked up. If he saw anything at all it would only be disturbances in the air as the reactive camouflage struggled to keep up with its surroundings. Miska fired the SIG twice, the crosshairs from the gauss pistol's smartlink overlaying the guard's face in her IVD. Two red holes blossomed on his face as her boots touched the composite surface of the cradle. The guard started to topple. She reached for the guard to lower him quietly to the catwalk. Miska's wiry build was a mass of compact muscle but, even boosted, at the end of the day she was small. Some might even say petite. The guard's dead weight shouldn't have been a problem but just as she reached for him a sudden gust of wind caught her chute. It pulled her over the mech catwalk's railings. She managed to keep a hold of the dead guard with one hand, her gauss pistol still in the other. The body was half hung over the railing as her chute blew around in the humid wind.

'Shit,' she hissed.

'Den?' a voice asked from below.

'Fuck my life,' Miska added.

'You okay?'

Miska heard the first voice confer with another. She knew that the moment the wind died she would swing back into the mech and probably pull the body over and they would be blown. She touched the SIG to the drop holster riding her thigh. The holster's smart material sucked the pistol in and she reached into her webbing for the chemical reaction wand. She touched

4

the wand to the stealth chute and turned it into carbon dust. Immediately she started to drop, swinging towards the mech cradle's superstructure. She let go of the guard's body before she pulled it off the cradle and reached for the superstructure. Her fingertips scrabbled at carbon composite, her ghillie suit getting in the way. She was falling. She managed to get a tenuous grip on one of the spars with her right hand. To her ears it sounded like she'd kicked a drum kit down a flight of stairs. Miska found herself face to face with another guard. She knew he couldn't see her but he would have heard the noise and she suspected that her reactive camouflage would make the night air look like a pair of curtains blowing in the wind. An expression of surprise crossed the guard's face as he tried to make sense of what was going on. He was, nevertheless, bringing his Kopis gauss carbine up. Miska knew that standard operating procedure for dealing with someone concealed with reactive camouflage was to fill the air with flechettes fired from the carbine's 30mm under-barrel grenade launcher. That would hurt.

Miska was holding on to the cradle's superstructure with her right hand. The drop holster was on her right thigh. Even with boosted reflexes she would be too slow but you had to try, didn't you? She started to move. The barrel of the grenade launcher looked huge. She saw the guard's mouth open to cry for help, or subvocalise a comms message. A crossbow bolt appeared in the guard's cheek. He spat blood through newly broken teeth and collapsed to the ground, far too noisily for Miska's tastes. She didn't need to check her IVD to know who had fired the shot. Hogg, Vernon, consecutive life sentences for conspiracy to commit kidnapping, aggravated vandalism, mayhem and assassination. Hogg had been a member of the New Weather Underground terrorist organisation and was an occasional penal legion conscientious objector. She might have enslaved them all and implanted nano-explosives in their heads, but combat was only for those who wanted it. Though they did get shore leave and spending money for combat time. On this occasion he had agreed to active service because it allowed him to 'kill corporate scumbags'. A member of the Sneaky Bastards' first squad, he was the only legionnaire armed with a printed compound crossbow.

Miska heard boots clattering on the walkway below as a third guard ran up the ramp to investigate the noise. The only sound the suppressed, subsonic round fired from a slugthrower made was the metal-on-metal of the rifle's internal mechanism. The noise came from the ground close to the mech cradle. Miska heard a grunt, followed by a clatter, as the third guard hit the deck. Again, making too much noise.

'Shh,' Miska whispered to herself as she climbed onto the catwalk. She checked to see who'd fired. According to her IVD Kaneda, Atsushi was stood on the cleared ground a little way from the mech cradle, covering it with his weapon. Even with the low light amplification of her artificial eyes Miska couldn't see Kaneda because the young *bōsōzoku* gang-member-turned-sniper was concealed by his own reactive camouflage ghillie suit. Hogg was a little way from Kaneda, by the corner of the neighbouring mech cradle. Hogg and Kaneda had their own problems, however. Two spider sentry drones, basically gauss squad automatic weapons with thermal imaging lenses and six legs, had skittered round the mech. The drones were searching for the two Sneaky Bastards. A third joined them. This one, however, made for the mech cradle and started climbing.

'Fuck, shit!' Miska muttered. She could hear the spider making its way slowly up the cradle towards her. Then it went quiet. She checked Kaneda and Hogg's position on her IVD. She could see the two spiders were slowly edging towards them. *Their audio sensors must be pretty impressive,* she decided. Kaneda's biometrics suggested that the sniper was completely calm. Hogg's showed a different story. Miska assumed that the spider drone on the cradle with her had stopped moving, that it was listening.

Miska loosened her M187 Tyler Optics laser carbine on its sling before bringing it to her shoulder. She tapped her toe on the catwalk and heard the metal-on-metal skittering noise as the spider sentry drone ran towards her.

'Hangman-One-Actual to all Bastard call signs, I am compromised, going hot,' she said over the hitherto silent comms net. The spider drone appeared at the top of the ramp. The reactive ghillie suit hid her from its lenses, momentarily. The heat-dampening properties of her inertial armour hid her from its thermal imaging, momentarily. She squeezed the trigger. The mech cradle was bathed in hot red light. Air particles exploded between the barrel of the carbine and the drone as she fired a three-round burst of harsh light. Superheated composites exploded and the drone collapsed to the ground.

Immediately Miska was forced to duck down as the other two spider drones that had been hunting for Kaneda and Hogg started suppressing her position with long bursts from their gauss SAWs. Electromagnetically powered rounds tore up the cradle all around her. The firing lessened and Miska risked a look. One of the drones was receiving hit after hit fired by the still-hidden Kaneda, but the subsonic rounds were struggling to penetrate its armour. Both the spider drones on the ground were attempting to acquire Kaneda. Miska fired a three-round burst at the other drone, and it exploded. The remaining one turned its SAW towards her. A crossbow bolt lodged in the spider's SAW's feed mechanism and then exploded. The wreckage of the drone slumped to the ground.

'Sneaky-One-Seven to Hangman-One-Actual, I'm coming up,' Kaneda told her over comms.

'Understood,' Miska answered. In her IVD she was aware of the Sneaky Bastards platoon breaking down into squads and then fire teams. She assumed that Triple S's troops in the hangar and the shuttles had been thrown into an uproar but she couldn't see or hear anything yet.

Miska moved quickly to the Medusa-class mech's hermetically sealed external hatch. She flicked the ghillie suit over her head, knelt down and attached a lock burner to the hatch, feeling the camouflaged ghost of Kaneda pass her as she did so. Now she could hear gunfire, the hypersonic scream of gauss weapons, an explosion that sounded like a 30mm fragmentation grenade going off. She readied her carbine before turning her back to the hatch, feeling like she always did in situations like this: that everything was taking too long. The lock burner finished its work and the mech's external hatch sprang open. There was a disturbance in the air as Hogg joined her by the open hatch, watching her back while she entered the mech.

Miska moved into the war machine's cramped cockpit, situated in its heavily armoured chest area. She sat on the ergonomically designed chair, felt it shifting into a comfortable configuration, noting, not for the first time, how much more comfortable Martian Military Industries fighting vehicles were compared to any others she had experienced. Miska closed her eyes.

Now we get to see if Raff's access codes work, she thought. Because if they didn't, this operation was going to go badly wrong.

She used one of the codes that Raff had given her and tranced into the mech's net.

Miska appeared in the virtual representation of the mech as a small, spiky, angry-looking cartoon version of herself. Her image was ghostly and transparent, the visual manifestation of the stealth programs she was running. Only Miska could see her icon, in theory anyway. She was carrying a club and wearing a pre-Final Human Conflict 'steel pot' helmet with the words 'Make war not peace!' written on it.

The mech's icon looked like a giant faceless samurai wearing armour constructed of ultra-modern stealth material.

For the purposes of viewing the mech base's communications network, the Medusa's icon's chest cavity was transparent. The mech base's net architecture was all smooth, stealthy, black ultratech lines and oddly subdued neon. It was doubtless designed by some overpaid military net architects to look professional and intimidating. It just looked like they were trying too hard. The base's net was an isolated system. There was only virtual wasteland around the stealth samurai figures representing the mechs, the data fortress that was the hangar, and the oddly hi-tech anachronisms of the cannons and ship's boats that represented the base's defensive weapon systems and Harpy heavy drop shuttles.

Subdued beams of flashing neon light represented the, presumably panicked, comms messages being relayed back and forth as it became apparent to the Triple S personnel that the base was being attacked. The isolated net's intrusion countermeasures were on full alert, a dome of black fire rising up around the network – but it didn't matter. Miska was already in and nobody seemed to be paying her transparent cartoon icon the slightest bit of interest. She pulled one of her fuzzy worms out of the pocket of her battle dress trousers. The worm was transparent, just like her, and she placed it on the virtual radio that represented the mech's comms systems.

'I'll just put this here,' she whispered to herself. Immediately the worm, containing Raff's access codes and a high-spec virus designed to suborn weapon systems, started to burrow. Cartoon Miska smiled and tranced out.

She was out of the seat and heading for the hatch as soon as her eyes opened, and she almost tripped over the nearly invisible Hogg on trance overwatch. Outside, everything was going smoothly if you ignored the on-going fire fight and the fact that she'd hoped to suborn the base's systems before Triple S had even known the Bastards were there. She made her way quickly up to the top of the mech cradle.

Kaneda was kneeling down, his ghillie suit thrown over his head so he could better see what he was doing. His accursed heavy barrel M-19 designated marksman's rifle was leaning against the catwalk's railing. Miska noted that the integral suppressor had been pulled back and replaced with a gauss push, designed to electromagnetically help the slugthrower's rounds into the hypersonic.

Kaneda had a case open on the floor in front of him and was rapidly assembling a Bofors rail sniper rifle. The sniper was a handsome, fresh-faced, wiry Japanese man in his early twenties. His air of youth had dissipated somewhat since the death of his abusive boss, the Yakuza lieutenant Teramoto Shigeru, at Kaneda's hands. Teramoto's death had apparently been the result of a 'friendly fire' incident. Now, as Miska watched Kaneda screw the long barrel into the sniper rifle and attach a gyroscopic stabiliser to the mounting rail, she caught glimpses of the *irezumi* tattoos that denoted the sniper's graduation from *bōsōzoku* gang member to fully-fledged member of the Yakuza. It appeared he was going up in the world.

'You should be able to do that under the ghillie suit, Kaneda,' Miska told him as she hunched down by the mech's head and took stock of the situation.

'I can,' Kaneda told her as he finished assembling the rifle, 'but this is quicker.' Kaneda pulled the ghillie suit back over his head and disappeared, except for a few disturbances in the air. He dragged the extended sniper's sleeve over the long rifle and that too disappeared. Miska was only aware of him taking position on the cradle because of her boosted hearing.

She pulled her own ghillie suit over her head and moved around the mech's head to survey the situation. The Sneaky Bastards first squad, of which Kaneda was a member, had split into three four-man fire teams and had taken up covering positions. Second and third squad were cautiously advancing between the two columns of mechs, still all but invisible, towards the concrete bunker and the drop shuttles, respectively. The biggest threat was the trailer-mounted point defence lasers. They were designed to shoot incoming artillery, mortar shells and missiles out of the air but they could be repurposed for an anti-personnel role. The Bastards were relying on stealth and having the mechs between themselves and the point defence lasers to keep them safe. So far the Sneaky Bastards had mostly been engaging the spider sentry drones, leaving small smoking piles of wreckage in their wake. There were, however, more than a few dead guards hanging from the mech cradles and lying on the ground.

Miska's audio dampeners filtered the otherwise deafening

roar of the Bofors rail sniper rifle firing. She assumed the electromagnetically propelled, hypersonic, half-inch titanium penetrator had just blown a sizeable hole in something, or someone. Despite the noise there was no muzzle flash, and the near-invisible Kaneda would still be difficult to spot.

Miska peeked sideways into the net again.

Now let's see if the command codes work. She turned to look at one of the point defence lasers. It was spinning, stopping, and then spinning in a different direction. It had been repurposed. It was searching for targets.

'Hangman-One-Actual to all Sneaky Bastards call signs,' Miska subvocalised over their own comms net. 'They've repurposed the point defence lasers, everyone hold their positions.' *C'mon,* she added silently. Things were going to get interesting very quickly if the virus with Raff's command codes didn't work.

'Heavy-One-Actual to Hangman-One-Actual, what about me?' Mass asked over a private link. Despite being the commander of the Heavy Bastards, Miska's virtually trained, currently hypothetical mech platoon, the Mafia button man had come in with the Sneaky Bastards. While parachuting in Miska had checked his biometrics. It hadn't looked like Mass had enjoyed the experience.

'Very quietly, Mass, I want you to make your way up to the third level of the closest cradle to you, the one I'm on.'

'Understood,' Mass said and then over the command net: 'Heavy-One-Actual on the move.'

'Sneaky-One-Seven to all Sneaky call signs,' Kaneda said over the comms net, 'we've got movement from the maintenance hangar.'

Miska glanced that way and saw a squad of Triple S guards making their way cautiously towards the mechs.

'Let them close,' Miska subvocalised over comms and then admonished herself for not using the correct protocol. She glanced at the net feed again. Suddenly all the mech base's systems and those of the vehicles present opened themselves to her. The expert system contained in the virus took over. It had a simple command: attack any personnel that weren't members of the Bastard Legion until Miska told it to stop.

Three of the point defence lasers were firing. Where the Triple S squad that had emerged from the bunker had stood there was now just red steam, the dirt streaked with glass.

'Hangman-One-Actual to all Bastard call signs. We've got control of the base's systems,' Miska announced over the command net. 'Heavy-One-Actual, the Medusa is all yours.' She heard movement on the cradle below her.

'Understood,' Mass replied.

Miska checked her IVD to see who was closest to her.

'Hangman-One-Actual to Pegasus-One and Two, we're ready for you.'

'Pegasus-One to all Bastard call signs, myself and Pegasus-Two are inbound,' replied McWilliams, an OG, or original gangster from the Hard Luck Commancheros prison gang, who was piloting the first of the two Pegasi assault shuttles. 'Please be advised, if you haven't switched off the air defences this will be a short flight.'

Then the ground shook. It had been a while but Miska instantly knew what it was. It was the thing that infantry feared the most.

'Hurry the fuck up, Mass!' Miska snapped, forgetting comms discipline for the second time. At least it had been over a private comms line.

Backlit by the hangar's lights a huge shadow was thrown across the ground.

'I mean it, Mass!'

The Mafia button man still didn't answer.

'Hangman-One-Actual to all Sneaky call signs, continue to hold your position,' Miska told them

The Medusa-class mech stepped out of the hangar. She guessed its comms had been taken offline due to whatever work they had been doing on it. That would explain why the virus hadn't suborned it.

With a thought, Miska dialled down the power on her M187 and prepared to 'lase' the mech. She could then send the targeting info to the inbound Pegasi, who could feed it to their missiles' guidance systems. The world went red again as the base's point defence system targeted the mech, to little effect other than scoring up its paintwork. The mech raised the 30mm chain-fed railgun it carried like an oversized carbine and fired a short burst at one of the offending point defence systems. The electromagnetically-driven cannon rounds tore the laser to pieces. The 200mm mass driver on its back unfolded and fired, and another point defence laser ceased to exist. The show of firepower was, as ever, awe inspiring and terrifying if you were that way inclined, Miska supposed. She might not have felt the fear but there was a sense of mounting concern, and she quite wanted Mass to get his Medusa up and running.

Another point defence system was sent tumbling into the jungle as 30mm rounds ripped into it. The enemy Medusa was moving towards the two columns of mechs. Miska knew that advanced sensor systems would be searching for her Sneaky Bastards. Suddenly all the umbilicals connecting Mass's Medusa to the cradle exploded away from the mech. It stepped out from the cradle, the 30mm railgun already firing. Mass put round after round into the other mech, shooting continuously as he moved far enough away from the cradle for the back-mounted plasma cannon to swing into place. Both weapons firing, Mass's mech advanced on the Triple S Medusa. Plasma fire ate through the other war machine's thick armour. Doubtless the Triple S pilot was competent enough but they hadn't expected the sheer ferocity of Mass's attack.

Mass concentrated all of his fire on the torso. It was the most heavily armoured area because it was where the pilot sat. Mass was firing plasma bolt after plasma bolt into the chest and concentrating the railgun fire in the same place. The Triple S mech came to a halt. Material that shouldn't burn flamed as the huge armoured humanoid figure became a pyre. It was quite beautiful, Miska decided, as she became aware of the base's forces broadcasting their surrender on all frequencies. She ordered the expert system embedded in the virus to stop killing.

CHAPTER 2

There was running. The Sneaky Bastards' first squad remained with the mechs. Second squad raced past the still-burning mech for the hangar. Third squad were running for the two Harpy-class heavy lift drop shuttles. Miska could hear the Harpies powering up as she walked between the mechs, making for the hangar.

'Hangman-One-Actual to Heavy-One-Actual, I want those Harpies covered by your mech,' Miska told Mass over the comms link, using her command override to cut through all the chatter.

'The ... uh ... what, boss?' Mass asked.

'The heavy drop shuttles, the mech carriers,' Miska told him. She could feel the heat of the burning mech as she closed with it. There was something primeval about the huge, humanoid-shaped war machine on fire. She felt the ground shake as Mass passed her in his own Medusa, railgun and plasma cannon levelled at the two heavy shuttles.

She sent a command to the virus to have the SAM

emplacements missile-lock the two Harpies. The virus responded immediately but Miska still wasn't happy. She knew she should have a hacker in the net. The expert systems were too vulnerable but she needed to be out here. There were a number of good choices for combat hacking, legionnaires who'd all but fulfilled the role when they had been career criminals. The problem was they presented the biggest threat to her failsafes, to the tiny nano-explosives she'd replaced the bomb collars with. The deactivation codes for the nanobombs were well protected but nothing was completely safe and these were people whose job it had been to break through computer security. Miska could have done it herself but she was supposed to be command now, something she had never wanted.

'Under the articles of conflict agreed upon by—' a husky-voiced woman started over the same comms link the Triple S commander had used to surrender.

'One of those Harpies leaves the ground by even so much as an inch and I'll blow you out of the air. Leave the engines cycling. If you're not out of that shuttle and face-down in the dirt in thirty seconds flat, I'll blow you into the air.' She cut the comms link. Her dampeners kicked in as the Bastards' two Pegasus assault shuttles screamed overhead, manoeuvring engines burning as they bled off speed. The two vaguely insectile, armoured pieces of airborne military tech, bristling with weapons, circled over the base. The first Pegasus touched down while the other covered it from the air. The loading ramp was already down, her Bastards sprinting from the shuttle. Time was key here. They had maybe twenty minutes before Triple S's quick reaction force reached their position. If they had fast-movers, atmosphere fighters, then they'd be there all the faster but that was what the multi-role missile launchers were for.

The Bastards had been able to take the mech base because it was far enough behind the New Sun's forces' lines that they were overconfident with their security protocols. Triple S were far too reliant on their automated systems as well. Such things were only as good as their weakest link, and said link was almost always found in the pinkware, a person. It appeared that her handler, Raff, had found the weakest link and exploited it. They would not have been able to pull this off without his help.

Thank Christ for the weird no-orbit rules, Miska thought. She could understand why the articles of conflict for this particular little mercenary proxy war stipulated no space combat. Ships were expensive and she wouldn't have wanted to risk the *Hangman's Daughter* in a space battle. The huge prison barge had been built as a troop carrier close to a hundred-and-fifty years ago. She might have been well armoured, designed to take a pounding getting troops into place, but she was no warship. The no-orbit rule insisted on by the New Sun megacorporation, the aggressors in this particular undeclared war, and Stirling Security Solutions' employer, was just one more thing that didn't make any sense. It did, however, mean a lack of satellite surveillance, and that meant that bases didn't have geosynchronous orbital coverage that could hit the Bastards with particle beam weapons, or drop a Quick Reaction Force on their head as fast as terminal velocity in the moon's .75G would carry them. It was, however, just another part of this war that didn't make sense.

The first Pegasus clawed its way back into the humid air. Even with her inertial armour's coolant system running hard Miska was covered in sweat. The air was so humid it was like inhaling liquid.

The passengers from the Pegasus were sprinting towards the

hangar, the low loaders and the heavy drop shuttles. Miska was gratified to see that the Harpy crews had emerged and were lying face-down in the dirt, covered by one of third squad's four-man fire teams.

The second shuttle came down to land but stayed on the ground, leaving the first Pegasus to provide aerial cover. Again, Bastards sprinted down the already-lowered ramp. Everyone knew their job. Their orders were simple. Steal absolutely everything except the missile launchers – they were going to leave those as a booby trap.

Seven large Maoris in battle dress inertial armour, carrying snubby personal defence weapons, came sprinting towards her from the second assault shuttle. They were members of the *Whānau*, or family. The *Whānau* had originally come from disparate mine gangs working the subterranean rock of Lalande 2. They had banded together for self-protection during the war with Them. Since the war they had become one of the biggest organised crime syndicates within the Lalande system, with a ferocious reputation for violence, born of their warrior heritage – so they claimed. Many of their ancestors had piloted mechs during the war. Even today a lot of them had worked in civilian mech piloting jobs like cargo handling, construction and mining. A few had even seen military service as mech pilots, and all of them, apparently, played on virtual mech simulations. Not surprisingly, when the opportunity to put together a mech platoon had arisen, the *Whānau* had all volunteered. The nine best had been picked for the armoured platoon commanded by Mass. The Mafia button man, or hitman, had become obsessed with heavy armour ever since he'd worn a Wraith combat exo-skeleton during the battle for Faigroe Station.

Miska startled the Maoris by flicking the ghillie suit over her head, practically appearing in mid-air. Suddenly seven snubby Martian Military Industries PDWs were pointing at her.

'Easy, boys. Where're the rest of you?' She was directing her question to the six-foot-four, powerfully built leader of the *Whānau* on the *Hangman's Daughter*. His details scrolled down her IVD. Kohere, Hemi, thirty-five years for distribution of narcotics but with a long history of violence, and suspected of being behind at least five murders. He had long, black, braided hair. The spiral and fern-like designs of chiselled out and dyed *tā moko* markings made his face look as though it had been carved out of hard wood. The two lower canine tusk implants protruding from his bottom lip made his face look brutal, like a monster from a fantasy viz. Miska had asked Mass about the tusks. He had told her that it was in tribute to his favourite viz, and that the fantasy in question had somehow been of import to the Maori people back on Earth at the time of its making.

Hemi stopped running, leaving the rest of his crew to sprint towards the mechs.

'There's a scout mech in each of the drop shuttles, they've gone to grab them,' he told her, his voice a deep, impassive growl. 'You want them with us, boss-lady?'

It made sense, most mech platoons went out with one or two Satyr scout mechs for recon and forward observation.

'Yeah, as soon as they're powered up I want you running them full-tilt, tell Mass,' Miska said. Hemi just nodded and resumed sprinting towards the mechs.

'Hey, boss,' Hemi shouted. Miska glanced behind her. He was jogging backwards. 'Did you want that lenshead with us?'

It took Miska a moment to work out what Hemi was talking about.

'Oh shit!' she groaned and changed direction making for the second shuttle, Pegasus 2.

Miska was pretty sure that Raff had been a journalist before he had been recruited and trained by the CIA. The Epsilon Eridani conflict had given him a chance to brush up on old skills. It also worked as an excuse to keep an unusually close eye on Operation Lee Marvin, the deniable black operation that had seen Miska steal the *Hangman's Daughter* and form the penal mercenary Bastard Legion. Pretend to be a journalist, however, and get treated like one. Of African-American descent, Raff had the kind of open, handsome face that made people want to tell him things. He had what Miska thought of as a gym body. He was in good shape but it was all show, she doubted there was any real endurance there. He was also bound and gagged and lying on the dirty floor of the Pegasus assault shuttle. Judging by the boot marks on his designer outdoor clothing, some of her Bastards had been using him as footrest. Miska would have laughed except for the attractive Hispanic still sat on one of the benches glowering at her. Torricone pointed at Raff and opened his mouth to say something. Fortunately Raff had his back to the other man.

'Shut the fuck up, hippy!' Miska snapped. Torricone looked as though he'd been slapped. Miska gestured for the ex-car thief, and her self-appointed conscience, to get out of the assault shuttle.

She walked him away from Pegasus 2.

'That—' Torricone started. Miska held up her hand. She knew Raff's ears would have been augmented to filter and amplify sound. Being able to listen in on people's conversations from afar was as good for a journalist as it was for a spy. His artificial eyes were almost certainly lenses as well. That's how war correspondents had got the name lensheads.

'Comms,' Miska subvocalised, opening up a private, secure comms link to Torricone as she turned to face him. His shaved head had a crown of thorns tattooed around it. He had an inked tear on his cheek, in memoriam for the gang member he'd killed in self-defence. It had been that killing that had resulted in him being sent to the ultra-max prison barge. She knew he had other tattoos, mostly religious iconography. His battle dress inertial armour covered a body that Miska knew was all hard, tight street muscle, little fat, and no pumped steroid muscles. *Not that you ever look at him naked in his pod, right?* There was anger in his brown eyes. There always seemed to be these days.

'Who is that guy?' Torricone demanded over the comms link. Respecting the chain of command had never really been his thing. 'You met with him on the *May '68*, the free port in the Tau Ceti system.'

Miska was getting an IVD headache. The various feeds – biometrics, gun- and helm-cams, lens feeds from the shuttles, the net feed, the tactical overlay, the comms icons – may have been minimised in her IVD but the sheer amount of information that was incoming was nearly overwhelming, and Torricone wasn't helping. Not for the first time Miska decided that she far preferred operating to command.

She watched the mechs stepping out from their surrounding platforms as she tried to decide what to tell Torricone. The platforms folded down onto the backs of the low loaders as their engines rumbled to life and they pulled away from the mechs, making for the drop shuttles.

'You're surprised I know war correspondents?' Miska asked.

'Bullshit, I watched you, it was more than that,' Torricone snapped, his eyes narrowing suspiciously.

Is he jealous? Miska wondered. She'd had a brief, ill-advised drunken fling with Raff when she'd found out about her dad's murder. Raff had carried a bit of a torch for her. She wondered just how much of that had been apparent when she'd met him on the *May '68*.

'Is he a spook?'

No, he's not jealous, Miska decided, absently wondering if that bothered her. *He is, however, very perceptive.* She also suspected that Raff would either kill Torricone, or ask her to kill him, if he thought the ex-car thief suspected anything.

'No, he's not a spook. Not everything is a conspiracy,' Miska told him, wondering how apparent her exasperation was when she subvocalised.

'No, but your plan to steal a prison barge and turn it into a mercenary penal legion was,' Torricone pointed out. The ground started to shake as the seven remaining Medusa-class mechs sprinted for the treeline. Moments later the two thin Satyr-class scout mechs, each of them half the size of the Medusas, sprinted by at a much higher speed, causing other Bastards busily going about their business to scatter out of their path.

'Well yes,' Miska admitted, 'that was a conspiracy, but a conspiracy of one. Two if you count my dead dad.' She was extremely conscious of the countdown in her IVD, the inbound assault shuttles full of Triple S (elite) and the lancing pain in her head. 'Look, I don't have time for any of this. If you're not going to carry a gun then just fuck off out of my sight, will you?'

Torricone narrowed his eyes. She wasn't sure if he was hurt or angry, and she certainly wasn't sure why she would care one way or another.

'Any wounded?' he asked. Their last mission had been a difficult one. A small-scale black op that had turned bad. They'd encountered some kind of ancient alien artefact. Raff, who'd set up the job, had called it a 'Cheat'.

'Not on our side,' Miska told him.

Since then Torricone had point blank refused to carry a gun. He'd augmented the rudimentary combat medic training he'd received from Miska's dad with lessons from the doctor. Miska hoped that medicine was all the doctor was training Torricone in. The imprisoned serial killer had some truly unpleasant predilections.

'That's a first for you, isn't it?' It was an unusually spiteful thing for Torricone to say. Now Miska narrowed her eyes. 'Sorry, that wasn't . . . Permission to see to any enemy wounded.'

'Go on, fuck off,' she told him. For a moment Torricone looked as though he was about to say something else but thought better of it. He turned and trotted towards the bunker.

What was that about? she wondered as she turned and headed back to the assault shuttle. She was more mystified than hurt, and conscious of what a waste of time it had been.

Miska drew her fighting knife and stood over Raff. She knelt down, cut his hands and legs free and then removed the tape covering his mouth none too gently.

'What the fuck!' he demanded as Miska sheathed her knife. 'Seriously, what the fuck?' he subvocalised, more reasonably, over a secure private comms link.

'Stop whining, lenshead, you didn't get beat on,' Miska said and then subvocalised: 'I didn't order it and I didn't know they were going to do it.'

Raff sat up, leaning against the folded-up bench seats.

'Colonel Corbin, I am a duly licensed war correspondent. The articles of conflict state that all operations will have an embedded—'

'Parasite packaging our deaths as entertainment for the core systems?' Miska asked, still keeping an eye on the countdown and checking on Mass's platoon's progress as they sprinted through the dark jungle. Through the feed from the lead scout mech she could see that the skyscraper-tall trees' thick inter-linked canopy was letting in only the odd stray beam of red light reflecting the gas giant overhead.

'Seriously though,' Raff subvocalised over the comms link, 'I need your co-operation so I can get a better idea of the scope and capabilities of your outfit.'

'My contract says you have to accompany us, it's less clear on the degree of co-operation that entails,' Miska said out loud. 'They're criminals, Raff, what do you expect? You're the enemy,' she added over the comms link. 'And never mind evaluating us, you're still on probation for walking us into that clusterfuck on Barney Prime.'

'I never met a criminal who didn't want to be famous,' Raff said and then subvocalised: 'The codes work?'

'Yeah,' Miska subvocalised back. 'You must have drilled into them deep.'

'One-time deal,' Raff admitted over the comms link. 'We're not going to get away with something like this again.'

We? Miska wondered.

'Stay out of our way,' Miska told him out loud. 'Get off the shuttle if you want but you get left behind if you're not back here when we're done, and I have a feeling Triple S are going to be pissed when they get here.' She walked down the ramp and back out into the jungle night and the hive of activity. She

25

was pleased. Everyone was doing what they were supposed to without having to be told. *If you want stuff stolen, criminals are the right people to ask*, she decided. The low loaders were driving up into their modular airlocked slots in the Harpies' holds. There was a steady line of cargo lifters and movers from the hangar to the heavy shuttles.

'Sneaky-Two-Actual to Hangman-One-Actual, I think we've got something you want to see,' the sergeant from the Sneaky Bastards' second squad told her over a direct comms link. Miska checked his position. He was in the hangar.

'On my way,' she told him, trotting towards the large poured-concrete building. The mech that Mass had put out of action was still burning, its flickering light illuminating the Bastards' efforts.

'Well now,' Miska said, grinning.

'Thought you'd like it,' the smiling sergeant said. Miska was pleased to see that, despite the find, the four-man fire team were still alert, looking outwards rather than inwards. Her legionnaires stole spares, ammunition, tools and anything else that wasn't nailed down. It was like watching locusts at work. She checked the countdown. Captured Triple S guards and support staff knelt, facing the wall, under the watchful eyes of another fire team from second squad.

'Oh, I like them,' Miska said, still grinning as she looked over the two Martian Military Industries Cyclops war droids. About the same size as a combat exoskeleton, the Cyclops were state of the art combat drones, capable of bipedal and quadrupedal movement. They had modular weapons hardpoints and a limited AI that allowed a pretty sophisticated level of autonomy. Matte grey with no right angles, their smooth lines helped lower their sensor signature and it looked like these ones came equipped with reactive camouflage. Both of them carried the same weapons load-out: a turret-mounted 20mm Dory/light multi-role missile battery combination. They also had ball-mounted point defence lasers at their shoulders and hips. In short, they were a fast and formidable weapon system. 'Good work,' she told the fire team.

Miska patched her comms into Pegasus 1. The assault shuttle was still circling the base. She piggybacked on the shuttle's more powerful transmitter to reach the *Hangman's Daughter* docked high above them at Waterloo Station.

'Hangman-One-Actual to Hangman-Actual,' she said. 'We've found you another body.'

She sent an order through the virus's expert system to automate one of the war droids. It burst into life, startling the fire team, but they made way for it as it ran across the hangar, leaping a cargo lifter exo-skeleton, and made for the assault shuttle. The second droid was reserved.

'Acknowledged,' the gruff voice replied after a few moments of lag. She couldn't be sure but she didn't think her dad was particularly enthused by her plan. Still, studying the Cyclops she couldn't help but feel that, despite the name, the head looked more feline than anything else. She pointed at the remaining war droid.

'I think I'll call it Kitty,' she decided.

'To LSM's face?' the sergeant asked. There was some laughter from the other three members of the fire team. Miska just smiled.

Miska had promoted her dad to legion sergeant major, effectively making him the highest-ranking non-commissioned officer. That said, even those that had been promoted to officer

27

knew that LSM Corbin was still the de-facto second in command of the Bastard Legion. He might have been an electronic ghost created from the uploaded personality of her father, existing only as an icon in the virtual construct they used to train the Bastard Legion, but he was still both feared and respected among the convict legionnaires.

Then the second Cyclops burst into life as well. Immediately another two limbs unfolded like switchblades from the mech's existing forelimbs. These new limbs ended in two slender chainsaw blades. Miska couldn't be sure but she suspected that the teeth on the chainsaws were synthetic diamonds fused to the titanium, just like her fighting knife. She liked that. It felt like synchronicity – after all, her dad had given her the knife when she'd made it through boot camp.

'What in the good goddamn!' her father demanded, his voice emanating from the war droid. Miska was delighted that some Martian designer had seen the need to equip the Cyclops with such a good quality voice synthesiser. 'I feel like a praying mantis carrying a pair of switchblades.'

'Hey Kitty,' Miska said brightly. 'Walk with me.'

'What did you just call me?'

Miska just nodded to the second squad fire team and made her way out of the hangar, now almost bare.

'Harpy-One to all Bastard call signs, we're fully loaded and buttoned up,' the pilot of the one of the captured Harpies said. They'd broadcast it on a frequency that, while not exactly open, wasn't going to take too much effort to break for people listening in. It was exactly the sort of mistake that criminals masquerading as military amateurs would make.

'Harpy-Two to all Bastard call signs, the same,' the pilot of the other Harpy said over the same frequency. Both the Harpies' flight crews had been picked from male members of the Sirius-based pirate fleet, the Scarlet Sisterhood. In fact Harpy 1's pilot's lover had fired on Miska while she'd been piloting one of the Pegasi during her last visit to Maw City, the pirate base in the Dog's Teeth asteroid belt.

'Hangman-One-Actual to Harpy-One and Two, okay, full burn for Camp Badajoz, we'll be right behind you,' Miska told them over the same frequency. It wasn't the sort of mistake an operator of her calibre made, but then you played the cards you were dealt.

She heard the roar of the Harpies' huge engines as hot winds buffeted her and anything that hadn't already been stolen or wasn't nailed down turned into so much flying debris. Miska knelt, shielding her face with her arm, and tried not to inhale too much dirt as the Harpies clawed their way into the sky like ancient rockets. They looked so ungainly, so heavy. Miska still struggled with the concept that they could fly. As the dust clouds swept past her, Miska realised that the Cyclops had taken a protective posture over her.

'Dad!' she muttered, a little embarrassed.

'Force of habit,' he told her. They continued walking towards Pegasus , even as it took off. Over by the bunker the burning mech was tottering. It fell over with a deafening thump, making the ground shake and sending yet more dirt into the sky. Miska and her dad's new Cyclops body just kept walking.

'No casualties,' her dad said over a direct comms link. 'Objective achieved. That's leadership.'

The Sneaky Bastards were folding back towards the landing area as Pegasus 1 came into land.

'No casualties is cool, not sure about the no action part.'

'Well you're a colonel now,' her dad pointed out. She wasn't sure but she suspected he was making fun of her. Working out of Waterloo Station and the mercenary contracts that entailed meant that the Bastard Legion had to have some semblance of a military hierarchy. She was in charge of six thousand possible combatants. She'd stopped short of letting Uncle Vido and her dad call her a general. It was a catch-22 situation, though. Waterloo Station might have required her to give herself a high rank, but the other mercenary officers didn't feel that she'd earned it. They were right, but she'd met enough officers to know that many of them didn't deserve to be in charge of an orgy in a licensed brothel.

'I thought you said that my plan was reckless,' Miska said as they reached the Pegasus. She was checking the position of all her people in her IVD. The Sneaky Bastards were all on board. She saw a figure sprinting towards the assault shuttle from the hangar. She checked his ident. He was one of the Hard Luck Comancheros who'd been helping strip down all the engineering equipment. He was supposed to have been on one of the Harpies.

'Move it, you maggot, or you get left!' It seemed that her dad had spotted the straggler as well.

Everyone's going to be so pleased he can join us on missions now. The thought brought another smile to Miska's face.

'I said your plan was just the audacious side of reckless,' he told her as the Comanchero sprinted past them and into the shuttle's cargo hold.

'Pegasus-Two to all Pegasus and Harpy call signs,' Joseph Perez, the pilot of the other assault shuttle, still hovering over-head and providing cover, said over secure comms. 'We've got two incoming fast-movers from the east, and two, no, three assault shuttles inbound from the same direction.'

Perez was another Hard Luck Commanchero. Miska and her dad had tried to break up the gangs initially, but their current thinking was to let each of the gangs use their specialities where it complemented military objectives. It might result in ghettoisation but frankly as long as Miska could stop them killing each other she was reasonably happy. She climbed into the assault shuttle's crowded cargo hold and knelt down. Somehow they managed to make room for the Cyclops to perch on its thin legs above the heads of the Bastards in the hold. The shuttle lurched into the air.

'What about phase two of the plan?' Miska asked over direct comms to her dad as she linked into the Pegasus's external lens feed. The assault shuttle dipped its nose and burned hard. Pegasus 2 followed as they flew into the jungle, weaving in and out of the huge trees under the thick, almost solid jungle canopy. Fire illuminated the mech base behind them as the vehicle-mounted launchers fired missile after missile into the air. Some of the missiles exploded almost immediately as the incoming aircrafts' point defence systems shot them out of the sky.

'Phase two is the other way around,' her dad told her.

CHAPTER 3

Miska had a map of the surrounding area overlaying her vision. Her IVD headache, what she was thinking of as her 'command headache', was worsening. She was trying to resist the urge to feed herself painkillers from her internal medical systems. She would only do that if she felt that the headache was compromising her concentration. Being in command felt like she was doing very little, physically anyway, yet somehow it was still tiring.

The Pegasus's utilitarian cargo bay was full. People and gear were packed in tightly, swaying as the craft weaved its way through the trees. The thick leaves of the huge trees' upper branches were so efficient at capturing sunlight that there was little foliage other than the multi-coloured patchwork of parasitical mosses underneath the dense canopy. That left more than enough room for assault shuttles, and even larger craft, to fly in between the massive trees.

Miska patched into the shuttle's sensor systems. They weren't running active sensors like radar and lidar – both were only of so much use in the jungle, but they could give away the shuttles' position. Passive sensors weren't showing any pursuit. She checked the net feed from the mech base but that had gone down. Triple S's own combat hackers would have made taking back net control a priority, particularly with their own missiles shooting at them. She checked on the Heavy Bastards' position. The mech platoon was less than a mile from the Turquoise River. Pegasus 1 and 2 were closing with them rapidly. She checked the Harpies. The heavy lift drop shuttles were still en route to Camp Badajoz. So far everything was going to plan.

Miska checked the external lens feed. Thin beams of reflected red light were making it through the jungle canopy. She could make out the Medusas' running lights as the shuttles overflew them. The larger mechs were making no attempt at concealment. She had to check the transponders on both the Satyrs to find the smaller, faster, stealthier scout mechs.

'Just look at all that ass,' her dad said, his voice emanating from the Cyclops. The war droid was drawing a few looks from some of the legionnaires on board. Ass was old USMC slang for armour. Back before the so-called Final Human Conflict, four hundred years before, it had meant tanks. While tanks still existed, there were just some places they couldn't go.

'Feeling more confident?' she subvocalised over a private link to the Cyclops but her dad didn't answer. Miska looked around at the legionnaires in the belly of the Pegasus with her. She wasn't sure when it had happened but, despite the horror stories that had come back from the Faigroe Station and Barnard's Prime jobs, many of them had stopped giving her the surly, insolent looks. Some of them were actively embracing the life of a mercenary in a penal legion, and the limited rewards that offered.

She wasn't sure when or how the change had come about. It

could have been the influence of the senior criminals, like the Mafia *consigliere* Uncle Vido, supporting her and taking officer's ranks in the legion. Or perhaps they had just decided that it was more interesting than being held in suspended animation. Plus they got to steal things and shoot at other people. Every so often Miska reflected that she was perhaps a bad influence on all these thieves and murderers. That said, she had the most enthusiastic, and therefore the best paid, legionnaires with her on this job. Even so, she still caught the odd resentful glance out of the corner of her eye. Like the one Torricone was giving her right now. She thought about opening up a direct comms link and demanding to know what his problem was this time. *You've got far more important things to concentrate on*, she chided herself. Torricone had been a pain in the ass since they had returned from their disastrous mission to Barney's Prime. That, however, wasn't what bothered Miska. What bothered her was why she cared, one way or another. Sure, he was pretty, but so what? *Not as pretty as the Ultra.*

'Pegasus-One to all call signs, I'm cutting the canopy now.' McWilliams's voice over the comms net shook Miska out of her somewhat guilty reverie.

Fucking concentrate! she told herself. From the external lens feed she watched as the assault shuttle fired its point defence lasers up at the canopy, using them as energy-inefficient cutting torches, further reddening the jungle darkness. Miska's stomach lurched as McWilliams jinked the assault shuttle, sluggish from all the weight it was carrying, out of the way of the falling greenery. She heard someone further forward in the cargo bay retch, an angry voice admonishing them.

Miska enlarged the feed from the spotter drone in her IVD. It took off from its cradle and flew through the smouldering hole that had been cut in the foliage. Above the jungle canopy, the distant star of Epsilon Eridani was just starting to brighten the horizon, though the gas giant, Epsilon Eridani B, remained large in the sky above them. The drone stayed low over the canopy, its reactive camouflage rendering it all but invisible. The drone's-eye view of the jungle top made it look like a vast green plain, broken only by distant hills and beyond them the imaginatively named Northern Mountains. Without satellite coverage and with the sensor range limited above and below the canopy, a spotter drone was their best bet of finding incoming aircraft.

'Pegasus-One to all call signs, two fast-movers inbound from the east,' McWilliams intoned over comms. Miska could just about make out the fast-movers in the spotter drone's long distance lens feed. They were burning hard, skimming over the tree tops at what looked like mere inches above the canopy. They had the smooth lines of sleek violence that Miska had come to associate with Martian Military Industries weapon systems. She was pretty sure they were Siren multi-role atmosphere fighters.

'Pegasus-Two to all call signs,' Perez added over comms. 'Passives are picking up heat behind us. I'd guess one, possibly more assault shuttles coming in fast and angry.'

That made sense. Leave someone to secure the base and then come after them.

'Shit,' Miska muttered out loud. Some of the nearby legionnaires turned to look at her, as did the head of the war droid that the copy of her dad's electronic spirit was wearing.

'Going to get expensive,' her dad said. Miska nodded. It was inevitable. They had attacked Triple S (conventional), a subsidiary that, as their name implied, handled the conventional part of the war on Ephesus. The QRF was most likely Triple S (elite), recruited from special forces veterans. Miska and her

Bastards had encountered them before. Triple S had their faults but their elite subsidiary had their shit together.

'Hangman-One-Actual to Pegasus-One, missile mine the fast-movers,' Miska said over the comms link.

'How many?' McWilliams asked.

'All of them,' she told him.

It was odd hearing a war droid groan.

'Hangman-One-Actual to Pegasus-Two, you're cleared weapons hot as well.'

There was a dry chuckle from Perez over the comms link. There was no two ways about it, missile combat was expensive, and thanks to the efficiency of modern point defence systems, often ineffective. That said, it was devastating when it worked and they had stolen much more material than the mission was going to cost.

Assuming we don't get shot out of the sky.

The Pegasi assault shuttles were designed to survive putting troops down in hot LZs, and then providing a degree of close air support if need be. But they weren't dogfighters, particularly when they were this heavily laden.

'All call signs abort, abort, abort. I need the Harpies to come in and pick up the mechs,' Miska said over an open frequency, hoping that Triple S would think that the Bastards had sloppy comms discipline.

And if they buy poor comms, hopefully they'll take the bait and won't think to look for the drone. She was starting to think her dad was right. This plan had too many moving parts. She was feeling trapped in the press of bodies. Helpless. She didn't like the way that her life was in the hands of the shuttle pilots now.

She felt the shuttle shift around her. Checked the lens feed.

Watched as Pegasus 1 manoeuvred under the hole the shuttle had cut through the canopy, the missile batteries, on their stubby wings, angling upwards. Both of the Pegasi would be trying to put trees between themselves and the inbound Triple S shuttles making their way towards them. Miska knew that the co-pilot in Pegasus 2 would be programming the missiles to use the trees as cover to close with the enemy shuttles. Ambush tactics were pretty much the only advantage they had.

'Hard scans,' McWilliams said over the comms, and she could hear the tension in his voice. 'They're flooding the jungle with lidar and radar.' It was a bold move on behalf of the Triple S pilots. Good news for them if they found the Bastards' shuttles, but it also gave their position away.

'We've got weapons lock,' Perez said.

'Let them close,' McWilliams told him over the comms link.

'I know how to do my job, old man,' Perez answered, but there was humour in his voice. The two Hard Luck Comancheros were old friends.

Miska checked the position of the Harpies. They had practically reversed their course and were burning hard for an artificial clearing by the banks of the Turquoise River to rendezvous with Mass's Heavy Bastards.

Then she checked the spotter drone. The two Sirens were almost overhead. Between the mechs and the Harpies they were about to enter a target-rich environment. Again Miska felt the shuttle shift slightly as McWilliams adjusted their position. Then it shook as McWilliams fired every single missile in the racks up through the hole in the canopy. Even through the assault shuttle's armour the sound of the rocket engines igniting was loud enough to trigger Miska's audio dampeners. She saw some of the other legionnaires put their hands over their ears.

She checked the feed from the spotter drone. She barely saw the missiles. The feed was full of red flashes and explosions powerful enough to shake the drone as the Sirens' ball-mounted point defence lasers took out missile after missile, but the aircraft had been too close to the canopy. One of the sirens was hit, thrown into a brief flat spin, the pilot managing to eject before the wreckage hit the canopy. Then something hit the spotter drone and the feed went down. Thoughts of yet more expenditure were replaced by worries about the second Siren.

Miska watched as Pegasus 2 waited until the last moment to fire all of its missiles at the two, now visible, enemy assault shuttles, hoping to expensively overwhelm their point defence systems. Harsh red light, fire and force filled the jungle under the canopy as Pegasus 1 and Pegasus 2 turned tail, their own point defence systems shooting down incoming missiles from enemy shuttles and launching counter measures as they fled through the jungle. Miska's stomach lurched as she felt successive shockwaves from nearby detonating warheads buffet the Pegasus. She heard the brief thunder of rail cannon rounds pitting the assault shuttle's armour and then they were out from under the canopy, over the riverside in the dawn's rising sun. The two huge Harpies were below them. The mechs milled around the heavy lift drop shuttles.

McWilliams brought Pegasus 1 up over the canopy by the riverside to check what had become of the second Siren. Miska wasn't sure what they were going to do if it had survived. The Pegasi couldn't take on a fighter with just rail cannons and point defence lasers. Fortunately for them, they could see more smoke rising from the jungle canopy, another parachute drifting down towards the treetops.

'What happened to the second shuttle?' McWilliams asked over comms. Miska could hear the urgency in his voice.

'The first one I took out, second one got tagged pretty hard, last I saw he turned tail and ran,' Perez answered. 'Will provide overwatch until Harpy-One and Two are ready to get their fat asses in the air.'

'Understood,' McWilliams said as he circled Pegasus 1 over the clearing.

'Dad,' Miska subvocalised over a direct link. The Cyclops's head shifted at a funny angle, rotating a lens so it was looking at her. It was a bit weird but better than him looking at her with one of his ass lenses mounted on the point defence systems on the war droid's hip joints. 'I'm bored.'

'What're you complaining about?' he replied. 'Parachute insertion, you killed a guy and shot up a spider drone. That's more than most colonels get a chance to do.'

Pegasus 1 dropped back through the hole cut in the thick canopy of trees and into the morning mist underneath. Even though the correct access codes for the day had been transmitted, the missile and laser batteries affixed to the huge trees, and in the various strongpoints around the hillside base, still tracked the shuttle as it came down towards one of the hilltop landing pads. Above and behind them, one of the Scarlet Sisterhood pilots was skilfully easing a lumbering Harpy through the same hole. Miska suspected the heavy drop shuttle was losing paint-work to the trees.

The rear cargo bay was coming down even as the landing struts touched the earth. Cool air conditioning was replaced by flying dust and grit kicked up by the shuttle, and, of course, the omnipresent humidity. Moments later Miska lost most of her visibility in a huge cloud of dust as the Harpy landed lower down the terraced hill on one of the reinforced landing pads. Miska pushed her goggles down over her eyes and made her way through the dust. She could feel the legionnaires pushing past her. They all knew their jobs. The stolen gear had to be thoroughly checked for back doors into their systems and other nasty surprises. Then it had to be catalogued, stored and other shit that Miska knew she was supposed to care about.

Another huge cloud kicked up as the second Harpy came down. Miska was vaguely aware of Pegasus 2 moving sideways in the air above them, a shadow in the dust as it came in to land. She spat, checked her IVD and made her way towards the platoon commander of the Sneaky Bastards. The Cyclops was a large metal insect moving through the dust cloud next to her. She tugged on the Sneaky Bastards' commander's ghillie suit, hanging down his back. He turned to face her.

'Tell your boys good work. Gear cleaned, upload their after-action reports and then you're stood down for twenty-four hours. I'll put some money in your commissary accounts above and beyond your combat pay. Have some drinks and then get some sleep.'

The platoon commander just nodded – he looked bone weary – and then turned and headed for the platoon's hooch.

'I don't get it,' Raff's voice said behind her. Miska didn't turn to look at him. Instead she was concentrating on the Offensive Bastards waiting in the landing pad's ready area, most of them leaning on their packs. The Offensive Bastards were her rifle company, the conventional force that was forming the back-bone of her fledgling legion. The legion she didn't have enough volunteers to bring to full strength, or enough resources to fully equip. Currently they were one full fighting company, the

Offensive Bastards; their recon platoon, the Sneaky Bastards; an under-strength combat exoskeleton squad, the Armoured Bastards; and their two brand-new mech platoons, the Heavy Bastards. In addition they had a significant amount of support staff, which included the ground crews for the two Pegasi and the recently up-armoured prison shuttle. With only two Armoured Personnel Carriers, they were, however, significantly under-equipped vehicle-wise and of course, all of this had on-going costs, most of which was being met by stealing the stuff they captured. The Ephesus conflict had been a boon in some ways, particularly financially, but it had also been something of a baptism of fire. In the two months they'd been in-country some of their leadership choices were working out, other not so much.

'Beat it, lenshead.' The Cyclops's voice modulator really was excellent quality. It picked out her dad's gruffness so clearly.

'It's all right, LSM,' Miska told her dad. 'Go and speak to the company commander, make sure they're ready to go.' The Cyclops glanced suspiciously at Raff. Not even her dad knew that the entire Bastard Legion was a deniable CIA black op. He just thought Raff was another annoying war correspondent.

'Yes, boss,' her dad said and then made his way towards the Offensive Bastards' company commander.

Miska turned to Raff. At least he wasn't looking at her with puppy-dog eyes. She hoped she'd beaten that out of him.

'You're going for FOB Trafalgar, right?' he asked. 'You think you've found it. That's why you were running the mechs, bringing them through the jungle.'

Trafalgar was a concealed Triple S forward operating base on the wrong side of the Turquoise River, somewhere in the held territory of the Ephesus Colonial Administration, the legions' current employers. MACE, or Military Active Command Ephesus, knew roughly where FOB Trafalgar was, but had yet to pinpoint it. The Sneaky Bastards were about to be tasked to look for it again. She wanted to join them but knew that sort of thing wasn't really her job any more.

'McWilliams, Perez, how're you guys doing?' Miska subvocalised over comms. She was watching Raff but not answering him. She could see the Colonial Administration's ground crews hooking up heavy gauge power cables to the Pegasi. Cargo exoskeletons were loading new missiles into the empty racks.

'We're good, boss,' Perez told her.

'Need time to recharge the point defence lasers and re-arm and then we're good to go,' McWilliams added.

'All right, stretch your legs and get some coffee,' she told the pilots.

'So why is your rifle company ready to ship out?' Raff asked. Miska just looked at him.

'You're not going after Trafalgar, are you?' he said slowly. They weren't, but the feint's secondary objective had been to try and get a reaction from FOB Trafalgar. Currently stealthed spotter drones were going through the area where MACE suspected the enemy FOB was located, using heat sensors to try and find it.

Miska still didn't say anything. Instead she just pointed at the newly christened Harpy 1. Raff turned to look at the huge heavy lift drop shuttle. The modular cargo bays were open. They could see the low loaders but the mech cradles were empty.

'Where are your mechs?' Raff asked.

Miska just smiled.

*

Nyukuti was waiting for her. The big Aborigine wore full combat armour, inertial armour battle dress with hard plates over the top, and a half-helmet, rather than the full-threat helmet that most of the Offensive Bastards preferred. He almost looked like a marine, except for the circuit tattoos on the nearly-black skin of his face. His eyes, implants, were unnaturally dark as well, presumably to enhance the intimidation factor. Before he'd been imprisoned on the *Hangman's Daughter* he'd been a stand-over man in the Lalande system, meaning he'd 'stood over' criminals as he tortured them into handing over their ill-gotten gains. A criminal dangerous enough to steal from other criminals, he was feared and respected as much as he was disliked onboard the *Hangman's Daughter*.

'Hey, Nyukuti, you want something?' Miska asked. She liked Nyukuti. He was weird but capable, and appeared enthusiastically loyal for someone with a nanobomb implanted in his head. On the other hand, Miska knew she couldn't trust any of them. Still, she was glad to see he'd recovered from the quite serious wounds that he had received on Faigroe Station at the hands of Triple S contractors.

Nyukuti was staring over her head. He towered over her, but then everyone did. She turned to see what he was looking at. One of the *Whānau* was walking by. She guessed he had been the member of the Heavy Bastards who hadn't got a mech because Mass had taken out the eighth Medusa. The Maori mech-jockey was glaring at Nyukuti, his face made all the more fierce because of his *tā moko* facial tattoos. Miska knew that in his stand-over days Nyukuti had targeted the *Whānau* often enough to gain their enmity. It was the kind of prison yard bullshit she didn't have time for.

'Nye!' she snapped. 'Down here!' He broke eye contact and looked down at her, smiling.

'I punched the platoon commander,' he told her. Miska stared up at him. She felt her 'command headache' worsen and decided that she could go off people quickly.

'Why did you do that?' she asked dangerously.

'He's a wanker,' he told her. 'I didn't kill him, though.'

Thank God for small mercies, she thought.

'You're his platoon sergeant,' Miska managed through gritted teeth.

'Not any more,' he said. He was grinning now.

'Let me guess, you were busted down to private again?' Miska asked. Nyukuti nodded. 'Major Cofino?' Miska asked. Nyukuti nodded again. 'And what were the good Major's orders?'

'CP.' They both said it at the same time. Close Protection. It seemed she now had a bodyguard. She struggled to think of anything more pointless. She wondered if her dad had a hand in this. Being an NCO had never sat well with Nyukuti but the sad thing was he had been good at it, perhaps because of his own military service before he had become a stand-over man. Though he had been dishonourably discharged.

'Stop being a pain in the ass, or I'll blow your head up, understand me?' Miska told him. He looked confused. He never seemed prepared to acknowledge he had a bomb implanted in his head. 'Fuck's sake, get your gear, and get in the shuttle, but I tell you you're going to be bored. I never get to have any fun any more.'

Nyukuti just smiled, grabbed his daypack and his MMI Xiphos gauss squad automatic weapon. Miska noticed that he'd added a 30mm grenade launcher to the under-barrel mounting rail. He shouldered the pack, slung the SAW and headed for the shuttle.

'Hangman-Actual to Hangman-One-Actual.'

Oh good timing, Miska thought.

'Uncle V, just the REMF I wanted to speak to,' Miska sub-vocalised back over the comms link. REMF stood for rear echelon motherfucker. It was a little unfair, after all Vido had thrown down with the rest of them on Barney's Prime, and she herself was supposed to be a full bird colonel, a REMF rank if ever there was one. Vido Cofino had been the *consigliere*, or adviser, to one of the most powerful Mafia families on Barnard's Prime before he had been sentenced to the *Hangman's Daughter* after being prosecuted under the RICO statutes. Now, recently promoted to major, he was putting his skills to good use as the Legion's intelligence officer, civilian liaison/negotiator and, if she was honest, her acting XO or executive officer. Her father may have been the Legion's second in command in all but name, but he was too involved in the training, and now, with his new war droid body, he would presumably be more hands-on operationally as well. That left Vido in the rear, handling things, always happy to help, as he built his own empire.

'You're pissed about Nyukuti?' Vido said. There was a bit of lag as the signal reached her from the *Hangman's Daughter* docked at Waterloo Station.

'And with you.'

'Want me to take him off combat duty?'

'No, that's just one less competent gun down here. I'll find something for him to do.'

'Best lesson I ever learned about leadership, you don't have to make the right decision, you just have to make a decision,' he told her. Miska spent a moment trying to decide if there was a hidden message in his words.

'What do you want, V?'

'Triple S and New Sun have lodged a complaint with Salik about the attack, citing theft and claiming that you executed prisoners ... again.'

'I didn't ...' Miska started. 'Theft? Haven't they ever heard of the spoils of war?' She knew it was part of the game but she found the politicking exhausting. Uncle Vido, however, seemed to love it. 'Fine, anything else?'

'Yeesss.' He sounded uncharacteristically hesitant.

'I don't have the time, V.' The Offensive Bastards were already making their way onto the two shuttles.

'The network security officer for the mech base we just attacked ...' Vido started. Miska already had a sinking feeling. '... Was found brain-dead in a sense booth. That's going to land on you.'

Miska looked around. She found Raff leaning against a poured concrete wall. She guessed he wanted to get on the shuttle at the same time as her to reduce his chances of ending up as footstool again.

'I want to know what happened,' she told Vido.

'You sure?' he asked.

'I didn't do it, V.' *At least not knowingly.*

'Okay, I'll get onto it. What do I tell Triple S? I'm guessing they're not getting their gear back any time soon.'

Miska started heading back towards Pegasus 1.

That if they liked that, they're going to love this, she thought.

'Tell them to go and fuck themselves,' Miska said, smiling.

CHAPTER 4

This time Miska had bagged herself a bench seat in the back of Pegasus 1, Nyukuti next to her. The Cyclops was balancing on four of its six limbs above the heads of the Offensive Bastards.

I'm spending entirely too much time in the back of assault shuttles, she decided. It wasn't just the boredom factor. The two Pegasi had seen a lot of action in the two months they'd been in-country. They weren't just doing the work of assault shuttles, they were also working as gunships and transports. McWilliams had been speaking to her about maintenance. They were robust, well-engineered vehicles, but everything was subject to wear and tear. These were the kinds of things that she had to worry about now. She preferred worrying about getting shot.

She checked Pegasus 1's external lens feed. Both shuttles were hovering above the Turquoise River, so named for its iridescent algae. Leaning trees, which seemed to defy gravity, formed an arched tunnel of greenery and multi-coloured moss over the deep river. The shuttles were holding back, hopefully beyond the sensor network that surrounded Port Turquoise. Waiting.

She couldn't tell if the Offensive Bastards were nervous or eager but then reading people had never been her thing. Nearly all of the legionnaires had seen combat in the two months since they'd arrived in-country. They had even lost people, but frankly the fighting had been pretty well-mannered so far. Most of the mercenaries in this conflict knew each other and socialised on Waterloo Station, and their parent organisations didn't want to pay out too much in death duties and lost equipment. What tended to happen was that shots were fired, to keep face, and then surrender was negotiated based on who was most likely to win any ensuing battle. It led to a lot of arguments among mercenary commanders but the casualties were kept low. This was one of the reasons that the 'violence of action' approach that the Legion was taking was working so well. That and she was treating it like a war rather than a game. But she was careful to observe the niceties of the articles of conflict, whatever her detractors might say.

Two flashing icons appeared in her IVD. She sighed. It looked like she was going to be another tourist in this battle. Her head throbbed as she opened the lens feed from the two Satyr-class scout mechs.

'You okay?' Torricone asked over a direct link. She hadn't even realised that she'd closed her eyes and been rubbing the bridge of her nose with her thumb and forefinger. Miska looked around. She also hadn't realised that Torricone was still on the shuttle. She found him sat on the deck close to the bulkhead that separated the cargo bay from the steps that led to the cockpit. He was watching her. She couldn't read his expression. There was just a slight moment of irritation as she wondered if he was stalking her.

'Fine!' she snapped and too late realised she'd said it aloud.

A number of legionnaires glanced her way. She saw Torricone frown. She was aware of one of the Cyclops's lenses swivelling around to look at her. She decided to concentrate on the lens feeds from the Satyrs. This battle was shaping up to be just like watching a viz, again.

Both the lenses had been extended on telescoping arms from the top of the scout mechs. They only just broke the surface of the river, iridescent water lapping at them, occasionally obscuring the view. Port Turquoise was the regional capital for the area. Half its waterfront was given over to a small-scale commercial port. Cranes, cargo-handling mechs and exoskeletons served a small fleet of flat-bottomed riverine drone craft that ran luxuries and construction and arboculture supplies for the vertical farms up and down the river, and brought harvested crops, meat and other animal by-products back to the port. The other half of the port had been a marina, not just for the wealthy, it seemed like everyone owned a river craft in Port Turquoise. Now, however, the waterfront had been fortified. Smartcrete bunkers and barriers provided blocking strongpoints in key areas. Between the two lens feeds Miska could see two heavily armed patrol boats in the water and one Medusa-class mech on dry land.

The two Satyrs moved a little closer to the port, the tops of their armoured, reactive-camouflaged hulls breaching the bright turquoise-coloured water enough for them to launch similarly camouflaged rotor drones. Two more blinking lens feed icons appeared in Miska's IVD. She opened them as well. As the rotor drones rose in the air, the town behind the port was revealed. It lay in a small basin of clear-cut hills in the shadow of the jungles. Before the current unpleasantness it had been home to about fifty thousand people, the majority of them involved in the gas mining industry, arbocultural industry, the port, or the

49

Colonial Administration. Until New Sun's mercenary forces had bewilderingly invaded.

The small town was set out in a neat orderly grid, and few of the buildings were much higher than three storeys. The shuttle port had been on one of the clear-cut hills around the town. It had been expanded into a military shuttle port and a base for the occupying mercenaries. The port was well protected, the town had a number of strongpoints with heavy weapon emplacements, but the majority of Triple S's defences were jungle-facing. It was the most obvious direction of attack. Which was exactly the reason that Miska hadn't come that way.

The rotor drones were busy mapping the town's defences, the missile launchers, point defences, the gunships, the four Medusa-class mechs and so on. They would be feeding the information back to the waiting Medusas as target packages. Then, between the tactical computers and the pilots, they would start prioritising and doling out the targets. The shuttles would head in once the missile launchers and point defences were dealt with. She just hoped that Mass and the others remembered their rules of engagement. People lived in that town. They were about to take thirty-foot-tall armoured behemoths in and start a fight among the people they were, in theory, there to 'liberate'. Miska felt the shuttle shift a little underneath her. They were waiting for Mass to start it all.

She saw the bow waves first. Six of the seven Medusas marching in a rough spearhead formation towards the port. Heads breaking the water first, huge metal hands tearing waterproof coverings from their weapons. Miska couldn't see the seventh Medusa as the two understrength mech platoons waded through the increasingly shallow water, glowing slightly from the water's residual iridescence.

Several of the shore point defence batteries exploded but Miska hadn't seen anyone fire yet. Then she saw a strange disturbance in the air and recognised it as a one of her fast moving scout mechs hidden by reactive camouflage. Another point defence battery was turned to wreckage by Dory fire from one of the nearly invisible Satyrs. The Triple S mech guarding the port was turning to face the water only to be hit by pellets of hydrogen superheated to a plasma state from Mass's mech's shoulder-mounted plasma cannon. At the same time he was firing the 105mm mass driver from the combination weapon the mech carried in its hands. The plasma bolts turned much of the enemy mech's armoured torso to burning liquid, then one of the electromagnetically-driven mass driver rounds shot straight through it and hit a cargo harbour crane behind the mech. The burning mech collapsed in on itself, sinking to the ground.

Hemi's mech was putting round after round from the larger calibre shoulder-mounted 200mm mass driver into one of the patrol boats just at the waterline. He used the flame gun element of his combination weapon and sprayed a line of napalm over the deck of the patrol craft. Enemy combatants leapt into the river, still burning as they sank beneath the water.

Missiles were blown out of the sky and then the launchers destroyed. Both the patrol boats were sinking now. The shore-side bunkers burst by the mass drivers were now both burning. Miska could make out infantry and light-skinned military vehicles fleeing the area. An APC jumped into the air, buckling as a mass driver round hit it. The mechs were still waist-deep in the river.

'Heavy-One-Actual to all Heavy call signs, watch your field of fire,' Mass warned them, a little hypocritically. Mass was taking his three-mech platoon through the marina. Hemi was taking his platoon through the commercial port. The firing was sporadic now. They were taking heavy weapons fire from vehicles and rooftop strong points but nothing that was giving them too much pause. As they climbed up onto dry land, Mass seemed content to let the Satyrs hunt the heavy weapons emplacements.

Missiles streaked across the rooftops from launchers in the hills surrounding the town. The mechs' point defence lasers blew them out of the sky before they got close. Depending on their configuration, all six mechs were firing their carried 105mm or shoulder-mounted 200mm mass drivers over the roofs of the town and into the missile launchers and point defence systems protecting the Triple S base. As soon as the point defence lasers were destroyed, the mechs launched missiles from the batteries on their backs. Targeting packages provided by the stealth rotor drones guided the missiles into defensive emplacements, heavy weapons and armoured vehicles that Miska would have loved to steal but that were too dangerous to leave in play. With the town's missile launchers and point defence systems down, Pegasus 1 and 2 started their approach.

All six of the Heavy Bastards' Medusas were advancing through the town now, their combination weapons raised to their shoulders, looking for all the world like two giant infantry fire teams. Miska wondered what had become of the seventh Medusa but she didn't want to distract Mass by asking. As individual mechs got hit they turned and checked the source of the fire. If the target was a significant threat, or their background was clear, they destroyed it with their own weapons fire. If not, they soaked up the damage and continued going. The two understrength mech platoons were trying to use the two- and three-storey buildings for concealment only, as even the indigenous hardwoods provided very little cover from railguns and lasers. More than one building was burning.

Miska watched as Mass kicked a soft-skinned light strike vehicle into the air and then removed the magazine on his 105mm mass driver, sliding home his second and final magazine for the huge weapon.

'Heavy-One-Actual to Hangman-One-Actual, they've got man-portable plasma weapons down here that are—' Mass started and then his mech staggered. For a horrible moment Miska thought the Medusa was going to topple over. Instead Mass's mech went down on one knee, a hand out to steady itself.

'Mech, mech, mech!' Hemi said over the comms link. Four Medusas had just walked out of the treeline and were heading through the Triple S hillside base towards the town. Miska assumed that Mass must have been hit by a mass driver round. The other five mechs, still shrugging off small arms and man-portable heavy weapons fire, immediately turned their weapons on the enemy mechs. Mass driver rounds and plasma bolts impacted on the Triple S mechs cratering armour plate or turning it to slag. This was the benefit of being trained by Miska and her dad. Even with mech combat they had trained her legionnaires in the primacy of aggression and violence of action. Counter attack as ferociously as possible, worry about the resources afterwards.

Mass's Medusa was back on its feet, advancing on the mech that had shot him, firing round after round from his 105mm mass driver. Miska could almost hear the clanging as the huge tungsten-cored electromagnetically-driven penetrators hit the enemy mech's thick armour.

'Heavy-Two-Two to all Heavy call signs, we have multiple

gunships preparing to take off from the pads to the south and east of us,' one of the *Whānau* mech jockeys said.

'Heavy-One-Three and Heavy-Two-Three, engage the enemy ass with your mass drivers, the gunships with your Vengeances,' Mass told them. Two of the Bastards' mechs, one from each of the sections, turned towards the south and east and knelt down behind two-storey buildings.

Each of the mechs had a slightly different configuration. One-Three and Two-Three were set up to destroy bunkers with the 200mm mass drivers mounted in the hardpoint on their right shoulders. The flamethrower element of their carried combination weapons would then be used to clear out any surviving enemy personnel in the busted bunker. Like all the other mechs they each had a missile battery, currently folded down against their back, mounted on their left shoulder hardpoint. Heavy-One-Three and Two-Three reversed their mass drivers so they were pointing to the north, the direction of the enemy mechs, and resumed firing. Meanwhile they each lifted their combination weapons to their shoulders and aimed the 30mm Vengeance railguns over the tops of the town's buildings. Each Medusa had a huge ammo hopper affixed to its lower back that chain-fed ammunition to the automatic cannon as the rounds tore up the hillside and shredded the VTOL gunships as they tried to take off.

'Incoming!' McWilliams shouted over comms. Suddenly the shuttle banked violently. Bodies slid into each other in the overloaded shuttle as people grabbed hold of whatever they could. Nyukuti thumped into her hard and squashed her against a member of first platoon. From the rotor drone's lens feed she saw what had happened. The Triple S mechs were targeting the shuttles, trying to distract the Heavy Bastards. Both were burning

54

hard and coming down low over the town in a rain of glittering chaff, bright flares and tiny sensor-confusing Electronic Counter Measure decoys. The air burned red as the Heavy Bastards and the shuttles' point defence lasers shot missiles out of the air. The shuttle bucked and more of the legionnaires were thrown about. Miska heard the audible snap of a leg breaking, which was followed a moment later by screaming.

'Medic!' someone shouted.

Fuck this noise, Miska decided.

'Hangman-One-Actual to Pegasus-One, you're going to put down in the plaza at Eighth and River Street. LSM, you're taking first platoon and going heavy weapons hunting in town,' Miska told them over comms.

'Understood,' her dad replied.

'Hangman-One-Actual to Pegasus-Two, you're going to take third and fourth platoon and drop them as close to the enemy Command Post as possible. I'll follow with second platoon.'

'Understood,' Perez replied.

'Permission for a missile run on the enemy ass once we've dropped you guys off?' McWilliams asked.

'Negative, Pegasus-One, I want all airborne elements in close air support once we're on the ground,' she told the Comanchero pilot. 'Offensive-Three-Actual, I want you to sweep south along the hill back towards the river, secure the landing pads and any of their VTOLs,' she told the commander of Third Platoon. She could hear something that sounded like railgun fire bouncing off the assault shuttle's armour as it came in to land. The cargo ramp was already down, the air fresher near the river. The Pegasus lurched to one side and she heard the screeching of tortured metal as the assault shuttle presumably crushed a car. First platoon piled out of the Pegasus accompanied by the

Cyclops. The ramp closed and they climbed into the air to the sound of more tortured metal and the poorly syncopated tattoo of railgun rounds bouncing off the shuttle's armour. The shuttle lurched as it was hit by a la-la, a multi-role, man-portable, light anti-armour rocket.

She could see Torricone kneeling over one of first platoon's legionnaires. He was cutting through inertial armour with the penny cutter scissors from his trauma kit to reveal a compound fracture that was slowly painting the deck red.

'Hangman-One-Actual to Offensive-Two-Actual,' she said to the lieutenant in charge of second platoon. 'You're going to sweep north—'

'Towards the mechs?' he asked. He sounded scared. She supposed it was reasonable but she couldn't wait to get out there.

'Leave the mechs to the Heavy Bastards,' she told him. From where she was crouched, by the bulkhead close to the ramp, she could see him nod. He didn't look convinced.

Miska contacted the commander of fourth platoon, their weapons platoon, and started splitting up his railgun, assault and mortar sections to support second and third platoon, leaving some with her to go after the CP, or command post. She was checking the feed from the rotor drones as she did so.

The Triple S mechs and the Heavy Bastards were exchanging heavy, hurried and therefore often inaccurate fire as they tried to close on each other. In the few moments that she had been concentrating on reiterating the orders to the Offensive Bastards, the jungle behind the Triple S mechs had become a burning mess of splintered branches and dense, bullet-ridden wood. The north part of town had all but been destroyed.

'Well, shit,' Miska muttered quietly.

Pegasus 1's ramp came down as the assault shuttle circled

over the Triple S base. Miska caught a glimpse of the Heavy Bastards closing with the Triple S mechs. Outside everything was thunder. Her audio dampeners kicked in, filtering out the excesses of hypersonic booms from large calibre railguns and mass drivers. Below her, on the hillside base, she could see third and fourth platoon securing the landing zone. They were engaged, taking fire. As Pegasus 1 came down to land she watched a la-la, fired from a back-mounted launcher worn by a member of one of the assault sections from the weapons platoon, arc into a concrete strong point and destroy it. Pegasus 1 touched down. She let second platoon rush out ahead of her. They split into three squads and went to cover. Miska and Nyukuti strode out after them.

'Hangman-Two-Actual to all call signs, please be advised we have an enemy stealthed Satyr somewhere in the city. Last engaged on the corner of Sixth and Pleasant.' Her dad's voice. His call sign was ad-hoc but everyone recognised his voice. His addition to the mission might have been last-minute opportunism but it seemed to be working out.

Pegasus 1 took off, leaving Miska and Nyukuti kneeling down in the shuttle's dust cloud. Miska heard and felt the snap of hypersonic rounds passing nearby. The noise of the incoming rounds was drowned out by one of fourth platoon's railgunners opening up. She saw strobing red light from one of the assault section's laser carbines. With all the shit in the air the lasers wouldn't be nearly as effective.

'Heavy-One-Actual to Heavy-One-Five and Heavy-Two-Five, detach from the platoon and hunt that enemy Satyr,' Mass said over the comms link. He sounded distracted. Miska was impressed he'd had the presence of mind to give that order. She glanced north. The Medusa that Mass was piloting flung an eighteen-wheeler at the head of one of the enemy Medusas. The truck caught the enemy mech high on its torso with enough force to send it to the ground hard. Miska was pretty sure she had felt the impact through the earth.

She was glad to see there was only a minimum of fucking about while second and third platoon were each joined by a railgun squad, an assault squad armed with the back-mounted la-las, and a mortar squad, before beginning their sweep north and south along the hilltop base, respectively.

Despite being blinded by dust she knew her surroundings from the surveillance images she'd studied while planning the mission, and the footage shot by the rotor drones. This part of the hillside base consisted of a series of fortified pre-fabricated cabins, known as hooches, used as barracks for the Triple S troops. They were connected by shallow defensive trenches and, in an excavated hollow defended by smartcrete barriers, there was a bunker with a commanding view of both the town and the jungle. She was pleased to note that the point defence systems, on this side of the hill anyway, had all been taken out.

She was left with a railgun squad, assault squad and mortar squad.

'Get set up, I want—' Miska started. Rounds impacting the earth all around interrupted her. She scrambled for the closest trench, Nyukuti by her side. The eleven men from fourth platoon did likewise. Further along the stretch Miska saw their attackers. A Triple S fire team. Miska immediately had her carbine to her shoulder and was advancing towards them. There was a loud pop as she fired the carbine's 30mm grenade launcher, filling the trench with razor sharp flechettes.

'—mortar set up, targeted on the bunker, la-las the same, stay well clear of the western approach, fire on my mark,' Miska continued as she stalked through the trench firing the laser, the beam beating the flechettes to their mark, possibly even burning a few out of the air en route. Nyukuti was following her down the trench, his SAW at the ready but there wasn't enough room to fire around her. The laser superheated the hard armour plate, causing it to explode. The flechettes found exposed skin. Steaming flesh blew out through destroyed armour. The fire team either went down or scrambled around the corner in the trench. One of the assault shuttles flew overhead raining down railgun fire on some unseen target.

'Railguns to provide security,' she finished as she reached the corner of her trench, slipping in steaming viscera, a humid blood mist hanging in the air over the corpses. The battery icon for her carbine was blinking in her IVD. She'd had to up the weapon's power to cut through all the crap in the air.

'Reloading,' she told Nyukuti. She heard railgun fire from nearby. Nyukuti nodded and came round her as she replaced the battery in her carbine, checking the rotor drones to see if either of them had eyes on her position. They didn't, and she didn't want to re-task them. She listened for a moment but even with her dampener she couldn't hear anything from around the corner of the trench. She removed a 30mm fragmentation grenade from one of the loops on her webbing.

'Frag out,' she warned Nyukuti, then knocked off the safety cap with her thumb, depressed the arming stud and threw it into the next trench. They were showered in more dirt as the frag exploded and then Nyukuti was around the corner, firing burst after hypersonic burst from his SAW. Miska followed, her carbine at the ready.

'Offensive-Four-Two-Three-Actual to Hangman-One-Actual. We have a drone in the air and a targeting solution for the CP,' said the corporal in command of the mortar squad she had been left with. Miska tapped Nyukuti on the shoulder to stop him. Both of them hunkered down in the trench, Nyukuti covering forward, Miska covering back the way they'd just come. The red miasma still hung in the air behind them. Nyukuti had made two more bodies in the trench in front of them. Miska checked the feeds from the rotor drones. As she watched, Heavy-Two-Two tackled one of the enemy mechs and brought it to the ground. Moments later she heard the clanging of metal hitting metal. Miska was pretty sure it was the last thing the Triple S mech-jockey had expected. He was flailing to get up. Heavy-Two-Two knelt on the enemy mech and extended the synthetic diamond-toothed chainsaw blades from his forearms. They were intended as arbocultural tools – the mechs used them as machetes when operating in the thick jungle. Heavy-Two-Two repurposed them, pushing the spinning blades into the armoured torso of the enemy mech in a fountain of sparks.

Heavy-Two-One, Hemi's Medusa, wrapped its arms low around the legs of the enemy mech he was fighting and then straightened up. With enormous mechanical strength Heavy-Two-One lifted the Triple S Medusa into the air and, with a clearly audible scream of protesting metal, dropped the mech over his back and onto its head. Miska couldn't help but grimace, there was no way that wouldn't have damaged some of Hemi's weapon systems.

Heavy-One-Two was covering one of the enemy mechs that was down on its knees, hands in the air.

Heavy-One-Actual, Mass's mech, was stamping on the Triple S mech that it had knocked over with the thrown truck. In many ways that was the problem with the Triple S mech jockeys. They treated their mechs as moving weapon platforms and thought in terms of strategy and tactics. Her Bastards, on the other hand, were thinking of this as a scaled-up prison yard brawl. They weren't interested in the 'rules' of mech combat. They didn't know better than to think of the mechs as anything other than thirty-foot-tall, armoured extensions of their own bodies. The Triple S jockeys had come for a war and got a street fight. It had worked in the Bastards' favour this time.

Miska checked on Heavy-One-Three and Heavy-Two-Three. They were both still covering the landing pads. As she watched, Heavy-One-Three fired its Vengeance railgun over Port Turquoise's rooftops, shredding a moving VTOL transport like it was so much confetti.

'Hangman-One-Actual to Heavy-One-Actual, can I borrow Heavy-Two-Three, please? He looks bored,' Miska asked.

'Be my guest,' Mass answered. He sounded out of breath.

Miska told the corporal in charge of the mortar section to send the targeting package to Heavy-Two-Three. Heavy-Two-Three stood up and started making its way through Port Turquoise towards the CP. A line of earth and powdered concrete erupted into the air from the impact of the 200mm projectile fired from the approaching Medusa's shoulder-mounted mass driver. The tungsten-cored penetrator left a glowing trench in its wake. The hypersonic round tore open the reinforced concrete front of the bunker. Miska let the assault squad fire a few la-las through the hole. Then she ordered the mortar section to start dropping the bombs in, and not stop until the CP surrendered. She heard the familiar pop of the mortars firing. This was followed moments later by an explosion and more dust filled the air.

'This is Miska Corbin. I'm assuming you all know who I am. You've got until the approaching mech reaches the CP to surrender,' she said over an open frequency. 'Or I burn you out.'

Heavy-Two-Three hadn't even covered half the distance before she received a message from the Triple S commander surrendering.

CHAPTER 5

Triple S's command staff had stumbled out of the command post into the waiting arms of Miska's Bastards. They were covered in powdered concrete, their eyes were bloodshot and they were more than a little dazed. The highest-ranking surviving officer from the mass-driver-gutted bunker staggered towards her, stuttering something about the articles of conflict. Miska reassured her that that they would be followed even as the Triple S officer was pushed down to her knees by one of the railgun squad's assistant gunners. All of this in the shadow of the Medusa. The mech, cradling its railgun/flame-thrower combination weapon as though it was an oversized carbine, looked for all the world like another legionnaire, a giant in combat armour.

Everything was in hand. Miska walked past the mech to look out over Port Turquoise. It was quiet now the Triple S rank-and-file had seemed eager to follow the order to surrender. The northern corner of town where her stolen mechs and their Triple S counterparts had fought was a mess. Rubble everywhere, buildings that looked as though somebody had taken a bite out of them, and huge craters in the surface of the road.

'Well, balls,' Miska muttered. She had been tight on the ROE, the rules of engagement. She had told Mass and the other mech jockeys to check their backgrounds when firing their weapons, to try and keep collateral damage to a minimum. That was probably why they had closed for hand-to-hand fighting so quickly. She hadn't liked making the ROE so tight. Her responsibility was to her legionnaires first and foremost, to give them the best possible chance to survive, but Port Turquoise was peopled by the very colonists that had hired them. It was difficult to liberate dead people.

She was aware of Torricone heading down the hill towards the town about a hundred feet to the north of her. Miska quickly checked her IVD. Two of her Bastards were KIA and several more were injured. She would review the gun- and helm-cam footage along with the footage from the drones and find out what happened. What they all could have done differently.

'What are you doing?' Miska asked Torricone over a direct link. 'We've got wounded.'

'They volunteered,' Torricone answered and then severed the link. She'd heard disgust in his voice. It was a flagrant disregard for her orders and he was going to have to be dealt with sooner rather than later. She didn't think Torricone felt that the last two missions, during which they'd both been in some pretty tight scrapes together, had bought him any slack. He just didn't seem to care any more. Not since they had come back from Barney Prime. What she couldn't work out was why he hadn't just elected to stay in suspended animation.

Miska saw the Cyclops war droid that her father's electronic spirit inhabited running on all six of its limbs through the hillside base towards her. The two Pegasus assault shuttles were still circling overhead. Doubtless Triple S relief forces were en route but forces employed by the Colonial Administration had set out in an ad-hoc flotilla of ferries, cargo boats, and a few ageing riverine patrol craft to occupy Port Turquoise the moment the attack had started. All the river craft were loaded to the gunwales with mercenary troops in the employ of Military Active Command Ephesus sent to relieve the Bastards. Miska had made it clear when she had gone to work for MACE that, like the USMC with whom she had served, they were an expeditionary force, a fighting force, not a garrison unit. They would be relieved.

'You know that whole galloping thing looks undignified, don't you?' Miska said as the Cyclops reached her.

'Gets me places quicker though. Being in this metal body, I don't know why we don't just let drones do all the fighting these days,' her dad said.

'Hacking, upkeep, and frankly humans are cheaper and more surprising.'

'I certainly think we were that. Where's he going?' The Cyclops pointed at Torricone with a metal thumb, a human gesture that seemed incongruous coming from the armoured war droid.

'See if he can help anyone in town,' Miska told her dad.

'You sign off on that?'

'Sure,' Miska lied. She had the disconcerting feeling that the Cyclops was staring at her. She was grateful that her dad didn't push the matter. Torricone was becoming a real problem, in more ways than one.

'ETA on your relief?' her dad asked instead.

'The forward elements are about twenty minutes out,' she told him, magnifying her vision, checking the river, but it seemed that the flotilla was still over the horizon. 'MACE have got a couple of high altitude surveillance drones up. No sign of Triple S response yet.' They would know that this situation wasn't going to be solved with a few shuttles full of their QRF. The captured mercenaries would complicate things as well. Their contracts would have stipulations as regarded the risks they would have to take from their own forces counterattacking in just such an eventuality. They might risk an air strike, though. Triple S definitely had air superiority in this particular conflict but that advantage was limited because of the terrain. 'How're things down in town?' she asked.

'Some of the Triple S combatants managed to make a break for it, but frankly I can't see them coming back, and they're just making their own repatriation that much harder. That said, we're keeping an eye out for them. We're keeping all the prisoners in the plaza where we landed. There's quite a lot of them.'

It wasn't quite a criticism. They had always known they were going to be outnumbered. It was more a warning that, although it might have gone their way this time, it could have easily gone the other way. She was aware of the recklessness of her plan. She was of the opinion that said awareness showed how much she'd grown as a person.

'You strip all their gear from them? Weapons, ammo, armour?' she asked. She particularly wanted the man-portable plasma weapons the Triple S troops had been using.

'Yes, but that's part of the problem. The gear we're taking off the troops, guarding the enemy mechs, the airfield, the raw materials for their military printer, securing the vehicles. We're stretched pretty thin.'

As ever, her dad wasn't wrong.

'I know that, Dad. This morning's smash and grab isn't me

going back to my bad old ways, I promise. No more Barney-Prime-style clusterfucks but we couldn't turn our nose up at this. We desperately need the gear and this will be the last chance we get to rob on such a scale.'

'Because the next time they'll have booby traps, literal and electronic,' he said.

Miska nodded. It was a worry. Triple S (electronic) would have their hackers going after the systems of all the hardware they had taken this morning, and she was light on the net support side because of the threat criminal hackers posed to her. As soon as they managed to get all their stolen war machines back to base, everything would be shut down until she had personally had the opportunity to purge their systems of malicious code and back doors.

'You found a weakness and you exploited it tactically.'

'Still need to work on strategy, huh?' Miska asked, smiling.

'Keep playing chess with Major Cofino,' her dad suggested. Miska had caught him and Uncle V playing a few games as well. That was the biggest threat posed by Vido Cofino, he made it very difficult not to like him.

'I hate chess,' Miska griped.

'Well done today, it was a ballsy move but it paid off.'

'By balls I'm assuming you mean ovaries?' she asked.

It was downright disconcerting hearing the war droid chuckling with her dad's voice.

'Prioritise the vehicles, only take things that are multi-role, and can be used in combat. Dump all the soft-skinned bullshit and I'll have Mass task the Satyrs to patrol for the ones that got away. We get back to Badajoz we're going to stand down for a day or two, and then no more hairy shit.'

'Understood,' her dad said. The Cyclops's head turned towards the river. 'Looks like our relief is here.'

Her IVD headache had become a two-day-long net fatigue headache. They had turned Port Turquoise over to the allied mercenaries in the relief force. There had been some wrangling over the 'spoils of war' but nobody had really wanted to tangle with Miska over it, so the Bastards had got their hardware. A staggered airlift had followed as they ferried the remaining VTOL gunships and atmosphere transports that the Medusas hadn't destroyed; the printer raw materials; captured arms and ammunitions, including some plasma weapons that Miska was very excited about; every single last piece of mech spare part they could find; the least damaged mech and the few armoured vehicles that hadn't been destroyed. They had also recovered the missing Medusa, which had got bogged down in the Turquoise River. All the vehicles and a number of the weapon systems had required checking for back doors, viral mines and other surprises that Triple S's electronic warriors might have left behind. It was exactly the sort of work that she hated. Simultaneously boring and repetitive but requiring a great deal of attention to detail, and she was the only one who could do it. The lack of combat hackers that she could trust, or intimidate to the extent she was sure they wouldn't betray her, was becoming more and more of an issue. She had discussed with her dad the idea of hiring actual mercenaries to work for them, combat-capable hackers that didn't have N-bombs in their heads, but that had its own set of security concerns.

The only thing that had cheered her up had been redesigning the net representations of all the stolen vehicles and weapon systems. She had done away with the dreary committee-designed aesthetics that Triple S used. In its place she made the net representations of the hardware look like vehicles and equipment from a pre-FHC conflict that had taken place in a country called Vietnam. The conflict had spawned a number of apparently classic, according to her dad, vizzes. He had thoroughly approved of the new aesthetics. The addition of the 'steel pot' combat helmet to her own cartoon icon came from the same conflict.

However, she still had to run the Legion while she was immersed in the net, as well as make sure she ate, used the toilet, and apparently she was supposed to sleep as well.

Triple S had kicked up a lot of fuss about what people were already calling the Bastard Offensive. Colonel Duellona, the commander of the Triple S forces in-system, had cited infractions of the articles of conflict, none of which were holding much water. It was at times like these that she really appreciated Uncle V. He seemed to love this bullshit, whereas she didn't quite understand why, despite them being on opposing sides of the conflict, she couldn't just go and shoot Duellona in the head. There were some pretty stringent rules to this war designed to limit unnecessary loss of life. Most of the battles came down to a brief exchange of fire, some posturing, and then whichever side had the clear disadvantage surrendered. Miska's response to the situation, which had been favouring Triple S and their New Sun employers, had been to hit hard and fast, ideally with the element of surprise, and do sufficient damage with the opening attack that the enemy wanted to surrender before things got any worse. While her tactics weren't, strictly speaking, against the articles of conflict, they weren't the 'done thing'. Previous to the Bastards joining the conflict it had looked more like a dance, or one of her dad and Uncle V's chess games. This had well-served the military contractors, mercenaries by another name, who were employed on either side. Miska, however, had turned up to fight a war.

Wage a war, she reminded herself. Now other people were supposed to fight for her.

She opened her eyes to pain lancing through her head. It was so intense that she was actually seeing white flashes. She suspected that her eyes needed some maintenance. She was lying in her collapsible cot in her hooch, drenched in sweat despite her lack of recent physical exertion. It was the humidity. The air seemed as much a sweaty liquid as a breathable gas, even at night. She was in need of some painkillers, a shower, a fifth of Scotch, about a day's worth of sleep and some PT, probably in that order.

Most of the Bastards had been stood down, though McWilliams and Perez had been working to get some of the other experienced and newly sim-qualified pilots up to speed on the VTOL gunships and atmo-transports they had captured at Port Turquoise. Ideally they would take some of the pressure off the Pegasi assault shuttles.

The Sneaky Bastards had gone back out. They were still searching for FOB Trafalgar. Apparently some of the surveillance drones that MACE had sweeping their side of the river had found some interesting heat signatures.

Miska lay there in her own sweat for a few moments and listened to the base. It was reasonably quiet, though she could hear Nyukuti snoring softly through the thin printed wall of the pre-fabricated hooch. Beyond that she could hear conversation and the occasional laughter from the nearby hooches. She felt the hum of the generators, heard the sound of the cargo-handling exoskeletons shifting supplies around, and she could just about hear the sound of the canopy rustling in the wind. When the wind picked up it could sound like thunder going through the thick leaves above them. Other than the wind and the creak of the enormous trees, the jungle was quiet. There was no indigenous fauna. Plants handled some of the roles in the ecosystem that would normally be filled by animals. Predatory plants weren't an issue without animals, but biting airborne seedpods and aggressive parasitical fungal spores were. The latter were causing more casualties than combat at the moment. Somehow the colonists, many of whom were Maasai, managed to avoid the worst depredations of the local flora. The colonists had left their homes in Kenya and Tanzania after it became progressively more difficult for them to pursue their semi-nomadic lifestyle in cosmopolitan Africa.

Miska could see the attraction of New Ephesus to the Maasai, but what she couldn't understand was why New Sun wanted the planet. It seemed to have little to offer in exploitable resources. The gas mining operations in Epsilon Eridani B's upper atmosphere, which provided fuel for the colony and passing spacecraft, were about the most valuable industry in the system. So far, however, New Sun had shown little interest in the gas platform aerostats. She understood why the colonists were fighting. That pesky self-determination seemed to get in the way of the all-consuming profit margin again and again. She just couldn't see where that profit was supposed to come from for New Sun. Raff was digging into it, and she'd asked Vido to do the same. So far, nothing. Raff was convinced that New Sun was a Martian-backed shell company, but the Martian threat was a familiar song sung by the CIA, in part to justify their existence. The song played well back home on Earth, where they lived in fear of the Small Gods' tech. In fairness it was tech that had allowed the Small Gods to dominate much of the Sol System.

Miska used her neural interface to add painkillers to her blood from her internal medical systems, noting that she would soon need to top up her supplies. Trying to act responsibly while in command was taking its toll. She swung up out of her cot. She knew she could get one of her Bastards to change her sweaty sheets but the enlisted marine in her wouldn't do that. She would change them herself, once she'd had a shower and located some Scotch.

'Sneaky-One-One to Hangman-One-Actual.' Sneaky-One-One's details scrolled down her IVD. Sergeant Robert 'Bob' Kasmeyer, the leader of the Sneaky Bastards' first squad. He'd grown up as an asteroid rat, run with the tunnel gangs formed by the children of other itinerant belt miners in the Sol system. Petty crime had turned to not so petty crime when he'd graduated to hijacking automated ore transports. He'd sneak on board the transports in their home port, disable communications and his accomplices would dock with the transports en route. Except that on his last job the automated transport had stowaways on board, in the shape of a tin-can habitat tethered to the sub-light ship. Kasmeyer's part in the murders had earned him a life sentence.

He had excelled during training, particularly at stealth operations, and seemed calm and patient. These qualities, and being able to think on his feet, had got him command of the squad. His preference to observe and provide information over contact with the enemy was just the sort of leader that the Sneaky Bastards needed. That didn't stop Miska groaning when she heard the message.

'Hangman-One-Actual to Sneaky-One-One, this had better be good.'

'We've found Trafalgar, repeat we have found Trafalgar.'

Triple S's hidden forward operating base on MACE's side of the river. It was good.

'Okay, I want you to get what you can, defences, numbers et-cetera, and then withdraw quietly. They can't know we know,' Miska subvocalised back.

'Er ... that's not really an issue,' Kasmeyer replied.

'You compromised?'

'I think you need to see this for yourself.'

Miska didn't bother with the lens feed from the squads' guncams. Instead she tranced in, appearing in the net as the stylised, spiky cartoon version of herself. Around her the computer-animated representation of Camp Badajoz looked like an old, squat, thick-walled fort from the Napoleonic War. It was the net architecture favoured by Salik, the mercenary broker who owned Waterloo Station. Cartoon Miska took hold of a flickering but dim neon line that symbolised the comms link between herself and Kasmeyer. Already accepted by the comms links encryption, she allowed herself to be sucked down the link.

Kasmeyer didn't have a net representation beyond a faint, roughly human-shaped wire-frame grid that represented the various electronic systems he was wearing/using. She knew that the armour he wore, and the thin shielding on the systems them-selves, would mask any EM signature. She was only able to see them because of her command access. She made herself tiny and entered the net representation of his Martian-designed Xiphos gauss SAW, going straight for the guncam. Her carbine's-eye view told her everything she needed to know.

73

Shit!

'I'm on my way,' she told Kasmeyer.

Rank had its privileges. One of Miska's was her own Machimoi combat exoskeleton. They had captured them when the Bastards had taken the *Excelsior* from Triple S during the battle for Faigroe Station. There had been enough to equip a squad of soldiers with the power armour and three left over. One had already been used to replace losses in combat and Miska suspected the same would happen to the other two, but until then she liked having her own ride.

She didn't bother to wake Nyukuti, who would have insisted on coming with her, but she did inform the MACE duty officer that she was going out. He tried to insist on her taking an escort but she didn't want to draw any more attention than she had to, and besides, she outranked him.

The Machimoi power armour was in a small pre-fab hangar on the edge of the terraced landing pads. There were lights on in the hangar but none of the support crew were anywhere to be seen, and sentry duty had been left to an unobtrusive surveillance drone. Miska did not approve.

Inside the hangar the Machimoi combat exoskeletons were ten-foot-tall, grey, nearly featureless, almost organic-looking suits of armour. The same smooth lines and lack of right angles that Miska had come to expect from all MMI tech. She sent a command to the armour and it split open for her. She clipped her laser carbine to the bottom of the ammunition hopper for the power armour's main weapon, a 20mm Dory railgun, and then climbed into the armour. The padding changed shape to securely grip her small frame. Her hands slid into the control gloves, feet into the control slippers. The Machimoi was by far and away the most comfortable combat exoskeleton she had ever piloted. Even more comfortable than some of the African models she had used, and far more comfortable than the Honey Badger and its variants favoured by the Corps.

The suit 'buttoned up' around her. Her neural interface connected with the exoskeleton's systems and suddenly she was a ten-foot-tall armoured killing machine. The feeling of power was palpable. She was wary of just how addictive it was, but couldn't stop a smile creeping across her mouth. She strode out of the hangar and into the humid night, Dory at the ready like an oversized rifle as the two stubby halves of the flight fin unfolded from the exoskeleton's back and slid together. Telemetry cascaded down her IVD. All systems appeared to be optimal. A quick run, the suit's servos amplifying her own muscle power, then she jumped into the air and she was flying. The neural interface meant that the suit's sensors were now her own.

Despite what she had seen through the guncam, Miska felt good. She knew it was reckless going out on her own but they were, after all, supposed to be in friendly territory. Ten-feet-tall or not, the vast scale of the trees was humbling. She flew through banks of steamy mist. Feedback from the Machimoi's sensors made the mist feel like sweat beading on her skin. Far below her the patchwork quilt of moss and lichens gave away to tall fungal forests – the bane of the foot patrols. All of this was visible in the suit's optics, which amplified beams of faint red light from the gas giant above that managed to penetrate the jungle canopy.

I need more moments like this, she decided. And then it was over and she was approaching the Sneaky Bastards' position. FOB Trafalgar looked like an anthill rising out of smaller, surrounding anthills on the hard-packed dirt floor far below the canopy.

An anthill that had been covered in stakes with headless bodies impaled on them.

Miska touched down close to Kasmeyer's position. With all of her legionnaires using their reactive ghillie suits even the Machimoi's excellent sensors were struggling to pick them up. She could only tell where they were by their transponder positions, which overlaid her vision.

'Hey, Kasmeyer. I take it you didn't do this?' Miska asked.

'The twelve of us?' he asked grimly. There were at least a hundred bodies arranged around the hill. Judging by their gear alone, at least some of them must have been Triple S (elite), the rest were presumably support personnel. Her people didn't do this. Probably weren't capable of doing it, and she was trying to think of any of the other mercenary units who were. She was coming up blank.

'What've you got?' she asked, as Kasmeyer threw the ghillie suit over his head and shoulders and became visible. He had a small build, his narrow face remarkable in just how unremark-able it was. Miska could see from transponder positions that the rest of the squad were remaining concealed, watching their back, including Kaneda and Hogg.

'The hill has been excavated. The bunker complex is well equipped. They've been recycling all their waste. It's even got a printer. It must have been set up either at the very beginning, or before the conflict started.' Kasmeyer didn't come across as frightened but she could see the tension in his face. Miska looked at the nearest corpse. Fungus had already started growing out of its neck stump. The largest fungal blooms made the impaled corpses look like their own species. Mushroom people. She was no expert but she didn't think they had long been dead. The corpses were still dripping despite the aggressive fungal growth.

'Any idea what happened?' she asked.

'The complex is partially collapsed. Lots of signs of violence but whatever happened it happened quickly. Lots of blood inside but I checked their weapons, most of them had a full magazine.'

That got Miska's attention. The Machimoi's head turned to stare at Kasmeyer.

'You sure?" Miska asked. "Most of these guys are recruited from SF. They're SEALs, SAS, KSK, people like that.' She didn't mention that they'd have top of the line implants, which meant wired reflexes comparative in spec to her own.

Kasmeyer just looked up at the Machimoi.

'Weird thing, they're all carrying slugthrowers. No lasers, no man-portable plasma weapons, no electromagnetics. All very low-tech. They don't even have gauss kisses on the weapons. They even had old-fashioned optical sights,' he told her.

That was weird. Miska could see the point in carrying slugthrower weapons. The higher the tech, the more chance of something going wrong. She often carried a shotgun herself as a backup weapon for her delicate laser carbine, and she still had a printed AK-47 that she had taken from Faigroe Station. To equip everyone with slugthrowers, however, suggested they were worried about an EMP. That didn't make any sense. It would be insane for a conflict like this to go nuclear.

She also couldn't work out why they had been out here. There had been rumours about the FOB flying around since before the Legion had arrived. Every transport crash, every lost soldier was attributed to a ghost force from Trafalgar. If, however, they had this many people, many of them ex-SF, then they could have caused absolute chaos behind the MACE's lines.

Miska used the Machimoi's optics to zoom in on the closest corpse's wounds. They were wide, brutal, surprisingly thick. The ragged skin around the neck wounds made it look as though the heads had been torn off. A combat exoskeleton would be strong enough to do something like this, but even the strongest would struggle to tear through MMI body armour.

What, then?

A new war droid?

A Small God?

Aliens?

'What's north of here?' she asked Kasmeyer, and then answered her own question by bringing up a map in her IVD.

'More jungle, you go far enough and you get to the mountains and the headwaters of the Turquoise. It's supposed to be swampy up there.'

Miska was running through information on the area as they spoke. The Maasai colonists on this part of the moon had spread out from Port Turquoise. They hadn't penetrated as far as the FOB yet; there were no arbocultural settlements further north than their current position. She was staring north now, the Machimoi's optics and sensors cutting through the night but revealing little more than steamy mist, spore clouds and seedpods floating on the warm breeze.

'You find their heads?' Miska added, nodding towards the closest mushroom-topped corpse. Kasmeyer just shook his own head.

'We've got something else to show you,' he said. Miska looked down at him. 'Kaneda found it, but your skel armour won't fit.'

*

Kasmeyer had Kaneda watch their back as Hogg led her into the tunnel complex within the hill. Miska's artificial eyes were good enough that even as they entered the tunnel she could make out the weathered lines on Hogg's face. Of an age with her father, Hogg was far too old for active service but he kept up with the younger legionnaires and his PT results and biometrics suggested he was more than fit enough. Miska suspected his fitness was down to his life as a fugitive, living rough in the wilderness.

The earthen tunnel smelt like people had died in here. The copper smell of blood mixed with shit. Hungry mosses had already crept in to feed on the biological waste. The tunnel was big enough for her Machimoi and Miska was just about to make such a comment when she saw the collapse ahead. It wasn't often that Miska enjoyed being small but this was one of those times as she squeezed through a freshly-dug hole in the pile of earth that blocked the tunnel, carbine at the ready.

It was so dark on the other side of the collapse that both of them had to use the powerful flashlights mounted on their weapons – there wasn't enough ambient light for her eyes to amplify it. Miska played her torch around the collapsed earth. She half convinced herself that it looked like something had come through the wall of the tunnel.

That's just your mind playing tricks on you, she told herself.

'Miska,' Hogg said from the darkness, his light playing over a large humanoid figure. It took a moment for Miska to realise what it was. It looked like an updated version of the venerable Wraith combat exoskeleton. The design was well over a hundred years old but they were robust and comparatively low tech compared to something like the Machimoi. They were still used by fourth-tier colonial militias and some police forces for crowd control. There were some on board the *Hangman's*

Daughter, designed for use in the unlikely event of a prisoner riot.

Instead of the venerable Retributor railgun that most Wraiths were armed with, there was a 20mm slugthrower cannon lying in the dirt next to the suit of power armour. Hogg pointed his light at a ragged, bloody hole in the front of the Wraith. Someone, or something, had rammed a pointed object straight through the heavily armoured chest of the combat exoskeleton.

'Okay, we need to leave,' Miska said. She was aware of Hogg nodding. She assumed that if Trafalgar didn't report in then Triple S command would send someone to investigate. They didn't want to be there when that happened.

She couldn't shake the feeling they were dealing with a new player.

She also couldn't shake the feeling that Triple S and New Sun would find a way to hold the Bastards responsible for this massacre.

CHAPTER 6

Salik had made it sound like an invitation but Miska recognised a summoning when she heard one. The massacre had hit the net a few hours after Miska and the Sneaky Bastards had been airlifted out of FOB Trafalgar. Carefully edited footage and heavily spun information made sure that the finger was pointed at the Bastards.

'Why us?' she muttered to herself as she tramped up Pegasus 2's cargo ramp, secured her pack and the M-187 laser carbine, and slumped down into one of the folding bucket seats. If she was honest she suspected that she knew the answer.

'Because you wanted to be the bad guy,' Torricone told her. He was sat on one of the seats on the opposite bulkhead, watching her. The other members of the Legion in the cargo bay, who were on their way up to Waterloo Station for some R&R, shuffled a bit and looked the other way.

'I'm not the bad ... oh wait, you mean because my mercenary legion is made up of enslaved violent criminals?' Even subvocalising the message her jaw moved a little. The other

Bastards in the shuttle would be aware of the exchange. If they suspected there was something between Torricone and herself it could go badly for him. On the other hand if they realised just how antagonistic he was being then it could make him a hero to some of the Bastards.

'Legion?' Torricone asked over the direct comms link. 'A couple of companies at most.'

Nyukuti trotted up the ramp just as it started to close and sat down next to Miska. It could be difficult to tell with him, but Miska suspected it wasn't so much that he was angry with her for going out without him the night before, as hurt. He was dressed in civvies but carrying one of the snubby MMI personal defence weapons. It seemed he was still taking his bodyguard/close protection role seriously.

'Surprised to see you taking a leave at all,' Miska subvocalised as she leaned forward, clasping her hands, staring at Torricone, the smile on her face more than a little evil. 'I thought you'd be out providing blood transfusions to sickly children direct from your bleeding heart.'

Torricone glared at her. 'Why don't you go and fuck yourself?'

Even over the roar of the engines as the assault shuttle took off, his voice carried enough for all the legionnaires in the cargo bay to hear. Next to her Nyukuti made to get up but Miska put a hand on his arm. The stand-over man froze for a moment but then relaxed back into his seat. Suddenly it was quiet in the back of the shuttle as it lurched forward and upwards.

Torricone's beautiful brown eyes held her stare. He tapped the side of his head, a careful measured movement. His finger touching the skin just above the single tattooed tear.

He's daring me to kill him, Miska thought. The public

challenge put her in a difficult position. She was, however, trying to get past the point where she had to kill anyone who stepped out of line.

'What the fuck is your problem?' Miska demanded, subvocalising over the direct comms link. The other legionnaires on board the shuttle were still watching the confrontation intently.

'It's too much, Miska, you're messing around with things ...' he left the rest unsaid but she was pretty sure that he was talking about the artefact they had 'jacked on Barney's Prime. The weird piece of alien tech that had somehow shielded them from the orbital strike by forces as yet unknown. Kaneda, Vido, Mass and Torricone had apparently seen nothing when they had jumped into the artefact, but all of them had been aware of the passing of time, the sense of being somewhere else, the sense of wrongness, and strange but indeterminate nightmares. Whatever had happened to them, it hadn't so much changed Torricone as reinforced previously held convictions.

'You're frightened,' Miska mused over the comms link. Torricone didn't say anything. 'So why not just wait it out in suspended animation? You've said it yourself: all I've got is enemies. This is just a matter of time.'

'Because between now and then you can do a lot of damage. If I'm going to live with myself when you're gone, I need to know that I did everything I could to mitigate that.'

Miska let his words settle in. She could still feel the other legionnaires in the shuttle's hold watching them. She narrowed her eyes, as though studying Torricone anew.

'No,' she subvocalised, 'I don't think so. I've met your mom ...'

'You mean you've had your ass kicked by my mom,' Torricone told her, no trace of humour in his voice.

'I did not ... I'm not sure that's anything you should be ... That's not my point.' She could feel Nyukuti watching the silent exchange now as well. *What? Am I flustered?* she wondered. 'You didn't have to grow up the way you did. You didn't have to steal cars. You did it because you liked it. Now you're walking unarmed into a war zone. Your problem is that you're just as much an action junkie as I am. The only difference is that you want to feel good about the bad things we do. That's not the way that works.' She leaned back in the bucket chair and crossed her arms, smiling.

'Unless you're a psychopath,' Torricone said out loud. Miska was pretty sure she heard a couple of sharp intakes of breath, but over the engines it might have been her imagination.

'Your leave is revoked, Private,' Miska told him. 'Report to LSM Corbin to discuss your attitude.' It felt petty but she had to at least give the impression there was discipline. Torricone let out a humourless laugh and shook his head.

'You could just get a room together?' Nyukuti suggested over a direct comms link. Miska turned to stare at him. He held up his hands and shook his head. The problem was that if the other legionnaires decided that this was all sexual tension then Torricone might not be long for this world.

There was clearly a lot of money in mercenary proxy wars. Waterloo Station was a lot grander than any military orbital habitat Miska had ever been posted to. The modular station was designed to be broken down and pulled by FTL-capable tugs to new colonial conflicts. There were other stations that did a similar job but none of them came close to the scale and success of Salik's operation.

Much of the station was given over to hotels of various

quality, alcohol and drug bars, restaurants, clubs, strip joints, brothels and sense booths. All ways for Salik to claw back the mercenaries' pay above and beyond his fifteen per cent. The station had offices for the representatives of the belligerents and the various military contractors to rent, and even modular barrack areas for those that didn't have their own ships to work from.

As Miska and Nyukuti made their way down the bustling Central Concourse past drunk and wasted mercenaries, barkers hustling their varied entertainments, serving drones and prostitutes of various genders, Miska noticed she was earning more than her fair share of glares. From various screens she could see footage from the massacre. It still surprised her just how much those who should know better lapped up propaganda. She guessed people just believed what they wanted to believe. She also noticed that she had a number of messages from Raff. They would all appear to be legitimate communications from a journalist to a commanding officer. What he really wanted would be encrypted. She just didn't want to deal with it right now.

Too many spinning plates.

Above her the transparent panes of the domed ceiling provided vertiginous views. Miska could see most of the rest of the torus and the centre spindle. Further up the spindle she could make out the smaller top docking torus. The long, slab-like mess of superstructure and armour that was the *Hangman's Daughter* was slowly rotating into sight. Miska was almost surprised at how much the ugly prison barge felt like home. That said, she would much rather be in-country than up here on the Station.

Salik's house was a tall, grey stone, nineteenth century

town house that, according to Uncle Vido, used to belong to somebody of import to the Napoleonic Wars. (Miska had forgotten who that was moments after she had been told.) The house had been transported block-by-block from London, or possibly Paris, or some other old place back on Earth. Waterloo Station's nineteenth century meets vice-Disneyland aesthetic notwithstanding, the antique house looked pretty incongruous on the habitat.

Miska paused and looked up again. Beyond the spindle and the other side of the torus she could make out a glorious sunrise as the bright but distant Epsilon Eridani peaked over the gas giant's horizon. The lights of the gas mining aerostats looked like glinting jewels in Eridani B's upper atmosphere. New Ephesus seemed very close to the station. The green moon's peaceful look belied the reality of the situation below the jungle canopy.

'You all right, boss?' Nyukuti asked.

'We get in there, I give the word and we kill everyone who isn't a Bastard. You cool with that?'

'I can't tell if you're joking or not,' Nyukuti told her. Miska headed for the front door. 'Seriously, what's the word?' he asked.

Miska supposed the hall to the town house was nice. It was certainly full of expensive, old and tasteful – she guessed – stuff, but it wasn't really her sort of thing. The servant drones in nineteenth century livery were a bit much, however. Drones shouldn't wear hosiery and wigs, she decided.

One of the drones showed her up the stairs and into the lounge, which she knew from a previous visit was actually called the drawing room, though she had no idea why. Apparently drawing rooms weren't supposed to be on the fourth floor but Salik liked to look out over his domain.

'Miska!' Salik stood up to hug her. She frowned a little but let it go. She liked Salik well enough but she never let herself forget who and what he was. Much of his fleshiness was artfully concealed in a well-tailored suit. Miska supposed she should be thankful that he wasn't doing his Napoleon cosplay thing today. Salik had a perfectly shaped goatee and lacquered, shoulder-length hair. He may have had the look of a well-turned-out Europhile but Miska knew he came from Arabian old money. Old money that had helped him set up his mercenary brokerage operation. 'What a pleasure. I'm sorry to call you away from your command but I'm sure you can appreciate the seriousness of the situation.'

'Not my problem ...' Miska started but then Uncle V was in front of her, hugging her as well. This she hadn't expected.

'You get you're supposed to salute, right?' she asked her executive officer. In his mid-sixties, Vido was in surprisingly good shape for his age. This was probably in part due to her dad's punishing physical training regime. With a white crown of hair, his features just beginning to flesh out and sag, he looked like somebody's favourite grandfather – something he both knew and capitalised on. That said, he'd done his bit with a gun in his hand when the cluster had been well and truly fucked, back on Barney Prime.

'Hey, boss,' he said out loud. 'Any chance I can do the talking?' he subvocalised over an encrypted comms link. Over Vido's shoulder she caught Salik frowning. He must have picked up the transmission. Vido let go of her and nodded at Nyukuti who'd wandered into the drawing room behind Miska, hands still on the PDW casually slung down his chest. Miska gestured at the stand-over man with her thumb.

'This is Nyukuti, he's my ...' she started. 'Well I don't really know, but he's one of my guys.'

'One of your slaves?' suggested a statuesque woman sitting on one of the two antique sofas. Olive-skinned, long pitch-black hair tied back in ponytail, she, like Miska, wore fatigue trousers and combat boots. A black sleeveless T-shirt completed the ensemble. A sidearm was strapped to her leg in a smartgrip drop holster. Colonel 'Ma' Duellona, the commander of the Triple S forces in the Epsilon Eridani system.

'Bodyguard,' Nyukuti supplied. Duellona ignored him. She just glared at Miska. Miska grinned back at her.

'Ma!' she said excitedly. 'Great to see you.' She sat down opposite Duellona on the other sofa and then squirmed a little bit. She was sure all the antiques were very nice but frankly she had sat on more comfortable seats in military vehicles. *Or perhaps you're just getting too used to the comforts of stolen Martian Military Industries equipment.* 'And you brought your pet monkey!'

Standing behind the other sofa was a short, dark-haired man with a wiry build and a face covered in stubble. He was wearing a mixture of rugged civilian and military clothing that practically screamed special forces to Miska. She had no idea of Resnick's rank, or even his first name, but she knew he was in charge of Triple S (elite) in the Epsilon Eridani system. Miska had never heard him talk at one of these meetings. She had, however, felt his cold appraising eyes run over her and Nyukuti when they entered.

Duellona opened her mouth to say something but the man next to her on the antique sofa put his manicured, long-fingered hand on her wrist. Duellona stared down at the hand as though a snake had just crawled over her arm and taken a shit on it. Miska could empathise. Tall, hawk-nosed, with slicked-back thinning blond hair that looked like a holdover from his youth as corporate young Turk, the word oily may well have been invented to describe Brennan Campbell. The highest-ranking New Sun corporate representative on the station, he had some complex job title that Miska had long since forgotten and replaced with 'executive douchebag'. He struck her as someone with just enough power to be dangerous but not enough to be genuinely useful. The kind of middle management brown-nose who was a menace to his underlings. It was always a real effort not to break his nose every time he opened his mouth.

'What I'm sure my colleague meant to say—' he started. His voice was smooth and even, doubtless the product of corporate, by-the-number, neural linguistic programming training.

'I'm sure Duellona is more than capable of speaking for herself,' Salik said as he sat down on a high-backed chair between the two sofas. This was the reason Miska liked him. There was no doubt in her mind that he was just another snake oil salesman in a world of snake oil salesmen but, his polite facade aside, he did not suffer fools gladly.

Vido joined Miska on the sofa. Nyukuti went and sat by the window, which looked out over a holographic projection that Miska suspected was supposed to be some old Earth city in the nineteenth century. Duellona glanced over at Nyukuti. It was clear that she didn't like the stand-over man sitting behind her. Resnick shifted slightly to get a better view of Nyukuti.

'We were having coffee,' Salik said. 'Could I get you and Nyukuti ... did I pronounce that correctly? ... a cup?'

'Have you got a beer?' Miska asked. A pained expression momentarily flickered across Salik's face.

'I'm sure we can accommodate,' he said, smiling again.

'It's not even ten a.m.,' Vido pointed out.

'I've no idea what the time is, I've had so little sleep over the last three days. Too busy upgrading the electronic security on all my new toys.'

'Jesus Christ,' Vido muttered.

'And murdering more than a hundred of my people,' Duellona spat with enough venom to make Miska wonder if she really believed their own bullshit propaganda.

'Oh, come on!' Vido started. 'You wanna play the propaganda game with your PR company out there, that's fine, but we're all adults in here. Don't piss on us and tell us it's raining.' Uncle V sounded uncharacteristically irritated. Miska suspected that dealing with Colonel Duellona's truculence and Campbell's bullshit was starting to tell on the *consigliere*. Her own behaviour wasn't helping but she was tired, pissed off, hated these games, and her talk with Torricone hadn't improved her demeanour.

'They're not soldiers, they're animals,' Duellona spat. She was pointing at Miska but talking to Salik. 'You know as well as I do that they've got no place in any civilised conflict!'

'Civilised conflict, will you fucking listen to yourself?' Miska demanded. She knew Duellona was trying to get a rise out of her but didn't care.

'She's too aggressive!' Duellona snapped. 'She kills too many people. That's not how this game is …'

'It's not a game!' Miska snapped, leaning forward in the sofa. 'You really care about your people? Really!' Duellona stared at her. 'Get them to surrender faster. Better yet, pack them up and leave. See you at the next war.'

'Miska,' Salik said. He spoke quietly but it was enough for

Miska to relent. 'It is in nobody's best interests that this conflict ends quickly.'

'I'm sure it's in the best interests of the colonists,' Miska snapped. *Christ, I'm turning into Torricone.*

'And New Sun's,' Campbell said. It actually irritated Miska that he was agreeing with her. It went quiet in the drawing room.

'I'm busy, so let's get to it,' Miska said. She was aware of Vido rolling his eyes next to her. '"The Bastards have been mean to us, they won two fights, captured a load of our stuff, took a load of our people prisoner, it's not fair wah-wah-wah." Is that about the sum of it?'

Duellona's face had gone a funny shade of puce. Miska knew from experience that she didn't like being spoken to this way, certainly not by a jumped-up corporal.

'That should calm everything right down,' Vido muttered.

'I want my frigate, my mechs, the other vehicles, the weapons you stole and all my people—'

'In that order?' Miska asked.

'—returned immediately,' Duellona finished.

'Yeah? Not really how this works,' Miska told her. 'You pay the repatriation costs to MACE, it'll go towards the war effort but you get your people back. The rest of it belongs to me. You want it? Come and get it.'

Duellona opened her mouth to retort but Campbell held up his hand to quiet her. She looked just about ready to snap the hand off at the wrist and slap him to death with it.

'Colonel Corbin,' Uncle Vido started. Duellona snorted with derision, but he ploughed on. 'May not have explained it in the most diplomatic of terms but she has the right of it. The Bastard Legion has not breached the terms of conflict in any way.'

'The massacre!' Duellona snapped.

'Was nothing to do with us and you know it,' Miska told her.

'It's out of our hands,' Salik said. 'The UN conflict inspector has stepped in. She's sent an investigatory team down to the site.'

'As have we,' Duellona told her.

'Fine, we're getting accused, we're sending investigators down as well,' Vido said.

'New Sun formally withdraws the accusation—' Campbell started.

'Should have thought of that before your PR team went to work,' Vido told him.

'What investigators?' Duellona demanded.

'With all due respect—' Vido started.

'Mind your own fucking business,' Miska finished. Vido was shaking his head.

'Who're you going to send, your doctor? He was a serial killer!' Duellona seemed angrier than the situation warranted.

'Keen botanist, though,' Miska told her. Nyukuti snorted with laughter and even Salik was struggling to hide a smile. Vido just shook his head and Duellona stared at her for a moment before turning to Salik.

'This is a mockery.'

'It's fair. You made the accusation, and you made it publicly. They get the right of reply, which includes finding out what actually happened,' he told her. Duellona stared at the mercenary broker as though she'd been slapped.

'What about Ashmead?' she demanded.

'What's Ashmead?' Miska asked.

'Captain Sophie Ashmead, Triple S (electronic),' Vido supplied. 'The officer in charge of network security for the mech base—'

92

'—You hit,' Duellona finished, glaring at Miska. Campbell, Salik and even Vido were all watching her carefully as well.

Fuck you, Raff, Miska thought. He had supplied her with the intelligence.

'The intelligence was third party,' Miska told them. It wasn't a complete lie. 'I didn't order her mind-wipe. I won't use them again.'

'Where did the intel come from?' Duellona demanded. Miska just shook her head. Duellona was on her feet. 'I'll crack your fucking skull open ...'

'Colonel Duellona!' Campbell snapped. It was about the last thing that Miska had expected.

'Is this the word?' Nyukuti asked from the window. An obviously seething Duellona glanced round at him. Resnick looked the stand-over man's way as well.

'No!' Miska and Vido said simultaneously. Miska noticed Salik watching the colonel warily.

'Colonel,' Campbell continued, 'currently you are disgracing yourself, and your company, but what is worse you are disgracing me. This is not the way we expect our contractors to behave. I suggest you leave.'

Miska was staring at Campbell wide-eyed. She had assumed that he was completely smooth between the legs. This display of balls was so uncharacteristic as to be unprecedented. Duellona pointed at him. Her finger was shaking she was so angry.

'Ma, please,' Salik said. Miska was suddenly aware of the liveried servant drone standing in the doorway carrying her beer. The drone had to move quickly to clear the way as Duellona stormed out of the drawing room. Moments later Miska heard the front door slam. The pained expression was back on Salik's face. The drone gave Miska her beer.

'I apologise,' Campbell told them.

'Shit, you're still here,' Miska said, genuinely surprised. Vido chuckled, and even Salik was smiling again.

'She has been under a great deal of strain recently. The reverses she has taken in the campaign, the murder of poor Sophie and now this massacre ... well, they've all taken their toll.'

'Who do you think killed your people?' Miska asked. Campbell gave a somewhat pained smile but didn't say anything. Miska wanted to push him further, ask why all his people were armed with slugthrowers, but she was pretty sure that she wouldn't get anything useful from him. He wasn't a useful type of person.

'While I have a great deal of sympathy for the good colonel, we have our shareholders to think about. I feel that Colonel Corbin may have made a good point,' Campbell continued. 'I believe that Triple S may be too hidebound in the way that they do things. Too used to the "done thing".' He actually made the sign for inverted commas in the air as he said it. Miska suspected that she wasn't the only person in the room who had a strong urge to grab his fingers and bend them back until they broke. 'We're starting to feel that Triple S aren't aggressive enough, and that perhaps we might need some blue sky thinking on this particular problem.'

'Blue sky thinking—' Miska started.

'What are we talking about here?' Vido interrupted before she could say anything offensive. 'Hiring us away from the Colonial Administration?'

Miska didn't like the sound of this at all, mainly because she didn't want to work with an asshat like Campbell.

'We don't have anything like the resources that Triple S do,' Vido pointed out. Miska took a sip from her beer. It was one of the nicest beers she'd ever tasted. She stared down at the glass for a moment.

'In part, Triple S have the resources they do because of our backing. You actually have a similar amount of personnel,' Campbell explained.

But not all of them are prepared to volunteer for active service, Miska thought, though she saw no reason to share this with the corporate snake sitting opposite her.

'But,' Campbell continued, 'it's too early for us to make such a commitment, untested, to your organisation. I think perhaps a small job first, see if we're compatible.'

'Can we do that?' Vido asked Salik. The mercenary broker gave it some thought.

'It depends. It can't contravene any of your current contractual obligations. Which means you can't do anything down on Ephesus,' Salik finally told them.

'But what about one of the gas mining aerostats?' Campbell enquired. Salik gave it some more thought.

'I would have to check with my legal team. There would be a nominal administration fee, but my sense of it is that would probably be okay,' he told the New Sun exec before turning to Miska. 'You going to do this?' he asked her.

Miska really didn't want to. She had started the Bastard Legion determined that she would take work from whomever, but the truth of it was she didn't like Campbell, didn't like Triple S and preferred working for the CA.

You're starting to think like Torricone, she chided herself. That was the clincher.

'If we can make it work,' she said cautiously. Even as she said it she didn't like the way it made her feel. Campbell held out his hand. Miska couldn't help but stare at it as if it was made of live slugs. Vido had to shake Campbell's hand for her.

'I'm surprised you're entertaining New Sun's offer,' Salik said, sipping from his coffee, after Campbell had left. Miska just shrugged.

'Might I have a beer now as well, please?' Vido asked. He was now slumped on the sofa. Miska had to resist the urge to apologise to him for her lack of diplomacy making his life more difficult than it needed to be.

'What are they doing here?' Miska asked Salik instead. 'What's this fight all about?'

Salik didn't answer. She knew he couldn't, it would be covered by client confidentiality, but something about his body language suggested that he didn't know. Not knowing something like that could come back to bite Salik. New Sun must have paid him a great deal of money just for him not to ask questions.

'This is the first time they've shown an interest in the gas mining operation,' Vido pointed out.

Miska couldn't shake the feeling that even with her Bastards' ballsy successes, Triple S (elite) backed by a sizeable QRF from Triple S (conventional) were a better choice for physically taking the aerostats, but the real fight for the gas mining operation would take place in the net.

'Will you check with your legal team and let us know?' Miska asked.

Salik nodded.

'You know this will sour things with MACE?' he pointed out. Miska nodded.

'I've never been popular,' she told him, and drained her beer.

'Hard to see why,' Vido muttered. She glared at him. 'Sorry, stressful couple of days.'

'Why don't you finish your beer and I'll meet you back on the *Daughter*?' she suggested.

Vido raised his glass in reply.

Miska stood up.

'Sophie Ashmead,' Salik said. Miska grimaced.

'I get it,' Miska said, 'you can't have that kind of thing on the station. Go after whoever brain-wiped her as aggressively as you like with my blessing. Beyond buying the intelligence I had nothing to do with it, but I can't burn a source or nobody will work with me.'

Salik gave this some thought and then nodded.

'Fair enough,' he said. It was another thing that she liked about him. He was an adult. He understood the rules. He stood up and hugged her.

'You be careful,' he told her. It sounded like the sort of thing that people always said, a useless platitude to someone in her line of work. Miska just smiled and headed for the door, Nyukuti in tow. It was only when she was out on the Central Concourse that it occurred to her that he might have been trying to warn her about something in particular.

CHAPTER 7

Miska knew she didn't want to get in bed with New Sun. She might try to take an amoral approach to choosing business but something about Campbell really bothered her. If Raff's suspicions about them being a Martian shell company were correct then that was another mark against them, though when it came to old Earth nations, particularly developing nations like America, you had to take their perspective on Mars with a pinch of salt. Much of it was propaganda that justified defence and intelligence spending. That said, the Martian regime was not a nice one: a bad mix of monopoly capitalism and Small Gods' cult-of-personality dictatorship.

It's only oppressive when you disagree, Miska mused. She was wandering down the Central Concourse. Nyukuti was a few steps behind her putting his CP training to use. She decided that she was going to see what the offer was from New Sun before she made a decision. She composed a few messages and sent them to the version of her dad who existed in the *Hangman's Daughter*'s systems.

'Corporal Corbin!'

It took Miska a moment or two to realise that someone had called out to her. It had been a really long time since anyone had called her that. Looking around at the various bars that opened out onto the Central Concourse she saw a hulking figure with a crew-cut in the kind of well-ironed shirt and slacks that suggested military personnel on a night out.

'Jones?' Miska asked grinning. 'Hey!' She crossed the distance and hugged the hulking figure. Even with her reinforced skeleton, the powerful return hug threatened to collapse her ribs. Jones released Miska and looked down at her. Jones still had the look of a fresh-faced farm boy, though Miska knew that she had to be in her mid-thirties by now, which still seemed old, somehow, to Miska.

'It's colonel now,' Miska told her. Jones smiled, though it didn't seem to quite make it to her eyes.

'So I heard,' she said, and again there was something in her voice. 'How long's it been? Four years? Just before you tried for selection.'

'That's right.' Miska noticed that the four other soldiers who had been sitting with Jones were either studiously avoiding looking at her by staring at their drinks, or just openly glaring.

'How'd that go for you?' Jones asked.

'Y'know,' Miska said, shrugging, a little distracted by the glares she was receiving.

'Don't mind them,' Jones said, taking Miska by the arm and steering her to a high stool just inside the bar proper, at the window. She concentrated for a moment and a serving drone turned up with two more beers almost as soon as they sat down.

'What's their problem?' Miska said, nodding back to Jones's table.

'You killed some of their friends at Port Turquoise,' Jones told her, grimacing slightly.

'Some of yours as well?' Miska asked.

Jones shrugged.

'That's why they pay us the big bucks, I guess.' She looked down at her beer bottle, smearing the condensation on the glass around with her thumb.

'You with Triple S?' she asked.

Jones nodded. 'Yeah,' she said, 'I am. That a problem?' She looked Miska straight in the eyes.

'Not for me. It's just a pay packet. You up here on repatriation leave?' Miska asked. When mercenaries were captured the victors rarely wanted the responsibility and cost of looking after prisoners. Most mercenaries had a clause written into their contract that the parent company would pay to have them repatriated. Part of the clause meant that the mercs were entitled to leave immediately after their repatriation.

Jones nodded.

'You at Port Turquoise?' Miska asked.

'Yeah, I was there when your boys turned up,' Jones told her.

'Well I'm glad we didn't kill you.' Miska glanced at Jones's angry comrades sat at the other table. 'You got repatriated quickly.'

'Triple S are pretty good about that. You've certainly shaken things up a bit.'

Miska shrugged again and took a sip from her beer.

'We're a new face, we've got to prove ourselves,' she said.

'The job's a lot more dangerous now that you're here.'

Miska leaned back on her high stool and studied Jones for a moment or two.

'Like I told your boss, surrender faster or leave. I'm here to wage war, not dance around posturing.'

Jones held up her hands.

'Hey, relax,' she said.

Miska could make out the fading white of implant scars curling around Jones's skull. It was good work, Triple S clearly paid well.

'You got something to say?' Miska asked.

Jones considered the question.

'Yeah, yeah I do. You can't blame us for wanting to minimise the risk, can you?' she asked. Miska didn't quite trust herself to answer. It sounded like rank hypocrisy to her ears. Profitable no-tears war. 'But what you're doing ain't right, okay?'

'Excuse me?' Miska demanded. She was vaguely aware of Jones's friends paying more attention, of Nyukuti shifting position slightly.

'Sending criminals out to fight professionals—' Jones started.

'They seemed to do all right against you guys,' Miska said and knocked back the beer.

'—slave labour to take our jobs.'

Miska had been pushing the stool back, sliding off it, as Jones said this.

'Everyone who fights for me volunteers and is paid,' Miska told her.

'They volunteer because you put bombs in their heads.'

'The bombs are the prison, the discipline ...'

'What discipline? They massacred a hundred—' Jones started.

'Triple S elite? Ex-special forces? Come on, you don't believe that bullshit, do you?' Miska snapped. She was more angry with herself for getting drawn into the argument than she was with

101

Jones, but the whole propaganda element of the conflict pissed her off.

'Good to see you again,' Miska muttered and made for the door.

'Miska!' Jones called after her. Despite her better judgement Miska stopped and looked back. 'I'm sorry about your dad. I liked him.'

Miska felt something in her chest. She swallowed hard but nodded.

'Miska ...' It was Nyukuti. She could hear the urgency in his voice. Jones, her table of friends, and about three-quarters of the people in the bar suddenly jumped to their feet and snapped to attention. Miska felt a sinking sensation as she turned around to see Colonel Duellona standing inches away from her. Resnick was outside the bar, close to Nyukuti.

'So you're going to use slave labour to undercut real soldiers?' Duellona asked loud enough for the crowd to hear. The hatred coming from the soldiers standing at attention was palpable. There was even angry muttering from the non-Triple S mercenaries in the bar.

'We're mercenaries, none of us are real ... wait, how'd you—?'

'Perhaps you and your scum need a lesson in the capabilities of real soldiers, Corporal Corbin.' Duellona had really emphasised the corporal.

'Wait, you're going to start a—' Miska began. She didn't even see the kick that knocked her through the window. It was too fast. Too strong. Unnaturally so. Lying in the glass, out on the Central Concourse, her left arm felt broken. She knew it wasn't, because of her bone reinforcements. But it still hurt like fuck, as did her side, and she didn't think that she was going to be able to move it much.

Duellona took her time walking around the now-broken window. Miska forced herself to her feet, glancing at Nyukuti. The stand-over man had his hands raised. Resnick was covering him with a gauss pistol.

'You shouldn't be able to do that,' Miska muttered through gritted teeth, and it was true. Miska had military grade cyber-ware augmenting high-end skills that she had worked hard to develop. She should have been able to get out of the way of, or at least block, something as slow as a kick.

'A disgraced tier-three special forces operator in charge of a crew of sick animals? Of course I can do this.'

Miska slapped the first blow out of the way, and too late realised it was a feint. She took a jab to the head that was hard enough to make her see lights. A blow to the stomach doubled her over. A knee to the face straightened her up again, broke her nose and sent her staggering backwards.

Duellona was making this look effortless but Miska just couldn't move fast enough to block. She tried to counter but Duellona battered the blows aside as though they weren't there. Miska grabbed for her SIG. 'I don't think so,' Duellona said. She kicked Miska in the hand, breaking it, and bouncing her off the wall. The last time she had felt this outclassed was when she had fought whatever it was that had inhabited Teramoto's dead body back on Barney Prime.

Miska was aware of other people joining the crowd to watch the fight, including some of her Bastards.

'Small Gods ...' Miska slurred. Duellona's elbow caught her under the chin with enough to force to launch her into the air. She was unconscious before she hit the ground.

*

'Do you ever win a fight?'

Her headache wasn't getting any better. She tried opening her eyes but the white strip lighting of the *Hangman's Daughter*'s medical bay felt like knives being pushed through the soft part of her head.

'Your fight's all over the net. It's being hailed as a triumph of real soldiers over criminal wannabes.'

It was with a not inconsiderable degree of irritation that Miska recognised Torricone's voice. She suspected it was her own fault. Her dad had probably assigned him to assist the Doc after she'd cancelled his leave.

'Win-lots-of-fights,' she slurred and then managed to push through the pain and open her eyes again. Though she almost puked when she sat up.

The operating theatre was stark, grey and very institutional, all the surgical instruments held in locked cabinets and drawers. The robot arms of the operating theatre's built-in automed were poised over her like a long-limbed predatory insect.

Doc, still the most non-descript man that Miska had ever met, was attaching a medpak to drive the gel that covered her hand. MACE's medical facilities were rudimentary at best. The Bastards had been making do with combat medics in the field. Anyone seriously wounded was medevac'd to the *Daughter* and the Doc's tender mercies. Everyone tried not to get medevac'd. The Doc had killed sixty of his patients with nearly untraceable poisons made from genetically modified plants that he had engineered himself, before he had been caught. He had told the court that poisoning his victims had been the only way to preserve their beauty. He was one of the more prolific serial killers on board. The Ultra had asked for the Doc for his Nightmare Squad but he was more valuable to the Legion as a medic.

104

Though if anyone was going to get away with killing someone on her watch, it would be the Doc. He finished attaching the medpak, and his colourless eyes looked down at her.

'The hand will take a day or two to heal. You're probably still concussed but the swelling is now under control, and I've done what I can for the bruising. You've got micro fractures in the reinforcement material on your jaw, but you'll either need to upgrade the facilities here, or take yourself to a 'ware clinic to get that seen to,' he told her. She wasn't sure why, but of all the criminals, even those with much higher body counts like the Ultra, it was the Doc who creeped her out the most.

'Thanks,' she said. He continued looking at her. Irritated that he was making her uncomfortable she instead looked over at Torricone. He was leaning against the reinforced doorframe. He smiled at her, irritating her further.

'You properly and publicly got your ass kicked,' he told her.

'Yeah, I was there. She was made of nanotech. She's either a demigod or one of the Small Gods.' Her mounting irritation wasn't helped by the defensive tone she heard in her voice.

'Was my mom a Small God as well?' Torricone asked with mock innocence.

The Small Gods were AIs of still unknown origin who had grown their own bodies from the Grey Goo Wastelands that had resulted from the nanobombing of Earth during the War in Heaven.

Grinding her teeth made pain shoot through her head. The Doc was still watching her.

'That was different, and I got some good shots in on your mom! Besides, it's not like hiding behind your mom makes you look cool, is it?' she demanded.

Torricone was laughing.

'I'm not trying to look cool,' he said. Miska just stared at him. 'I am saying if you go around claiming that she's a Small God, it's just going to look like you're a sore loser.'

He was right. She knew he was right. That annoyed her more.

'Just fuck off will you, T?' she told him. His smile faltered but he nodded and left the OT.

'People have noticed,' the Doc said quietly. Miska turned to stare at him. She assumed what he saw was a mass of swell-patches and bruises looking back at him.

'Noticed what?' she growled. The Doc just looked at her.

'You'll get him killed,' he finally said.

'You care about that?' she asked. Because she really didn't right then and there.

'He is useful. This work is more interesting to me than the alternative. I like the fungal infections on this world. They have a compelling and alien beauty.'

Miska squeezed her eyes shut as the throbbing in her head intensified. She opened her eyes again as Nyukuti entered the OT. He had not timed it well.

'Some fucking bodyguard you are!'

Nyukuti looked between Miska and the Doc. Then he backed out of the OT.

Miska slid off the operating table. Her legs almost went from underneath her and she had to steady herself by holding on to the table. It was only then she realised that she was just wearing a backless hospital gown.

'Who undressed me?' she asked. The Doc opened his mouth to answer. 'Wait, I don't want to know. Are you trained to do forensics?' It was a long shot, she knew.

'Not specifically, though I did spend some time working with the coroner's office in Capital City.'

'Of course you did,' Miska muttered. It had probably made him a more efficient murderer.

'The *Daughter* has a good library of forensics pathology skillsofts. It's not as good as actual training but it will do in a pinch. Would you have me join the investigators looking into the Trafalgar massacre?'

Does this guy ever blink? Miska wondered.

'Yeah, I really want to know what happened to them. They had fungus growing out of the wounds, you'll love it.'

Doc gave this some thought and then slowly nodded, smiling slightly.

'Will Special Agent Corenbloom be joining me?'

Miska suppressed a slight shiver. It was as though the Doc had read her mind. Though the disgraced FBI agent was of course the obvious choice to accompany him.

'We'll see,' Miska said. The problem was she still had to talk him into it.

Why did I let my dad talk me into only taking volunteers for active service? she wondered. It had been so much easier when people just did as she told them or she blew their heads up.

'Vido, where are you?' she subvocalised over the comms link. She'd put her clothes back on, somewhat gingerly as a surprising amount of her left side – as well as her face, arm, hand and stomach – still hurt. She didn't care what was being said. She could accept getting a kicking, like the one she had at the hands of Torricone's mom. She knew there were better, stronger, more experienced fighters out there. She was self-aware enough to understand the limitations of her own skills, but Colonel Duellona had breezed through her as though she didn't exist.

As Miska made her way through the bowels of the ship

towards the hangar deck she tried to find the least edited footage of the fight to play back. Duellona had done her job well. It hadn't looked like Pavor/Phobos, the entity that had taken over Teramoto's body, cutting through Miska and the other Bastards in the warehouse back in New Verona. Instead the Triple S colonel had made it look as though Miska was just hopelessly outclassed in terms of skill level, rather than technology. Torricone had been right, though. If she started screaming that Duellona was a Small God then she would just be labelled a sore loser and a conspiracy theorist. It would have the opposite effect to what she wanted.

'I'm back at Camp Reisman,' Vido answered. That meant he was back in his suspended animation pod in GenPop, or general population, and tranced in to the VR construct that Miska and her father used to train the Bastards.

'What was the verdict as regards the gas mine operation?' she asked.

'Legally do-able but it'll ruffle feathers at MACE,' Vido told her. She could tell he didn't approve. 'You're going to do it, aren't you?'

'Probably,' she told him.

'Are you just doing this to piss off Triple S? Because we've got lots of other ways we can do that.'

She didn't really want to analyse the answer too carefully.

'Any other business?' Miska asked.

'Mostly routine stuff. The Ultra reached out to me. He wants Gumbhir on his squad.' She could tell that Uncle V didn't enjoy talking about the Nightmare Squad, Miska's scorched-earth option. 'Want me to speak to Golda?'

Miska gave the question some thought.

'What do you think?'

'I think Gumbhir's sick enough but I think Grig will probably kill them all anyway.' Vido meant Rufus Grig, a British vigilante, and the only other person on board the *Hangman's Daughter* with special forces experience.

As far as you know. Miska was thinking of the people who had murdered her father, hidden somewhere in the ship's criminal population.

'But?' Miska asked.

'Golda will try and build an empire . . .' Vido told her.

'Like you,' Miska said.

'Well, yes,' Vido said. She suspected he was suppressing a little irritation. 'But I'm not sure that's a bad thing. He's effectively run an insurgency. Frankly, I think we can use him in a command position, but he should be made to work for it. Gumbhir's an animal but I think Golda getting what he wants is actually the gain for us.'

'Enlightened self-interest?' Miska asked.

'Indeed.' It was practically Uncle V's mantra. He attributed his success to it, well, at least until he fell afoul of the RICO act and ended up in a maximum-security prison barge.

'Where's Golda now?' she asked.

'He's in here training,' Vido told her after a slight delay.

'Okay, I'll speak with him once I've talked to Corenbloom.'

'Uh huh,' Vido said. She could tell he didn't approve of the crooked FBI agent either. Few criminals did approve of law enforcement when they ended up sharing the same prison air. 'Look, I know you don't want any old-life problems landing here but some beefs run deeper than others. It's worth keeping Mass and Corenbloom away from each other. I don't think Mass could help himself.'

Miska wanted to ask but she couldn't shake the feeling it just legitimised whatever the problem was. Instead she closed the comms link down.

Corenbloom, Franklyn, had been a special agent in the FBI's Criminal Investigative Division. Although he was a trained behavioural analyst in the CID's violent crimes section, he had used his position to set up a protection racket for criminal street gangs in New Erebus, a ski resort and vice capital on Barney Prime's night side. He had finally been caught after he had arranged to have his partner, who had been his accomplice in the protection rackets, killed because he had insisted on a larger cut of the profits. Hated by his victims and the Mafia, whom he had acted against to protect his 'clients', it was astonishing to Miska that nobody had managed to kill him in the exercise yard under the *Hangman's Daughter*'s old regime. Even now nobody wanted to work with him during training and he hadn't volunteered for active duty.

She could see the prisoners, wearing printed battle dress uniforms and carrying heavy packs, running around the cavernous hangar deck. They were escorted by guard droids. The lead droid had a screen mounted on it. From the screen the image of her dad exhorted them to try harder in the way that only a Corps training sergeant could. His voice echoed through the hangar. She opened a comms link to her dad.

'Gunny ... sorry, force of habit, LSM, I need to speak to Private Corenbloom.'

'I prefer Gunny,' her dad's gruff voice replied. Miska smiled. 'Where are you?'

'Over by the Centaurs,' she told him as she made her way towards the two captured Martian-built eight-wheeled armoured personnel carriers. She leant against the one that had been configured as a mobile command post and waited. Her hand felt numb now but the rest of her still hurt from the beating, despite the painkillers. She could see a figure jogging towards her.

Corenbloom had been a big, powerfully built man when he'd gone to college on a football scholarship. Judging by the images she'd seen of him during his FBI days he'd tried to keep himself fit but too much riding around in cars and sitting behind desks and he'd surrendered to middle age spread. Her father's punishing PT schedule, however, was slowly turning him back into the man he had once been.

Corenbloom reached the APC covered in sweat. He held his hand up, asking for a moment. Miska nodded. He bent at the waist as he fought to recover his breath.

'You want to ditch the pack, private?' Miska asked.

He just nodded, hit the quick-release straps and shrugged out of it and then looked her up and down.

'Who kicked your ass?' he asked. Miska didn't answer. He shrugged as if it wasn't important. 'This about Trafalgar?' he asked. He wasn't an unattractive man, Miska decided, despite his age. His close cropped hair and carefully trimmed goatee were both more salt than pepper. It was the eyes that bothered her, again. They were like black chips of ice. It wasn't that they made him look evil or insane. Just calculating. Like he was measuring you all the time.

'Yeah. Salik reckons he can get you and the Doc on the investigation team. I want to know what happened.'

'Why?' he asked. Miska decided that this was a guy that she would not like to play poker with.

'Because we're getting blamed.'

'So? Ride it out, nobody believes the propaganda.'

111

Miska thought back to what Jones had said to her, to Duellona playing to the crowd.

'You believe that?' she asked.

He thought about it briefly and then shook his head.

'No, people believe what they want to believe. Truth, facts, actual information often have very little to do with it until you're trying to prove something in a court of law, and even then ...'

'Such cynicism,' Miska said.

Corenbloom just shrugged.

'This an order?' he asked.

Here we go, Miska thought.

'And if it is?'

'I thought active service was only for volunteers,' he said.

'Yes, but the deal for active service remains the same, shore leave and share of the money. I'm not negotiating.'

He nodded, mulling over what she had told him.

'Can I show you something?' he finally said.

'I don't have time for games,' she said.

'It's no game and I promise you it'll be worth it.'

Now it was Miska's turn to study the disgraced FBI agent. She was really struggling to get a read on the guy, though if she was honest, working out what other people were thinking or feeling had never been her strong point. She was, however, mildly curious.

'Fine,' she relented. He picked up his pack and made his way across the hangar deck. He moved over to the bulkhead close to one of the shuttle airlocks. Then he looked at her expectantly.

'What?' she demanded.

'We have a lot in common, you and me. Both disgraced ex-employees of the United States Government. Both people that the rest of the Legion would like to see dead.'

'Well, let's be besties,' Miska suggested. 'We could have a sleepover and you could braid my hair.'

'I was sorry to hear about your father's murder.'

It was like someone had thrown a cold bucket of water over her. Then she got angry.

'Don't let the hand fool you, motherfucker, I'm still more than capable of beating you down.'

He made a calming motion.

'I'm sorry. I wasn't trying to upset you. The fact that you're asking me to look into the massacre means that you know what I used to do for a living.'

'What makes you think that's anything to do ...'

'Because I play Go with Kaneda, and before him, Teramoto. I know you believe that your father's killers are on board, and I'm guessing that you think it's all part of a black op of some kind.'

'So you decided to cut out the middle man?' Miska asked. It was clear that the Yakuza had Corenbloom looking into her father's murder for leverage. She didn't like this, didn't like it all.

'Yes, though they did hire me so I'd appreciate it if you didn't tell Kaneda that I've come direct to you.'

'The Yakuza have been keeping you alive in here, haven't they?' Miska asked. He didn't answer. It made sense. Most of the Yakuza on board came from the Lalande system. They'd never crossed paths with Corenbloom, and the disgraced FBI agent's problems with the Mafia would only have made him more attractive as an ally. 'What do you want?' She was starting to feel that she had been utterly played. As though Corenbloom had been waiting for an opportunity to have this talk.

'First of all I want a commission. Second lieutenant's fine. I'll work my way up.'

'As what? You want a squad?' she asked.

'Intel. It's where all the best people go and hide from combat, as I understand it.'

Miska resisted the absurd urge to defend Uncle V.

'That means you'd be reporting to Major Cofino,' Miska pointed out.

The smile that played briefly across his lips seemed to contain little in the way of actual humour.

'Major Cofino,' he mused. 'You know he once tried to have me killed?'

'I have no time for your prison yard bullshit,' she told him. He shrugged.

'Just business, never personal,' he said, 'but I want something else.'

'What?' she asked.

'I want you to let me go.'

'You and everyone else.'

'When I bring you your father's murderers.'

Miska stared at him.

'You know I could drop you into a VR torture program, leave you there until you tell me what you know.'

'No. You wouldn't. You're a high functioning psychopath. At a guess you're a latent ASPD of the risk-taking subtype. That level of cruelty isn't your thing.'

'No, it's not,' Miska admitted. 'But I think you know enough to know that people aren't real to me unless I like them.' She took a step towards him. Head down. 'And I don't like you,' she whispered and looked up at him. There was just the slightest flicker in his mask of calm, realisation that he might have overplayed his hand.

'I can be of use to you in other ways,' he told her.

'Talk fast, because you're beginning to piss me off.'

'Run a security lens check on the corner here,' he said pointing to where the edge of the airlock met the bulkhead. Miska was getting more than a little fed up of this. It must have shown on her face. 'Please.'

She sighed and connected to the *Daughter*'s security systems via her neural interface, the results appearing in her IVD. She frowned and then ran the check again, and then a third time.

'You see it?' Corenbloom asked. Miska ignored him and looked around at the nearby lenses.

'It's a blind spot,' she finally said. It wasn't a small blind spot, either.

Corenbloom nodded and then pointed at two tiny figures scratched into the black painted metal of the airlock's frame. Miska zoomed in on it. It looked like the letters E and C. She turned back to Corenbloom.

'Escape Committee,' he told her. Corenbloom reached down and touched the letters then held up his fingers. There were little flecks of black paint on them. 'This has been done recently as well.'

'How do I know this wasn't you?' Miska asked. Suddenly she was starting to question just how cooperative the prisoners had been recently.

'Not my sort of game,' he said. 'Besides, consider Occam's Razor. Do you really think that nobody on board wants to escape?' On balance she suspected she believed him. 'I mean, you've already had one escape.'

'Lomas Hinton is dead,' Miska said. Hinton hadn't come back on board after shore leave in Maw City. Though to be honest she had no real proof that he was dead. She looked down at the two letters scratched into black paint.

'You really are a rat, aren't you?' she asked. It was petty and she knew it but he didn't rise to the bait. He just watched her, impassive. 'You go looking for my father's murderers, how are you going to get the rest of them to talk to you?'

'That's my problem,' he said. Miska suspected he would manipulate the Yakuza and the Bethlehem Milliners to do his legwork. 'Do we have a deal?'

Miska still didn't like this. She didn't like it all. More so than Vido, Teramoto, even the Ultra, this somehow felt like getting into bed with the devil.

She nodded.

'When do you want me to leave for Trafalgar?'

CHAPTER 8

Miska was taking one of the access ladders up to the *Hangman's Daughter*'s bridge. Judging by how out of breath she was by the time she reached the bridge deck, it was obvious she needed the exercise. Just another thing she was angry with herself about.

I'm a fool. She had been lulled into a false sense of security by the combat and support elements of the Legion appearing to be so cooperative of late: embracing their training, embracing the work, getting paid, enjoying the myriad pleasures of Waterloo Station. Of course they wanted to be free. Of course they wanted the bombs out of their heads and, if they could get away with it, they would want the *Daughter* and the not inconsiderable hardware on board. It occurred to her, not for the first time, that with the weapons and training the prisoners had access to it would not be difficult for them to knock over and take control of one of the smaller colonies.

Miska reached the bridge deck and made her way along the short corridor. The ship's systems recognised her and the blast door opened. The bridge was as quiet as ever. Hologram displays

117

illuminated the gloom, showing local space in various different spectrums, telemetry and system diagnostic data cascading through the air. She made her way up to the raised captain's workstation that gave her a commanding view of the other two bridge levels. Through the two storeys of wraparound windows Miska could make out the lights of Waterloo Station on her left as they slowly revolved around it on the top docking torus. Various shuttles and occasionally larger ships moved around the station, and through its three slowly spinning tori, she could see the torches of their manoeuvring engines flickering off and on. Epsilon Eridani glowed in the distance. The revolving docking torus slowly brought the red glow of Eridani B into view.

At the back of her head she had still known that she couldn't trust any of the prisoners but now the need for the healthy paranoia that was a job requirement returned more fiercely than ever. Who was in the Escape Committee? Vido, Mass, Kaneda, Nyukuti? Torricone? Torricone seemed a very likely candidate, assuming the other prisoners would trust him, which they might not, given the erroneous conclusions they were jumping to about him and herself.

The captain's chair suddenly felt like a very lonely throne. She spent a moment or two brooding, then her neural interface reached out for the *Daughter*'s systems and Miska tranced herself in.

Miska appeared in what looked like a bare, institutional smart-crete corridor. She was in Camp Reisman's command post, the virtual reality construct designed to behave as close to reality as its USMC-hired programmers could make it. She had appeared in the empty corridor so she wouldn't just materialise in front of any of the legionnaires, and thus break the construct's verisimilitude. The training construct wasn't the stylised animation of the net. It was set up to look like actual reality. Her icon was pretty much a one-to-one representation of what she looked like but without the swell patches on her face and the medgel all over her hand.

'Vido,' she subvocalised as she opened a direct comms link to her XO, 'I'm in the CP, where is Golda?'

'He's just outside in the rest area, waiting for you,' Vido replied. He sounded a little harassed. Miska suspected there was considerably less sitting around in cafes bullshitting with his friends in the Legion than there had been in his previous job.

'Can I get a minute with you to talk about the gas mining job once you've spoken to Golda?' Vido asked. Miska sighed internally but agreed as she made her way out of the CP.

Outside, the camp looked like so many she had lived in throughout her entire life, first as a military brat and then as a leatherneck when she had joined the Corps. Printed smartcrete buildings, parade grounds, vehicle parks and workshops, the mess and, beyond the boundaries of the camp itself, the various customisable training environments. At the moment the training was concentrating on jungle warfare for obvious reasons. All of it was overseen from the tower in the centre of the CP that overlooked the entire base, much like a spaceport control tower.

Golda was sat at a plastic table underneath an awning that stuck out from the side of the CP. It was used as a break area for the CP's staff. There were a number of other tables and chairs scattered around, a few dispensing machines. Golda was sipping from a cup of lemon tea.

The Leopard Society boss looked deceptively spindly despite all the PT that her father had put the prisoners through. He was tall, his head shaved, and he wore a slight smile on his face that Miska had come to connect with intelligent criminals who felt they had the upper hand in some way. His BDU's looked clean and pressed, which suggested that whatever training he had been doing hadn't been that strenuous. He stood up and saluted as she approached. Miska didn't like this. She had spent most of her military career in various special operations groups where military discipline had been much more relaxed. However, her father had insisted that this was important. Though nobody saluted in the field to avoid becoming sniper-bait.

Aheto-Cudjoe, Golda. A senior boss in the pan-African Leopard Society crime syndicate. He was Congolese by birth, from an affluent middle class family. Aheto-Cudjoe had apparently turned his not inconsiderable intellect to crime at an early age, though that had not prevented him from getting an undergraduate degree in business management and economics, and a postgraduate degree in international relations. Selling hacked counterfeit weapons for popular net-based sense games had apparently financed both degrees. He had graduated from Oxford University in Kinshasa, and a mixture of practically applied intelligence and ruthlessness had seen him rise through the ranks of the Leopard Society. When the Kenyan authorities had cracked down on one of the Leopards' most profitable human trafficking rings, and gone on to openly declare war on the Society, Aheto-Cudjoe had been the mastermind behind the retaliatory Glass Desert insurrection. The Crocodile Society, the Leopard Society's military arm, had used asymmetrical warfare against the Kenyan police and judiciary so effectively that eventually the military had to be called in. Aheto-Cudjoe's well-publicised trial had been more than a little controversial. He was convicted of killing two *Nyota Mlima* SWAT team members during his arrest. His defence had argued, quite convincingly, that Aheto-Cudjoe had been acting in self-defence. Certainly they had not been able to gather enough evidence to convict him of any of the other criminal activities he had most certainly been involved in.

'Colonel Corbin,' Golda said and bowed slightly, gesturing for her to join him at the table before sitting down again. Miska did the same and ordered a soft drink from one of the nearby dispensing machines. A tiny serving drone brought the drink to their table. 'I understood you wanted to see me?'

'And I'm guessing you can work out why,' Miska said warily. She didn't think she was a stupid person, far from it, but she also knew there were some really smart prisoners on board the *Daughter*. Golda was definitely one of them.

'I think whenever white people hear the words jungle and warfare they automatically think of black people.' The smile was still there. The sunglasses were making it more than a little difficult for Miska to read him. She could order him to take them off, or even make them disappear with a thought, but she couldn't shake the feeling that it would be an admission of weakness.

'Oh bullshit,' Miska muttered. 'You grew up in a nice suburb of Kinshasa and spent most of your adult life in the shadow of the *Nyota Mlima* spoke, selling immigrant workers to off-world colonies as disposable slave labour. So don't come like that with me.' *Nyota Mlima 2* was one of the huge equatorial orbital elevators, or spokes, that reached up from the surface of the Earth into high orbit. The first *Nyota Mlima* had been destroyed by kinetic orbital bombardment during the War in Heaven. Its towering ruins had been turned into a huge memorial garden.

Golda watched her for a moment or two and then smiled.

'Allegedly,' he added. 'Let us not pretend.' His English was heavily accented but perfect. 'You are interested in Bobo, not me, for the Ultra's atrocity squad.'

'And you have been holding your people back from active duty with the Legion until you had some leverage to bargain for position,' Miska said. She felt a little bit of pleasure in Vido's words that Golda would be just as much, if not more, of an asset than Bobo Gumbhir who, under Golda's command, had become known as the 'Glass Desert Cannibal'.

'I am not sure that Bobo is who you think he is,' Golda told her. 'Every act of terror, every atrocity, was carefully calculated and psychometrically tested in simulations to work towards our ultimate aim. Bobo is a thoughtful and quiet man who relishes peace as much as violence.'

And that might well have been the truth, but all that Miska knew was what Gumbhir was actually capable of. After leaving a trail of mutilated and often partially-eaten bodies all over Sub-Saharan Africa, he had been caught red-handed, the blood of a Nairobi judge's family still smeared all over his face. He had killed seven of the police officers who had tried to arrest him. More to the point, the Leopard Society had almost succeeded. They had almost convinced the Kenyan authorities to leave them to operate with impunity.

'What do you want?' Miska asked. She had discovered that prisoners loved to talk as a result of having so much time on their hands. She was watching as a Pegasus assault shuttle, escorted by four Machimoi combat exoskeletons flying in diamond formation, came in to land on the other side of the parade ground.

'A commission.'

It seemed to be a popular request today.

'You want a squad?' she asked, considering making him the same offer she had made Corenbloom.

'I assume that you're aware that I am more than capable of looking after myself. I have nothing to prove. I will also assume that you are aware that my talents lie in the strategic rather than tactical.'

Miska knew he was right. He was more experienced than she was at running combat operations, albeit a particular type of combat operation, but she had to balance that with just how much power she could risk turning over to this extremely dangerous individual.

'Where?' she asked. She suspected he would be best off running combat operations. What he didn't know about warfare he was more than capable of learning, probably more so than she was herself. She wasn't, however, going to turn over command of live troops in the field to someone who hadn't commanded them in that field. She just couldn't, Marine Corps doctrine was too ingrained in her thinking.

'Vido Cofino is stretched working as your executive officer and the Legion intelligence officer. Let me take some of the latter responsibilities off his shoulders.'

Intelligence, again. Miska was thinking back to her earlier conversation with Corenbloom.

'And what do I get?' Miska asked.

'I will speak with Bobo, that is all I can do ...'

'Oh bullshit!' Miska snapped. 'You're a smart guy but don't treat me like I'm an idiot.' She let some of her actual anger leak through. 'I know who pulls the strings.' She saw the muscles around Golda's mouth tighten.

'Very well. Bobo will join your atrocity squad.'

'And?' Miska demanded. Golda watched her through the dark lenses of his sunglasses for a few moments.

'Members of both the societies that I have a degree of influence in are free to volunteer for active duty, if they wish. I suspect many of the Leopards won't, though some have skills that could be put to use in a support capacity. I suspect many of the Crocodiles will.'

'I appreciate you talking so openly about it,' Miska told him. He just nodded. He took his sunglasses off. His eyes were a deep green colour, like the sea.

'What do you think you're doing here?' he asked. There was no challenge in his voice, only curiosity.

Miska frowned. 'Building a mercenary force.'

'If you were smart you would realise that you have a perfect opportunity to create a force that is a perfect synergy between a military and criminal organisation. You may as well realise this now, because I assure you Vido Cofino and his associates have.'

Miska wasn't quite sure what to make of his words.

'If the Legion is being subverted then I would know about it,' Miska told him.

'I don't mean subversion. I mean sometimes you need a military solution and other times ...'

That she could understand. On more than one occasion they had relied on individual legionnaires' criminal skills rather than their military ones. Golda appeared to be stating the obvious. Miska frowned again.

'You have a problem with Major Cofino?' she asked. She only just stopped herself from calling him Uncle V.

'I have a great deal of respect for Vido Cofino, and I look forward to working with him more closely.'

For the second time that day Miska couldn't shake the feeling that jaws of a trap had just closed around her. The jaws of a leopard.

Miska found Vido in one of the rec rooms in the CP. He was bullshitting with some of his fellow wiseguys. Mafia old boys, mostly *caporegime*, or street bosses, and *soldatos*. They were of an age with Vido, or older, making them too old for active service. Miska and her father had to be a little careful putting them to work. They were trying to limit Vido's empire building, but they also didn't want to insult the old boys. Everything was a balancing act and they hadn't found anything appropriate for them to do just yet. They were up on their feet and saluting as Miska walked into the room. Somehow they made their salutes seem like old country, gentlemanly courtesy. She had them stand at ease and exchanged a few words before dismissing them. Everything was friendly, everything pleasant. She had no doubt that any one of them would have killed her in a heartbeat given the opportunity.

'Hey Vido,' Miska said by way of greeting. The programming on the training construct was so good that he even looked tired here.

'Hey boss. How'd it go?' he asked meaning the meeting with Golda. Miska sent a message to her dad.

'Pretty much as you said,' Miska told him.

'He held out for influence?' Vido asked.

'Just like you,' Miska pointed out.

'Makes you wonder why the Yakuza are being so quiet,' he said.

Why'd he say that? Miska's paranoia asked. *Is he trying to introduce a seed of doubt here?* Teramoto's death on Barney Prime had been something of a blow for the Scorpion Rain

Society, the largest and most influential Yakuza society on board the *Daughter*. It wasn't clear who was going to emerge as the Society's new leader. Though rumour had it that Kaneda, who had been a member of the Bethlehem Milliners, a bike gang associated with the Yakuza, was now a fully-fledged member of the Society and rising swiftly through the ranks.

'This about Corenbloom?' Miska asked. If the Yakuza had been protecting the crooked FBI agent from the Mafia then it was just another reason for friction between the two organisations.

Vido frowned.

'You know what gets me about that guy?' Vido asked. 'He was good, I mean really good, and he went after some bad people, worked high profile cases. You know he worked on the Ultra investigation. Nearly got him in New Erebus. He was consulting with the local Feeb on Sirius 4 when they took him down. He just loved the street too much. He wanted to be like the people he put away.'

'He said that you tried to have him killed,' Miska said and then kicked herself. This was the kind of real-world bleed into her organisation that she couldn't allow. Vido shrugged. He would never incriminate himself, he was a lawyer and a criminal after all. Miska knew some of it from the *Daughter*'s files. Corenbloom had become too ambitious. He, along with another corrupt FBI agent, a number of corrupt cops, and their criminal allies had tried to push the Mafia out of New Erebus. It had turned bloody.

'He tell you he had Mass's girlfriend killed?' Vido asked.

That explained why Mass hated Corenbloom so much.

Her dad walked into the meeting room. He didn't bother coming to attention or saluting with only Miska and Vido present. Instead he just nodded at Vido, who nodded back. Her dad was another person who Vido had made friends with despite the legion sergeant major's best efforts to resist such a friendship.

'You got your ass kicked,' he said. Miska sighed. 'How'd that happen?'

'You seen the footage?' she asked. Her dad nodded. 'Should I be that outclassed?'

'Martian nanotech?' he asked.

'At best. It felt like I was fighting Teramoto, y'know after he was ...' she told them.

Her dad turned to Vido. 'That legal here?' he asked.

Vido was shaking his head. 'No, strictly forbidden under the articles of conflict, as mandated by the UN conflict inspector,' he told them. 'To be honest, some of the hardware they're using, and now we are because we stole it from them, is borderline.'

'Anything we can do about it?' LSM Corbin asked.

'Not unless we can prove it, and we'd better have really good proof. I can dig into it but I've not managed to find much on Duellona or Resnick,' Vido told them. Miska and her father exchanged a look. 'What?'

'They came from nowhere, high-end military skills,' her dad said. 'Could be off-the-book members of the Spartans.'

Spartan was an umbrella term for Martian special operations units.

'Martian boogie men?' Miska asked. 'Reds under the bed?'

Her dad shrugged.

'We could hire a PR company?' Vido said, though the resignation in his voice suggested that he knew his question was a waste of time.

'Not a chance,' LSM Corbin scoffed. Miska was shaking her head.

'Well, at least give the journalist ... Raff, a chance. I've spoken to him, he's a good guy, sympathetic. He could tell our side of the story. Stop letting the guys tase him and tie him up,' Vido told them, somewhat irritably Miska thought. She couldn't help but smile. She noticed her dad was doing the same thing. 'I'm serious, boss.'

'No amount of PR is going to change who and what we are,' Miska said. *Or what I've done*, she didn't add. 'But we'll let the lenshead ride along next time.'

'And you won't tase him or tie him up?' Vido checked.

'Sure,' Miska said. Uncle V didn't look reassured. She decided to change the subject. 'The gas mine job, you think it's a bad idea?'

Vido shrugged. 'We've got a good relationship with MACE, with the Colonial Administration. Why jeopardise that?'

'They're grown-ups,' LSM Corbin pointed out.

'There's no way this isn't going to feel like a knife in the back to them, no matter the realpolitik,' Vido insisted.

'Where are you on this?' Miska asked her dad.

He gave the question some consideration.

'I'd rather fight for the colonials. I think New Sun are assholes—'

'Untrustworthy assholes,' Vido added.

'—but we're either mercenaries in a free market economy or we're not,' her dad continued, 'and I quite like the idea of making Triple S look stupid.'

Miska was a little surprised that her dad was prepared to go for the plan.

'What is it they actually want us to do?' Miska asked Vido.

'Most of the gas mining aerostats are automated. They have a number of control platforms that are actually manned

– human oversight, maintenance teams, storage depots, that kind of thing. New Sun are talking about a coordinated effort, attacking them all simultaneously. From the control platforms they can take control of the whole operation in the net.'

'Why not just hack it?' LSM Corbin asked.

'Whoever's running security will have their own hackers, and besides, it's always easier from within a system,' Miska told her dad. 'Who's running security for them?'

'The Dogs of Love,' Vido told them.

'Competent but unimaginative,' her dad said. Miska was nodding in agreement.

'L'Amour's a good guy,' Vido pointed out.

'You don't think you're getting a little too sentimental for this job do you, Vido?' Miska asked.

A shadow passed over Uncle V's face.

'I just don't like burning relationships with so little gain.'

'How many?' Miska asked.

'Eight platforms,' Vido told her.

'We don't have the shuttles,' her dad said.

'They're just giving us one platform. Campbell told me it was a test of our abilities,' Vido explained.

'As opposed to us humiliating Triple S at their own mech base and in Port Turquoise?' her dad asked.

'Like I said, this is a bad idea,' Vido told them. 'They also want us moving all of a sudden. The moment we say yes they'll send over the schematics. Operationally it's up to us but we move four hours after accepting the job. They're holding up the operation for us.'

At this news her dad did not look happy.

'That's not much time,' he told her.

Miska shrugged. 'We've both gone out with less prep.

Time-compressed run through the job in VR?' she suggested.

'Who?' Vido asked. 'Everyone who's combat ready is down on the planet. Everyone up here is on leave, they'll all be drunk.'

He had a point.

'I've got a really bad idea,' Miska told them.

CHAPTER 9

Miska had overridden Uncle V's objections and managed to curtail a major argument with her dad on the grounds of practicality. They'd only had four hours to plan and run time-contracted VR simulations based on the intel provided by New Sun. Her dad had left her with the distinct impression that their 'discussion' was not over yet. She could see his and Vido's point. It looked like she had gone back to her bad old ways. She hadn't. Or at least she didn't think she had. Miska needed to know if the Ultra's Nightmare Squad could be controlled. This was the best way to find out.

That was how she found herself in the passenger bay of the *Hangman's Daughter*'s remaining prisoner transport shuttle. The shuttle had recently been up-armoured and armed, retro-fitted as an assault shuttle, which was how it had started its life. It was no Pegasus but it would do in a pinch. Trying to control the ancient, armoured hulk of the shuttle in the upper cloud layer of Eridani B was proving something of a trial of fire for the newly sim-qualified pilot.

'Ah! Fuck!' Miska shouted as she banged her gel-covered right hand on her seat's armrest. The shuttle was being kicked around so much in the upper atmosphere that she felt like she was on a small boat in the middle of an angry ocean. Atmospheric interference from the bad weather, however, would go a long way towards hiding the shuttle from the gas mining aerostat's rudimentary sensors.

'You're not combat ready,' Rufus Grig said, looking at her medgel-covered shooting hand. He was in charge of the power armour element of this hastily cobbled together operation. He was standing in one of the *Daughter*'s ancient, but also recently upgraded, Wraith combat exoskeletons. The front was unbuttoned and his head was visible under the peeled-back armoured plate. In his mid-thirties, Grig was of Afro-Caribbean descent but came from London. With freckles and short dreadlocks, he was a handsome man, Miska supposed, but his dark eyes were dead – there was nothing there at all. His eyes made his face look slack somehow. An ex-member of Britain's SAS, he had stood up to some local thugs where he lived in London and then come home to find his entire extended family butchered. That had resulted in a torture and killing spree that had culminated in a hostage situation. It had only ended when a number of Grig's erstwhile colleagues had breached the tower block where he was holed up and taken him down non-lethally. He hadn't said anything during his trial. The judge might have been more lenient had it not been for what she had called 'the astonishing brutality' of his crimes.

Miska had approached the vigilante shortly after she had taken control of the *Daughter*. Grig had made it perfectly clear that she was no better than all the other scum on board and that given the chance he would kill her – thus setting off all the N-bombs, or so he believed – and rid humanity of six thousand pieces of human excrement. Miska still half expected him to try it.

The Nightmare Squad was the worst of the worst. She was still surprised that Grig had agreed to work with the Ultra. The Ultra, for his part, remained convinced that Grig was just as much a serial killer as he himself was and merely needed an excuse.

'She'll be fine.' The Ultra whispered but somehow his voice still carried. Even though he was wearing Miska's own space-suit, his long platinum silver hair tied back, he looked like an alabaster statue of classical perfection given motion. He remained the most beautiful guy Miska had ever seen. She'd never been comfortable with how it made her feel when she looked at him, mostly because she knew it was artifice – a created look that was the product of technology, not impossible genes. He had been sculpted.

Grig looked unconvinced by his squad leader's words.

'How's Skirov's reconstruction coming along?' the Ultra asked, changing the subject. He must have had the knife he was toying with printed. Miska hadn't seen the design before, though the blade was titanium with a fused synthetic diamond edge, just like her own. To her eyes the Ultra's blade was almost elegant in its functionality. It looked like the most practical killing knife she'd ever seen. Miska wondered how many of the Ultra's artfully murdered victims had met their ends at the edge of a blade like that.

'Slowly,' Miska finally answered, taking her eyes off the knife. Skirov was a warewolf, a heavily reconstructed cyborg made to resemble a machine version of the old Earth werewolf myths. He had replaced too much of his body with machinery and ended up divorced from his humanity, becoming a psychotic murder machine. He had been extensively deconstructed before he, like the Ultra, had been sentenced to solitary confinement aboard the *Hangman's Daughter*. Miska had been putting a small amount of the money the Legion earned into having him reconstructed. *Another killing machine in the arsenal*, she thought.

'Be nice to have a puppy,' Bean said, though his Scottish accent was so thick that Miska had to run his words through her head a few times before she could work out their meaning. The intention was for Skirov to join the Nightmare Squad when he was fully reconstructed. Like Grig, Bean was wearing a combat exoskeleton. Unlike Grig's, Bean's suit was the spare Machimoi. His narrow, weasely face, with its hollow cheeks and wild, manic eyes, looked out at her from the unbuttoned power armour.

Bean, Swanky. Sentenced to consecutive life sentences for eleven proven murders and suspected of many, many more. Bean had lived in the wilds of the Scottish parklands with his 'family', a clan of incestuous, torturing, murderous cannibals, who based their existence on an old folk tale. They had moved around the vast wilderness feasting on campers, hikers and other visitors to the park. Rumour had it that they had been able to do so for so long with the co-operation of the Scottish tourist board who felt their presence in the park helped encourage the more macabre visitors. After the family had been caught in an extensive police operation and sentenced, they had been split up and sent to different prisons. Swanky had ended up on the *Daughter*. Frankly, he disgusted Miska, and he knew it. She looked up to find him watching her again. He smiled, his filed-down and capped teeth like pointed canines, a line of drool running down his chin.

'What do you think, Fatman?' Bean asked the closest person he had to a friend.

Kaczmar, Charles. Like Miska, he was an ex-marine.

Unlike Miska he had kidnapped, tortured and murdered over thirty people before dumping their bodies into space. He had been working as a miner in the Sol System's asteroid belt. Nicknamed the 'Fatman' he had only been caught when one of his victims had survived long enough in vacuum to be picked up by a passing ore freighter. A one in a million freak occurrence. The victim, one of Kaczmar's co-workers, had recognised the Fatman, identifying him to the authorities on Ceres, before succumbing to his wounds and the ravages of vacuum. Kaczmar hadn't put up a fight when the SWAT team had stormed his bunk area. When asked why he'd committed the murders he had told the prosecutor that he was bored.

He certainly lived up to his name, Miska thought. He was four hundred pounds of pure butterball. That said, there must have been something under that sea of fat because, somehow, he managed to keep up with her dad's gruelling PT routines – but without losing any body fat. Miska suspected he was some kind of freak of nature. The gyroscopic harness he wore, which supported the Sarissae railgun, had needed to be altered before it would fit his corpulent bulk. The Ultra insisted that Kaczmar had a genius level intellect. If that was the case then Miska hadn't seen any indication of it, and it certainly wasn't on display now as he turned his huge, hairless head towards Bean, his little piggy eyes staring, his facial features like a tiny island among the folds of fat, and farted audibly in answer.

Bean giggled like a nine year old.

'A well thought out and considered answer,' Bean told his huge 'friend'. At least, Miska was pretty sure that was what he'd said.

'You know how to use that?' Grig asked Bobo Gunhir, the second cannibal on the squad.

For someone who had struck fear into the great and good of Kenya and *Nyota Mlima*, the so-called Cannibal of the Glass Desert looked surprisingly normal. Solidly built, his hair cropped short, a neatly trimmed goatee covering his chin, he looked much more like a soldier than a criminal. Miska found this a little reassuring.

The 'that' Grig was referring to was a Martian Military Industries Appolion plasma rifle. It had been one of two man-portable plasma weapons found when the Bastards had captured the frigate *Excelsior* from Triple S, after the battle of Faigroe Station. Incredibly expensive, it fired hydrogen pellets that had been superheated to a plasma state. It was a devastating weapon. Gunhir paused while attaching a PDW over the Appolion's barrel as a secondary weapon, and looked up at Grig, studying him for a moment.

'In Kenya we called this weapon the Tears of the Sun. We used them to assassinate prosecutors, judges, high-ranking police officers and other dignitaries in their armoured vehicles. Please be assured, I know what I'm doing.'

Grig nodded. Miska could understand the vigilante's concern. As eager as she was to see the Appolion in play, she wasn't keen to lose it, and Gunhir's part in this was pretty crucial for a newcomer to the squad.

'You good?' Miska asked Nyukuti, sitting next to her. He had just finished attaching his PDW to the mounting rails underneath the barrel of a printed, magazine-fed 30mm grenade launcher. The stand-over man looked over at her and nodded. Given his capability for torture, Miska had asked the Ultra why he hadn't wanted Nyukuti on his squad. The Ultra had told her that the stand-over man didn't want to hurt people enough. Sadly, Miska had known what he meant. For Nyukuti torture had been a means to an end, for the rest of the Nightmare Squad hurting people was the end, and now she had to make sure they all stayed on the leash. She knew that Grig wasn't happy. Part of the agreement he had with the Ultra was that they would only go after really bad people. They were about to attack an aerostat full of gas mining civilians and mercenaries just doing their jobs. Grig reminded her of a spree-killing Torricone. She had been happy that talking Grig into the op had been the Ultra's problem, not hers. One Torricone was more than enough, even if this one was a torturer and mass-murderer.

'Everyone ready?' she said at the same time as the Ultra. He smiled and gestured to her. 'No, it's your command, I'm just along for the ride,' she told him.

Or because you're bored, or because you've got something to prove, the voice inside her suggested. She tried to ignore it.

'You all know what you're doing. We stick to the plan and it will be just fine,' the Ultra told them. She hadn't heard an implied threat in his voice but she was aware of a number of very dangerous individuals shifting uncomfortably. Over the comms link Miska heard the Ultra give the shuttle pilot the order to rise out of the gas clouds. Miska enlarged the feed from the ageing shuttle's external lenses in her IVD. She saw tendrils of cyanide-laced hydrogen swirl around the shuttle, reaching out for it as it rose out of the clouds towards the gas mining platform.

The aerostat mine looked like a technological mushroom covered in industrial hardware. Interconnected pre-fabricated machine rooms, tool sheds, atmosphere flyer hangars, storage bladders and sleeping quarters sprouted haphazardly from the spars of the mushroom's superstructure. Trunk-like appendages hung from the refinery machinery at the base of the mushroom. These huge tendrils, dangling into the planet's stormy upper atmosphere, harvested the gas giant's hydrogen and helium-3. Miska could make out the lights of the numerous automated aerostat platforms in the upper atmosphere. They fed on the huge planet's resources like a swarm of blood-sucking mosquitoes.

There was an assault shuttle docked with the aerostat atmosphere-mining platform. It belonged to the Dogs of Love mercenary collective employed by the Colonial Administration and under the command of MACE. The tactical information overlaid in her IVD made her aware of their own shuttle missile-locking the Dogs of Love's shuttle. She watched hypersonic tracers from the prison shuttle's new railgun batteries turn the aerostat's bolted-on weapon emplacements into so much scrap with short controlled bursts, only a minimum of collateral damage.

Despite the upper atmosphere turbulence, Grig and Bean had buttoned up their combat exoskeletons and, along with the Ultra, who had also sealed his borrowed spacesuit, made their way towards the airlock.

'Piper Sierra to unknown shuttle, please be aware that the articles of conflict prohibit all space warfare. Your attack is an act of piracy and will be dealt with as such.' The voice was calm, just a hint of tension. Miska assumed that it was one of the mercenaries rather than one of the miners.

'I think it's best if you handle this,' the Ultra told her over a private comms link.

'They've got two combat exos in the air,' Grig relayed over the group comms. 'Look like older generation Honey Badgers to me.'

'Okay, the shuttle will hunt them, we engage only if fired upon, stick to the plan,' the Ultra reminded them.

'Piper Sierra, your gas mining station is within a planetary atmosphere and therefore a legitimate target. If that shuttle attempts to leave its dock we'll blow it out of the sky. This is the Bastard Legion, surrender now.'

'Let's go,' Gunhir told them. Despite him being a newcomer the Ultra had put him in charge of the boarding element. If Kaczmar minded he hadn't expressed it in any way.

'Piper Sierra to the Bastards, aren't you supposed to be on our side?' the voice asked. Miska could hear a little more tension now. She didn't answer. The Dogs of Love would fight. They would have to if they ever wanted another mercenary contract in the Epsilon Eridani system. Miska managed to stand up, somewhat unsteadily, as the deck bucked underneath her. In the external lens feed she watched as Grig and Bean jumped from the shuttle's airlock, the Ultra, in Miska's spacesuit, wrapped tightly around Grig's Wraith. The torches on their flight fins lit up as they jetted underneath the aerostat in between the dangling tendrils of the huge vacuum hoses.

Miska picked up her boarding shield and followed the others towards the airlock, moving from handhold to handhold as best she could, the molecular hooks on the soles of her boots helping her remain on her feet.

The shuttle was now playing hide and seek in between the superstructure with the two Honey Badger combat exoskeletons. She heard the faint staccato drum beat of electromagnetically-driven 20mm rounds powdering against their shuttle's much improved armour. In the external lens feed the upper atmosphere glowed red as the shuttle's point defence lasers destroyed incoming missiles fired from the Honey Badgers' back-mounted launchers. It was a very unfair fight. The two Dogs of Love Combat Exoskeletons had little going for them except their manoeuvrability. Any cover they found was quickly chewed away by the shuttle's railguns as it chased them around the aerostat. A stray round caught one of the Badgers' flight fins and sent it spiralling down towards the gas clouds.

Miska had taken up position at the corner of the corridor that led down to one of the shuttle's airlocks. Gunhir was next to her. On the other side of the corridor Nyukuti waited with Kaczmar. She heard Kaczmar chuckle.

'He'll be so tiny,' the huge serial killer said quietly. His voice was soft and surprisingly high pitched.

'Are you in this, Fatman?' Gunhir asked him. Kaczmar just grunted at Gunhir by way of reply.

In the external lens feed Miska saw the other Honey Badger dive after his plummeting mate.

'Let them go but keep an eye on them,' Miska subvocalised to the shuttle's pilot and co-pilot, receiving an acknowledgement back. She was also keeping an eye on the DoL assault shuttle but it hadn't moved. The Dogs of Love might have to put up at least a token resistance but they weren't prepared to risk a resource like an assault shuttle. *Very wise*, Miska decided, though not the way she would have played it.

She checked the lens feeds from Grig and Bean. They were standing on an EVA walkway just outside one of the aerostat's airlocks. Bean was attaching his very expensive plasma thermite frame charge to the external airlock while Grig covered him. When he'd finished Bean stepped away from the airlock, putting his back to the aerostat's hull, unclipping his Dory railgun and readying it as the frame glowed white, turning thick metal and hardened composite molten as it burned through the external airlock. Grig placed an armoured hand in the centre of the airlock, pulled the glowing, molten-edged rectangle of dripping metal and composite out of the airlock, and let it fall into the crushing depths of the gas giant. He stepped into the airlock and attached another plasma thermite frame charge to the inner airlock door while Bean watched his back.

We very nearly look like soldiers, Miska thought, as the prison shuttle docked with the aerostat. Strobing light from the laser torch mounted on the ceiling over the shuttle's airlock entrance bathed the corridor in red light as it cut through the aerostat's external airlock door. Nyukuti moved down the corridor and kicked in the glowing rectangle of metal. The re-sounding clang echoed through the prison shuttle. Through the feed from Nyukuti's helm-cam, Miska could see him attaching a hydraulic ram to the aerostat's internal airlock door before returning to his position on the other side of the corridor with Kaczmar. The strobing light started again. Nyukuti nodded at Miska as he readied his grenade launcher, his own boarding shield leaning against the wall. He got down on one knee, using the corner of the corridor as cover.

Miska checked the lens feed from the Ultra. It was blank. She had expected no less. She was still going to have to discuss that with him.

Miska was gritting her teeth. She just wanted it to start. The time waiting for her action 'hit' seemed to stretch out in front of her and into eternity. Waiting for the laser cutter to do its thing was interminable.

Then came the clang of the hydraulic ram beating on the aerostat's cut-through internal airlock. Nyukuti was already firing the grenade launcher. The first three-round burst of 30mm grenades was in the air before she heard the clang of the airlock hitting the aerostat's deck. In Nyukuti's hands the grenade launcher looked like a massively oversized carbine. He adjusted for the weapon's recoil, fired another three-round burst, then another and finally a fourth burst, emptying the magazine. He ducked back behind the corner. The defenders hadn't even started returning fire yet. All four of the Bastards turned away, closing their eyes, hands over their ears, mouths open. All the multi-spectrum stun grenades went off in quick succession. Even with her artificial eyes polarising, the bright phosphorescent glare managed to creep through her eyelids. Her audio filters had shut down her hearing. She was effectively deaf for the time being though she would still be able to receive direct comms. The stun grenades were individually designed to overwhelm protections like audio dampeners, polarising goggles and artificial eyes. Nyukuti had fired twelve of them. It must have been hell for the defenders in the aerostat.

A few moments after the final explosion she opened her eyes and looked at Gunhir. He signalled for them to move down the corridor. Miska nodded and readied the boarding shield. She held it in her right arm. The medgel covering her hand allowed her to grip it just enough. She had the SIG Sauer GP-992 in her left. She could shoot with her left but she wasn't nearly as good. She had the pistol resting in a small indent in the shield but she didn't clip it in place. She was excited.

Gunhir touched her shoulder, the signal for her to move down the corridor. She did so. Nyukuti advanced next to her, his reloaded grenade launcher clipped to the boarding shield. As her hearing returned she heard the rapid popping noise as he fired fragmentation grenade after fragmentation grenade into the aerostat. The shockwaves from the detonations rocked them as they advanced. Through the holes cut in the airlock all Miska could see was the orange bloom of nearly constant explosions. They were getting shrapnel in the airlock corridor. She felt it hit the shield and the moulded ceramic armour plates strapped to her legs. The inertial armour hardened to absorb the impact. Her head was pulled back as a fragment bounced off her half-helm. She couldn't make out any targets yet but she was mostly a shield carrier in this fight. Then she saw it. A silhouette wading through fire, force, and the storm of shrapnel like some impervious demigod. Miska knew she should be afraid. Instead, she found she was smiling.

'Skel! Skel! Skel!' she shouted out loud and over the comms. Skel was short for combat exoskeleton. Gunhir was firing immediately, putting plasma pellet after plasma pellet dead centre in very quick succession. Miska could feel the heat of the weapon as it was triggered in close proximity, felt her skin blister. Her hair was mostly tucked under her helmet but she was a little worried that it was about to catch fire. Miska's hearing cut out again as Kaczmar fired his railgun. The front of the Honey Badger was lit up. Gunhir had emptied a very expensive magazine into the combat exoskeleton and was rapidly reloading the plasma weapon. The tungsten-cored penetrators fired by Kaczmar's railgun were splashing into the Honey Badger's now-molten chest at hypersonic velocity and travelling straight into the merc wearing the armour. The Honey Badger tottered and fell over.

'Grenade!' Nyukuti screamed. It had bounced off his shield and landed just in front of him. Miska didn't have time for anything else. She just hunkered down behind the shield, aware of Gunhir doing the same behind her. The fragmentation grenade exploded. Miska's own shield hit her in the face and she found herself lying on top of Gunhir some distance back down the corridor. Her head, arm and most of the front of her body felt like one big bruise. She managed to push herself on to her feet with Gunhir's help. Somehow Kaczmar had stayed upright. It looked like Nyukuti had bounced off him. Miska noticed that Kaczmar had blood running from his ears. The fool hadn't worn any ear protection and was probably deaf now. He was, however, still laying fire down the corridor.

'Skel! Skel! Skel!' Nyukuti shouted. Instinctively Miska raised her shield, her wired reflexes slowing the moment down as she sped up. It looked as though her shield was being eaten away. Then she felt the impact. The arm holding the shield felt broken. Then the impact picked her up off her feet, spun her in mid-air and slammed her into the wall. She felt someone grab her and drag her back around the corner to momentary safety and saw Kaczmar move with surprising speed as he ducked back around the opposite corner. Nyukuti was in the air. Miska half expected to see him torn apart by the Retributor fire but a stray round must have caught his shield or just winged him. He slid to the ground and half crawled, half dived back round the opposite corner.

'It's wild fire!' Miska shouted over comms as she took a fast-release thermal smoke grenade from her webbing with her good arm, flicked off the cap with her thumb, depressed the arming button and threw it round the corner. The Honey Badger jockey either wasn't risking direct fire, which was reasonable, or had panicked and wasn't using his Retributor's smartlink targeting system. Either way it had saved their lives.

'La-las!' Nyukuti shouted over the comms link. Miska pushed herself up, trying to get the shield into position so it protected Gunhir as well as her. The two light anti-armour missiles exploded in the air.

When she came to Miska felt like somebody had beaten on her with a sack full of hammers. She'd only been out for a second

144

or two but that amount of time was crucial in a fight like this. She forced herself to move through the pain. Opposite her she saw Nyukuti slowly pushing himself to his feet. Kaczmar was some way further down the corridor, but he wasn't moving. Miska glanced behind her. Neither was Gunhir. She grabbed the plasma rifle. She didn't have time to run a diagnostic on the notoriously finicky weapon. She just checked that it was loaded.

'Lay down smoke,' she told Nyukuti over comms. He started removing smoke grenades from his webbing and throwing them down the corridor. She was pretty sure that the remaining Honey Badger would try and capitalise on the missile strike. 'Draw its fire,' she told Nyukuti. He hesitated for a moment but then unslung his Xiphos squad automatic weapon, leaned around the corner and fired off four grenades from the SAW's under-barrel launcher. Then he ducked back as the returning Retributor fire ate away the bulkhead. Miska lay on the floor and rolled out into the open and found herself looking at a corridor of hot smoke. The smoke would confuse the Honey Badger's thermographics. She hoped. And with Nyukuti drawing the combat exoskeleton's fire they wouldn't expect her to just be lying in the centre of the floor. She hoped. Nyukuti fired two quick bursts and then ducked back round the corner as more returning Retributor fire ate away yet more of the bulkhead. Miska felt the hypersonic 20mm rounds flying overhead, saw their passage in the eddies they made in the hot smoke. She held the Appolion plasma rifle awkwardly in her left hand, forcing her right, which felt broken but she knew wasn't, to grip the weapon as well, despite the medgel covering the hand. 'Now fall over,' she subvocalised over the comms. She was aware of someone else talking to her over the comms link but she ignored it, she had to concentrate. The Honey Badger's Retributor sounded again. She was aware of Nyukuti falling backwards as though hit. Even in her periphery it hadn't looked convincing, but he had stopped firing.

At first she wasn't sure if it was her mind playing tricks on her or if it was actually the Honey Badger moving down the corridor through the smoke, very cautiously. Miska felt sweat beading on her skin. She shut down the comms link. She needed to concentrate. It was the Honey Badger. The combat exoskeleton's Retributor was moving from side to side in the smoke.

Just a little closer, Miska whispered to herself. The first shot went wide, just glancing off the Honey Badger's shoulder, making it glow. The second shot went straight through the Retributor, burning through the weapon, splitting it in two and then catching the combat exoskeleton in the armoured face. The third round hit centre mass, the chest area. Behind the thick armoured plate was the pilot's compartment. Miska fired again and again until the magazine counter in her IVD read zero. It was a very expensive way to kill. The Honey Badger was frozen mid-stride, burning. Nyukuti emerged from round the corner, covering the combat exoskeleton with his SAW. Kaczmar had sat up and Gunhir was stirring. The boarding shields had saved their lives. Miska opened up the comms link message that had seemed so desperate to get her attention.

'-render. Repeat, we're offering an unconditional surrender to the Bastard Legion, please acknowledge ... please ...' Words were replaced by sobbing. It was the same voice as before but tension had been replaced by terror. Miska assumed that the Ultra had a blood-stained knife pressed to the man's throat.

'This is Colonel Miska Corbin of the Bastard Legion, we accept your surrender.'

CHAPTER 10

'Smells like barbecue,' Kaczmar growled. His voice sounded wrong because he couldn't hear it any more. Miska could smell the Honey Badger pilot cooking as well. She was staring at the combat exoskeleton. Watching the armour burn. Something didn't sit quite right with her about this but she wasn't sure what. Miska was not feeling her warm, post-combat rush. She shook her head, momentarily worried that Torricone's bleeding heart was somehow contagious.

Gunhir had staggered to his feet and retrieved the Appolion, changing the magazine.

'That thing's expensive, try to use the PDW if you have to,' Miska told him as she retrieved her gauss pistol. She wasn't really expecting trouble but she was still going to act as though she was until she was happy that the aerostat was secured. Miska checked the feed from Grig's and Bean's combat exoskeletons. Both of them were standing guard over prisoners. Bean was watching over the Dogs of Love mercenaries in what looked like a briefing room. They were all down on their knees, hands behind their heads. Grig's prisoners looked more comfortable. He had the civilian aerostat staff sat around tables in a rec area. There may have been a few stragglers hiding in the aerostat but she couldn't see them wanting to start anything. She noticed that Gunhir was swaying.

'You okay?' she asked.

'Hit my head pretty hard, it's reinforced but still,' he told her.

'Nyukuti, check him out,' Miska told the stand-over man. All the Bastards had now received rudimentary field medic training. Nyukuti slung his SAW and moved to Gunhir. Miska was pleased that Kaczmar was covering the corridor that led to the aerostat without being told. Not that he would have heard her anyway. They hadn't even left the shuttle yet.

'Miska?' Even over the comms the Ultra's voice sounded like sex.

Get a grip! she told herself. She was trying to ignore how much pain she was in.

'Report,' Miska told the Ultra over the comms link.

'Lieutenant Larouc has very graciously provided us with access codes for all of the aerostat's systems,' he told her.

'Good of him, thank the lieutenant for me, and you can probably stop terrorising him now.'

She was answered by a soft chuckle.

'I've stimmed him,' Nyukuti told her. If he was concussed Miska was pretty sure that wasn't the thing to do.

'You weren't really paying attention during the field medic training, were you?' Miska asked the stand-over man. Nyukuti looked at her for a moment or two.

'You are a tiny blood-painted goddess who I have dreamed. We should return to Australia and stain the sands red,' he told her.

Miska pursed her lips.

'Maybe another time,' she told him.

'I feel fine,' Gunhir told her.

'You go and see the Doc when we get back to the *Daughter*, you understand me?' Miska told him. Gunhir nodded. 'Okay, Nyukuti you're on point, then Gunhir and me, Kaczmar brings up the rear, diamond formation.' Gunhir and Nyukuti nodded. Miska put her hand on Kaczmar's shoulder and communicated her orders via hand signals. As she turned away from the huge serial killer she felt a massive fleshy hand on her shoulder. She almost flinched away from his touch but instead turned back to face him.

'Thank you,' he shouted. Miska stared at him while the feeling that something just wasn't quite right intensified. She just nodded. Then the shuttle's ageing fire control system woke up and sprayed the burning combat exoskeleton with flame retardant foam.

The prison shuttle had docked at the passenger airlock. There was a small passenger lounge and a series of suit-lockers. The airlock had apparently doubled as an EVA exit as well. The Dogs of Love mercenaries and a few of the aerostat's security staff had tried to fortify the lounge area with strategically placed crates of raw material for the aerostat's printer. They had partially closed the interior blast doors to the surrounding corridors to use as cover as well. Miska suspected that the stun grenades had done their job but it had been the fragmentation grenades that had done the real damage. Though she also saw flaps of bloody skin and limbs that were consistent with the damage done by railguns. There would have been little left of the bodies hit by Kaczmar's Sarissae. She had her SIG in her hand as she surveyed the carnage wrought by her fire team. The others were covering the bodies. There was the occasional sob or moan but there were very few wounded, and those were deep in shock. Miska noticed that Kaczmar had a wide grin on his face.

'This was everything the Corps promised but never delivered,' he said.

The corridor leading to the Command & Control had been painted red and was spotted with corpses. Each of them had been efficiently dispatched, their left and right common arteries cut. Miska was grateful that there were no civilians among the dead. What she couldn't understand was how the Ultra had done it without them responding. There were four bodies leaking precious blood into the corridor leading to the C&C. Nobody was fast and stealthy enough to do all four without any of them getting a shot off. One, yes, maybe two if you were good, but not all four. The precision of the cuts was extraordinary. This was viz/sense game nonsense. It was nearly impossible to kill like that. She felt Gunhir's eyes on her. The door to the C&C slid open.

Command and control was a utilitarian collection of consoles illuminated by strip lighting and the holographic displays of the various systems, some of which showed local weather patterns in the clouds below the aerostat. The closest things the C&C had to comfort were the ergonomic chairs and the peeling magnolia paint.

All the civilian staff were cowering in one corner of the room, many of them with tears running down their faces. Opposite them, the Ultra was leaning against one of the consoles. Miska was less than pleased to see that he was naked. He held his dripping knife in his left hand. His left arm was bloodied to the elbow, like a red opera glove. A gangly man with a goatee wearing the uniform of the Dogs of Love mercenary cooperative was sat on one of the chairs next to the Ultra and he looked scared shitless.

'You the Dogs of Love commander?' Miska asked the man, presumably Lieutenant Larouc. He nodded. 'I'm here to discuss nominative determinism.'

'Did you go commando in my spacesuit?' Miska asked the Ultra. She wasn't entirely sure if she liked the idea, or was repulsed by it. Possibly both. They had sent Larouc and the C&C personnel to join the other prisoners that Grig and Bean were guarding. Kaczmar was standing guard by the door to C&C and Nyukuti still seemed to consider himself her bodyguard. He was hanging back but keeping an eye on her. Gunhir had been given the unenviable job of liaising with Triple S.

'I stashed your spacesuit in a safe place. I will retrieve it before we leave,' he told her, not answering her question. Miska was trying not to stare at his beautiful naked body.

'I gave you the suit because it is combat spec, equipped with reactive camouflage.'

'And it helped me gain entry to the aerostat,' the Ultra told her, 'as did the very high spec lock burner that seemed to have just the right code for access through the maintenance airlock.' The lock burner belonged to the Legion but New Sun had supplied the codes. Other than by brute force it was supposed to be very difficult to gain entrance to a sealed habitat or ship via the airlock for obvious reasons. They were always the most heavily defended systems.

'Something to say?' Miska asked him.

'Did it not seem ... too easy?' he asked. Miska turned to look at him. His sculpted face hinted at genuine concern.

'Not from where we were standing it wasn't.'

'We took on something close to a platoon of trained soldiers,' he pointed out.

He was right. It had been a bold strategy. It was something that a suitably equipped SF squad wouldn't think twice about, but that wasn't what they were.

'And beyond guarding the prisoners, Grig and Bean did very little,' he continued.

No, because you were killing on an industrial level, Miska decided not to say. She noticed that Nyukuti was paying attention to this conversation as well.

'Why did you take the suit off?' Now Miska changed the subject.

'Slowed me down, restricted movement and the senses, and also I was no longer operating in vacuum,' he told her.

'But no armour, not even clothes?'

He smiled.

'I'm an exhibitionist,' he told her.

Miska narrowed her eyes. He had total confidence, being naked didn't faze him in any way, but an exhibitionist he was not. She was putting the pieces together.

'You're a chameleon, aren't you?' she said staring at him. She knew her emotions were muted compared to other people's but she still felt astonishment. If every single skin cell in his body were self-replicating nanotech reactive camouflage then he would effectively be invisible. It explained so much. How he had been able to murder so many people before he had been caught. The Dogs of Love mercenaries must have thought that they were fighting a ghost. 'That's Martian tech,' she hissed, keeping her voice low, 'illegal nanotech.' She thought about it some more. 'It's not even Martian tech, that's ...' her voice trailed off.

'Small Gods,' he finished for her.

She stared at him. There had been lots of stories about the Ultra concerning his tech. It had been classified when he'd been captured. She had assumed that the rumours of Martian and Small Gods tech had been exaggerations, imagining instead that he was some millionaire savant who could afford the very best cyberware.

'What the fuck are you doing on board the *Hangman's Daughter*?' she demanded. 'You should be locked away in a Hotel California.' The Hotel Californias were government black sites where they tended to 'lose' high value prisoners. The Ultra just shrugged. Then something occurred to her. 'Did you kill my father?'

The Ultra was shaking his head before she had finished asking the question.

'No,' he told her, 'think about the timeline.'

He was right. She had seen the Ultra's arrest in the news. It still didn't make sense that they would have put him on board the *Daughter* rather than disappear him and try and reverse engineer the tech. Perhaps the case had just been too high profile for that.

'Jesus Christ!' she spat as something else occurred to her. 'You are a completely illegal ...'

'Weapon,' he supplied along with an arched perfect eyebrow.

'I didn't ... I mean we are in breach of so many of the articles of conflict, not to mention intersystem laws. When we get back you're going to have to ...' She stopped and looked up at him.

'Go back in my box?' he asked.

'I'm sorry,' she told him. It was ludicrous. She was apologising to a monster whose body count was at least in four figures but she found herself meaning it. There was something oddly vulnerable about him, like a child with an old soul.

Are you fucking crazed! the beleaguered remnants of her common sense screamed at her.

'I understand,' he told her. She knew it was ridiculous but his sad smile was breaking her heart.

Get a grip! You're being played! she told herself.

'Are you a Small God?' she asked him. 'A demigod?'

Grey silver eyes looked at her as he considered her question.

'I don't know what I am,' he told her. She opened her mouth to ask another question.

'Boss,' Gunhir said from one of the workstations. A holographic display in front of him showed a Triple S Pegasus approaching the aerostat high above Epsilon B's swirling storm fronts. 'Major Resnick and some of his people are en route to relieve us.'

'Resnick?' Miska frowned. It was the first time she had heard mention of Resnick's rank. She knew that the Triple S part of the operation was being handled by Elite, the military contractor's SF contingent. She had made the same agreement with New Sun as she'd had with MACE. The Bastards were an offensive force, not a garrison. She knew enough to not want her people mixing with civilians. They were a blunt instrument, not a colonial police/peace keeping force. She had, however, expected Triple S (conventional) to take over from them.

'Are we going to do this dance again?' Nyukuti asked. He had been with them on board Faigroe Station when their employer had betrayed the Legion and sent Triple S to deal with them. He

154

had been badly wounded by the Triple S mercenaries during the ensuing conflict. They had nearly killed him. On the other hand, he had killed one of them with his sharpened metal boomerang.

Miska ran the feed from the weapon- and helm-cams into the aerostat's comms and opened an on-going feed to the *Hangman's Daughter*.

'Hangman-Actual to Hangman-One-Actual, you okay?' Uncle V asked from the virtual CP in Camp Reisman.

'Yeah, just a little bit worried about Triple S pulling another Faigroe Station,' she told him.

'I can set up a QRF but it'll have to come from Ephesus, so it won't be all that Q, if you know what I mean,' Vido told him. Miska knew that they were stretched too thin. They needed another shuttle the same size as the Pegasi and enough volunteers for a permanent QRF on the *Daughter*. She was hoping that Golda might be able to help her with that, though she would need to integrate members of the Leopard and Crocodile Society into the rest of the company and the other platoons. None of which was going to help her this time.

'Nah,' Miska said. 'If it goes off it'll be over a long time before they get here, just monitor the situation,' she told him.

'Okay. I'm going to have second platoon and Pegasus-One stand-to for my own peace of mind,' Uncle V told her.

'Understood,' Miska told him. It wouldn't do any harm and she liked that Vido was showing initiative.

'If it's any consolation I think it's too public,' he told her.

'Nyukuti, relieve Bean, I want you looking after the prisoners,' she told him.

He opened his mouth to protest. She knew he would want to stay close to her.

'Not now,' she told him. He nodded and left C&C. 'Hangman-One-Actual to Nightmare-Two-One?' she asked over comms.

'Two-One here,' Bean answered.

'I need you to go and get my suit and stow it in your armour's storage compartment,' she told him. 'Nightmare-One-Actual will tell you where it is. Then get back to the briefing room as quickly as possible.'

'Understood,' Bean told her.

'Hangman-One-Actual, to all Nightmare call signs. We may have trouble in the shape of Triple S (elite). I'm going to meet them in the departure lounge. It kicks off, we use Contingency-Three. Any questions?'

Nobody said anything. She turned to the Ultra and gestured towards Kaczmar with her thumb.

'Make sure that dumb fuck knows what's happening,' she told him. 'He'll need some cyberware in his ear when we get back to Waterloo Station.' The Ultra nodded and crossed the C&C to communicate with Kaczmar.

'This is Colonel Corbin to Major Resnick,' she said, opening a comms link to the approaching shuttle.

'What is it, Corporal?' Resnick answered.

Mature, Miska thought. She could feel Gunhir watching her again.

'Were you a friend of Major Sheldon's?' she asked. Major Sheldon Cartwright had been the officer in charge of the Triple S contingent that had come to Faigroe Station to kill the Bastards after they had taken it. Resnick didn't answer. 'If you're planning a burn, I just thought you should know that it didn't end well for old Sheldon.'

'Why don't you grow up and try and act like a professional

long enough for us to do the changeover, you fucking amateur?' he asked.

Real mature, Miska thought. What bothered her most was that SF operators didn't behave like this, even if they didn't like each other. There was always too much at stake and it just wasn't professional. It showed the total contempt that he had for her and the Bastards.

We're still kicking your ass and taking your jobs, Miska thought with no little satisfaction.

'Okay, it's going to happen real fast,' she told him. *So we don't have to spend too much time in each other's company*, she didn't add. 'We'll meet you by the airlock. You send two of your people, and they run to relieve my guys watching the prisoners, we get on our shuttle and you do what you want.'

'You need to get a hold of your fear,' he told her. *Fear?* Miska wondered. *We've been killing Triple S since we got here.* She decided not to tell him that as well. It was clear that he was trying to goad her. 'I'll tell you how we do this—' he tried to continue.

'No, we do this my way or we walk off right now and you guys can have fun and games chasing the prisoners round the aerostat,' she told him. There was no answer. 'Asshole,' Miska muttered.

'If it goes bad do you want me to save money or cry the Tears of the Sun?' Gunhir asked. He was talking about the use of the expensive plasma rifle.

'Cry me a river,' Miska told him as she headed for the door.

Nyukuti caught up with them at the devastation that was the small departure lounge by the airlocks. They stood among the mangled dead and waited by the airlock that they had cut through. There was a clang as the Triple S Pegasus docked at one of the other airlocks a little further down the departure lounge.

'Are we killing these guys?' Kaczmar shouted. Miska turned towards him.

'No! Not unless they move on us! And shut up!' she shouted back slowly, hoping that he could read her lips. He just stared at her, the look of concentration on his tiny face nearly lost among the folds of fat.

'Open the airlock,' Resnick told her over an open comms link. She was currently in control of the aerostat's systems. She sent him access and the airlock opened. The Triple S operators came out of the airlock weapons at the ready, scanning the area, looking very professional. An eight-strong squad, two of them wearing Machimoi combat exoskeletons, and Resnick himself. Both the Nightmare Squad and the Triple S mercenaries were trying to look as though they weren't pointing guns at each other.

Resnick walked over towards them, staring at Miska. She suspected that he was trying to intimidate her. She wasn't really feeling it.

'Messy,' he said.

'I want to see two of your guys running to relieve my people guarding the prisoners,' Miska told him.

Resnick looked around at the carnage.

'So you hit a soft target with overkill but then shit yourself when real soldiers turn up?' he asked her.

'What are you trying to achieve here?' she asked him. 'If you wanna fight then throw down. If not, then you obviously don't like us so let's get on with our day.'

Resnick was looking them over, an expression of disgust on

his face. He paused for a moment when he came to the Ultra.

'Why is that man naked?' he asked.

'Fuck this,' Miska said reaching the end of her patience. 'Guys,' she said out loud but opening a direct comms link to Grig and Bean. She didn't want to use their names or call signs in front of Resnick. 'Leave the prisoners, make your way to the rendezvous.'

'Aye,' Bean answer.

'Understood,' Grig replied.

'Good luck finding your prisoners,' she told Resnick.

He nodded at two of his people. One of them, a blonde woman, caught Miska's eye. She looked familiar but she couldn't quite place her. If she did know the blonde woman then it had to have been from her time in the marines, or the CIA's Special Activities Division.

'You people fucking disgust me, you're a disgrace—' he started but Miska just turned and walked away, making her way towards the prison shuttle. Gunhir and the Ultra followed, as did Nyukuti, though he kept an eye on the Triple S operators. Kaczmar remained, staring at Resnick. Miska stopped by the ruined airlock and turned to look at the huge serial killer. She could only see one side of Kaczmar's face but it looked as though he was studying Resnick. He leaned forward.

'I'm hungry!' he shouted at Resnick. The commander of Triple S (elite) in the Epsilon Eridani system took an involuntary step back. Miska couldn't help but laugh. Kaczmar turned his back on Resnick and the Triple S squad and lumbered after Miska and the others.

'Tell Kaczmar he can go into Waterloo Station restaurant of his choice, and eat as much as he likes,' Miska told the Ultra as they made their way into the prison shuttle.

'A dangerous proposition,' the Ultra mused, 'but I shall pass that on.' Then, a few moments later as they were walking down the corridor past the melted and burned remains of the Honey Badger: 'I'm out of this conflict, aren't I?'

'I'm afraid so,' Miska told him. He nodded but Miska was sure she detected sadness in his expression.

Between them they managed to dump the destroyed Honey Badger in the departure lounge area. The aerostat's emergency systems sealed the ruined airlock as soon as it detected the prison shuttle disengaging. Grig and Bean had left through a different airlock. They rendezvoused with the shuttle in the upper atmosphere. All of them were sat in the prisoner transport area. Bean and Grig were still in their combat exoskeletons.

'That man does not like you,' Gunhir pointed out, meaning Resnick.

'I know, and I'm such a likeable person!' Miska said. 'Though you'd be surprised how often that happens.'

'Maybe it's the whole slavery thing?' Grig suggested.

'Oh, you love it really,' Miska said but Gunhir was right. Resnick's dislike of her seemed disproportionate and very personal. She ran through some of the gun- and helm-cam footage, taking the best images of each of the operators, putting it into a text message, encrypting it and then sending it to one of Raff's dead letter drops. She wanted to know who they were, particularly the woman.

The journey was going to be a bit of a trek. Waterloo Station was about as far away from their position as it was possible for the station to be, despite orbiting a satellite of the planet whose atmosphere they were just leaving.

A blinking icon asking if she wanted to accept an incoming comms link appeared in her vision. She accepted it and a grainy image of Corenbloom and the Doc appeared in a window of her IVD. She guessed that Corenbloom had wedged his helmet in a tree to film them both. In the background FOB Trafalgar looked even more like an anthill than ever with UN and New Sun investigators crawling all over it. It was night down on Ephesus. The investigators had set up huge lights to illuminate the scene of the crime. On a flat piece of open ground she could see where all the body bags had been laid out. As she watched, an investigator in a brightly coloured hostile environment suit came out of one of the tunnel system exits.

'Guys, what've you got? Did we do it?' Miska joked. There was a bit of a lag.

'It wasn't us,' Corenbloom said, smiling. 'It's weird stuff. Whatever did this came on them suddenly. Natural weapons of some kind, traces of a super dense wood in the wounds. Whatever they used was hard enough to go through combat exoskeleton armour, and whoever was wielding it was strong enough to push it through.' The disgraced FBI agent did not look happy.

Miska frowned. 'Are you saying the trees did this?' she asked.

'You know some of the so-called mangroves are ambulatory?' the Doc asked. 'Actually, they are less like mangroves and much more like the *kahikatea* trees native to New Zealand back on Earth.'

'That's great, Doc,' Miska said. She had heard of the walking mangroves in the swampy land north of where they had found FOB Trafalgar. 'But there's a big difference between trees that move slowly to catch the light and a tree that kills a mercenary company made up of experienced pipe-hitters, know what I mean?'

'Not really,' Doc said. 'But the root, branch and trunk

structures of the Ephesus-Mangrove heavily resemble mammalian musculature.'

'So what are you telling me?' Miska asked. 'An unknown alien plant species that was missed by the extensive planetary survey?'

Neither of them answered but Miska suspected that the Doc was so excited by the prospect he might even have a facial expression. Corenbloom looked less happy.

'The UN people are freaking out down here. They're talking about suspending all hostilities, first contact protocols, even planetary evacuation.'

Miska pursed her lips. That wasn't good news but all it really meant was that they would have to go looking for another job.

'How are New Sun behaving?' Miska asked.

Even with the lag Corenbloom seemed hesitant in answering.

'Poker-faced,' he finally said.

I'll bet, Miska thought.

'And?' she pushed.

'It's just a hunch but I don't think they're all that surprised,' he told her.

Again Miska found herself wondering why New Sun were there.

'Colonel Corbin,' Doc said. 'Epsilon Eridani isn't a very old star, maybe a billion years.' That sounded old to Miska. 'I've read the survey, and there were some questions the surveyors couldn't answer. The plant life is very advanced for a moon in a system that young. The exobotanists couldn't understand why the moon was so fecund with flora when the sun is so far away. This is connected to some kind of heat exchange from Epsilon Eridani B that the physicists don't quite understand.'

None of this sounded like something an ex-marine should concern herself with, Miska decided.

'What are you telling me, Doc?' Miska asked.

'One of the possibilities was that the ecosystem, and perhaps even the planetary mechanics, had been tweaked somehow,' Doc told her.

Miska let that sink in. It definitely sounded like something well above her pay grade.

'If that's the case could this … I don't know, have some kind of ramifications for biotech?' she asked.

'Almost certainly,' Doc told her. She made a mental note to ask Raff if biotech was part of the New Sun portfolio. She suspected it was.

'So who tweaked the ecosystem?' she asked. Doc didn't answer. There was that feeling at the back of her mind again. Something wasn't right. Something about this made her think of the artefact they had tried to steal on Barney Prime: some supposedly ancient alien doodah that had released a truly horrible entity that had inhabited Teramoto's dead body. It had also saved them from the orbital bombardment. A boon and bane but any way you looked at it, weird shit that she didn't want to have anything to do with.

'Okay, thanks, guys, is there anything more you can do down there?' she asked.

'No,' Corenbloom answered. 'We've got more than enough to prove the Legion didn't do it. So it's just a matter of dealing with the PR fall-out but I think that the UN is going to want to keep this pretty quiet.'

'Okay, talk to Vido, you're on the next shuttle back to the *Daughter*,' she told them.

Corenbloom nodded but she was pretty sure that the Doc looked disappointed.

The clanging noise that the shuttle made as it slotted into the plug-like docking port of the *Hangman's Daughter*, and was then sucked slowly into the mother ship's superstructure, sounded different to any other dock. It sounded like home to Miska.

'Good work, everyone,' she told them as they exited the shuttle onto the *Daughter*'s cavernous hangar deck. Surprisingly there was nobody doing PT today but the guard droids were there to escort the Ultra back to his pod. It wasn't much of a reward for his part in the job. The rest had been given shore leave but would have to store all their battle gear first. Though they were allowed to carry handguns and knives on Waterloo Station. They had strict ROE for barroom brawls. If the other guys drew a knife then they could, same for guns. They were under orders to help each other out if they saw another Legionnaire in trouble. The two most important ROE for shore leave was to never start a fight but to always win them. It was the only way for her people to get peace and quiet from the other mercenary companies. Many of whom still barked when her Bastards walked by – a reference to the explosive collars they had worn during their first job.

A blinking icon appeared in her IVD. She opened it. In the window she saw Uncle V in the control room. He did not look happy.

'You need to see this,' he told her. Miska looked around. There was a comms screen next to the airlock. She patched the message through to that. It was a net news viz. She immediately recognised the slaughter just outside the airlocks on the aerostat.

'... the level of barbarity involved beggars belief,' the war correspondent was saying, 'Those not killed in the initial

164

onslaught were subsequently tortured to death while trying to surrender.'

The image changed to an ashen-faced Triple S (conventional) mercenary stood by the blast door to the C&C. She could hear the sound of retching in the background. Through the open blast door they could make out Lieutenant Larouc and some of the Masaai crew suspended in the air by hooked chains. They had been peeled open layer by layer, like a medical dissection. There was something familiar about their grotesque postures. It took Miska a moment to realise where she had seen scenes like this before. The Ultra's file. This was how he liked to kill.

'We should have seen this coming,' Nyukuti muttered. He was right. They had been set up. Royally suckered. She had walked them right into it.

'Salik wants to speak to you,' Uncle V was telling her but she was barely listening. She had just remembered where she had seen the blonde woman before. She had been a Marine Raider, like Miska, but she had been based on Earth. She had been involved in some kind of scandal involving the torture of enemy combatants in some brushfire European conflict. There had been deaths involved. 'We've had death threats from the Dogs of Love,' Uncle V continued. That was a shame. She liked L'Amour, their leader.

'I'm angry,' the Ultra said quietly. Miska glanced over at where he stood, looking naked and pure. She knew how he felt.

CHAPTER 11

Miska was staring at the footage playing on the view screen next to the airlock. It showed Resnick talking to her on the aerostat, among the dead. It had clearly been shot by one of his squad's helm-cams. Resnick's face was blacked out.

'You people fucking disgust me, you're a disgrace ...' he told her and Miska just turned and walked away with the others. Except Kaczmar. Kaczmar had stayed and when he had leaned towards Resnick the Triple S (elite) commander had flinched away. It had been an act, all of it. His words had probably been scripted. There was no way a guy like that was frightened of someone like Kaczmar. A list of Kaczmar's crimes was scrolling down the screen accompanying footage of the crime scenes, his arrest, and the trial. The footage had to have come from out of system, which meant New Sun/Triple S had been planning this.

Hell, they've probably got some kind of revenge think tank consultancy, she decided. The footage changed to a murder scene on board the aerostat. A reporter was explaining how the murders fitted the 'Fatman's' MO. The UN investigators would be over the moon about reporters tramping all over the crime scene.

Miska was shaking she was so angry, mostly at herself. She had walked right into this one.

She flinched away as she felt a hand on her shoulder. She spun to find herself looking up at the Ultra.

'I can . . .' he started.

'No,' she told him. Anything he did now would just make matters worse. 'Get him cleaned up and then take him back to his pod,' she told the guard droids. The look of hurt on the Ultra's face was obvious this time but he nodded before the droid took him away. 'Not him,' she told the guards as they started to take Nyukuti away. 'Get changed into civvies,' she told him. 'Make sure they're armoured, draw a PDW, you're with me.' It wasn't that she felt she needed a bodyguard so much as she wanted another gun because of the sheer number of people that were pissed at her.

Nyukuti nodded and then pointed at his neck.

'You need to get that seen to,' he told her. It took her a moment to work out what he was talking about. Then she remembered the burns on her neck that she had received when Gunhir had fired the plasma rifle too close to her skin. She touched the blisters and some of her hair just crumbled away. It was the least of her problems.

The med bay was pretty much the last place that she wanted to be. She would have taken care of the wound herself but it was starting to look like time was of the essence. The Doc was still returning from the surface. Torricone was dressing the burns while she pointedly ignored him and spoke to Uncle V, who was still in the CP at Camp Reisman.

'Miska, you've got to take the call from Salik.' Vido was practically begging her. She didn't want to speak to Salik right then. She needed time to marshal her forces, work through what was going on, and come up with a strategy to deal with it, but things were happening too quickly.

'Put him through,' she told him. Salik appeared in her IVD. He was sat at his desk. It would be one of his absurd liveried servant droids filming him. He would be looking at her animated comms icon.

'Miska, I'm sure you know what's coming next,' he said, his voice full of regret.

'It wasn't us. Well, some of it was us. The civilian personnel and all the DoL who surrendered quickly enough were alive when we left. Resnick had them killed to frame us ...'

Salik held his hand up.

'Miska, please. The murders all fit the MO of the individuals in this so-called Nightmare Squad you took with you. There's footage of you standing among the bodies of some of your victims ...'

'They were combatants!' She was screaming now. She pushed Torricone away as he tried to apply medgel to the wounds. She was on her feet. 'It was a fight, a hard fight. They sent two combat exoskeletons after us! I can send you over the helm- and gun-cam footage!'

Salik was motioning for her to calm down.

'It's out of my hands. The UN has stepped in. It's being investigated as a war crime.'

'It is a war crime! Just not ours! And this is an extra-legal area. The Colonial Administration hasn't even asked for UN recognition. They have no jurisdiction here. If they did we couldn't operate.'

Salik's expression looked pained.

'They have no jurisdiction here yet. They are already talking about shutting us down because of what happened at FOB Trafalgar. If there is some kind of first contact situation then they can legitimately claim jurisdiction. Look, Miska, the fact of it is I need to remain in the UN's good graces in order to do business. That means trying to keep a lid on some of the worst excesses that can happen during war time ...'

'But you know that we didn't do it, don't you?' she howled at him.

'It doesn't matter what I know, it doesn't even matter what I can prove. It matters how it looks.'

Miska stopped. She just stared at the comms window in her IVD. To Torricone it must have looked as if she was staring into space.

'You're fucking kidding me?' she finally managed to mutter.

'All the Bastard Legion's active duties are suspended. They are confined to whichever base they are currently stationed at, and prohibited from carrying arms pending an investigation.'

'What about Triple S?' she demanded.

'They're not currently under suspicion,' he told her.

'So much for innocent until proven guilty,' she muttered. 'If we're being accused then I want my people looking into this,' she told him. Salik looked pained again.

'Miska, please, think about this. Your people are a serial killer with a keen interest in botany, and a disgraced, corrupt FBI agent. How do you think that will look?'

'I don't care.'

'And perhaps that's the problem. Have you spoken to Vido about this? Your father.'

Suddenly Miska didn't trust herself to speak.

'Just make it happen,' she managed.

She severed the comms link and found Torricone watching her. She held up a finger in warning.

'Can I finish dressing your neck?' he asked.

Miska just nodded. She sat down, still trembling. The medgel felt cool on her neck as Torricone applied it.

'I only heard half of that conversation,' Torricone said.

'Just don't,' she tried to warn him.

'You seem to feel you've been unfairly treated,' he continued, apparently unaware of just how much danger he was in. 'Maybe you might want to consider how the victims felt, regardless of who killed th—'

Miska was screaming. She somehow carried Torricone across the med bay by his neck and slammed him against the wall. Her knife had appeared in her hand. She was only partially aware of someone entering the med bay.

'Miska!'

A hand grabbed her knife arm as the blade plunged towards a terrified Torricone's chest. She was picked up and slammed into an operating table. Nyukuti appeared over her, trying to say something. She neck-locked him with her legs and then straightened them, skipping off the table and taking Nyukuti to the floor.

'Miska!' her dad's voice from one of the view screens cut through her fury. The tip of her knife was millimetres from Nyukuti's eye.

'I'm sorry,' Miska said. She was sat on one of the stools in the med bay, breathing heavily. Nyukuti was leaning against the wall. He nodded. Torricone didn't look mollified by her apology in the slightest.

'Fuck you,' he told her. Miska looked sharply up at him. 'You just can't take responsibility for your actions, can you? Whether you did it or not, those people are dead because of the choices you made. Think about that the next time you're feeling sorry for yourself!'

Miska was on her feet again. Nyukuti pushed himself off the wall and interposed himself between them.

'Just piss off, mate!' he told Torricone. Torricone turned his stare from Miska to the stand-over man.

'What?' Torricone demanded.

'Seriously, I don't want to get killed over whatever this is,' he said, pointing between the two of them. Torricone kept staring at Nyukuti. The stand-over man didn't turn away. 'How far do you want to take this, brah?'

Torricone leaned around Nyukuti.

'I'm fucking sick of this,' he told her and stormed out of the med bay.

Nyukuti moved away from Miska before turning to face her.

'It would be a lot simpler if you just fucked him,' he told her.

She stared at him for a moment and then burst out laughing.

'I am standing right here,' her dad said from the screen. That just made her laugh harder.

Nyukuti cleared out to let her talk to her dad. Her dad was watching through the screen. She could see Camp Reisman's CP in the background.

'You can kill as many of them as you want if you can tell me how a temper tantrum will help our current situation,' he said. It felt like the telling off from a parent it was. Worse, she knew he was right.

'You're right. This needs some properly focused killing,' she muttered, sounding like a sulky teenager even to her own ears.

'You haven't lost it like that for a while,' he said more gently. Now she looked up at him.

'I hate things like this. Being the target of lies. Feeling that there's nothing you can do about it. Feeling helpless ...' She went back to staring at the cracked tile flooring.

'We might have been the target here, but you get that you're not the victim, right?' he asked.

'Honestly?' Miska looked back up at her dad. 'Not really. I didn't want those people to die, didn't want them to suffer the way they did, but I didn't know them. Torricone may well have been right, but I don't feel anything for them. Does that bother you?'

'Not as much as it seems to bother Torricone,' her dad said.

Miska's eyelids narrowed into slits.

'What's that supposed to mean?' she demanded.

'It means you lost it because someone you feel for purposefully hurt you,' he told her and then crossed his arms.

'Oh bullshit!' she snapped.

'I thought you hated lies.'

Miska went very quiet.

'What are you going to do?' he asked a few moments later.

'Send Corenbloom and the Doc to the scene of the crime, and then I'm going to go and talk to someone.'

'Who?' her dad asked but Miska was on her feet heading for the door.

'You need to take a shower!' he called after her. 'You look like you've just killed a whole bunch of people!'

*

Showered and changed, Miska had Vido liaising with Salik and the UN investigators, trying to get Corenbloom and Doc onto the aerostat. The UN had demanded that all the weapons and armour used in the attack be turned over to them. That further pissed Miska off as the railgun, the plasma rifle and the Machimoi combat exoskeleton were all expensive bits of kit that were too complex to just print, even with *Daughter*'s military grade printer. She had, however, agreed and some of Vido's 'old boys' were handling the exchange. After all, the Bastards had nothing to hide.

All through her shower she had been thinking about Torricone. Her dad had been right. The last time she had lost it like that had been when Raff had told her that her dad had been murdered. She had known for a long time that she had an anger management problem, what her psych profile described as a tendency to fall into psychotic rages, but she'd had a lid on it ever since she'd joined the marines. Torricone was pissing her off. There was no doubt about it. More to the point, he was trying to. Even so, what she had done wasn't right.

Do you care? she asked herself. After all, he was basically a weapon with a bomb in his head.

Miska checked Torricone's whereabouts with the *Daughter*'s systems.

'Of course,' she muttered.

'Come to finish the job?' he asked as she entered the multi-denominational chapel. Torricone was on his knees in front of a, frankly scary, hologram representation of Christ on his cross. Not for the first time Miska thought that religions could do with more cheerful iconography.

'I came to ... to ...' she started. He turned away from the

hologram to regard her, one eyebrow raised. The hologram blinked out, plunging the institutional room and its bolted-down pews into gloom.

'Apologise?' he asked. 'You?'

'I apologise when I'm ...'

'Wrong?' he suggested. He looked more intrigued than anything else.

'Fuck this!' she snapped. 'I knew you weren't going to make this easy.' She turned to leave.

'Easy?' he demanded. 'You nearly killed me, Miska.' Now he sounded angry. 'Do you get that we're not actually toy soldiers? That we're living, feeling people, just like you? It's bad enough that you put bombs in our heads—' he tapped the side of his skull '—but we also have to live in fear of you just flipping out and killing us when you hear something you don't like.'

'I'm sorry!' It had practically exploded out of her.

Torricone didn't say anything. He glanced behind him at where the hologram of Christ on his cross had been just moments before.

'I mean, you pick a fight every time you see me, what's that about? Are you just trying to hurt me?' she asked more quietly. 'Do you not get that I don't care about these things, that I'm not ... wired up properly?'

Why are you telling him this? Her internal voice was a scream.

'You certainly seemed to care earlier,' he said softly.

That made her stop.

'It wasn't about ...'

Torricone just watched her.

'I like you, Miska.' He pointed between the two of them. 'I know ... everybody knows that there's something between us,

174

even if you won't admit it. It's going to get me killed.'

'Maybe,' she said, looking down. 'So what? We both know that nothing can come of it. You going to pull my hair every time you see me?'

'It's not like that.'

'Then what's it like?' Miska hissed, the venom in her voice surprising her. *Because it did hurt. Every time.*

'I got a second chance.'

Miska frowned. Pavor/Phobos, the Small God entity that had inhabited Teramoto's body, had run Torricone through with a sword. The car thief should be dead. Only jumping into the artefact had kept him alive. He had been fully healed when they had emerged from it some hours later.

'So, what?' Miska nodded to where the hologram of Christ had hung in the air. 'You're resurrected? Got religion? Is that why you're so fucking judgemental? Maybe you want to martyr yourself like Christ? Make mommy proud of you for once?' She saw him flinch just a little at this last. It didn't make her feel good.

'I've never not had religion,' he told her, 'but if I get a second chance then what kind of a coward would I be if I didn't speak up? Because somebody's got to. What you're doing is wrong and you need to stop.'

She regarded him carefully. It wasn't anything he hadn't said before. *Except this time …?*

'Maybe you're right about us,' she said carefully, 'but you keep doing what you're doing and that'll fade and you'll become just another irritant.'

She turned to leave.

'See, that's the thing,' he said. Miska paused. 'Neither of us can be what the other one wants.'

Miska left the chapel.

The Central Concourse was strangely quiet as Nyukuti and Miska made their way down it. All the viz screens still seemed to be playing the story of the massacre on the aerostat.

'Hangman-Actual to Hangman-One-Actual,' a very harried sounding Vido said over a direct comms link. 'Look, don't shoot the messenger but I've got some more bad news for you.'

'What?' Miska subvocalised through gritted teeth, trying to ignore the stares from the few bar patrons on the Central Concourse.

'The *Sneaky Bitch* just docked,' he told her.

'What?' Miska demanded as she approached Raff's hotel. She had no idea what he was talking about.

'The Crimson Sisterhood. Captain Gosia Tesselaar's ship,' Vido told her. Then it clicked into place. It was one of the corsairs that had attacked them when they had left the asteroid belt freeport of Maw City in the Sirius System.

Shit! she thought. It was the last thing she needed at the moment, but frankly unless they started firing on the *Daughter* it was going to be a case of having to wait and see what they were up to. She knew that Tesselaar wanted all the male members of the Crimson Sisterhood pirate organisation released from the *Daughter*. This included the captain's own man, who was currently down on Ephesus as part of the flight crew of one of the big Harpy drop shuttles, along with a number of the other Crimson Sisterhood pirates. Just for a moment she was tempted to give Tesselaar what she wanted for a quiet life, but that would set a dangerous precedent.

Suddenly Miska found herself standing in the shade. She looked up to see a large, implant-scarred, bullet-headed individual that she suspected had been injecting himself with silverback gorilla hormones. Glancing around she realised that there were several more approaching her and Nyukuti. She guessed they were members of the Dogs of Love.

'So this is—' the gorilla started. He stopped when Miska levelled her gauss pistol at him.

'I don't have the time,' she told him. 'Vido, there's nothing we can really do about the *Sneaky Bitch*,' she subvocalised over the comms link. 'We're supposed to be confined to the ship.' She heard a pop from behind her and then a cry of pain as Nyukuti shot one of the DoL mercenaries with a hardgel round from his PDW's over-barrel 25mm grenade launcher. 'Make Salik's security people aware that they're known pirates.'

'Will do,' Vido told her.

'Back off,' Miska told the gorilla, gesturing with her gun.

'I've still got a few people on the station. I can see if we can get eyes on Tesselaar and her people,' Vido said over the comms link.

'If you can do that without getting us into more trouble, then sure,' Miska told him. She glanced behind her to see Nyukuti practically back to back with her, his PDW at his shoulder, covering the DoL mercs trying to surround them.

'What's up?' Vido asked.

'The dogs are circling,' Miska told him. 'No offence,' she said to the gorilla. 'Look, tell your people we didn't kill your guys … well, we killed some of them but it was a fight. We certainly didn't torture anybody to death, that was Triple S when they relieved us.'

Somehow the gorilla didn't look convinced, but they were all backing away from the guns, helping the merc that Nyukuti had shot to his feet.

'Miska …' Nyukuti said.

'You seeing this?' Vido asked over comms. Miska risked glancing up at one of the viz screens, and then opened a window for the footage in her IVD so she could keep an eye on the retreating DoL mercs.

The footage showed Medusas sweeping out of the jungle into Port Turquoise, weapons blazing. She watched one of the mechs turn their flame gun on a four-storey building. Triple S conventional had just retaken the town. It didn't look as though they were being nearly as careful with collateral damage as the Bastards had been, but then Miska was starting to understand the lengths to which Triple S would go to punish those who had defied them. The footage showed gunship-escorted Harpies and VTOL transports in the air high above the wide Turquoise. There were landing craft, patrol boats and fortified barges carrying troops and vehicles below the shuttles and aircraft down the river itself. Miska knew that Camp Badajoz would be the next target.

'I don't give a shit, Vido,' Miska was subvocalising over the comms as she walked into the hotel, Nyukuti in tow. 'Contact Salik, contact MACE, tell them that I'm not having my people, or my gear, captured by Triple S. They have a choice, either we fight and we get paid for it, or we pull off-planet and head back to the *Daughter*.'

There was an automated reception screen but much of the ground floor of the hotel was taken up with a bar. Frequented by journalists, the hotel bar was clearly meant to cater for a more moneyed clientele than many others nearby, though it still kept to the faux-Napoleonic decor that ran throughout the station. There were very few customers at the moment. Most of them would either be down on the moon covering New Sun's offensive, or still reporting on the aerostat massacre. Still, it was nice not to be looked at with seething hatred for once. The few lensheads in the bar just looked shit scared of her.

'MACE has been pushing to let us fight, but the UN are saying no and Salik's backing them,' Vido told her. That was what it had all been about. Remove one of the stronger, more capable forces from the Colonial Administration and then make an aggressive push.

'Fine, get our forces ready to evac,' Miska told him.

'Nobody is going to like that, Miska,' Vido told her.

'Then get them ready to do it under fire,' she said and then cut the comms link. She was giving some thought to going over to the New Sun offices on the station and shooting Campbell in the face, a lot.

'Stay here,' Miska told Nyukuti. He opened his mouth to protest. 'Seriously, not today.' He closed his mouth again and nodded.

Miska knocked on the door to Raff's room. It hissed open for her. Raff was standing looking at the wall, which had become a huge viz screen. He was watching footage of Triple S (conventional) rappelling onto rooftops in Port Turquoise, vicious one-sided gunfights, and burning vehicles.

'They're learning from you,' he said when the door closed behind her.

'We safe to talk?' she asked.

'It's been swept,' he told her and then pointed at the small white noise generator on the bedside table. The device would inhibit any attempt to listen in on them with long-range microphones. 'Can't say the visit was all that subtle.'

'You're embedded with us,' she pointed out.

179

'Yeah but everyone knows I'm not welcome, and then you come running to me when this happens.'

'Maybe I want to tell our side of the story.'

Raff turned to look at her, one side of his face illuminated by the huge wall screen. He concentrated for a moment and the grisly images from the aerostat massacre appeared on the wall screen.

'This is why you have journalists with you,' he told her.

'Oh bullshit, Raff!' Miska snapped. She was tired of getting lectured. 'The lensheads covering this are in bed with New Sun's PR company.'

'Of course they are,' Raff told her. 'They have a good working relationship. The journos get what they need from New Sun and Triple S, and you're letting me get tied up in the back of a shuttle. Guess who controls the narrative?'

'I run a slave legion made up of hardened criminals, so positively spin that for me!' she shouted at him. 'Do you just want to be a sanctimonious prick, or are you actually going to be of some fucking use?'

Raff sighed and went and sat on the bed. Miska glanced at the footage from the aerostat that still covered the wall.

'Can you change that over?' she asked. Raff studied her for a moment or two and then concentrated, switching it back to Triple S's offensive down on Ephesus.

'That bothering you?' he asked. There was something in his voice, suspicion maybe.

'Did you get my message?' she asked.

'Yeah, the net on this station isn't up to much information-wise. Sports, porn and gun template catalogues is fine, information on war criminals with spec-ops backgrounds is sketchier.

But the woman you pointed out, I recognised her from that mess during the Rotterdam drug wars.'

'That it?' she asked.

He shrugged. 'I'm pretty sure one of the other guys was ex-SAD, Fifth Special Forces originally. I think he was a counter insurgency specialist. Dishonourably discharged. SAD recruited him ...'

'When you were looking for morally ambiguous operators,' she finished for him. Like her, she didn't add.

'Rumour has it he went too far even for us.'

'So Resnick's got a squad of sick bastards,' Miska said.

'So they frame you for the aerostat massacre. That's assuming you didn't do it. I mean, you took some very sick people with you. Your very own atrocity in a box.'

Miska turned to stare at him.

'That look like me?' she asked, meaning the aerostat massacre. 'You've tried to get me to do those kinds of things in the past, to send messages. Have I ever done it?'

'Not for me, not for the company. For yourself? I'm less sure. I mean, what are you going to do when you catch up with the guys who killed your father?'

'That will be medieval,' Miska admitted, her voice cold.

'And like I said, you set up your Nightmare Squad for a reason.'

'To scare people.'

'Good work. Why did you take them on this job?' Raff asked. She realised what he was doing. A confrontational debrief, to get to the truth quickly. On the other hand at least he wasn't hitting on her.

'To see if I can control them,' she told him.

'And can you?' he asked.

It was a good question. *Was I in control or was the Ultra?* she wondered. One thing she was sure of: she didn't control the Ultra.

'I'm having a difficult day, Raff. I'm in no mood for an interrogation. Are you part of the problem or the solution?'

He sat up on the bed.

'Okay, I'm sorry. I don't have much in the way of good things to tell you. This looks really bad.'

'But it's bullshit,' she said. Raff just looked at her. 'I mean it, Raff, we didn't do that. Okay, I mean we did some of that, but we weren't fucking peeling people.'

'They didn't have long to set that up. They couldn't have known who you were taking until shortly before the op happened.'

'So they've got from when we left the aerostat until we get back to the *Daughter*, maybe two hours.'

'Then they're running through their files on the Nightmare Squad's past crimes, got them in their IVDs, trying to recreate them.'

Something occurred to Miska.

'Did anyone get eaten?' she asked.

Raff stared at her.

'Jesus Christ!' Raff exploded. 'You're going out on jobs with fucking cannibals?'

'Hey, this was your idea,' Miska pointed out.

'This wasn't ... Okay, look, so this is a hastily set up series of copycats. The investigators are going to see through it pretty quickly.'

'And go after Triple S?'

'Maybe, maybe not. If Resnick's a Spartan then he fades away, maybe they serve up the rest of the squad. Triple S and

New Sun use their influence to keep the whole thing as quiet as possible. Nobody notices the retractions in the news, and you're still the bad guys as far as everyone can remember.'

'We're always going to be the bad guys,' Miska said, 'but Triple S are going to get caught, right? Sure, they get us out of the way. They do their little offensive—'

'It's not a little—'

'But as soon as it gets investigated we're back in the game and I go fucking head hunting. Make sure I'm drinking my next beer out of Resnick's hollowed-out skull.'

Raff stared at her.

'What?' she demanded.

'We're left with one of two possibilities. Either they only need the short-term gain to achieve whatever the fuck it is that they're trying to achieve here,' he suggested, 'or—'

'It's just the first part of the strategy to deal with us,' Miska finished.

'Possibly both.' Raff looked as though he was wrestling with what he was about to say next.

'Don't,' she told him. 'We leave now, our rep is fucked. It looks like we lost. We cut and run and we committed a war crime to boot. Nobody will touch us and nobody will hire us to fight Triple S in the future, and I really want to see them again.'

'They're fighting wars in ways you won't … *can't* fight.'

'The lies?' she demanded.

'The PR, the media part of the campaign, whether you like it or not it matters.'

'Where's Resnick?' she asked. Raff looked at her, saying nothing.

'You really going to make me beat it out of you?' she asked.

'You just don't like having friends, do you?' Raff asked. He sounded more irritated than hurt. 'He's in-country.' Resnick was down on Ephesus and on active duty.

'There's a ship just docked,' she told him and then explained about the *Sneaky Bitch*.

'Okay, I'll look into it,' Raff grudgingly told her.

Miska turned and headed for the door.

'What are you going to do?' he asked her.

Overreact, Miska thought.

'See if you can speed up the whole "we're innocent" thing,' she said over her shoulder, and left the room.

'Vido?' Miska said over the comms link, ignoring protocol as she made her way towards the elevator on Raff's floor in the hotel.

'Hey Miska,' Vido's beleaguered voice finally answered when she was riding the elevator down to the ground floor. 'Sorry, I was speaking to Salik. The UN and Salik are happy for the Bastard Legion to withdraw to the *Daughter*. Frankly I think they'd be happy if we just left.'

'I hear a problem,' Miska said.

'Triple S are saying that they will fire on us if we try to pull out,' Vido explained. The elevator doors opened. The bar was a scene of utter destruction. The DoL mercs that had hassled them in the street were lying around among broken furniture and smashed glass. Nyukuti was sat at the bar. His PDW lay on the wood next to a very large glass of bourbon that the stand-over man was taking sips from. The barman was cowering behind the bar, and there were several journalists hiding behind overturned tables as well.

'They came back,' Nyukuti told her as she emerged from the elevator. She could see in the mirror behind the bar that his face was a mess.

'So I see,' Miska said. She noticed that Nyukuti's folding boomerang sword was imbedded in a wooden carving of the Duke of Wellington, its blade bloodied. One of the DoL had pushed himself to his feet and was staggering towards Nyukuti. Miska had had quite enough for one day. She drew her SIG Sauer GP-992, dialled the velocity down to subsonic via her neural interface with the gauss pistol's smartlink, and then shot him in the back of the knee. He howled as he went down. He doubtless had subcutaneous armour but it still would've hurt.

'We didn't fucking do it!' she told the DoL mercenary as he rolled around on the floor clutching his wounded knee. 'And you're going to feel pretty fucking stupid when the truth comes out in a day or two!'

'Miska?' Vido asked over the comms link, more than a little concern in his voice.

'I'm sorry,' she told Uncle V over the comms link, 'We're just diploming with the DoL.'

'Oh, right.' Uncle V sounded more than a little dubious.

Miska sat down next to Nyukuti but swung the stool round so she could see the rest of the bar.

'Tell Salik and the UN that we are non-combatants. We are withdrawing from the theatre of operations. If we are fired on then not only will we assume that we're combatants again but we will take that as a breach of the articles of conflict and defend ourselves with every means at our disposal.'

'Including space assets?' Vido asked.

'Including the *Daughter*,' she told him. She heard the *consigliere* sigh over the comms link. 'Get our people out of there, Uncle V,' she said softly.

'Understood.' He sounded exhausted.

'One more thing,' she said, 'I don't care how you do it but get

185

the Nightmare Squad down on Ephesus. I want them outfitted for a lurp,' she told him, meaning long-range reconnaissance patrol, 'but tell the Ultra he has to go as low tech as possible, no electromagnetics, no lasers or plasma, just slugthrowers.' She was thinking about how the dead Triple S (elite) at FOB Trafalgar had been armed. 'And tell the Ultra he needs to stay in contact with me.'

'Why?' Vido asked.

'I don't care how they do it but tell them to bring me Resnick, alive.'

'Okay,' Vido said. She could tell he thought it was a terrible idea but it sounded like he was too tired to argue with her.

Miska was aware of Nyukuti sagging down onto the bar next to her.

'What?' she asked turning to look at him. He just pointed at a viz screen in the corner of the mirror behind the bar. She saw the words 'Breaking News' on the screen. Miska was really starting to fear the news. She contacted the bar's public systems via her neural interface, enlarged the viz screen so it filled the mirror, and then turned the sound up so it drowned out the moans of the beaten mercenaries behind her.

'... with my head in a lead bucket all the way from the Sirius System.' The smartly dressed young man on the screen looked very familiar to her but Miska couldn't quite place him. He was sat next to Brennan Campbell, who was definitely on Miska's shit-list. The sympathetic expression on Campbell's face looked about as sincere as a prison daddy telling his bitch that he won't come in his mouth. *I've been around convicts too long*, she decided. They were both being interviewed by some viz-presenter clone.

'But surely you knew that coming here, to the conflict in

Epsilon Eridani, would be a death sentence?' the interviewer said.

'I had to,' the young man said. 'Look, I've done some bad things in my life, I know that and I'm happy to serve my time, but she's fu … she's evil.' Miska realised that they were talking about her. 'She targeted the role model prisoners first, murdered them in front of us. Then she put the worst in charge. The serial killers, sex offenders—'

'No I didn't!' Miska shouted at the viz screen.

'—they ruled by gang rape.' The man broke down, sobbing. 'I'm sorry,' he managed. Then Miska realised who he was. On the large screen she could see where the prison tattoos had been removed. He'd been spruced up considerably, given a hair cut, new clothes, but there was no mistaking Lomas Hinton, convicted drug dealer and, apparently, a consummate actor. Hinton had not returned from shore leave on Maw City. With a thought, Miska sent the detonation code for the tiny nanite explosive implanted in his head. Nothing happened. The signal returned to tell her that the N-bomb did not exist.

On the screen Campbell was patting Hinton's shoulder. The New Sun exec looked like he'd seen acts of sympathy before but hadn't really understood them.

'New Sun employed the Bastard Legion, didn't they, Mr Campbell? How do you explain this sudden reversal?' the interviewer asked.

Now Campbell was all mock contrition.

'Well, Cynthia, that was a disastrous lapse in judgement, and I can assure you that those responsible no longer work for New Sun,' Campbell told the interviewer. 'As soon as I realised what had happened I was in contact with Colonel Duellona. She sent Triple S (elite) to deal with the situation but sadly they didn't get there in time. The Bastard Legion's so-called Nightmare Squad had fled before the true extent of their crimes was discovered.

'I can't emphasise enough just how brave Mr Hinton has been in coming forward. He still had one of the N-bombs in his head and expected to be killed immediately. Fortunately New Sun had the surgical facilities to remove the N-bomb.'

The camera closed in on a fresh scar on the side of Hinton's head.

'We're sorry for the part that we played in this morning's terrible atrocity. It is unfortunate, the rather selfish anti-capitalist stance that the self-declared Ephesus Colonial Administration has chosen to take. It is the kind of resistance to a free market economy that needs to be opposed wherever it is found, but this is not the way that New Sun fights wars.'

Now he turned to face the camera. It was all clearly rehearsed.

'I want the Colonial Administration to know that New Sun will make reparations to them, and to the Dogs of Love mercenary collective, for our part in facilitating this outrage.

'Things have moved very quickly today. Mr Hinton only arrived a few hours ago from the Sirius System—'

The *Sneaky Bitch!* Miska thought.

'—but we think we have a way that we can help this situation. To all members of the so-called Bastard Legion, I have this message: we know that you are being forced to fight in a war you must know is unwinnable against professional soldiers. You are being fed into a meat grinder for the gain of an evil, possibly insane woman. Our ships and our facilities on Waterloo Station, and down on Ephesus, are all currently broadcasting jamming signals, though obviously we cannot keep this up for long. But if you can make it to one of them then we have the surgical facilities to remove the nanite explosives from your heads.'

188

Miska stared at the screen. The interviewer was asking a question but all Miska could hear was the sound of blood rushing in her ears.

'C'mon,' she managed and strode out of the bar, Nyukuti in tow. She needed to calm down and then contact Vido. Find out who was out and about. Who was in a position to take New Sun up on their offer. And, if they made a move towards a New Sun facility, then she would have to kill them.

Miska's cyberware included a degree of protection against electrocution. This could, however, be overwhelmed. A shotgun with large capacity magazines firing taser darts was more than enough to do that. Even with the armoured clothing she was wearing, there was still too much bare skin on display. She was peripherally aware of Nyukuti getting hit as well. The 30mm hardgel stun rounds, fired from two under-barrel grenade launchers, were overkill. She didn't even feel the hooks in the capture net bite into her skin and deliver another fifty-thousand volts. She just flopped around on the ground, unconscious.

CHAPTER 12

Miska hadn't been paying attention.

You're taking this too personally, she told herself. She'd let her emotions get the better of her, dropped her guard, and now her entire body hurt. She suspected the pain was the result of all the muscle contractions from being ridiculously over-electrified. Even for someone with her military grade cyberware, she was lucky her heart hadn't given out.

Her hands and ankles were strapped to some kind of reclining chair. There were restraints around her stomach and her head as well. Someone really didn't want her moving around too much. It sounded like she was in a cavernous space, she suspected the hold of a ship, and there were at least four other people in there with her.

'Ow,' she said with some feeling as she opened her eyes. She was right, it was the hold of a ship and, with Captain Gosia Tesselaar standing over her, Miska guessed it was the *Sneaky Bitch*. 'Hi!' Miska said much more cheerfully than she felt.

Tesselaar looked every inch the belt pirate. Like she'd

stepped straight out of a viz. Statuesque, wearing a red sleeveless one piece and thigh-high boots. Red was the colour of the Crimson Sisterhood, the pirate organisation that terrorised the Sirius System. Both her arms were covered in sleeves of tattoos, and she had red hair down to her ass. Implants animated her hair, which seemed to respond to Tesselaar's moods. A large slugthrower pistol rode her hip. All she was missing was a tricorn and a cutlass.

'Gosia! Great to see you again. Is this about a conjugal visit?'

Gosia glared at her with red, obviously implanted, eyes. Miska smiled sweetly.

There were three more people in the hold with her. A tall Native American, so heavily built with obviously boosted muscle that she was worried his skin was going to split. He had long braided hair that was shaved at the sides, and tribal tattoos running up his neck and onto the side of his head. He wore a duster and bristled with weapons – many of them non-lethal.

With him was an equally tall Asian woman, who wasn't quite as heavily built as the Native American, but still looked like she could put you through a reasonably sturdy wall. Her hair was shorn, her tattoos were less tribal and more pictorial, and she also wore a duster over leather pants and a vest, and was equally heavily armed.

The third member of the 'Duster Crew', as Miska was starting to think of them, was a very short, very stocky, heavily bearded white guy. She suspected he had been going for a biker look, except his endomorphic build, probably due to growing up in a high gravity environment, made him look like a dwarf in one of her fantasy sense games.

She was pretty sure it was the kind of thing the 'dwarf' was sick of hearing. So: 'You know you look like a dwarf in a sense game?' she asked.

He actually growled and took a step towards her.

'If you've electrocuted and tied me up and I'm still not intimidated, do you really think growling will do the trick?'

'I thought you were supposed to be some bad-ass special forces operator?' the dwarf asked. He had a Norwegian accent. It got better and better.

'Well,' Miska began, 'I was having the shittiest of shitty days and I have to admit I let my guard down. So good work, team! I'm guessing you three were the take-down crew?' she asked. Nobody answered. It was getting embarrassing. She suspected that they had some military experience between them, but it looked like three amateurs had captured her. That said, they hadn't been mucking around. Emptying the magazines of an auto-shotgun loaded with sabot taser darts was a pretty sound plan.

Miska looked at Gosia.

'Gun tramps?' she asked.

'Bounty hunters,' the Native American rumbled.

'Cool,' Miska said. 'Well, now you're going to have to let me go or have the deaths of some six thousand people on your hands.'

'Not our problem,' the Asian woman said. Miska smiled at her but then turned the smile on Gosia.

'No, but it is Gosia's, unless she wants her honey to lose a quite vital lump of his cranium.'

'Try it,' Gosia told her.

'No, because I don't want to kill him yet. Besides, I'm sure the hold is shielded enough. Doesn't matter, your gun tramps—'

'Bounty hunters,' the Native American repeated.

'—will want their bounty, which means you'll have to move me, and then the signal will find him. Even if it doesn't there's a threshold on how long I can be away before it triggers them all.' Which was half true and half a bluff. It was a bit more complicated than that.

'I told you last time,' Gosia said leaning in close enough for Miska to practically taste the stale cigarette on her breath. 'He's better off dead than your slave.'

Miska narrowed her eyes. Then something occurred to her.

'Where's Nyukuti?' she asked.

'Who?' the Asian woman asked.

'The Aboriginal guy with me,' she told them.

'Left him on the street,' the dwarf told her. 'No bounty on him.'

Miska wasn't sure if that was a good thing or not. If Vido had been monitoring then he would send people out to get him. If not, well, the Bastards weren't popular on Waterloo Station at the moment. The best-case scenario would be Salik's security people picking him up.

She squirmed around in the chair she had been tied to. It was similar to a dentist's chair, only with straps. It was oddly comfortable, yet suspiciously stained.

'I'm strapped into your sex chair, aren't I?' Miska asked Gosia.

The Asian woman smiled, the dwarf chuckled. Gosia slapped her. It was surprisingly hard.

'Ow,' Miska said. 'So you're going to let old what's-his-face die, then? Fair enough.' She'd have to find another way to escape.

'No, you're going to let all the Crimson Sisterhood on board the *Hangman's Daughter* go,' Gosia told her.

'Shan't,' Miska replied. She may have been being childish but frankly this was almost a welcome break from just how bad a day she was having.

'Yes you wi—' Gosia started.

'So we're still in the Epsilon Eridani system then?' Miska checked. She guessed that Gosia wouldn't want to stray too far from where her people were. Gosia stared at her. The bounty hunters exchanged a few looks.

'We're going to dump you in a time-contracted torture sense program. You know as well as I do that everyone breaks eventually. So how long you want to suffer is up to you,' Gosia told her.

'This all right with you guys?' she asked the bounty hunters. 'Could mess up the trial.'

'Not our problem, we'll have been paid,' the Asian woman told her. Miska had to admit that she had a point.

'Well anyway, good luck trying to force me to trance in to your torture porn program. You'd need one hell of hacker to get past my counter—'

Miska found herself standing in the middle of a purple-coloured cartoon forest with a comfortable looking quilted floor. All the flora was made out of fabric. Frolicking, animated plush unicorns in all manner of colours gambolled by. Miska had some vague idea that this was from some children's educational sense game that had been popular when she was a child.

'Oh, this is a nightmare,' Miska muttered. 'Fine, I give up, you can have the codes.' A friendly unicorn trotted over to sniff at her. Miska tried to summon her attack software, in the form of a club with which to beat the unicorn flat, but nothing. Even allowing for how long they'd had when she was unconscious it was impressive just how extensively they'd hacked her integral computer and neural interface.

'Do you want to give us the codes?' Gosia's disembodied voice echoed through the soft fabric forest. Miska held up her middle finger. 'Just let us know when you've had enough. The safe word is Star Kitten—'

'Star Kitten?' Miska didn't bother trying to hide her disgust.

'Only use it when you're ready to talk. Abuse it and we'll just check on you when we feel like it.'

The problem was Gosia was right. Everyone did break eventually. Miska knew she should probably just spare herself the pain. The other problem was that she wasn't built that way. Her dad and her sister had always said that she was stubborn. She braced herself. Then it felt like every single one of her nerve endings had been dipped in acid and the screaming began.

It had felt like an eternity. They had disabled her internal clock, so she had no idea how long it had actually been. With pain as a new constant she had intended to come to terms with it. Make living with pain her new reality and thus deal. That hadn't worked. It had just really hurt. The verisimilitude of the sense program, in terms of sensory input if not environment, was so good that she had screamed until her throat bled. She was left lying on the comfy fabric forest floor in a puddle of red drool being watched by fucking unicorns. She knew she should just give in. She would break. But that in turn meant she would become a broken person. A different person. A weaker person. That, she couldn't allow. Just telling them as a matter of practicality she could rationalise. It was the only sensible thing to do in the situation. And then the pain disappeared.

'Why'd you stop? I didn't say Star Kitten, you fucking

pussies!' she managed, staining the forest floor with some more red drool. 'What is this? Aversion therapy for fucking unicorns?'

'Sorry about that. I had to sample and loop your pain to spoof the program.'

The voice came from nearby and sounded familiar. Miska had a sinking feeling but it was still better than the constant agony. She looked up. Che Guevara was sat nearby, stroking one of the unicorns. Miska returned to her face-down position. As horrifyingly twee as her surroundings were, they were at least comfortable.

'I hate being rescued,' she muttered, the quilt-like forest floor partially muffling her voice.

'That's good. You're not being rescued, just being offered an opportunity,' the sentient communist virus told her.

'Wait, are you the same one I met on Faigroe Station?' she asked. She knew the virus tended to go where it felt it was 'needed' to fight the forces of capitalist oppression.

'The same one.'

'Does that mean Joshua's body is on board?' she asked. The sentient virus had possessed Joshua, an undercover data warfare expert who had been in Triple S's employ.

'All of Joshua is on board, although he is still in here with me, just taking a backseat for the time being, but yes, I am currently the *Sneaky Bitch*'s data warfare officer. They're very impressed with me. Particularly because of the ease with which I hacked your systems.'

'I'll bet,' Miska said, though it certainly made sense now. 'What an extraordinary coincidence.'

Che just smiled at her. Miska couldn't shake the feeling that there was more going on here. Either that or she was being stalked by a sentient computer virus that thought it was a pre-FHC Communist folk hero.

'How're you finding being human?' she asked, largely for something to say. She was still trying to pull herself together.

'I started off human, a long time ago,' he said almost wistfully. That got her attention. 'I'd forgotten how much I appreciated a good shit.'

'Lovely,' Miska said. She was aware of someone moving behind her. She pushed herself up and looked. It was her, writhing on the forest floor, body painfully contorted, agony etched into her silently screaming face. It was the spoof program, what Gosia and her crew would be seeing in the real world. She knew it would be accompanied by some similarly spoofed biometrics. Che had rendered both her and himself invisible to them. For a moment she couldn't look away.

'I had no choice,' he told her. He genuinely sounded sorry, even ashamed of himself.

'How long?' she asked.

'Five minutes,' he told her.

It had felt a lot longer. She turned away from the image of her immediate past.

'You said you weren't here to rescue me?'

'I'm going to return use of your integral computer and your neural interface to you,' he explained.

'Good of you,' Miska told him. Her initial thought was to open every door on the *Sneaky Bitch*, including the ones to the outside. *Well maybe not the ones to the cargo hold I'm in*, she decided, modifying her plan. Given time she could work herself free. *Mind you, I probably shouldn't kill Joshua/Che, either*, she thought.

'There are conditions,' he told her. Miska sighed. 'You can't kill anyone on board.'

'Not kill anyone …!' Miska exploded. 'I'm killing every last one of these fuckers. Horribly! I may get some of my people and come back here and kill them again just to be on the safe side!'

'Then you can stay here and frolic with the unicorns,' Che told her.

'If I stab you in here with an actual unicorn?' she enquired.

'I'm serious, Miska.'

'You think I'm not? Why can't I kill them? I mean they're fucking pirates!'

Che looked momentarily embarrassed.

'What?' Miska demanded.

'They're my friends,' he admitted.

'You can make new ones!'

'Do you want out or not?'

'Fine.' Miska sighed. 'I won't kill any of them.'

Che studied her for a moment or two.

'Yeah, you're going to have to try a bit harder than that to convince me,' he finally said.

Miska threw her hands up in the air.

'Seriously, Che, they're not going to stop. Sooner or later I'm going to have to kill them. I may as well get it over and done with now.'

'Those are the rules, take it or leave it. And I'll be watching.'

'The gun tramps, they're not crew. I can kill them, right?'

'No.'

'Fine! I'll go back to the torture!' she said and crossed her arms.

'You can't be serious!' He was starting to sound more than a little peeved with her. She wasn't serious but she felt like digging her heels in.

'Anyway, what's your interest?' she asked. Che narrowed his eyes. He was probably suspicious of the change in subject.

'I am aware of what's going on in-system at the moment. I suspect that, despite yourself, you're on the side of angels this time—'

'You know me, Che, fighting the good fight. Keeping the colonies safe from megacorp abuses.' She offered him a fist bump, which he ignored.

'Except when you change sides and go to work for New Sun.'

'Oh, you know about that.' Miska withdrew the proffered fist. 'Well, I am a mercenary. Highest bidder and all that.'

'Yes, it's why you're not being fully rescued,' he told her.

'Anything you can tell me about what's going on? I don't suppose you know what New Sun is up to?' she asked.

'No,' Che said. 'But I suspect the situation is being manipulated by the Small Gods.'

That got her attention.

'Really?' she asked. 'Mars?' She was thinking about Deimos, the entity that had inhabited Teramoto's corpse.

'Mars is always involved in colonial conflicts to one degree or another. Triple S and New Sun are just fronts for Martian interests.'

'You brought Hinton here? Cut a deal with New Sun?' she asked.

'We brought Hinton here but the captain knew that Triple S had been in contact with Maw City about you. She made a deal with them in the Sirius System. Hinton was part of the deal, as was the bounty hunters taking a crack at you,' Che told her.

Miska knew that with her out of the picture they could totally trash her reputation.

At least it was confirmed. Miska was giving some thought

to going to the nearest Martian Embassy and asking them to leave her alone. *Well, stop picking fights with their proxies*, she chided herself. Then something occurred to her.

'I won't kill anyone if you get my gun and my knife back,' she told him.

Che stared at her for a moment, a unicorn nuzzling his face.

'Let me see if I've got this straight, you promise not to kill anyone but you want me to give you weapons?' he asked.

'Yes,' she told him, nodding enthusiastically. 'My dad gave me that knife, I'm not leaving it here with these assholes.'

Now it was Che's turn to sigh. He seemed to decide it was the best deal he was going to get.

'Very well then.' He faded away.

Miska found she had access to her integral computer. The first thing she did was change her icon from the realistic looking one to the spiky cartoon version of herself, complete with her steel helmet. The second thing she did was beat a unicorn to death with her club.

The torture program was in a wooden crate in the hold of the *Sneaky Bitch*'s net icon. Miska didn't know anything about historical sailing ships but she was pretty sure that the corsair's virtual representation was supposed to be a seventeenth or eighteenth century pirate vessel. They nearly always were. Miska recognised the common element. The virtual ship had sails, cannons and was made of wood.

She was using one of the stolen stealth programs that had come with *U.S.S.S Jimmy Carter*, the electronic warfare ship she had stolen from the NSA. So far it was proving a lot more sophisticated than the *Sneaky Bitch*'s intrusion countermeasures, the visual manifestations of which appeared to be some very unconvincing pirate mannequins. She crept out of the hold and up the wooden steps onto the deck and looked out over the smooth, black, glass-like ocean that represented space. In the distance she could make out another ship. Miska turned around and glanced up at the masts. There were no sails up. The ship was still on the ocean. The *Sneaky Bitch* was running cold and silent. They didn't want to be seen by the other ship.

They're a long way from home for piracy, she thought. She picked up a telescope from the rail and in doing so snuck into the corsair's passive scanners. She looked at the other ship through the telescope. She recognised it, or at least the type. The net icon was of an ironclad from the First American Civil War. It was a US government ship. She was pretty sure she knew which one as well. She interrogated the ship's systems and her hunch was confirmed. It was the *U.S.S.S Teten*, the FBI destroyer that was part of the multi-agency taskforce that had been assigned to capture her and recover the *Hangman's Daughter*. They had no jurisdiction in the Epsilon Eridani system, and any aggressive move against the Legion could be seen as an act of war, but that didn't mean they couldn't take delivery of a bounty. It was a bold move for Gosia. The last time the *Teten* and the *Sneaky Bitch* had encountered each other they had been exchanging munitions. That said, Gosia and her crew weren't wanted for piracy in the Epsilon Eridani system.

'It never rains but it pours,' Miska muttered to herself. She wondered if her sister was still on board the FBI ship.

A map and a pair of compasses represented the navigation system. Miska confirmed her suspicions. They were still in-system. Gosia wouldn't want to be too far from her people on the *Daughter* if she thought she was going to get the information she wanted from Miska. Miska was still, however, several light minutes away from Waterloo Station. The icon for the comms system was a signalling mirror. Miska folded herself down and flung her consciousness out across space in an occulted black beam of light.

The lag was killing her, but slowly and surely she was getting the *U.S.S.S Jimmy Carter* – or the *Little Jimmy*, as she called the stealth ship – systems up and running. She was mostly programming it for autonomous flight. Finally she was as ready as she was going to be.

She received three-minutes-old footage of the hollowed-out raven skull, which was the Little Jimmy's net representation, detaching from the *Hangman's Daughter*, which looked like a cross between an old prison hulk and some mythological funeral barge. The *Little Jimmy* made its way as stealthily as possible out of Waterloo Station space. Again, the New Sun's ban on space warfare made this easier than it otherwise would have been. When the *Little Jimmy* spread its sails and accelerated there was no way that Waterloo Station traffic control wouldn't pick them up, but by that time the ship would be gone.

Miska hated math, even computer-assisted math. The trick was to decelerate far enough away to fold away the sails and bleed off heat as discreetly as possible, but still keep enough velocity to drift in on the *Sneaky Bitch*. All the while relying on the stolen ship's top of the line stealth systems to keep her invisible to the pirate corsair's passive scanners. They couldn't risk lidar and radar if they wanted to remain invisible to the *Teten*. Trying to work out the math for this, even with the help of the *Little Jimmy*'s dumb AI navigation so-called expert system, had given Miska another headache.

There was a horrible, disorienting, wrenching sensation as she ceased to exist in the *Little Jimmy*'s systems as the ship accelerated. Minutes later she existed again and the lag was down to nearly negligible milliseconds. Miska folded the sails down and bled the heat off. Heat would be the biggest threat of discovery. Now she needed to let the *Little Jimmy*'s admittedly excellent autopilot handle the extremely difficult manoeuvres that would be required, using only its compressed gas manoeuvring systems. She would have to move quickly now. She dropped one of her fuzzy worms. This one was yellow in colour. It burrowed into the wood, merging with the *Sneaky Bitch*'s systems. It contained one of the most sophisticated NSA intrusion programs that Miska had found when she'd stolen the *Little Jimmy*. Then she spoofed the security lenses in the hold she was being held in, occulted an instruction to one of the maintenance systems and tranced out.

Miska half expected all sorts of alarms to go off when she tranced out but they didn't. She was impressed with Che's spoof program despite herself.

Her body was still a mass of aching muscles but the twelve hours or so she'd been away from Waterloo Station had at least given her hand, and some of her other bruises, contusions and burns, time to heal.

A wheeled maintenance droid was trundling towards her. She frowned. Someone had painted a disturbing clown face on the front of it. It extruded a small, spinning circular blade.

'Now wait a minute, haven't you got anything a little less spinny?' she asked as the blade moved closer to her right wrist restraint. 'No, I've changed my mind, I'm pretty sure I can free myself.' She grimaced and closed her eyes. Something sprayed up into her face. She risked opening one of her eyes. The wrist restraint had been cut but the circular blade had gouged a chunk out of the medgel encasing her right hand. Miska very quickly undid the rest of the restraints as the maintenance droid trundled back from wherever it had come from and she was free.

Her gauss pistol and the knife her dad had given her were waiting just outside the door to the cargo bay. She strapped on the knife's sheath and SIG's smartgrip drop holster. She drew the pistol, holding it somewhat awkwardly in her left hand as she made her way as quickly and as quietly as she could towards the closest airlock. She heard voices, and boots on the metal deck coming towards her. She cursed mentally and moved into the first room she saw.

Miska found herself in a tiny cramped bunkroom filled with various spare parts and tools. She was face to face with a short, slight, frizzy-haired woman wearing grimy overalls and a peaked cap.

'Sorry,' Miska told her and hit her in the throat, not quite hard enough to kill her, but hard enough to leave her short of air and unable to speak for a little while. Miska listened as the footsteps passed the tiny berth. She hoped they weren't going to check on her. When she was sure they were gone she left the room. The woman was writhing on her bunk clutching at her throat.

Pistol outstretched, Miska – very aware of the time – moved quickly through the *Sneaky Bastard*'s cramped corridors. She had just one more corridor to go. She was pleased that she hadn't heard them sound battle stations, which meant they hadn't detected the *Little Jimmy*.

She rounded the corner. She supposed it was inevitable that the big Native American gun tramp and the dwarf had chosen this particular corridor for a discreet rendezvous. Miska was only slightly amused to see that their rendezvous involved a stepladder. They both stared at her. She stared back.

'I'm so sorry,' she told them, 'this is going to seem really harsh.'

They were going for their weapons. Miska already had hers ready. Even though it was her off-hand the smartlink super-imposed crosshairs in her IVD, showing her where the bullets were going to hit. The first three-round burst tore into the side of the dwarf's knee with sufficient force to take his legs out from underneath him. His head bounced off the top of the stepladder on the way down.

The big Native American had actually drawn a PDW that he seemed intent on using as an oversized pistol. Miska went down on one knee. Her first three-round burst disintegrated the gun tramp's left kneecap, the second his right.

'Toss the gun!' Miska told him, 'Or the next burst goes into your balls! And you might want to think about how pissed I am with you right now!'

He was roaring. He aimed the gun at her and Miska had to throw herself around the corner as he squeezed off a long, undisciplined burst.

'Really!' she demanded. She cursed Che. It was really difficult trying not to kill people.

Further up the corridor she heard voices. A head popped around a junction. She wasn't sure but she thought it might have been Joshua.

'Duck!' she shouted and fired a long burst in his general direction. The face disappeared back into cover.

Miska peeked round the corridor to the airlock. The Native American fired off another long burst.

'Jesus!' Miska ducked back behind the corner. Kneecapping a stationary person was one thing. Hitting a moving arm with your off-hand, even with a smartlink, was what her dad called viz-bullshit.

She heard the satisfying clang of the *Little Jimmy* docking with the *Sneaky Bitch* and then cries of surprise from forward.

Right, enough mucking around. She came round the corner low and fired off the rest of the magazine. The recoil on the gauss pistol, even on full automatic, was negligible. She used the smartlink to aim as much as possible but was hoping that filling the air with rounds would solve the problem. A round caught the PDW's ceramic magazine, shattering it; another caught him in the arm and he dropped the weapon. She was now taking fire from forward as she rolled into the airlock corridor and up onto her feet, quickly changing the gauss pistol's magazine. The Native American was thrashing around on the floor and roaring in pain and anger.

Miska started running and then threw herself into the air, hitting the deck on the other side of the two prone gun tramps and rolling to her feet.

'Oh god!' she howled. Her accumulated injuries and muscular pain from the extensive tasering had not left her in the best state for gymnastics.

In some pain, she spun around to cover the corridor behind her. The Native American was reaching for another weapon with his uninjured left hand.

'For fuck's sake!' Miska muttered and shot him in his left arm. It was much easier at near point-blank range. The airlock hissed open behind her. Her yellow worm had worked. She backed into it. The airlock hissed shut. Gosia, Joshua, the other gun tramp and two other crew in Crimson Sisterhood colours ran into the corridor. Gosia and the two crew leapt the Native American and the dwarf. The external airlocks on the *Sneaky Bitch* and the *Little Jimmy* opened behind Miska. Gosia looked angry, she was screaming at Miska, hammering on the airlock. Miska smiled, waved cheerily and mouthed the words 'Star Kitten' to her and then headed into the *Little Jimmy*.

Miska targeted the *Sneaky Bitch*'s weapon systems with the *Little Jimmy*'s lasers on the way out but there was only so much that Gosia could do as the *Teten* flooded space with radar and lidar, missile-locked the corsair and almost managed to do the same to the *Little Jimmy* before Miska set sail and accelerated.

Oddly, Miska was in a much better mood. Her kidnapping had proven a distraction. Provided perspective on her problems back on Waterloo Station. That didn't, however, mean that New Sun could get away with talking trash about her and her Bastards.

CHAPTER 13

'Where the fuck have you been?' The fact that her dad was swearing, let alone at her, admittedly over the comms, illustrated just how frightened he'd been.

'Got kidnapped, escaped again, it was a thing,' Miska told him. She'd used her engine to get into the correct orbit around Ephesus for Waterloo Station but then run silent and cold on the approach. She was relying on the *Little Jimmy*'s superior stealth systems to prevent her having to explain the presence of the stolen NSA ship in Epsilon Eridani space. She didn't care how liberal the 'authorities' were. Besides, as far as she knew the *Teten* was still in-system.

This is your life now, she thought as she used the compressed gas manoeuvring thrusters to invert the *Little Jimmy* as it came in beneath the *Daughter*'s superstructure and docked with one of the underside maintenance airlocks.

'What kind of answer is that?' her dad demanded.

'Bounty hunters,' she told him, wondering where Vido was. She quickly explained what had happened.

'You want to go after them?' he asked.

Yes, she thought, but although the *Daughter* outgunned the *Sneaky Bitch*, the corsair was faster and more manoeuvrable, and the prison barge wasn't really set up for pirate interdiction.

'No,' she told her dad, 'but we see that ship again we shoot first and ask questions later, I don't care who her boyfriend is. Did we get everyone off-world and back to the ship?'

'Yes, pretty much everyone's back in their pods. Except the Ultra and his people.' Oddly, for matters pertaining to the Ultra, her dad didn't sound as though he disapproved.

'I don't like him, his people, or his methods, but I think you were right to put someone down on the ground. Depending on what you want to do here, we need intel,' he told her.

Miska spun round in the bucket seat in the *Little Jimmy*'s cockpit and looked at the airlock hatch on the floor of the ship. She should probably trance in to Camp Reisman and talk to her dad and Uncle V but being electrified into unconsciousness wasn't the same as getting sleep and she was dog-tired.

'Nyukuti?' she asked.

'Came back, when he came to. I think they left him in the street. He was a bit banged up but none the worse for wear.'

'Nothing back from the war crimes investigation?' she asked.

'No, Vido thinks that Triple S will be doing everything they can to slow it down.'

'Is Vido getting some rest?' she asked. He had sounded desperately like he'd needed it the last time she had spoken to him.

'Er ...' her dad said. Miska frowned. Then she ran his image through the projector in the cockpit. He became a twelve-inch hologram stood atop the main console.

'What?' she asked. Then she remembered New Sun's offer to remove the N-bombs. 'Did he desert?' she asked, dreading the answer. A blinking link to a news viz appeared in her IVD. 'I'm not going to like this, am I?'

Her dad didn't answer.

She opened the link.

'. . . no sexual abuse among the Legion. Colonel Corbin made it absolutely clear from the first that she would not tolerate sexual violence in any form when she killed all the sex offenders, and anyone who'd ever hurt a child.'

Vido was in the same real-world studio, being interviewed by the same media clone as Campbell and Hinton had been.

'I see. And the allegations that she has sexual relations with many of the prisoners and the virtual ghost of her father?'

Miska hadn't heard that one. Her breath caught in her throat. Her hands bunched into fists. She glanced at her father's hologram, he was stony faced but she knew him well enough to know he was seething.

'Utter nonsense,' Vido told her.

'But the electronic recording of her father is a tyrannical force within the virtual environment where the convicts' minds are imprisoned.'

'Only in so much as he's a marine sergeant major, so what do you expect? A fairy godmother?'

'But you're slaves kept in line with explosives in your heads?'

'We're prisoners, a penal legion in the truest sense of the world, but active duty is for volunteers only. The bombs in our heads are our prison while we're working.' He leaned forward. 'They're to protect people like you. They're to protect the likes of people who spread horrible lies from the consequences of coming face to face with the victims of their propaganda. The thing I don't get is why you feel the need to make up stories, we're a pretty colourful bunch.'

For a moment, the media clone looked decidedly uncomfortable.

'You were a member of the Cofino crime family, weren't you?' she asked, changing the subject.

'Obviously I'm not going to discuss that,' he told her. 'But let me say this. I ended up on the *Hangman's Daughter* because of cause and effect. Imagine if the people who invented and disseminated such lies were subject to cause and effect.'

'Mr Cofino, please, Corporal Corbin ...'

'Colonel,' Vido corrected her.

'Colonel Corbin attacked the gas mining platform with some of the most horrific criminals on board the infamous *Hangman's Daughter*. Do you honestly expect people to believe that they didn't commit those atrocities? Your blaming of Triple S smacks of a conspiracy theory.'

'We expect people to believe the result of the evidence from the UN's investigation that New Sun is trying so hard to suppress at the moment. And we're hoping that media organisations, even those who have received contributions from PR agencies tied to New Sun,' he said with some significance, 'will report those results with the minimum of spin.'

'But Miska Corbin is a psychopath,' the interviewer insisted.

'Undoubtedly, but she's a lot of fun,' Uncle V told her. 'Many of us have done monstrous things, but we're not all monsters, and those of us that are, are on a pretty tight leash.'

'Until someone tells lies about you?' The way the interviewer said it made it sound like she'd gone off-script. Miska suspected she was scared. That pleased Miska, Vido was right, there should be consequences for talking shit about people, even if it was just a bust nose.

'I didn't say that,' Uncle V said. 'You're putting words in my mouth.'

'I'm sorry,' the interviewer sputtered. Uncle V gave her one of his more disarming smiles.

'I'm just saying there's no need to lie. The truth is much more interesting.'

It appeared that the interview was over. Uncle V exchanged some pleasantries and shook hands with the still somewhat frightened-looking interviewer. Miska ran over what she'd seen of the interview. He'd not revealed anything that people hadn't already known, certainly nothing operational. She wasn't sure if it had done any good. She suspected that he/they might have come across as a little intimidating but at least their side of the story had been told.

'We discussed this when you were away,' her dad told her. 'Decided it was the way to go.'

'Vido's idea?' she asked.

'Golda's.'

Well, he's getting stuck in, Miska thought.

'Not the way I would've done it,' she admitted.

'We did discuss fire-bombing the PR offices,' her dad told her, coaxing a smile out of her.

'Let's not dismiss that just yet,' she said and it was his turn to smile.

'My instinct was to say no but we're a conventional force now, we're not running black ops. I think the silence was hurting us.'

Miska nodded. They were one big black op but she couldn't tell her father that.

'You need sleep,' he told her. She nodded again. She could have gone on longer if needed, but frankly there was no real gain.

'They take Badajoz?' she asked.

Her dad nodded. 'MACE abandoned the camp. With us gone they were stretched too thin. Their forces retreated west.'

This meant the uninhabited jungle highlands on the western side of the river to the north of Badajoz, that supposedly had no strategic significance, were completely open to New Sun. She desperately wanted boots on the ground, wanted to send the Sneaky Bastards into the north, but there was no way to get them onto the ground without people noticing. She could repurpose the Nightmare Squad but she wanted them hunting Resnick. Besides, she suspected Resnick would head north eventually.

'There's one other thing,' the twelve-inch hologram of her dad said.

She had known this was coming since she'd seen Hinton's interview.

'How many deserted?' she asked.

'We've got about fifty people unaccounted for,' he told her. 'Including Torricone.'

She tried to swallow but couldn't. She was glad that the pressure building up behind artificial eyes couldn't turn to tears any more.

'Send me the list,' she managed.

'Miska—'

'I've got to get some sleep, Dad. But the list first.' She severed the comms link.

A few moment later the fifty or so names appeared in her IVD. She battered her fist off the cockpit console, boosted muscle denting the hardened composite material. She had no idea how Torricone had got to her like this. This wasn't the way she conducted herself, it wasn't the way she worked. She tried to think of the Ultra. The way she felt about him. Tried to block out Torricone with lust but it wasn't working. She was furious with him. Not his desertion, his defection, his betrayal – she was angry with him for the way she felt.

Angry enough to kill?

She screamed. Then she sent the codes to detonate the N-bombs in all fifty of the defectors' heads. There were of course no N-bombs to detonate. Presumably New Sun had already had them surgically removed. A dry sob wracked her frame. It was relief. She pulled her knees up to her chin and hugged her legs.

Sleep had finally come with the help of chemicals. She was less fatigued but she did not feel rested. She was still lying in her bunk on board the *Little Jimmy* in her PJs, but she had tranced in to Camp Reisman. Outside the CP it was business as usual. Not everybody volunteered for active service but everyone trained. She knew that those who had returned from active service were being left to sleep. They were owed shore leave but even as quiet as Waterloo Station was at the moment, due to Triple S's offensive, the station still wasn't a healthy place for the Bastards to hang out.

She would have preferred to have the meeting outside the CP under the awning. This was despite the humidity that simulated the conditions down on the planet within the VR training construct. However, this meeting was better had out of sight of the rest of the Legion for the time being.

The door to the smartcrete bunker hissed open and she made her way to one of the larger meeting rooms. Her dad, Vido and Golda were all sat at the featureless utilitarian table. They stood up and saluted as she entered.

'Nobody's watching, gentlemen,' she told them, as all four sat back down.

'You okay, boss?' Vido asked. She just nodded. 'The interview?'

'I wasn't here, you made a call.' That was all she was prepared to say about it.

'The deserters?' her dad asked.

'Their N-bombs have been removed,' she told them.

'You tried ...?' Vido started.

Miska nodded curtly. She didn't like the look of concern on Vido's face. Her dad at least had the courtesy to cover his concern. Golda was just watching her, an expression of detached interest on his face.

'How come so few deserted?' she asked.

'We didn't trust New Sun,' Golda told her. He looked over at Vido. 'Words were had.'

'Mass got into it with Torricone,' Vido told her. 'Tuned him up a little but ... They probably shouldn't be in a room together any time soon.'

'Somehow I don't think that's going to be an issue,' Miska told him.

'Your FBI agent and the doctor are back,' Golda said. 'We've kept them awake so they could speak with you.'

A hologram flickered into life over the table. Corenbloom and the doctor were at one of the workbenches in the med bay. The disgraced FBI agent was slumped over the dull grey bench. The doctor had propped his head up on his elbows but even he looked tired. There were four guard droids standing not-so-unobtrusively in the background.

'Franklyn,' the Doc said and nudged Corenbloom.

Nice to see they're bonding, Miska thought. Particularly as the ex-FBI agent's job had been to hunt down people like the Doc. Corenbloom sat up and slapped his face a little. If the Doc looked tired then Corenbloom was clearly exhausted. Miska noticed that Vido was struggling to hide the apparent disgust he had for the ex-FBI agent.

'Well?' her dad asked.

'The long and short of it is that they're reasonably sure it wasn't us,' Corenbloom told them. 'I could go into detail if you want but basically it was a series of sloppy copycat killings. It didn't help that we use the same weapons as Triple S, but the ballistics and knife wounds don't match our gear.'

'Well, that's great, isn't it?' Miska said. 'When are they going to release that information?'

'That's the problem. They can't tie it to Triple S either. They handed over weapons and equipment that they say Resnick's squad wore when they relieved you but we suspect they were the wrong ones ...' Corenbloom's words faltered as his eyes flickered.

'The time of death places Resnick's people at the scene of the crime,' the Doc continued, 'but that's circumstantial at best. They were careful. We suspect they wore clean suits, they left very little evidence.'

'Let me guess, they wiped the memory on all the security lenses?' Miska asked. The Doc nodded and then he shook Corenbloom awake again.

'What?' he asked. The Doc just pointed into the lens that was shooting the holographic image. 'Oh yeah, so basically they're holding back on the announcement because New Sun's lawyers are telling them that if they implicate Triple S in any of this there will be hell to pay.'

'But they are implicated,' her dad said. Even to Miska's ears it sounded naive.

'Doesn't matter what you know, it matters what you can

prove,' Vido and Corenbloom said at the same time, and then realistic net icon and hologram glared at each other.

'So they're holding back·on the announcement?' Miska asked. Corenbloom nodded. 'But we can tell people, can't we? I mean they're free to try and sue me.'

'It'll be better coming from the UN investigator,' Vido told her. 'We lack credibility and we could do with less emphasis on the amount of contempt you have for the law.'

'There's something else,' Corenbloom added. 'Between the possible first contact situation at Trafalgar, and the war crimes, the UN are quite close to calling in a peacekeeping force.'

'I don't suppose they'd employ us for the job?' Miska asked. There were a few smiles around the table,

'With respect, Colonel, I think they feel that you're part of the problem but basically they're looking for an excuse,' Corenbloom told them.

Miska nodded again. She knew when she was being warned.

'Okay, thank you both, get some sleep,' she told them. Corenbloom glanced at Vido and then the hologram flickered off.

'So we're going to be exonerated,' Miska said.

'Of that,' Vido added.

'Eventually,' her dad said.

'So what do we do now?' Miska asked.

'What do you want to achieve?' Golda asked. 'After all, we're not getting paid.'

It was a good question. She wanted to know what New Sun were up to but that wasn't enough justification for military action. She knew that Raff would want to know as well. He, and by he she meant her employers in the CIA, would also want any evidence of Martian and/or Small Gods involvement.

Miska would quite like Colonel Duellona exposed as well, if for no other reason than it would explain the beating she took at the other woman's hands. But none of this was justification for an unpaid mercenary action and in terms of Small Gods' tech, she needed to keep whatever the Ultra was quiet. *Except you sent him right out on a mission immediately after saying you wouldn't.*

'Have we heard from the Nightmare Squad?' she asked.

'Nothing yet,' Golda told her.

'We're burning money staying here,' Vido pointed out.

'We got anywhere else to be?' Miska asked. There was always going to be down time, which was going to burn money, though she had to admit the docking fees for Waterloo Station were exorbitant.

'What do they want?' Miska asked.

'New Sun?' Golda asked. Miska nodded. 'Does it matter?'

'It's bothering me,' Miska told him.

'It never hurts to know what your enemy's objective is,' her dad said, 'and they are the enemy.' These last words were growled. They hadn't talked about the allegations made but she knew her dad. Rage was bubbling under the surface. God help the people responsible if he ever got hold of them while he was wearing the Cyclops.

'They want the north, right? The highlands, the mountains?' Miska said. 'That's why they crossed the river, that's why Trafalgar wasn't near anything strategically useful.'

'But if there's something up there why don't they just send a force directly? Why such a big military action?' Golda asked.

'They want the planet,' Vido said. 'That's clear.'

Miska agreed with him. The military effort was one big distraction, however they justified it. They wanted the planet for

218

some reason and that reason wasn't the gas mining operation.

'But Miska's right,' her dad said, 'too much emphasis on the north.'

'Which is uninhabited, and the survey says there's nothing of value up there,' Golda said.

'Surveyors have been bribed before,' Vido pointed out. 'To leave things out of the report that can be exploited at a later date.'

'Golda's right, why don't they just go to whatever it is?' her dad asked. 'They've managed to set up a no-orbit rule, presumably to hide something. So fly to whatever it is, set up a concealed camp.'

'What if they can't fly to it? FOB Trafalgar was extremely low tech. What if advanced tech doesn't work up there?' Miska asked.

'How would that work?' said her dad.

Miska shrugged.

'Are we forgetting that there's something down there killing people?' Vido asked. He looked less than happy. She suspected that his encounter with the artefact on Barney Prime had been more than enough 'alien' for Uncle V.

'The Doc said there's something odd with the flora on Ephesus. He suggested that it had been tampered with, somehow advanced along its evolutionary path,' Miska told them. 'I think this is all to do with biotech. I mean, leaving aside something that can ram wood through a combat exoskeleton, imagine if you could shut down your opponents' advance weapons systems? No plasma, no laser, electromagnetics, drones or aircraft.'

'But how does this help us?' Golda asked. 'I mean, are we going to get involved? The war is all but over. Even if we are exonerated and MACE hires us, we may still be on the wrong side of a losing war. New Sun and Triple S have played this well.'

'I still want to drink beer from Resnick's hollowed-out skull,' Miska mused. Vido stared at her, horrified, her dad laughed and Golda smiled.

'Who shoots at us if we get involved again?' Miska asked. 'I mean, the UN know we're innocent—'

'Of this,' Vido pointed out once more.

'—and if the UN knows then Salik knows. MACE, frankly, need us, so that leaves New Sun's forces who were shooting at us anyway.'

'But we're not getting paid,' Golda protested again. Her dad was nodding.

'Vido, can you contact Salik and MACE? Tell him what they both already know, and that we're back in the fight if Salik wants his cut and MACE need our help. I fancy taking Badajoz back.'

'Sure?' Vido asked. Miska nodded.

'Gunny, sorry, LSM,' Miska addressed her dad, 'you and I are going to work up a plan.' Her dad nodded. 'We go low tech, slugthrowers only, and no gauss kisses, no air-bursting bullets, in fact nothing more sophisticated than armour-piercing and tracers.' This raised an eyebrow but her dad nodded again.

'We may have to print some new weapons and ammo,' Vido told her. She sighed at the cost but he was right.

'What would you like me to do?' Golda asked.

'Unless you've managed to develop sources already, then, other than helping Vido, I want you to wait,' she told him.

'For what?'

'The Nightmare Squad to contact us.'

*

Miska opened her eyes as she tranced out. She climbed out of the bunk feeling like she'd been lying in bed too long. She looked up at the weapons clipped above her bunk.

The AK-47 copy that she had taken from Faigroe Station as a memento was actually going to get some use it seemed. The carbon composite weapon had been printed from a template that Che had provided when he helped organise the miners on the asteroid station to rise against their corporate masters. Modified to fire a 9mm long caseless round, it was otherwise the same as the pre-FHC weapon that had been favoured by terrorists and freedom fighters all over the world. She'd replaced the stock, pistol grip, and the rest of the furniture with found Ephesus hard wood as a project.

She picked her laser carbine up and started removing the under-barrel grenade launcher from its mounting rail. She would attach it to the AK-47 instead.

She briefly considered taking the big Mastodon revolver that had been handed down through her family. It was such a basic weapon that she couldn't see how anything could go wrong with it. But she was saving the revolver for a special occasion. For when she caught up with her dad's killers. She would take the old Glock and the Winchester shotgun that had come from the *Daughter*'s armoury. The Bastard Legion was going old school.

CHAPTER 14

Miska strode across the hangar deck accompanied by the sound of gunfire. The industrial white noise generators couldn't quite drown out the racket of the legionnaires zeroing their weapons on the range that Miska'd had the *Daughter*'s maintenance droids build. VR simulations were all well and good but sometimes you just had to live-fire. She'd ordered all the slugthrowers that they were taking with them to be equipped with old-fashioned optical sights. Many of them were still slick from the printer, which had been working overtime. If they were right about tech not functioning properly down there then they couldn't rely on the weapons' smartlinks to feed them targeting information. She was pleased that her dad's training regime, which was based on the USMC's own, had involved learning to shoot properly before relying on smartlinks. She was also pleased that her right hand was pretty much healed and back to normal.

The plan was to drop a fire team from the Sneaky Bastards platoon's first squad to recon Camp Badajoz. That would be Kasmeyer, with Kaneda, Hogg and one other. The Harpies, with the mechs, and the Pegasi, with the Offensive Bastards, would hold off. A decision would be made depending on what the Sneaky Bastards found. The current plan, however, was to use the Sneaky Bastards as forward observers for the mechs. The Satyrs would take out the camp's point defence systems and SAM emplacements. The mechs would act as walking artillery until they were close enough to engage Triple S's armour. At which point the Pegasi would add their own firepower against the Triple S mechs and land the Offensive Bastards, with support from the Armoured Bastards, as and when they could. They had a couple of different contingencies in place, and of course it could all change depending on what Kasmeyer and his fire team found.

She saw Mass heading towards her with the rest of the Heavy Bastards from his two armoured platoons. All of them were wearing full combat armour – padded inertial armour undersuits with load-bearing, hard ceramic plates over the top of them. Normally vehicle pilots would just wear inertial armour but they had packs on their backs and all of them were carrying M-19 carbines.

'You boys look like you're ready for a lurp,' Miska said, meaning a long-range reconnaissance patrol.

'Never know, boss,' Hemi growled, just the slightest smile on his face.

'Sorry, it's been a busy few days, but good work in Port Turquoise,' she told them.

There was some smiles and nods from the big *tā moko*-covered Maoris.

'You give me a moment, guys?' Mass asked. Most of the Heavy Bastards looked at Hemi, who nodded. He smiled at Miska and they continued on their way towards the two Harpies attached to the *Daughter*'s rear airlocks.

Miska frowned. 'Everything okay?' she asked. Up close she could see the bruises on Mass's face, presumably from his disagreement with Torricone. Despite what Vido had said, she was pretty sure that Mass wouldn't have been able to stop a really committed Torricone.

'They're tight knit. They all know each other from home. They resent some Italian guy being in charge of them. I get it. I'd feel the same way if things were reversed.'

'You could always go back to the Machimoi,' Miska suggested, smiling.

'And give up my armoured giant? You must be kidding,' he told her. She knew that Mass had developed a major armoured war machine fetish, she'd seen it before. 'The answer's for us to get more mechs so you can promote me, then Hemi can run the two platoons,' he continued. She opened her mouth to tell him that wasn't imminent. 'I know, I know, I'll have to earn it. When haven't I?'

Miska smiled as she heard her father's amplified voice from somewhere on the hangar deck, shouting at some poor legionnaire who'd fallen afoul of him.

'Still, I've learned a new word,' he told her. '*Pakeha.*'

'What does that mean?' she asked, adjusting two of the magazines in one of the pouches attached to the front of her load-bearing plate.

'I'm guessing it's Maori for nice Italian guy.'

She smiled again and then pointed at his face.

'You okay?'

He grimaced. 'Torricone and I are going to have another little chat the next time I see him,' Mass told her.

Miska nodded. She didn't say anything but she couldn't see that going well for Mass either. Torricone had been taught to fight by his mother, and Miska knew from personal experience that Mother Torricone was hard.

'What's with all the gear?' she asked, changing the subject.

'Hope for the best, plan for the worst,' he said. 'Most of it will be stowed before we go to work.'

Miska smiled.

'I'm going to go and get them squared away,' he said and headed towards the Harpy that had his mech on board.

Just for a moment Miska felt like she was part of some legitimate military organisation. She could almost pretend that the vast majority of people on the hangar deck wouldn't cut her throat or do much, much worse given the choice. Including Mass.

'Hey!' Mass called. Miska turned around to face him. 'Whatever else finally happens here. What they said about you. That ain't right.' He gestured around the hangar deck. 'We know the truth.' He turned around and continued heading for the heavy drop shuttle. Miska found herself smiling.

Then she noticed that the buzz of activity had died down. A lot of people were standing around with the look on their face that suggested that they were watching something on their IVD, or in their helmet's heads-up-display. She saw there was a flashing icon from a news feed in her own IVD. She wanted to ignore it but knew she couldn't. With a heavy heart she opened the news feed.

It took her a moment to work out what she was seeing. She saw the suspended terraces of an arboculture plantation hanging between the huge trees. It was on fire. Troops in MMI armour and carrying MMI weapons were brutally murdering the tree-farming colonists. At first she thought it was Triple S. Then she saw the insignia on the uniforms. Then she read the headline: 'Fresh atrocities committed by the Bastard Legion.' She could barely hear the presenter in some virtual studio talking about 'punishment squads' that she, Miska, was supposed to have sent to the planet as revenge for MACE suspending their contract. Then she saw the face of the 'punishment squad's' leader. The grotesque snarl on his face as he put a pistol to the back of a sobbing woman's head and squeezed the trigger, murdering her in front of her children. She was vaguely aware that Torricone's squad were made up of some of the other deserters. She was vaguely aware that Torricone was being described as a serial rapist, a trusted lieutenant, and her lover. Everyone was staring at her. She couldn't think straight for the screaming in her head. She felt a hand on her shoulder. She spun around, almost reaching for a weapon. Not out of instinct but because she wanted to hurt someone.

'Don't burn, goddess,' Nyukuti told her. 'None of this is real.'

Miska stared at him. She knew that he believed that only his dreams mattered, that they were real in a way the waking world wasn't. It wasn't something she believed but somehow his words were getting through to her. Maybe it was just his tone of voice, soft, deep, mellifluous. Maybe it was his beaten face, partially covered in swell patches. The price he had paid the last time she lost her temper and hadn't been concentrating on the task at hand.

'We need you cold. He needs you cold.' This last was whispered.

But last night I tried to kill him! she wanted to tell Nyukuti. Dark eyes watched her as though he knew, somehow he knew. She noticed that both her dad and Vido were trying to contact her.

'You know what they have done,' Nyukuti told her and

suddenly the screaming stopped, in fact all the noise on the hangar deck didn't so much stop as go away. And she was calm. New Sun/Triple S had committed one of the most heinous crimes possible.

She didn't open the links to her dad and Vido's incoming calls, instead she had one of the security lenses focus on her and feed the image to every screen in the hangar deck, the shuttles, Camp Reisman and anywhere on board where the prisoners, her legionnaires, could see it.

'New Sun and Triple S have sequestered some of our people,' Miska said, 'They can't do this. We're going to make an example of them.'

There was no cheering. Nothing like that, but as the legionnaires returned to work they did so with renewed purpose.

She felt eyes on her. She looked up to see Raff – wearing inertial armour and carrying a pack, M-19 carbine and sidearm – standing at the top of Pegasus 1's cargo ramp, watching her. She nodded and turned towards Nyukuti. He was wearing full combat gear as well, carrying a slugthrower squad automatic weapon.

'You look beat to shit,' she told him. 'You good to go?'

Nyukuti didn't dignify her question with an answer. He just fell in next to her as she strode towards Pegasus 1.

The shuttle shook as they hit Ephesus's atmosphere. Miska was standing, holding onto one of the handrails. The Cyclops war droid was locked in place, standing over her like a huge metal insect bristling with weapons. The two platoons of Offensive Bastards were strapped into the seats that ran along either side of the assault shuttle's cargo hold. She had the funny feeling that they were watching her when she wasn't paying attention

227

but then looking away if she looked towards them. They no doubt wanted to know what she was going to do if they found Torricone and his sequestered 'punishment squad'.

Sequestration technology, implanting neuralware that effectively allowed an operator, or an AI expert system, to puppeteer a human being, was among one of the most illegal technologies in human space. A number of nation states, including America and its colonies, still executed those caught using it. It was so obvious that Torricone and the others had been sequestered. She knew that there was no way he could ever act like that. The problem was she didn't have access to the neurosurgical tools that would be required to remove the sequestration implants. That was even assuming the Doc had the skills required to do the surgery. And of course Torricone had deserted.

The Rules of Engagement: if they are under arms then they are a legitimate target, she told herself. The reassuring thing was that she was pretty sure she could do it. The worrying thing was just how much she didn't want to.

She was trying not to think too much about how close to sequestration what she had done to the legionnaires was. But even if she could have, she wouldn't have used sequestration. She had put them in a horrible situation, narrowed their choices, but they were still themselves, however bad that was. It was a fine line, but it was enough for her.

She had spoken to Vido. All he had said was that he was going to handle the PR angle. He had sounded angry, a cold anger. He had sounded like he'd had quite enough.

The UN had protested but any way you cut it, Salik had the power in the sky over Ephesus at the moment. Miska did wonder if the UN were in touch with the *Teten*. Could they call the FBI destroyer in to help, until a peacekeeping force turned up? That would complicate things. Golda had spoken to Salik, made it clear that the Bastard Legion were going planet-side. That they were going to deal with these war criminals and anybody who stood in their way. MACE were fighting a losing battle against Triple S (conventional) and (armoured) in the west. They were too busy to object. By all accounts Salik was not happy but he did not try and stop them.

They were through the fires of atmospheric entry. Cooling thermals rising from the jungle were causing some chop but she'd experienced worse. She received a heavily encrypted comms link request. She opened it.

'I'm not in the mood for any more bad news,' she said.

'Define bad news.' It was the Ultra. She shared the link with her dad in the Cyclops.

'Where the fuck have you been?' she asked. It was difficult to make out the Ultra's surroundings in the encrypted feed. It was being shot from Bean's helm-cam, apparently. It looked as though he was standing at the bottom of a hill but nearby she could make out what looked like hooches. Some kind of military camp, then. Even for night the camp looked dark. She couldn't see anybody else moving around. At least the Ultra was clothed this time, though he only wore inertial armour and he still only appeared to be armed with a knife.

'Moving from atrocity to atrocity,' he told her. 'Following our so-called punishment squad. Torricone and some of the others have been sequestered.'

'We know.'

'We thought we were tracking Resnick's people,' the Ultra explained.

'Where's the punishment squad now?' Miska asked. She couldn't quite bring herself to use Torricone's name.

'They rendezvoused with Resnick,' the Ultra told her.

'That doesn't make sense,' her dad said. 'Why not leave Torricone and the others in play, committing more crimes, getting us into more trouble?'

'We can't get into more trouble,' Miska told him.

'That's the most optimistic thing I think I've ever heard,' her dad said across the comms link. She was surprised to see a small smile on the Ultra's lips.

'I mean as far as the punishment squad goes. Five atrocities or fifty, it's the same effect. Ties us up, gives them more time,' she explained.

'They need Torricone and his people back to either hide the evidence of the sequestration, or . . .' the Ultra said.

'Use them as a human shield against us,' Miska finished.

'Make us fight each other,' her dad said. 'I really don't like these people.'

'Everyone's got to make it personal,' Miska muttered.

'What do you want us to do if we encounter Torricone and the others?' the Ultra asked.

'Why're you even asking me that? You know the ROE.'

The Ultra stared for a moment or two.

In the shuttle the Cyclops's head looked between his legs, lens focusing on her.

'We're going after Resnick and his people,' the Ultra told her after a moment or two.

'There's something else up there, something truly dangerous,' she told them.

The Ultra nodded. 'I'm curious,' he said.

On the shuttle the Cyclops was shaking its head. It was kind of an incongruous gesture for a war droid to make.

'Where are you now?' she asked.

The Ultra did not answer. Instead he just nodded to Bean, who panned the camera around.

'Oh,' Miska said.

'We left a couple of presents for you as well,' he told her.

'Personally I would have opened with this,' her dad said as the Cyclops looked around Camp Badajoz. Miska was doing the same, her artificial eyes amplifying the faint red light that managed to penetrate the jungle canopy. There had been a fight. That much was clear. Triple S had laid down a lot of fire both from slugthrowers and actual flame guns, which, outside of the huge flamers carried by bunker-busting mechs, wasn't a weapon that a modern army tended to use.

The camp itself was a natural amphitheatre with hills on the south, west and east side. The CP, many of the hooches, and the shuttle/gunship landing pads were built into the hillside, along with SAM, point defence and artillery emplacements. Ammunition storage, machine shops and the mess were in the basin formed by the hills. The northern, jungle-facing perimeter was a raised trench system made of bulldozed earth. Miska, Nyukuti and the Cyclops her dad was wearing were looking down on the base from just below the brow of the southern-most hill.

Her own mechs were kneeling down behind whatever large, solid cover they could find. They were organised in a rough circle around the perimeter, though she'd ordered Mass to make sure that the north was particularly well defended. What she couldn't understand, however, was why the Triple S mechs were frozen in place like petrified giants. They had creepers crawling up them as well.

The hillsides were covered by row after row of impaled,

headless bodies. All of them wearing Triple S uniform. Miska hadn't checked all the bodies but she was pretty sure that most of them were Triple S (conventional) and support staff.

'I sent him after Resnick,' Miska said by way of explanation. The Ultra was nothing if not focused.

After the Ultra had shown her what had happened to Camp Badajoz, Miska had sent the Satyr scout mechs in for a fast recon. When they had confirmed the Ultra's intel the rest of the Bastards had joined them. She'd had mech and infantry secure the camp. Pegasus 1 was providing air support from above and the Armoured Bastards were splitting their time between patrolling and nesting in the nearby trees to provide overwatch. She had the Satyrs patrolling the perimeter using their reactive camouflage. Kasmeyer's fire team were scouting to the north but she had told them not to go too far.

'I kind of want to meet whoever is doing this and shake their hand,' Miska said.

The Cyclops turned its head towards her.

'These were just soldiers,' her dad told her.

'You're right. We need to go and get Resnick, Duellona and that oily fuck Campbell and feed them to whatever this is,' she suggested.

'That's a better idea,' her dad admitted.

Nyukuti chuckled. He was an unobtrusive shadow wherever she went, despite his armoured bulk.

'Sneaky-One-Actual to Hangman-One Actual,' Kasmeyer said over an open comms link.

'Hangman-One-Actual, what've you got?' Miska asked. She was seeing light-amplified footage from Kasmeyer's helm-cam. She accessed the helm-cam footage from the other three members of the scout team. The forest just outside the camp looked diseased somehow. She saw several canisters the size of old-fashioned oil cans. They had biohazard signs on them and were riddled with holes.

'Looks like Triple S rolled them down the hill and shot them up,' Kasmeyer told them. 'Smells fucking horrible, chemical stench.'

'Okay, get out of there,' she told them. 'Get back here. Hangman-Two-Actual will assign you a search area in the camp.' From the helm-cams she saw the scout team move quickly away from the chemicals.

'Sneaky-One-Seven, to Hangman-One-Actual,' Kaneda said over open comms. According to her IVD he was heading back towards the trench system in the north. 'This seems to be where much of the fight was. I'm seeing lots of fire damage here as well.' She accessed his helm-cam. He was right. They were moving through a large area of recently burned moss and scorched root structure. It looked like a green hell.

'Offensive-Two-Actual,' the lieutenant in charge of the Offensive Bastards second platoon said over comms. 'You need to see this.' Miska minimised the feed from the scout team and opened up Offensive-Two-Actual's helm-cam feed. He was up by the landing pads. Aim-lights attached to their M-19s played over the light-amplified images of the same containers that the scout team had discovered. These ones weren't riddled with bullets. Instead they were strapped into plastic pallets by the side of the landing pad as though they had just been unloaded. Nearby, a cargo-handling exoskeleton looked frozen mid-movement. There was no pilot but there were bloodstains in the pilot area.

'Looks like death-strength defoliant,' Offensive-Two-Actual said. He moved around and shone the aim-light onto the rifle-like apparatus. Their barrels ended in nozzles and they had canisters the size of a small fire extinguisher attached to them. They were in crates that had been smashed open in a hurry, and it was clear that several of the squirters were missing. 'Looks like we've got some military grade super-soakers as well,' Offensive-Two-Actual added.

'Offensive-Two-Three-Actual,' the sergeant in charge of second platoon's third squad said. 'We've got some flame guns here as well.' Lights played over opened crates with the flame guns and fuel canisters. Again they were next to the landing pads and again some of the weapons were missing.

'Pass them out?' her dad asked.

'Hell yes,' Miska said. 'Check them first but make that happen.'

'Didn't do them much good,' Nyukuti said, tension in his usually calm voice.

'Depends,' her dad said. 'It might have enabled Triple S to break out and make it to the river.'

Miska glanced at Nyukuti. He didn't look convinced. She didn't think they had enough information to support her dad's idea just yet.

'I don't think they had time to equip everyone with them,' Miska told the stand-over man, and then to her dad: 'Do it quickly, and make sure there's a good mix of defoliant and flame gun.'

She heard him start giving orders over the comms.

'Sneaky-One-Three to Hangman-One-Actual,' Hogg said over open comms a little later.

'Hangman-One-Actual, here'

'I've got something I need you to see yourself,' Hogg told her. He sounded hesitant, as if the last thing he wanted to do was tell her this. She enlarged the feed from Hogg's camera. She saw two bound and gagged Triple S support personnel wriggling

234

around on the ground. They had been left in the shadow of the Camp's CP. The Ultra's 'presents'.

There was a great deal of activity as Miska made her way down the hill towards the CP accompanied by the Cyclops and the ever-present Nyukuti. Second Platoon was busy delivering the squirters and flame guns to the other platoons.

One of the headless bodies impaled on a stake caught her eye. Fungus was already starting to grow from the severed neck but Miska recognised the powerful build.

'*Semper Fi*, sister,' she told Jones. Then she continued down the hill. She was glad that the Bastards hadn't been responsible for Jones's death.

'Hangman-One-Actual to Heavy-One-Actual,' Miska said. 'I want both your bunker-busters on the northern perimeter. Anything happens I don't want them to mess around. They burn whatever it is and we ask questions later. If it doesn't come from the north I want them to move position, same rules. Burn it, burn it with fire.'

'Heavy-One-Actual to Hangman-One-Actual, understood,' Mass said. Moments later the mechs started changing position. Infantry scurried out of their way. Miska could feel their footfalls through the earth as she reached the CP. Hogg was standing over the two captives. He didn't look happy.

'Rejoin your fire team,' Miska told the ageing terrorist in an attempt to forestall what she suspected was about to come. He didn't move. 'You're going to be difficult, aren't you?'

'Flame throwers, defoliants, really?' he demanded. 'I came down here to kill corporate assholes. Not help you murder the forest.'

'Seriously, dude, if it's trying to kill you then it's self-defence,'

Miska told him. He opened his mouth to argue further. 'We are trying to kill corporate assholes but we need a moment here, so could you please just go away so I don't have to blow your brain up?'

'Or I shoot you,' her dad added.

'Or Nyukuti hits you with a boomerang,' Miska suggested, mostly for variety. She was quite impressed that Hogg held his ground.

'What are you going to do with them?' he asked and nodded towards the two captives.

'Decoupage,' Miska told him. Hogg frowned. 'I'm a slaver and a killer, not a torturer.' The two captives seemed quite excited by this and were rolling around on the ground making squealing noises through their gags. 'How about this, if you don't fuck off right now I'll shoot both of them in the groin?' she suggested.

'Miska ...' her dad said from the Cyclops.

The two captives seemed even more agitated now. One of them had managed to sit upright and was trying to scream 'fuck off' at Hogg through his gag.

Hogg stood glaring at her. Miska drew her Glock. The two captives were in a frenzy now. Hogg walked away.

'I'll put him in for a discipline,' her dad told her.

'Everyone's being so fucking difficult,' Miska muttered. Truth was that Hogg had kind of reminded her of Torricone. She looked at the two captives, and held her gun to her lips. 'Shhhh,' she told them and then removed the gag from the one who'd sat.

'In as concise and straightforward a manner as possible, tell me what happened here,' she said to him.

The captive was a fleshy man in his mid-forties. His soiled

overall suggested ground crew to Miska. He looked between Miska, the Cyclops war droid, and Nyukuti.

'Oh my god, you're the Bastards aren't you?' He sounded terrified.

'Don't believe the hype,' Nyukuti told him.

'More concisely than that,' Miska suggested.

The man just stared at her.

'Now!' her dad demanded, his voice emanating from the Cyclops, making both captives jump.

'We hid, it's why we're both alive,' the man told them. 'We didn't see much, but roots grew out of the ground ... through people ... vines lifted them into the air and tore them apart.'

'So the jungle came alive?' Miska asked. It sounded ridiculous saying it out loud but it was what all the evidence had been pointing towards. After what Doc had told her about the ambulatory trees she suspected that it was some kind of natural self-defence. She could respect that. She just couldn't let it kill her people.

'It was more than that,' he told her. 'There were ... things ... people.'

Miska felt Nyukuti turn to look at the man.

'People, are you sure?' her dad asked.

The man nodded and opened his mouth to talk but a private from the Offensive Bastards second platoon ran up and handed Miska a flame gun and Nyukuti one of the squirters full of biohazardous defoliant. Miska thanked him and sent him away.

'People,' she prompted.

'I saw them, in the flames, before the mechs stopped working,' he told them. This wasn't good. It suggested some kind of EMP effect that was somehow strong enough to affect military grade shielded equipment had been used against the tech.

'Why did the mechs stop working?' her dad asked. The man just shook his head, it was clear that he didn't know.

'What did they look like?' Nyukuti asked.

'Not human,' the man told her.

'Can you be more specific?' Miska pushed.

He just stared at her. It was clear that he didn't have much in the way of an imagination.

'Look,' he told them, 'I saw one of the combat exoskeletons get hit with something that looked like an arrow, a wooden fucking arrow, and it went straight through, killed the pilot.'

Miska wanted to call bullshit but it tracked with what she'd seen at FOB Trafalgar.

'Resnick?' Miska asked. She had thought it impossible for the guy to look more afraid than he already was. It was clear that he'd already soiled himself. That was fair enough, he'd had a difficult day. First he'd seen his friends massacred by wood nymphs, then he'd been taken prisoner by the Ultra and his band of merry serial killers. It was enough to make anyone soil themselves. She was still a little surprised when he pissed himself at Resnick's very name. He was trembling. Shaking his head. 'Really?' she asked.

'You don't understand ... those people ...'

'Are they a more immediate threat than me?' Miska asked and put the barrel of the Glock to his head. The other captive was trying to scream through her gag, drool running down her chin.

'Miska ...' her dad said.

'I have a family,' the captive told her.

'Fair enough.' Miska wouldn't actually go after someone's family. She shot him in the head, then a second time. Double tapping out of habit.

The Cyclops was moving towards her. Miska suspected her dad was about to disarm her, so she held up a hand to forestall him. She was surprised and impressed that he stopped.

'Remove her gag,' she told Nyukuti.

He shook his head.

'CP,' he told her. He was right. A close protection detail's job was to look after their subject, not be at their beck and call. He couldn't protect her if he was mucking around with a gag. Miska had the Glock in one hand, the flame gun in the other.

'I'll do it,' her dad muttered. She could hear the disgust at what she'd done in his modulated voice but he reached down and removed the gag.

'I don't have a family, I'll tell you!' the woman practically screamed at them.

Miska could hear her dad telling everyone not to worry about the gunshots and go back to their tasks over the comms.

And she told them. Resnick's squad of war criminals were all ex-special forces guilty of heinous acts. They were Triple S's own pet atrocity makers. They were called the Double Veterans. On Ephesus their job had been to run black propaganda missions to make the Bastard Legion look bad. It wasn't much more than Miska and the others had already figured out. The male captive had died for nothing. Still, it was nice to get it confirmed.

'Where did they go?' Miska asked as she attached the flamer to her AK-47 by joining the mounting rails. It would make for an awkwardly bulky weapon but it would make it much easier to carry both weapons and bring them to bear when needed.

'They went north,' the woman told her. 'They had a flotilla down by the river. They had the conventional troops hold the line while they ran.'

Miska nodded.

'How many?' she asked.

'Four squads,' the woman told her. Miska guessed that could mean as many as forty-eight soldiers. 'Three squads of the Double Veterans ...'

'And?' Miska knew what was coming next.

The woman couldn't meet her eyes.

'Your people,' she finally said.

'You knew?' Miska demanded through gritted teeth. She glanced at the man she'd shot. It went some of the way towards explaining why he was so frightened.

She was aware of the Cyclops 'tensing' next to her. Again it was too human a move for the war droid. She suspected that her dad was readying himself to stop her executing this woman.

'When they give you what you want, you stop,' Nyukuti, her stand-over man bodyguard told her.

'Thank you,' Miska said, then she holstered the Glock and walked away. Nyukuti and her dad fell in beside her.

At first she thought it was snow caught in the lights of the mechs. Then she realised it wasn't so much falling as just drifting through the camp, sticking to whatever surface it landed on. It looked like pollen, only larger.

'Tell everyone to cover any exposed cyberware, goggles, ear protectors, gloves,' Miska told her dad as she slid her own goggles down and they adhered to her skin. She did the same with the ear defenders on her half-helm.

Then the screams started. They began human, but quickly became inhuman and were cut off by a wet tearing sound. Then came the flat hard staccato of metal being propelled by old-fashioned explosive chemical reaction. Tracers in the air to the north. Then fire. All the fire.

CHAPTER 15

Just for a moment Miska was transfixed. The two flame-cannon-equipped Medusas were dragons breathing fire as they lit up the night, and the treeline to the north of the camp burned. Then she was heading towards the flames. The carved wooden stock of the AK-47 nestled into her shoulder. With the flame gun bolted to it the weapon had become bulky, a struggle for even her boosted muscles to hold in position.

Miska could hear the faults being reported in the mechs, in the shuttles, in the combat exoskeletons. The crosshairs for her smartlink to the AK-47 were blinking on and off in her IVD. She brushed some of the pollen fall off the weapon with her left hand.

'Hangman-One-Actual to all call signs, unless crucial keep reports of your faults off air. If you are combat ineffective then fall back to exfil area three. Switch off your smartlinks, go to your optical sights,' she said over open comms and it quietened down. She didn't like the way Pegasus 1 was wobbling around overhead, however.

Something was slithering across, no, *through* the earth towards her. Nyukuti had seen it as well. She heard the flat, hard staccato of his slugthrower SAW. Saw the earth ripped up in the light of the flickering muzzle flash.

'The defoliant!' Miska shouted at him. He glanced at her, clearly none the wiser. 'The fucking squirter!' she told him. She moved her hand from the AK-47 to the flame gun and squeezed the trigger. Fuel shot through the blue pilot flame and ignited into a line of dripping fire. She played it over the ground. An inhuman squealing noise filled the air. Nyukuti let the SAW hang down his front on its sling. The SAW's cassette magazine was too bulky to allow the squirter to be attached by the mounting rails. He sprayed the burning ground with the powerful defoliant and an acrid chemical stench filled the air but the thick vine or creeper that had been burrowing through the earth towards them was now whipping around above ground. Suddenly it disappeared as though yanked back.

Miska reached up to the gas mask on her helmet and slid it down the groove that ran between the goggles' lenses. She pulled it over her nose and mouth. It clicked into place and then she felt the suction as it adhered to her skin.

'Masks on!' she ordered over the comms. 'Spray the ground, deny it to them!' She was looking around trying to see what was going on. She could see the Cyclops doing the same thing. The war droid just wasn't armed for this fight. Nyukuti was watching her back.

It was clear that they were being attacked from the north. The entire treeline was burning now. The pollen fall was a black rain silhouetted against burning, skyscraper-sized trees. Even the mechs, gushing flames, were dwarfed by the wall of fire. She could hear slugthrower fire and see muzzle flashes all over. It was self-evident that the perimeter had been breached. Flame guns squirted fire all over, and bits of the camp were burning. Other than the two Medusas configured for bunker busting and their flame guns, the other six mechs were pretty quiet. She heard the occasional hypersonic scream from their 30mm rail guns. Their rate of fire didn't sound right, but other than that they seemed to be searching for targets.

There was cannon fire from Pegasus 1, and moments later the assault shuttle fired two missiles. They shot overhead. Exploding plasma blossomed in the north between the perimeter and the wall of fire. Moments later Heavy-One-Actual, Mass's Medusa, fired its plasma cannon, twice, in the same area. Miska heard screaming coming from all over the camp.

'Gunny!' she shouted. The Cyclops's head swivelled round to look at her. 'Get the survivors into groups, then move back to back, three-sixty coverage, fold into the defenders in the north. They lay down the defoliant, deny the ground.'

'Understood,' he said. His modulated voice didn't sound right and he was moving strangely. She watched as more and more pollen drifted towards him.

'Wash him down,' Miska told Nyukuti.

The stand-over man turned his squirter on the Cyclops and started spraying the war droid with the biohazardous defoliant.

Miska glanced up. Pegasus 1 kept veering from side to side, as though the pilot was struggling to keep control of the assault shuttle.

'Hangman-One-Actual to Heavy-One-Actual and Pegasus-One, what are you shooting at?' she asked over direct comms. She was aware of her dad giving orders over open comms.

Screaming nearby. Miska spun round to see one of the Offensive Bastards yanked up into the air by vines dangling down thousands of feet from the huge sky-scraping trees. The vines ripped the man apart, his innards raining down. Higher in the trees she saw one of the Machimoi caught in the vines like a fly in a spider's web.

'Gunny, they need to watch above!' she told the Cyclops. The war droid was moving better now. She knew that he would pass on the warning as soon as he could.

'Fuck! Shit!' Mass snarled over comms. She could tell he wasn't subvocalising.

'Heavy-One-Actual, get a grip,' she snarled back. The shoulder-mounted plasma cannon on Mass's mech didn't seem to be folding away down his back the way it should.

'Heavy-One-Actual here, apologies but I've got system after system going down ...'

'Pegasus-One to Hangman-One-Actual, we've got things in the perimeter,' McWilliams told her.

'Can you be more specific?' Miska demanded. She was still making her way towards the northern perimeter. She watched as roots exploded through the ground and impaled one of the Offensive Bastards. Moments later the roots and dead Legionnaire were engulfed in flame. She saw Corenbloom and Raff sprinting towards her.

'... no,' McWilliams offered. 'Miska, I've got vines trying to wrap themselves around the shuttle. I've got systems going down all over. I've either got to put her down or get out of here.'

'Get out of here,' Miska told him, 'meet you at exfil point three.'

'Sorry boss, call if you're gonna evac,' he told her. Above her the shuttle pulled up, tearing away from the writhing vines that were trying to entrap it.

Trying to evac would just get messier. They needed to get things under control.

About three hundred feet to Miska's left a Satyr scout mech appeared as its pollen-covered reactive camouflage failed. Roots burst from the earth all around it and dragged the mech to the ground. Miska was gratified to see legionnaires sprint towards the mech and begin spraying it with the defoliant. Screaming vines were sucked back into the earth.

Raff and Corenbloom reached Miska, both of them gasping for breath. Corenbloom was doubled over but Raff was attaching one of the defoliant squirters to his carbine-configured M19. She noticed that the 'journalist' had liberated two other canisters of the defoliant. She also noticed that Corenbloom was watching Raff's practised ease as he handled the weapons.

'What have we got?' she demanded. They'd come from the north. Raff was just shaking his head. *So much for the intelligence professional*, Miska thought, somewhat uncharitably.

'They've come for the heads,' Corenbloom told her.

'Who?' she demanded. They were still moving towards the north. Small groups from all over the camp were doing the same. She heard the whipsnap of passing bullets. Tracers shot by too close for comfort.

'Gunny, tell them to only use the squirters and the flamers in camp, until everyone reaches the north perimeter, and everyone needs to check their targets!' Moments later she heard that going out over open comms. She turned back to Corenbloom. 'Who?'

It was clear that he didn't know how to answer her question. He was covered in sweat and shaking.

'Women,' Raff told her, 'made of wood.'

Corenbloom was nodding.

One of the Machimoi flew unsteadily overhead, tearing

through the vines reaching for it. Something flew up from the ground and embedded itself in the combat exoskeleton's head. *Was that a fucking arrow?* The blind Machimoi flew into the ground. Roots exploded out of the dirt all around it. They ran towards the combat exoskeleton. The Cyclops was there first but her dad didn't have the tools needed for the job. Miska arrived second. There was indeed an arrow sticking out of the Machimoi's head, though the arrow looked as though it had been grown rather than made. Miska saw where the roots had cracked the combat exoskeleton's armour. She squeezed the trigger on the flame gun and played it all over the Machimoi. Moments later Nyukuti and Raff were squirting the defoliant all over the roots. The roots whipped around in the flame, accompanied by the inhuman screaming, but they released the Machimoi. The pilot, blinded by the loss of the combat exoskeleton's head, was thrashing around on the ground, his finger still curved around the trigger of his Dory railgun. The Cyclops knelt on the Machimoi to stop the flailing.

'Easy, son,' her dad told the Machimoi pilot, as he prised the railgun out of the combat exoskeleton's hand. 'You need to unbutton.'

Miska assumed her dad had a comms link with the Machimoi pilot as well. She was checking to the north, looking around the Cyclops towards the network of trenches and earthen ramparts. She heard the Machimoi unbutton.

'Jesus Christ! Did you guys just flame me?' the pilot demanded. He sounded panicked. He sounded young. Then he was screaming. Miska swung round. It took her a moment to work out what was going on. Roots had grown through the back of the Machimoi and into the pilot and were now dragging him down into the earth in a fountain of blood accompanied by the sound of rending flesh and snapping bones. The Cyclops stood up, one foot on the bucking Machimoi, and pointed the combat exoskeleton's own railgun into the passenger compartment. He squeezed the trigger. At this range the hypersonic ripping noise was a physical force buffeting her. She went deaf as her implants and her helmet's audio dampeners sought to protect her hearing. There was movement to her left as roots grew up around the Cyclops's legs. The chain that fed the Machimoi's railgun with ammo was severed from the, presumably, crushed ammunition hopper on its back. The Cyclops quickly fired off what remained into the ground at point-blank range. Dirt exploded into the air.

'Move!' Miska shouted over comms. She triggered the flame gun again, squirting fire all over the Machimoi's bloody passenger compartment. The lines of flame were getting shorter and weaker. The Cyclops stood up but staggered as the roots around its leg tried to drag it back down. 'Nyukuti, Raff, squirters! Cyclops's legs!'

They must have heard because they were immediately squirting the defoliant all over the staggering war droid as it tried to tear itself free. Corenbloom added fire from his flame gun as well.

Something hit Miska in the chest hard. She staggered. Tried to remain upright but ended up sitting down on her ass, hard. She looked down at the hard armour breastplate that covered her chest. She could see the score on the plate where the bullet had hit her. Friendly fire. Suddenly the air was full of tracer fire from the north.

Assholes! She had told them to just use flame guns and the squirters in the camp.

'Contact!' It was Nyukuti who'd shouted. It was followed by

the sound of short burst after short burst being fired from his slugthrower squad automatic weapon.

'All call signs, watch your fields of fire!' her dad shouted over comms and then the Cyclops hunkered down, forming a barrier between them and the incoming bullets with its own armoured body. Raff and Corenbloom were also firing their M19s south. Miska pushed herself to her feet and then she saw the 'contact'.

She could sort of see why Raff had described them as women. They had a faintly female shape but they looked like living skeletons made of branch and bark walking slowly towards them. They wore natural crowns or crests of twigs, or had branch-like horns, or hair made of leaves. Their arms ended in root-like structures that writhed like snakes. There were five of the tree-creatures walking towards them. They were a childhood memory – twig figures Miska had made with her mother in those brief years she had been alive, given nightmarish form. They were out of range of the squirters and the flame guns.

'Reloading,' Miska told the other four over comms as she ejected the canister on her flame gun and kicked it away, replacing it with one of the spares. She brought the AK-47 up to her shoulder. Through the optical scope the tree-things didn't look much better. They were taking their time closing with them. She took her time playing the scope over each of the five approaching creatures. Some had hollow sockets where eyes should be, others had fibrous or resinous growths that might have been eyes but there were too many of them and they were in the wrong places. She saw the impacts from Raff, Corenbloom and Nyukuti's shots. The bullets blew splinters off the creatures, staggered them, but still they kept coming. She aimed at one of the figures. The crosshairs on the old-fashioned sight settled over the creature's throat. Miska squeezed the slugthrower rifle's trigger with the pad of her finger, firing a three-round burst. The wooden stock kicked back into her shoulder. The first round was a tracer, the phosphorescent tip making a line of light through the humid jungle night air. The round caught the tree-creature in the upper chest, knocking it back. The recoil made the rifle climb. The second round missed. The third round was a 9mm long, armour-piercing bullet of the type that had been developed during the war with Them. Designed to kill terrifying armoured alien bioborgs, the AP round hit the tree-creature in the face. The force of the bullet knocked the head back. Some splinters and sap went flying but that was about the extent of it.

Well shit, Miska thought. She was aware of tracers hitting the Cyclops's armoured body, which protected their backs from their own troops. The phosphorescent-tipped rounds went spinning off into the air. Then the Cyclops opened up with its back-mounted Dory railgun. One of the tree-creatures was snatched backwards by the hypersonic 20mm rounds and turned into so much kindling in mid-air. *That's more like it.* Though the Dory didn't sound right as it fired. She heard a sound from behind her. Something fast-moving and hard hitting armoured plate. She'd heard the noise before when large calibre weapons hit armoured vehicles, but it didn't sound right somehow. She was turning around as she heard the sound again. The Cyclops's legs went from underneath it. Horrified, Miska saw the arrows sticking out of the war droid's head and its chest. Roots grew from the arrow crushing the Cyclops's head, burrowing into its chest cavity to destroy its power source, its CPU. *That is not your dad,* she told herself, while still hoping he'd had time to evacuate his electronic ghost back to the *Hangman's Daughter* on a tight beam uplink. *Your real dad is dead.*

She turned back to the tree-creatures. Their slow movement through the heavy pollen bloom was an obvious power play. They were trying to intimidate the Bastards before they were in flame gun and squirter range. It wasn't a completely ineffective tactic, Miska decided. Though she was far more worried about the thing shooting the arrows. She switched the AK-47 to the grenade launcher manually. She had no real idea if the switch had worked because her IVD had long ago stopped talking to the AK-47's smartlink. *C'mon, c'mon*, she thought. It had been a long time since she'd fired anything without using a smartlink and grenade launchers weren't the most accurate of weapons. She allowed for the big projectile's drop, aiming the weapon at the tree-creature's head but hoping for the larger chest cavity. She squeezed the trigger. There was the popping noise of the 30mm under-barrel grenade launcher firing. The grenade hit the approaching tree-creature in the chest, the armour-piercing tip pushing through the branch-like ribs before the explosive charge detonated. It left a pair of legs and a wooden spine swaying in the humid breeze before it toppled over.

'HEAP grenades work,' Miska said over open comms. She was still aware of 'friendly' rounds sparking off the now-dead Cyclops behind them. 'Nyukuti, you'll lay down suppressing fire, Corenbloom, Raff, you'll reload your launchers with HEAP grenades.' She didn't wait for acknowledgement. Instead she just knelt down and worked the pump on the 30mm grenade launcher, ejecting the other three grenades in the weapon's tubular magazine into her hand. She pushed them into the drop pouch that rode her left hip to sort out later. Then she quickly reloaded the launcher with her last four HEAP grenades, working the slide to put one in the chamber. She aimed at another one of the creatures. A grenade exploded behind the advancing line.

'Take your time,' Miska told the other three over direct comms. 'Aim for their heads to hit their chests,' she said and fired. Another of the creatures exploded.

'Reloading,' Nyukuti told them. He ejected the empty cassette from the SAW, grabbed another from one of the large pouches hanging off his belt and slid the cassette containing two-hundred rounds of vacuum-packed caseless ammunition home. Then he was down on one knee, ejecting the grenades from his under-barrel launcher and replacing them with HEAPs.

Take your time, she told herself, *exhale, squeeze.* The popping sound. The AK-47 slamming back into her shoulder as she fired. The grenade missed but exploded close enough to one of the tree-creatures to send it flying. She was aware of more explosions. Corenbloom and Raff missing. Panicked fire. No help from technology. The tree-creature that she'd knocked over got up. Something about the cast of its wooden face told Miska it was angry. They charged. They were really fast.

There were more explosions behind the sprinting creatures as Raff, Corenbloom and now Nyukuti missed again. Miska took her time and aimed before firing. Her wired reflexes slowed everything down to slow motion. The grenade in the air was heading straight for the charging creature closest to her. It was dead on target. It would hit the creature's chest cavity and blow it apart. Then the creature moved. The grenade exploded harmlessly behind it as it closed. Miska aimed again and squeezed the trigger. The feed mechanism on the grenade launcher jammed. Miska moved her right hand from the AK-47's grip to the flamer and squeezed that trigger. Flame squirted out of it, engulfing the wooden figure. It kept coming. Miska's left hand worked the slide on the grenade launcher and ejected the final HEAP grenade. She knelt to pick it from the dirt. The burning tree figure reached for her. Miska pushed the grenade back into the launcher and worked the slide to chamber it. Burning root-like tendrils wrapped around her throat and lifted her into the air. Her unprotected chin burned. The tendrils were crushing her armoured neck protection. Then Nyukuti was there. He fired his grenade launcher at point-blank range into the creature's chest cavity. Due to her wired reflexes, Miska had the luxury of thinking: *Shit!* Then the grenade blew.

There was a lot of strangely resilient wood and armour between Miska and the explosion. Her inertial armour helped deaden and distribute the force of blast to minimise the impact. She was still thrown backwards, head-over-heels, to bounce off the dead Cyclops before sliding back to the ground, landing head-first. She was barely conscious, in fact unconsciousness seemed quite a welcoming idea. She was vaguely aware that the force of the blast had blown Nyukuti into Corenbloom, taking them both to the ground in a tangle of limbs. She heard that in-human screaming noise again. She saw the burning, one-armed head and torso crawling towards her.

'Oh c'mon!' she shouted as she forced herself to move, knowing that whatever she did it wouldn't be fast enough as she tried to roll into a crouch.

The ground shook. She was thrown into shadow. The huge chainsaw bisected the burning wooden torso and head of the creature and drove down into the earth, spraying dirt everywhere.

Miska sat back against the Cyclops and looked up at the Medusa-class mech. Friendly rounds sparking off its armour, roots growing up around its legs, the pollen fall coating it, but somehow Heavy-One-Actual was still moving.

'Thanks, Mass,' she told him over direct comms.

'Told you, boss, when your time comes ...' the Mafia button man replied. His comms link was a mess of static.

Raff finished off the remaining tree-creature with a HEAP and then sprayed it with defoliant to be on the safe side. Corenbloom and a very dazed looking Nyukuti were getting to their feet.

'Nye, you good?' Miska asked over direct comms, taking the time to look around, get an idea of the broader picture.

'Yes boss,' the stand-over man replied.

'You and Raff spray down Heavy-One-Actual with defoliant, get him back in the fight,' Miska told them. Raff moved to obey, as did Nyukuti, albeit somewhat slower.

What little exposed skin that hadn't been burned and blistered felt like it was full of splinters. She suspected that her gas mask had partially melted to her skin. Her body felt like one big bruise. Again. But the excellent Martian-made body armour they had stolen had absorbed the majority of the blast. Her head throbbed and she felt sick, possibly a concussion. She suspected she wasn't thinking as straight as she might but she could move.

The wall of fire behind her illuminated the scene. Up on the landing pad she could see bursts of fire from the flame guns and railgun fire from Pegasus 2 and the two Harpy heavy drop shuttles. It was difficult to tell from this distance, but it looked like one of the Harpies' domed engine housings was buckled. She could see figures around all three shuttles. She was pretty sure they were using squirters to wash down the Pegasus and both the Harpies.

She watched as vines tried to drag one of the Medusas up into the air. It was lifted off its feet but managed to cut itself free with its one still-working chainsaw. It dropped thirty feet to the jungle floor and made the earth shake. Another one of the

Medusas was being pulled down to its knees by roots that had burst from the earth to envelop it. As she watched it managed to burst free as well.

'We've got no weapon systems left,' Mass told her over the static-filled comms link.

'Mass, there are crates full of that defoliant over at the landing pad, get all the mechs over there. They smash it on anything they see growing out of the earth.'

Mass didn't reply over comms, instead he made the huge mech nod its head.

'Hangman-One-Actual to Pegasus-Two and Harpy-One and Two, what are the chances of you guys giving us danger-close air support in the form of missiles?' she asked.

'We're grounded,' Harpy 1 replied.

'We can try,' Perez told her from Pegasus 2. Again the comms connection was awful. 'But we have systems glitching all over the place and our friendly-recognition system is down. We've only got active laser targeting left.'

That was bad news. The friendly-recognition system could locate every Legionnaire and Legion vehicle to ensure it didn't actually get hit.

'Okay do it,' Miska told him. 'Avoid the landing pads, the northern defensive area and the mechs.'

Harpy 2 had not answered but she was aware of the heavy drop shuttle's engines firing up.

'Hangman-One-Actual to all Bastard call signs in the northern defensive area, do not, I repeat, do not fire to the south, four friendlies inbound,' she told the legionnaires in the trench system.

'We have to move!' Miska told Nyukuti, Raff and Corenbloom. They just nodded. Over on the landing pads she could make out the fire from Pegasus 2 and Harpy 2's engines as they clawed their way unsteadily into the air. 'Run!' Miska told the other three and they did, heading around the fallen Cyclops and aiming for the trench system to the north. There was nothing tactical about it, just a straight sprint, moving as fast as they could. She saw roots burst through the earth, more of the tree-creatures seemingly growing out of them. The air filled with red light from the two now-airborne shuttles' tertiary targeting systems.

'Hangman-One-Actual to all Bastard call signs, prepare for danger-close air support, repeat, danger-close air support!' she shouted over open comms. *Get your heads down,* she thought. Then tracers were flying towards her from the trench system. *Which part of don't fire to the fucking south was hard to fucking understand!* she screamed inside.

Her legs went out from underneath her. She face-planted hard. Nyukuti was stood over her again. Spraying her legs down with the defoliant, sending the roots that had grabbed her squealing back into the earth. Over his shoulder she saw the missile engines light up in their cradles. Suddenly Pegasus 2 ejected one of its batteries. It hit the ground and exploded. The force of the blast bounced Pegasus 2 into one of the trees and knocked a nearby Medusa off its feet. Then the night air was full of missile contrails. Miska was back on her feet running towards the trenches, looking at the tracers arcing towards her.

Are they trying to kill me? It was all she had time to think before a round glanced off the side of her head, shattering her goggles on her left side. She staggered, almost went down, but Nyukuti was there by her side again, dragging her towards the closest trench. Then they were taken off their feet by the hot wind pushed by the shockwaves from multiple warheads exploding.

Miska landed on top of Nyukuti in the trench. Fire and force blossomed around her everywhere she looked, plasma, high explosive, clustered area denial weapons that buried into the ground before exploding, anti-personnel sub-munitions that exploded into shrapnel at head height. Both the shuttles burned hard to gain height, buffeted by the rising shockwaves. The landing pad looked like an island amid the fire. She saw two of the mechs among it all. From her perspective it looked like they were wading through a sea of flames. It was beautiful.

It took her a moment to realise what she was seeing as her vision filled with rapidly approaching fire.

'Move!' she screamed at Nyukuti as she dragged him to his feet. All around her legionnaires scrambled as one of the burning skyscraper-sized trees fell towards them.

CHAPTER 16

Everything is shit, was Miska's first thought. It was raining dirt. *On the other hand you're not dead,* she told herself. *Somehow.* She was looking up at an enormous tree trunk curving away from her. This particular part of it wasn't burning but further along the huge trunk it was a one-tree raging forest fire.

Miska touched her eye and the glove came away sticky and red. The wound burned as well, presumably because of the defoliant that coated everything. She was pretty sure that her gas mask was no longer working. She pulled it off, and then screamed as some of the fused flesh came away with it. That was when she realised that not only was her eyesight a bit grainy, she could only see through one eye. *It gets better and better.*

'You all right, boss?' Kaneda had appeared, kneeling next to her. Kasmeyer was kneeling next to Nyukuti. Ash was falling from the sky like snow but at least the pollen fall had stopped. Miska stood up. Everything was on fire. Much of the earth had been burned to glass. There were pools of burning, bubbling plasma. There were huge craters everywhere. Pegasus 2 and

Harpy 1 hovered, unsteadily, in the air overhead. She saw one of the Medusas being helped to its feet by another. Much of their armour looked like so much slag.

The air was filled with the acrid chemical smell of the defoliant. Her own internal filters would protect her from the worst of it but she felt her exposed skin, her throat, and her nasal passages burn. She tried to spit the taste out of her mouth but it wasn't going anywhere soon.

'We just got our asses kicked,' someone said nearby.

Miska smiled, turned towards the source of the voice.

'You see any tangos?' she asked, meaning targets, the enemy. She climbed out of the trench and looked around at the devastation. Then she started giving orders.

Miska was frustrated at having to abandon Camp Badajoz when they'd fought so hard for it. She knew the forest fire would eventually burn out thanks to moisture and the inevitable rain but the tree fall had made using the base impossible and she simply didn't have the resources to do anything about it.

Twenty were confirmed dead, five more missing and presumed dead. Frankly it was a miracle they hadn't lost many more but they'd stuck together, watched each other's backs and for the most part acted tactically sensibly. Other than the friendly fire, but Miska wasn't completely sure that hadn't been an attempt to kill her. After all, it would be difficult to find out who'd actually fired the shot with gun- and helm-cams down. Perhaps the shooter had been hoping that the pollen would somehow prevent the N-bombs from detonating and killing them all.

Somehow they hadn't lost any of the mechs but all were damaged to some or other extent, and were reporting multiple system failures. The Satyrs had joined the Offensive Bastards in the trenches firing on the tree-creatures, occasionally having to be washed down with the defoliant mid-combat. They'd only lost the one Machimoi. Two had remained in the trenches and had to be treated similarly to the Satyrs. The rest had pulled back to exfil point three with Pegasus 1.

They'd washed the shuttles, the remaining Machimoi and the crouching mechs. Miska hated to think what prolonged exposure to the nasty defoliant was doing to her people. She now had those doing the washing wearing hostile environment suits. She hoped it wasn't too little too late. They were setting up a decontamination station at exfil 3. It was a risk, they were still behind enemy lines, but she didn't want them heading back up to the *Daughter* with any of that pollen on them in case they infected the ship. Somehow she didn't think that Triple S or New Sun were terribly interested in Camp Badajoz any more.

Hogg was cleaning and dressing her eye. It hurt.

As an ex eco-terrorist, Miska knew that he must be appalled about what they had done to the jungle. In fairness it had been in self-defence. She was wondering why he wasn't currently giving her a hard time about it.

'You don't seem very upset about what we've done to your beloved forest,' Miska said.

He stared at her for a long time.

'I understand what happened here,' he finally said, clearly holding back emotion. 'But this,' he pointed all around. 'This is a goddamned travesty, a disgrace to our entire species, and you enjoyed yourself, didn't you?' He was using tweezers from his medkit to remove splinters of goggle from her eye.

Something must have shown on her face, she decided. He was right, though, it had been pretty intense, even by her standards.

But she kept on coming back to the friendly fire incident. Had someone been trying to kill her? One of the shooters who'd killed her dad?

'Let's just say you probably don't want to push that line of questioning too far,' she told him.

'This wasn't why I signed on,' he told her.

Miska chuckled. Then she thought of Torricone. It was like a knife between her ribs when she remembered what had happened to him. What Triple S had done to him.

But Hogg wasn't Torricone. He was more like the Ultra's pet vigilante, Rufus Grig. Hogg had found a cause that had made him feel good about those he killed. It was just another excuse as far as Miska was concerned.

Hogg applied medgel to the burns that covered most of the bottom part of her face and over her eye. 'What would you have done?' Miska asked nodding back towards the ruins of Camp Badajoz.

'In fairness, probably the same as you,' he told her, distracted as he adhered a medpak to the back of her neck to drive the medgels. 'We were too late. We needed to try and communicate with them but I think that Triple S had already started this war.'

Miska couldn't decide if he was being a little too pragmatic for someone as idealistic as he apparently was.

'I need to speak to you,' Hogg told her.

'Go ahead,' Miska said.

Hogg looked around at the other legionnaires nearby. Miska followed his eyes. As far as she could tell everyone was busy going about their business.

'We could do with a degree of privacy,' he told her.

'Nobody is paying us the slightest bit of attention,' she

pointed out. If they were to walk off into the woods together then that would just draw more attention to them.

He leaned forward.

'We'll talk later,' he whispered.

'Hogg—' she started.

'Boss, we've got something I think you'll want to see.' It was Mass's voice over the still-static-filled comms. They hadn't been able to reach the *Hangman's Daughter* since the attack.

'Is it important?' Miska subvocalised over comms, cursing that he couldn't send images to her IVD.

'Could be.' Mass's response was annoyingly non-committal.

'Where are you?' she asked. Mass told her.

'Your right eye will try and compensate for the loss of the left. You're going to lose between twenty-five and forty per cent of your depth perception until you get it replaced. You've got pretty high grade milspec artificial eyes, so it will probably be lower than higher,' Hogg explained.

'Cool, I'll look like Snake Plissken.'

'I've no idea who that is,' Hogg told her.

Miska sighed and wished her dad were here. He would have known what she was talking about. She stood up.

'Did you kill the captives?' he asked her.

'Only one of them,' she told him. 'He was part of the problem.'

Hogg watched her. She couldn't read the expression. She gestured towards his crossbow.

'Ready to go and kill some corporate scumbags?' she asked.

'I absolutely am,' he told her.

'So what am I looking at?' Miska asked. She was standing in a partially demolished concrete bunker. It had been used for

261

storing missiles for the gunships and transport when she'd been stationed here.

In a darkened corner of the bunker she saw two open-topped cars, each about the size of a small truck. The cars had armour bolted onto them. Four long telescopic legs, that looked hydraulically driven, were folded up underneath them. On the front of each car there was a 20mm cannon, plus what looked like a very old-fashioned heavy machine gun mounted on one side, and an automatic grenade launcher mounted on the other. A double SAW was mounted on the rear of each of the vehicles. All the weapons had that recently-printed look to them, all of them were protected by a ballistic shield, and all of them were old-fashioned slugthrowers.

'That looks like the worst quad mech ever,' Miska said. She glanced at Hemi and Mass. Hemi was grinning, she suspected mostly at Mass who was looking at the two open-topped mechs with reverent awe. *Yep,* Miska decided, *Mass's got armour fever bad*. Even Kaneda, who'd apparently found them, had a slight smile on his camo-painted face.

'They're Waders,' Mass told them.

'It looks like a well-armed mule,' Kaneda said. Miska was inclined to agree.

'They're modded agricultural mechs, they use them to get through the mangroves. Look what those sick bastards have done to them.' Mass was clearly impressed. The two Waders were clearly very primitive bits of kit. It made sense to take machines like this north.

'Why'd they leave them?' Miska asked.

'They didn't,' Kaneda told them. 'Tracks in here suggest that there were at least ten more of them.'

That's a lot of potential bad guys, Miska thought.

'These were spares,' Hemi suggested, 'or those things killed too many of their people and they didn't have enough to make it worthwhile taking them.'

'Check them for booby traps,' she told them.

'Because you're going north, right?' Mass asked.

Miska turned to look at him.

'Probably into more of those tree-things and we can't risk taking mechs or air support in there,' she told him. 'Want to get yourself killed just because you want to try out a new toy?' she asked.

'And to impress you,' Mass said still grinning. It was infectious.

'Still bucking for promotion, huh?' she asked him.

Mass gripped Hemi's arm.

'Need to get out of this young man's way,' he told her.

'Until that day?' Miska asked. Her smile had gone.

'Until that day,' Mass agreed. His smile had only left his eyes.

Exfil point three was a grotto-like clearing in the jungle. The pool at the base of the waterfall was of sufficient size that there was a slight break in the overhead canopy to let the light in, which in turn meant that the pool was surrounded by non-fungal undergrowth, a relative rarity on Ephesus.

The shuttles, with the exception of Pegasus 1, were parked back in the shadows under the canopy. The mechs, having been defoliated and then decontaminated, were being loaded into their cradles. Most of the Bastards were preparing to head back to the *Daughter*. There was just no practical way to transport them into all into the north, not with the pollen fall, as much as Miska wanted to. She'd had Hogg collect some of the pollen. She would have it taken back to the *Daughter* for the Doc to look at, though she already had her suspicions as to what it was. The weird arrows had given it away. That was not a practical way to deliver a weapon in this day and age.

She had managed to get through to the *Daughter* and spoken to her very worried dad. The copy of him that had been wearing the Cyclops hadn't managed to upload, so he hadn't assimilated the Camp Badajoz experience. Miska wasn't sure she'd helped much when she told him what a buzz it had been.

She had let her dad in on the plans. It was clear that he hadn't liked them, but he hadn't argued. The UN still hadn't released the news of their innocence of the aerostat massacre. The whole punishment squad thing was complicating that. MACE and the Colonial Administration seemed prepared to accept that the punishment squad were either sequestered or, to their minds more realistically, a rogue element. *Whatever*, Miska had thought when her dad was telling her this. MACE were happy to deal with the Bastards again, but the UN was hampering this. Her dad had told her that Vido was handling the PR and legal problems.

She had the remaining members of the Offensive, Sneaky, Heavy and Armoured Bastards gather just under the jungle canopy, in sight of the waterfall, that fed the pool, that fed the tributary river that snaked through the trees to join the Turquoise. The river was much narrower this far north than it was down by Port Turquoise. She had to move her head to look at all her Bastards because of her loss of depth perception. A few of them were walking wounded, and they would be medevac'd. A number of them hadn't got their goggles down quickly enough and the pollen had destroyed their artificial eyes. Others had prosthetic limbs that no longer worked. Most of them had the thousand-yard stare – last night's fight had been intense and against a terrifying foe that none of them understood. A few were perfectly composed. She knew what that level of fearlessness in the face of what they had faced last night meant, especially in a prison population. They were the psychopaths. They were probably the people that she was going to be addressing. The people she needed.

'What we did last night was as incredible as it was unprecedented. Those things walked through Triple S conventional, while Triple S elite ran away,' she told them. It wasn't entirely clear that was what had happened but it was starting to look more and more like the truth. 'Well, we're not impaled on spikes. They didn't take our heads.' That wasn't entirely true. They'd lost a few heads early on in the fight. 'I'm not going to bullshit you, I'm going north to where those things live. I'm going to hunt Resnick and his black propaganda squad, these so-called Double Veterans. I'm going looking for our sequestered people.'

She heard a lot of muttered '*fuck that*'s, saw some of them shaking their heads at the mention of 'those things'.

'I'm willing to offer double combat pay,' she told them. That got the attention of some of them. She could see them doing sums in their heads. She wasn't actually entirely sure how she was going to pay the double time as, strictly speaking, nobody was paying them at the moment, but Resnick, Triple S and New Sun had all really got under her skin.

'Triple,' Mass called from the ranks. There were a few half-hearted cheers.

'Two-and-a-half times normal combat pay,' she told them, 'my final offer.' She could work out how to make that come true later. 'I need nine people; we'll be taking flame guns and defoliant,' she told them. She was also going to take all the 30mm HEAP grenades she could find. If possible she wanted the belts that fed automatic launchers on the Waders filled with HEAP grenades.

Mass stepped forward, as did Hemi. Miska had expected this. She nodded at them both. Mass returned an ironic salute.

Corenbloom stepped forward. Miska looked at him and raised an eyebrow. He shrugged.

'Golda ordered me to, he wants an intelligence element with you,' he explained. Something about the story didn't quite fit but she let it go. He'd held his own during the battle.

'I'll go,' Hogg said stepping forward, leaning on his compound crossbow.

Miska nodded to him. She was intrigued to know what he had to say.

Raff stepped forward as well.

She shook her head. Raff was more than capable of looking after himself. Her people knew that embedded journalists were allowed to carry arms but it would look weird if she didn't object.

'This is the story of a lifetime,' Raff told her. 'There's no way I'm missing out on it. I'll carry my weight, besides,' he looked at the rest of the Bastards present, 'nobody else seems to be in a hurry to volunteer.'

He had a point.

'You gonna let this lenshead put you to shame?' she asked them. She was a little surprised to see a few shameful faces looking down.

'We'll go,' Kasmeyer said as both he and Kaneda stepped forward.

'Is that it?' Miska asked. Nobody seemed terribly eager to meet her eyes but, frankly, she didn't blame them.

'Just seven then?'

'Eight,' Nyukuti said.

It would have to do.

The undergrowth started to wave around in the downdraft as Pegasus 1 appeared overhead, sinking down through the gap in the trees. A positively ancient-looking flat-bottomed riverine patrol boat hung by cargo straps underneath the assault shuttle. Pegasus 1 lowered the boat, which they had 'borrowed' from MACE, into the calmer part of the waterfall-fed pool.

'Get the Waders on board,' Miska told Mass and Hemi.

CHAPTER 17

Miska drove the boat. It had been the least sophisticated riverine patrol boat that she had been able to find in the short amount of time they had. Made of hardened plastic, protected by ceramic armoured plate and run off a screw-shaped impeller hydro-jet, the patrol boat had been stripped of the majority of its systems and all its weaponry – most of which had been electromagnetic or laser based. It had a satellite uplink, GPS and sonar, largely for finding river debris, but Miska had turned them all off.

The two Waders – she hesitated to call them mechs – were stowed back to back on the flatbed, their telescoping legs folded away underneath them. Should they be attacked while still on the river, the Waders would provide the firepower. The front Wader's legs would be extended so it could fire over the patrol boat's wheelhouse.

'So we're just going upstream in the hope that we discover something?' Corenbloom asked as he leant on the side of the wheelhouse.

Miska sighed. It had been peaceful piloting the boat, the

reflected red light of the gas giant occasionally breaking through the cathedral-like jungle canopy high above, dappling the water. She had been desperately trying to remember everything she had learned about small boat handling as a Recon Marine.

'Resnick's people went upstream in a flotilla,' Miska told him, 'and eventually they'll run out of river. We'll be able to find the boats and follow them then.'

She could see Kaneda and Kasmeyer forward of the wheel-house. Kaneda was lying on the deck close to the turret that used to contain one of the boat's railguns. Kasmeyer was practically perched on the bow watching the river ahead. The two Sneaky Bastards were taking it in turn on watch. She knew the others were doing something similar port, starboard and aft. If nothing else they were keeping an eye out for the occasional monstrous branch that fell from the huge trees; the 'spore mines', huge sub-surface fungi that exploded when knocked; and bite-seed swarms.

'How're you going to track through the mangroves?' Coren-bloom enquired.

Miska glanced over at him. 'You're going to dive down and look for footprints under water.'

'Seriously.'

She sighed again. Nobody seemed to get her sense of humour.

'It's more difficult but there are ways and means,' she told him. Recon had taught her to track. She and her dad had been teaching it to the Sneaky Bastards as part of their own recon-naissance training. Between Kaneda, Hogg Kasmeyer and her-self there should be enough trained observers to find Resnick's path through the waterlogged mangrove swamps. That wasn't her issue. What worried her was how long it would take. Which was why—

'You're relying on the Ultra to track Resnick and leave a trail of breadcrumbs, aren't you?' Corenbloom said, interrupting her thoughts.

'Relying is a strong word.' She wondered briefly how Corenbloom had found out about the Nightmare Squad's presence in-country, was it that obvious? Probably Golda, she decided. Corenbloom was desperate to make friends. Golda could be a useful ally for him.

'Problem with that?' she asked.

'The Ultra? Maybe if I was still a profiler, career FBI. This is kind of interesting. Makes sense as well.'

That got her attention.

'Well, he sort of had a rule. I'm not even sure it was that codified. Almost an algorithm. He only killed parasites.'

'By his definition, surely,' Miska said. She felt better without such excuses. If you're going to kill just get on with it. Don't dress it up.

'Let's say they were pretty popular definitions. He killed people that he didn't feel contributed in any way: lawyers, estate and letting agents, politicians, oligarchs who were all take and no give, and their useless spawn. There's no doubt he was a monster but I think he was trying to help. He wanted to kill and thought these people would be the least damaging people to murder.'

'You think that's why he's helping me?' she asked. 'There are no good or bad people, just differing points of view, and I'll work for the one that pays.'

'I know you've refused to commit atrocities,' Corenbloom pointed out.

'That's hardly a particularly sharp moral compass,' Miska told him. 'If I'm on the side of angels it's normally for an easy life.'

'We're after some bad people.'

Miska turned to look at Corenbloom.

'We are some bad people. If you think what you're doing is about making amends, you're fooling yourself,' she told him. Corenbloom held up his hands.

Miska wasn't best pleased that he was here. She would have preferred him working on finding her dad's murderer, and somehow she didn't think this job was going to require an intelligence element. This was all about the seek and destroy.

Corenbloom pointed at her eye. 'Think they were aiming at you?'

Miska shrugged. 'I'm going to assume that it was an accident.'

She checked behind her to where Hemi and Mass were tinkering with the Waders. 'I need to worry about your history with him?'

Corenbloom looked over at Mass, spending some time studying him.

'We did some damage to each other, it's true. None of it really matters now, I guess.' He turned back to Miska. 'So not from me.' He nodded towards Raff, who was standing guard on the starboard bow. 'The lenshead was pretty good in a fight.'

Miska glanced back at him.

'A lot of war correspondents are. He'll probably get some kind of prize for that footage, not to mention a tell-all exposé of us nasty mercenaries.'

'It was more than just skillsofts. He'd been trained.'

'Lots of them are before they embed,' she told him. He looked unconvinced. For someone who'd worked for the CIA she didn't think she was a very good liar. 'You talked to him?'

'A bit. Maybe I should some more.'

'You investigating something?'

'Always.'

Corenbloom headed aft to give Hogg a break from watch. Miska saw Mass watching as the disgraced FBI agent walked by on the other side of the Waders to avoid the Mafia button man.

'Maybe a bit more investigating and a little less crime back in the day would have helped?' Miska muttered to herself.

'It's getting dark, maybe somebody with two eyes should drive,' Mass suggested.

Miska's remaining functioning eye was protected behind the drop-down goggles on the half-helm she had borrowed for the mission. The goggles formed a hermetic seal that had proved protection enough against the pollen bloom at Camp Badajoz. This meant she still had nightvision capability in her remaining eye. Some of the legionnaires with artificial eyes, who hadn't got their goggles down quickly enough, had ended up blind. Thanks to her reduced depth perception, though, she had to move her head from side to side so often that it was actually starting to hurt her neck.

'You know it's not a mech, right?' Miska asked.

'I used to have a gin palace moored in the marina back in New Verona,' he told her.

She guessed that a gin palace was some kind of boat. 'Did it ever leave its moorings?'

'Frequently. Sometimes I wasn't even drunk.' He smiled. Miska guessed it was what passed for charm in his world. She took a step back, rubbed her neck with one hand and gestured for him to take the wheel with the other. He stepped forward, and just for a second looked slightly nervous and then that was gone, replaced by his normal confident smile.

272

Miska leaned against the side of the wheelhouse and waited.

'I saw you talking to Special Asshole Corenbloom earlier,' Mass said.

'Yeah, it's a small boat, that'll happen, but I want you to know you're still my favourite organised criminal from Barney Prime,' she told him. 'Y'know, except Uncle V.'

'He's a charmer, no doubt,' Mass said and then took his eyes off the turquoise water to look at her. 'I guess that means you see Torricone as a disorganised criminal, right?'

Miska pushed herself off the edge of the wheelhouse.

'What's that supposed to mean?' she demanded, lowering her voice.

Mass met her glare.

'It means people are talking,' he told her.

'You mean people with fucking bombs in their heads?'

'Yeah, them. How you doing on the recruitment front?' he asked. The sudden change of subject took her by surprise.

'What the fuck ...? Look I get you're still pissed off about T ... Torricone kicking your ass—'

'He did not—'

'—but do you see me cutting that sanctimonious asshole any slack?'

'That sanctimonious deserter asshole,' Mass pointed out. Miska stared at him. 'Things like that don't help.'

'Things like what?' Miska asked. She wouldn't have been surprised if her voice had actually lowered the water temperature.

'You know what I mean.'

'I really don't, Mass.'

'Then you've got nothing to worry about.' Mass sounded more frustrated than anything. She wondered if he actually

273

thought he was doing her a favour. 'If he comes back, chances are he'll be killed.'

'Another threat, Mass? Torricone, me when my "time comes"?' It would be so easy to end this particular problem right now but she'd be killing out of anger and it probably wouldn't do mission morale much good. 'Anyone else you want to add to your hypothetical list?'

Mass couldn't help himself, he glanced back at Corenbloom. Miska leaned in close to him.

'I mean it, Mass, don't fuck about on this one!' she hissed.

He nodded.

'I get it,' he told her. Something in his tone made her think he'd seen enough of what lay ahead of them at Camp Badajoz to realise the mission was too important compared with whatever problems he'd had with Corenbloom back in the world. Miska decided she wanted to be somewhere that was away from the button man.

'Hey,' he said as she walked away. Somewhat reluctantly she turned back to look at him. 'You want them to follow you then you've got to be the big dog, the cellblock daddy. We respect strength.'

Miska tapped the side of her head. 'How big a dog do you want?'

Mass was already shaking his head.

'You gotta earn that shit,' he told her.

'Like you, like Vido?'

'Vido's respected, so's Golda, and Hemi, and presumably whoever's in charge of the Yak at the moment – because they've all got influence, they've got soldiers. But they're not the big dog.'

'Who is then?' Miska asked.

'You created the problem when you let him mix, when you let him train with us.'

'The Ultra?' she asked, confused. His Nightmare Squad still kept pretty separate to the rest of the prisoners, but Mass was already shaking his head.

'Red,' Mass told her. 'I wouldn't fuck with Red, and I don't know anyone who would.'

Miska made her way forward past the wheelhouse. It was getting dark under the canopy as night fell. Her one remaining eye amplified the sparse ambient light.

Red, the huge professional convict who had killed so many people inside that he'd earned himself a pod in solitary, was a problem. She wanted him to volunteer for active service but she and her dad were the closest thing he had left to screws, authority figures he could set himself up in opposition to. He had very publicly announced that he would not be their slave when he had been allowed to train with the rest of them. The Ultra didn't want him in his squad because he wasn't nearly sick enough. Besides, guys like Red murdered guys like Kaczmar, Bean and, if they could get away with it, Grig, to improve their reputation in prison. Miska certainly didn't like Mass's suggestion. She was pretty sure that as well-trained, augmented and experienced as she was, Red would tear her apart. Still, it was a problem for another day.

Kasmeyer was leaning against the front of the wheelhouse. His eyes were closed but Miska could see he was still awake. She knelt down next to him.

'Kasmeyer,' she said quietly. He opened one eye to look at her.

'Boss?' he asked.

275

Kaneda was perched on the bow of the boat, on watch. He glanced behind him towards Kasmeyer and Miska.

'How're you doing?' she asked.

There were a few moments where he just looked at her. It was a stupid question, she'd never been good with the sort of easy small talk that officers were supposed to do to make their people feel better, to bolster morale.

'I'm good,' he told her finally. Kasmeyer was a quiet guy but, as far as she could tell, a good squad leader. He sought the path of least resistance, avoided a fight where he could, but tended to bring home the intel they needed. Miska had wondered if he was just so non-descript everyone ignored him. Miska's only worry was that he wasn't aggressive enough for what was to come.

'Why're you here?' she all but blurted out.

Kasmeyer blinked.

'I thought you wanted people?'

More like needed, she thought.

'I do ...' she started.

'You can't figure my angle?' he asked.

'That obvious?'

'Kinda understandable.' He nodded towards Kaneda. 'Someone's gotta watch his ass,' Kasmeyer said. There was something about the way he said it. Nobody was quite sure who was in charge of the Scorpion Rain Society at the moment. Vido, Golda, Teramoto when he'd been alive, had all made plays for rank in the Legion. Power and influence as they saw it. Kaneda, if he was rising through the Yakuza's ranks, hadn't. She was, however, starting to wonder just who was in charge of the Sneaky Bastards' first squad, or possibly the whole platoon. There were a lot of Bethlehem Milliners in the Sneaky Bastards.

276

It was a solid power base for Kaneda, who'd been a member of the *bōsōzoku* gang before he had been promoted to a member of the Yakuza.

Miska and her dad had tried to split up the gangs initially but it was pointless. Every military base of any size that she'd ever been to had its own gangs. The same went for any ship beyond a certain size as well. She'd been on carriers that had all but ghettoised. There were no-go areas depending on who you were and what you represented. But she did object to the gang politics when they blew back as operational problems.

Miska nodded towards Kasmeyer's SAW, which was propped up on its bipod and laid out alongside him. 'You ready to use that?'

Again he didn't answer immediately. Miska had never entirely trusted people who had to think before they spoke.

'I'll be honest with you, I don't want to but I will,' he told her. She frowned. The last thing she needed was any more reluctant soldiers. She opened her mouth to tell him so. 'I didn't kill those people,' he suddenly blurted out.

Kaneda glanced back at him.

It took a moment for Miska to work out what he was talking about.

'The hijacking?' she said, remembering his file. He'd snuck on board an automated ore transport to let his accomplices on board. Then they'd discovered stowaways.

'I didn't want to kill them,' he told them.

Didn't want to cop a plea either, Miska thought. If what he was saying was true, and Miska's gut reaction was to believe him, then he could have turned in the others for a reduced sentence.

So I guess he's loyal.

277

'I can do my job.' He sounded like he was trying to convince himself as much as her.

'Well, you'll mostly be shooting at trees and people who really deserve it.'

'What about the sequestered deserters?' he asked.

That gave her pause, but only for a moment. 'Somebody's shooting at you, you shoot back.'

He nodded. He was scared. That was clear. She supposed it was a natural reaction to the circumstances. She suspected that even the guys on their side were terrifying to Kasmeyer. She just couldn't shake the feeling he was frightened of something else. She glanced over at Kaneda. He still had his back to them.

'Get some sleep,' she told Kasmeyer. It sounded like the sort of thing a commanding officer was supposed to say in these circumstances.

'You hear that?' Miska asked quietly as she crouched down by Kaneda. She meant the conversation with Kasmeyer.

The world under the jungle canopy would have been in near total darkness now had it not been for her nightvision. The river was continuing to get narrower. As a result it was the lower branches that were arching over the river, making the leafy ceiling that much closer. Huge building-sized roots grew into the water.

'He'll be fine,' Kaneda said, not looking at her, continuing to scan the river.

'Like you were on Barney Prime?' She wasn't sure why she'd said it. Miska had watched some of his gun-cam footage in Kaneda's after-action reports. He was becoming quite the accomplished sniper. Quite the killer. She had remembered his initial reluctance to kill in a football stadium carpark out in the desert on Barney Prime.

He didn't answer her but he tensed, just slightly.

'My father—' she started.

'You've figured out that certain interests are protecting Corenbloom and you wish this to continue,' he said. Miska just nodded and then felt a little foolish. He wasn't looking her way. 'There will have to be considerations.'

'A power play?' she asked.

Now he looked at her, something in his expression she couldn't read, anger, contempt, sadness, or perhaps the suspicious absence of any emotion.

'I am not Teramoto,' he told her.

Miska just watched him until he turned back to the river. If Teramoto had been the abusive father that had helped give birth to this new, colder, Kaneda, then Miska had been the mother. Something about that didn't quite sit right despite his usefulness.

Raff was stood on the starboard side next to one of the Waders. He had his M-19 at the ready, the squirter full of defoliant still attached to it. He was taking his turn on watch but he looked pretty relaxed.

Miska didn't want to risk using comms. She had her suspicions about who and what the tree-creatures were and as low tech as possible was still currently the best option. Talking out loud to Raff where it could be easily overheard meant that she had to respect his cover as an embedded war correspondent.

'How're you doing, lenshead?' she asked.

'Not enjoying this soldier-boy shit,' he told her. 'But I'm getting good stuff, and I look like a goddamned hero in the footage I shot at Camp Badajoz.'

'Assuming the pollen doesn't crawl in your brain and eat it,' Miska said brightly. His expression soured. She noticed that Raff's half-helm had its ear protectors and goggles down, however.

'Hey,' he said as she tried to pass him. She stopped. 'Any idea what hit us last night?'

Miska's face screwed up in mock concentration. 'Woodland elves?' she finally suggested.

'You know you're going to look really hostile in the footage, right?' he asked.

'I'm not hostile. I'm lovely, downright fluffy. I just don't like you or your kind,' she told him and tried to move on again.

'Hey,' he called again.

She stopped, again, and let out an audible sigh.

'What?' she asked.

'No joke. Those things are dangerous. What're you going to do when you find them?'

She moved in close to him, standing on tiptoes to be close to his ear.

'Diplomacy,' she told him. 'Corenbloom suspects you.' This last she whispered so quietly that she barely made a noise. She hoped Raff's boosted hearing picked it up but nobody else's had.

Raff's expression didn't change. 'You're not exactly known for your diplomacy,' he told her back as she walked away.

Corporal Hemi Kohere was sat with his back against one of the Waders watching the dark riverbank go by. He was holding a weapon that looked half club, half knife. Made of wood, it was intricately carved with individual tooth-like blades embedded in the head. The blades reminded Miska of the circular teeth of a hammerhead shark. It was a wicked, if not entirely practical-looking, weapon. Between the archaic weapon, the inverted lower canine tusk implants, and the wooden-like quality his *tā moko* tattoos gave his face, he did not look as though he'd be out of place with the ferocious jungle spirits of this moon.

'What's that?' Miska asked.

'It's called a *māripi*,' Hemi said. His accent was lovely, Miska decided, his voice surprisingly soft. 'Supposed to be shark's teeth. My ancestors used to get them the hard way. They'd wade out into the sea. Cut themselves and wait for the sharks to come. Punch them in the mouth.' He looked up at Miska, one eyebrow cocked.

'Sure,' she said, laughing, though she could half believe it. He smiled.

'Local hard wood. Carved it myself, though I had to use a laser, the wood here's really tough, has to be to hold the trees up. The teeth are titanium with a fused synthetic diamond edge,' he told her with obvious pride in his voice.

'Yeah, my blade's the same,' she told him. She sat down next to him and drew the double-edged, black-bladed knife that her dad had given her when she'd finished boot camp. She passed it to him. He handed her his *māripi*. It had a heft to it but it was surprisingly well balanced and felt comfortable in her hand. Hemi inspected the diamond-fused titanium cutting edge of her knife, the ring on the end of the hilt. He looked at her questioningly.

'It's based on a sword that belonged to my favourite character in a sense game I played growing up,' she admitted.

Hemi laughed.

'A person made this,' he said, holding her blade up, 'not a machine.'

'Yeah, it was the armourer on the base where I trained, he was a friend of my dad's.'

'It has *mana*,' Hemi said and handed it back.

'Thanks,' she said, though she only had a vague idea of what *mana* was.

'And it's been used,' he said.

'You get all that from just holding it?' Miska asked.

'Just playing the odds,' he said.

She laughed and handed the *māripi* back.

'I like your thingy—'

'*Māripi*,' he supplied.

'—as well.'

He shrugged. 'Can't use mechs, maybe we can't use guns.' He held the *māripi* and made a striking motion with it. 'I'll bite these *maero*.'

'*Maero*?' Miska asked.

'Wild people, evil faeries who lived in the woods in the south island of Aotearoa back on Earth, where my people are from.'

'Aotearoa?' Miska asked.

'Land of the Long White Cloud,' he told her.

'I've never heard of it, pretty name though. I thought the Maoris were from New Zealand.'

Hemi just laughed.

'We're not facing *maero* though, are we?' he asked.

'What makes you say that?' she asked.

'I saw what happened to the Cyclops.'

'Yeah?'

'So the arrow hits. Roots grow out from it and wrap around its head, crushing it. Where'd the extra matter come from? It can't create it out of thin air.'

'The Cyclops itself.' She had suspected the same thing.

'So something is modifying the matter at a molecular level,' he said. It was clear he was much more than just some dumb gang leader, regardless of how ferocious he looked. 'Which means ...'

'Nanotech,' Miska supplied. She'd been thinking the same thing herself, but then she'd been trained about this sort of thing in the Marine Raider Regiment, and then more comprehensively when she'd joined the CIA.

'But the defoliant works on it, which means that the nanites must have some kind of flora component to them.' He looked sideways at her. It sounded ridiculous but she thought back to what Doc had told her about Ephesus's flora, how it appeared to have been tampered with or engineered at some point in the past. She knew Them, the aliens that humanity had fought some hundred years ago in a sixty-year-long war, had been composed of naturally occurring bio-nanites. Their original form had been a sort of extremophile coral.

'You put this all together yourself?' she asked.

Hemi shrugged.

'I like reading, sense documentaries, vizzes, that kind of thing. I was doing some courses in VR when you interrupted my sentence,' he told her. There was no reproach in his voice that she could hear. He was just providing her with information.

Maybe that's something we'll have to look at, she thought. If individual legionnaires wanted to learn stuff beyond their training she certainly had no objection.

'Any ideas where it's coming from?' he asked.

'A few,' she admitted.

'Pretty sophisticated stuff, any idea how you're going to deal with it?'

'You're going to hit it with your *māripi*,' she told him.

This time his laugh was a proper belly laugh. It seemed to echo through the jungle. Heads turned their way. She noticed Nyukuti staring at Hemi for a moment or two.

'Dude, shut up,' Miska hissed but his laughter was infectious. She nodded towards Nyukuti when they had stopped laughing.

'There a problem there?' she asked.

Hemi turned and looked at Nyukuti.

'He hurt some friends of mine,' he finally said, the smile gone now. 'Everyone breaks but *Whānau* don't break easily. Too proud. But with him it would have been better if they'd broken easier. Every minute a year when he dragged them into his dreams.'

Miska knew that when Nyukuti had been a stand-over man he had used custom-made sense programs to torture the criminals he preyed on into giving up their loot.

'You didn't answer my question.'

'I want to fight him, not kill him. I just want to know which of us is stronger,' he finally said. Then he turned back to look at her. 'But another day.'

It wasn't ideal, she decided, but it would have to do.

'Nyukuti,' Miska said, as she sat cross-legged on the deck next to where he was stretched out. Hogg was sat a little way off looking out over the boat's stern at where they'd been.

'Boss,' the stand-over man said.

Miska glanced down at him. He looked perfectly relaxed. He somehow managed to simultaneously look as if he was in a world of his own and completely alert at the same time. She'd not quite worked out how.

'Yeah, you're good, aren't you?'

He nodded. The biggest worry about Nyukuti was that his loyalty was all a lie. That he was lulling her into a false sense of security until she took him for granted.

'I am good, boss-lady,' he told her. 'This is exciting.' He held both his arms up, spreading his fingers and then moving his hands one over the other. 'Last night the dreaming world and the false world started to come together. I think they will merge at the head of the river.'

Miska digested this.

'Okay, sure,' she finally said.

'Burn cold and paint the world red,' he told her.

She nodded. 'Good talk,' she said, and started to get up.

'Do you want me to kill Torricone?' he asked.

She froze. She felt a coldness inside her chest. Nyukuti was watching her, intently.

'Someone shoots at you, you shoot back,' she told him. 'Same as it ever was.' Nyukuti nodded. 'Now can you give me some space here? I want to talk to Hogg.'

Nyukuti watched her for a moment more and then nodded and got up.

'I wondered when you'd get round to me,' Hogg said as Miska lay down on the deck, hands under her head. She was looking up at the nearly impenetrable canopy of leaves and branches. This far up the river the canopy seemed close, even claustrophobic. The air was also starting to cool, though it was still humid. It had that just-before-a-storm quality to it.

'You know, I knew your uncle,' he said.

Miska had been thinking about their next move but suddenly Hogg had her attention.

'What? When?' she asked.

'During the Occupation,' he told her. He meant the Cult of Ahriman's occupation of Sirius 4, nominally her home world. She knew that Hogg had been part of the resistance, before he had become a terrorist.

'He was in the resistance,' Miska said. She knew bits of the story but none of that generation liked to talk about the Occupation, about how her granddad had died.

'Eventually,' Hogg said. Miska wasn't sure what to make of that. 'His brother and both his sisters were in the British part of the expeditionary force.'

'I know, Mum coordinated with the resistance through him, after she'd dropped planet-side ahead of the main invasion force.' It was how her mum had met her dad. He had been doing the same thing in the American sector. This was family mythology.

'I know,' Hogg told her. 'I worked with her and your dad.'

Miska sat up and stared at him for a moment.

'My dad?' she asked. He nodded. She thought back to when they'd defrosted Hogg to ask questions about the Che virus, before they'd infiltrated Faigroe Station, the Legion's first job. She had talked to her dad about Hogg. He had given no indication of knowing the terrorist. Miska knew that her dad took secrecy seriously. He did not talk about his work, but even so this had operational relevance, he would have said something. 'He never—' she started.

'I know,' Hogg said. 'Doesn't recognise me at all, and I know the difference between genuinely not recognising someone and blanking them for some secret-squirrel bullshit.'

'Hogg, are you lying to me?' she demanded.

'For what reason?' he asked.

Paranoia was creeping in. Was he someone's agent? An operator? Had he killed her dad?

'So what were you and my parents doing? How come you waited until now to tell me?' Miska asked.

'That's a long conversation,' he told her. 'And we need to discuss quid pro quo.'

And there it was, another grafting convict, Miska thought. She couldn't say she blamed him.

'What do you want?' she demanded.

'What do you think?' he asked.

You and everyone else, she thought.

The pitch of the boat's engine changed, Miska felt the boat slow.

'Miska?' Corenbloom said from where he was standing by the rear Wader. 'I think you need to come and see this.'

'What is it?' she asked, without taking her eyes off Hogg.

'A breadcrumb,' Corenbloom told her.

CHAPTER 18

It had started to rain. They had only heard it at first. A distant percussion on the canopy high above them. Miska knew from bitter experience that the water would build up and build up on the nearly impenetrable canopy, until there was enough weight to bend the huge leaves – and then the jungle would be filled with waterfalls. Some of them had enough volume of water behind them to do serious damage. Miska had seen mechs knocked over, gunships forced into the ground and boats sunk. It was just another hazard they would have to look out for. *Along with a forest full of ex-special forces mercenaries, sequestered slaves, and plant-based bioborgs*, Miska thought. But that wasn't her problem, right now. Her problem was her own people.

Ahead of them the river widened out again into a turgid, swampy area. The trees were smaller, though still huge; the canopy was lower, though still far above them, and now broken by the storm-brought waterfalls. The trees that dominated the swampland had silver coloured bark, much of it spotted with huge fungal growths and crawling mosses. Their root structures made Miska think of a loosely clenched hand with too many fingers. These were the ambulatory mangroves, the walking trees of Ephesus, though Miska knew that for the most part they moved too slowly for people to see. Deeper into the 'mangrove' swamp Miska could see the higher ground. There, stepped waterfalls rose up into the highlands of the imaginatively named Northern Mountains.

They had found Resnick's 'flotilla'. Four boats a bit bigger than the Bastards' own and a handful of other smaller and individual watercraft. They had been tied off to branches sticking out over the river. None of the legionnaires were looking at the boats, however. They weren't even considering how much bigger Resnick's force obviously was compared to theirs. All their attention was focused on the 'breadcrumb'.

'It's called canoeing,' Corenbloom said.

Someone had nailed what Miska assumed was a member of Triple S (elite) to a tree trunk. He had been stripped to the waist. Had two gunshot wounds to his chest, close range, judging by the powder burns, and another close range V-shaped wound in his head. Miska had seen it before as well. It wasn't just an execution. The close range, the upper forehead, the exposed brain matter, it was designed to mutilate the body. The corpse's hand was pointing north.

She glanced at Corenbloom. 'Grig?' she asked. He nodded. It seemed the Ultra was showing the way.

'Kaneda, Hogg, I want you on the banks, check the tracks, I want to know how many Waders and which way they went. Go careful, Resnick's the kind of asshole who'd leave booby traps behind.' Hogg nodded, and both he and Kaneda leapt off the boat and onto the muddy bank.

'Mass, move the boat upstream, find a place to tether it, and then you and Hemi get the Waders ready. I want the rest of you on watch,' she told them. People started to move.

Another half-naked member of Triple S (elite) had been nailed to a tree. He had two gunshot wounds to the chest and one in the head. It was called Failure Drill and a lot of special operation forces units taught it. Her dad taught it to the Legion. What her dad didn't teach was to claw the bodies afterwards. This corpse was pointing north as well. Miska knew that a lot of the Leopard and Crocodile Society members had implanted claws in their fingers so she assumed this was Gunhir. She glanced over at Corenbloom in the other Wader a little way off. He was looking up at the body.

Both the Waders were stood in a pool about halfway up a stepped waterfall. The going had been slow and uncomfortable. The hydraulic systems were anything but smooth, and without anything resembling a sensor system finding a solid footing was more luck than judgement. They had almost gone over more than once, and one of the legs had plunged into a sinkhole that had come close to taking them under. Nyukuti had been bounced out of the cupola, though he'd managed to hold on to the side. It was a more interesting journey than even Miska liked. The rain, or rather the sky waterfalls, were an added misery. The Waders' cupolas were waterproof but that meant they held water inside as well. Each of the Waders had a pump but they just weren't quite up to the job. As a result the Waders were slowly filling with water, to the point that Miska was starting to consider bailing. Not that they had any receptacles big enough to make such an activity worthwhile.

All of them were wearing their rain ponchos but it didn't matter how advanced the materials were, their wicking properties, whether they were designed to 'breathe', somehow the rain was finding its way inside. Miska was wet and cold, and even her normally upbeat mood was taking a beating.

She knew the other seven legionnaires were less than happy too. Kaneda and Hogg had found tracks suggesting that twelve other Waders had gone north. With a minimum of four people to a Wader, that meant they were looking at as many as forty-eight enemy combatants, if not more, the majority of whom had special forces training and experience. Miska had tried to re-assure them that they were just going to have a look, that if the opposition was too much they would turn back. They hadn't seemed very reassured and if Miska was honest she wasn't going to look, she wanted Resnick dead.

'Boss?' Mass asked.

'We keep going,' she told him.

Mass started swearing at the Wader as it lurched forward.

It seemed that the mangrove swampland was a series of broad waterlogged terraces underneath the jungle canopy. They had come to a broad open area at the top of the stepped waterfalls they had just negotiated. The water was no longer turquoise up here. It was a white/grey colour and full of floating tree debris brought down by the torrential rainfall. Some of it was big enough to threaten the telescoped legs of the Waders.

They had found another corpse pointing north. Half-naked, he had been very extensively beaten to death. Miska had seen victims of mob violence that looked less beaten. His torso looked like a solid mass of bloodied bruise, his face a pulped, unrecognisable mess, and he'd been scalped.

Hemi brought his Wader up close to Mass's. Miska looked across at Corenbloom.

'Kaczmar?' Miska asked.

Corenbloom nodded.

'The scalping's new,' he added.

She just nodded, there wasn't much else to say.

'Keep some distance between the Waders!' she called. 'Mass, follow the arrow.'

'Jesus fucking Christ,' Mass muttered, shaking his head.

Everyone's got a line they don't want to cross, Miska thought.

She glanced around at Hogg on the heavy machine gun. He looked less than pleased as well. Nyukuti, on the grenade machine gun, was just looking up at the body thoughtfully as the Wader set off on its lurching way again. She could only see the back of Raff's head on the twin SAW mount at the back of the Wader.

'Well that's perfectly fucking horrible,' Hogg muttered behind her.

Miska hadn't been watching ahead, like she should have been. She kept seeing movement in her peripheral vision. It didn't track with the kind of movement that she would expect from people trying to be sneaky, nor did it seem like boats or archaic mechs. Instead the movement seemed to be coming from the trees. But she could not be sure if it was her mind playing tricks on her or not. Either way it was a serious breach of concentration.

She turned round to look at the latest directional atrocity. The body had been butchered in the truest sense of the word. All the choicest cuts and 'edible' viscera had been laid out on a flat part of one of the roots. Teeth marks in the kidney let them know that a bite had been taken out of it. The body had been scalped as well. The arm was pointing north again, up another stepped waterfall that Miska wasn't looking forward to traversing.

'This is sick,' Mass said.

'If it's frightening you then imagine what it's doing to them,' Miska pointed out, though she was reasonably sure that Resnick's people weren't seeing these bodies. That might make it worse. The Nightmare Squad were hunting them. Picking them off one at a time, making them feel helpless.

The Wader rocked from the bow wave of Hemi's approaching machine. Miska didn't like having both the Waders so close together but if they couldn't trust their comms then anything too complex to be relayed by hand signal had to be done verbally. She could see Kasmeyer had gone pale in the other archaic mech.

Miska's head shot round, convinced that she'd seen something moving in her periphery, again. She'd noticed Hogg, Nyukuti, and Kaneda in the other Wader had done the same a couple of times.

'Bean,' Corenbloom called over to her. It was clear that the disgraced FBI profiler had been studying his fellow inmates. 'Though again the scalping is new. I suspect that Kaczmar and Bean are starting to bond.' Miska could tell by the tone of his voice that Corenbloom didn't like the idea of this. Miska wasn't sure she liked it herself.

This is what you wanted, she told herself, *your own pet atrocity. Well, this is what it looks like.*

'I think this is the Ultra testing his people,' Corenbloom suggested. That made a degree of sense as well. Make sure they were up to the job. Though she also wondered how much of this was revenge for Triple S trying to copycat their 'work'. Miska nodded. She signalled to Hemi to take the point in his Wader as they started their ascent.

Jesus Christ, Miska thought. She heard muttering from behind her in the Wader's cupola, retching from the other Wader. Kasmeyer. She was beginning to have serious doubts about him, though she guessed that throwing up was probably a perfectly reasonable response to what they were looking at.

It looked like a medical diagram. Skin and flesh peeled back, the body's interior revealed, displayed, but somehow it reminded Miska of a pinned butterfly she'd once seen in one of her dad's pre-FHC vizzes.

'This will be the last one,' she said out loud. The Ultra had done this himself. She wasn't sure how she felt about that.

You knew he was a killer, she told herself. Only that wasn't quite true. She had known that he was a monster.

They were on another broad, open, waterlogged, terraced plateau. Through a rare gap in the canopy above them, probably the result of the torrential rain, Miska could see the shadows of the mountains. It was daytime again; they'd travelled through the night and Miska was starting to feel the fatigue seep into her bones. She had seen the others yawn as well. They'd had precious little sleep in the last forty-eight hours.

The body was pointing towards land to the north and west of them. A fungal forest was growing on the muddy banks. Miska wondered just how close they were to the source of the Turquoise.

Lightning threw the distant mountains into sharper relief. Miska looked away from the flare and saw an inhuman face in the water. It sank into the greyish murk.

'Mass, hull down!' she ordered. 'Check the water!' She signalled the other Wader to do the same thing. The Wader started lowering itself as thunder rolled across the sky. It was a dangerous move. If they were about to be attacked from the water with the stilt-like legs extended they were just too exposed, one good hit and the Wader was done for. Though for all she knew whatever she had just seen in the water was this very second attaching demo charges to one of the legs.

'Incom—' Raff managed before cannon rounds flew overhead and impacted into the tree with the corpse, making fibrous wounds in the wood. The corpse was now little more than a few limbs nailed to the tree as green tracers flew overhead. Miska glanced behind them as the Wader's cupola sank into the water, three-quarters submerged. She could see cannon round tracers arcing in towards them from the distance. They were splashing into the water behind Hemi's Wader as well. The Wader's sudden loss of height was momentarily confusing the long distance fire but Miska knew that wouldn't last long. They were taking fire from at least three different positions south of them, back the way they had come. Judging by the cannon fire, three of the Triple S Waders had skirted around behind them, or been camouflaged well enough to hide from them as they passed. That wouldn't have been difficult in the poor light and heavy rain with no decent optics or sensors.

'Mass, get this Wader moving and keep it moving, swing round a hundred and eighty degrees and back it up towards the land,' Miska shouted. 'Nyukuti, signal the others to do the same, I want you to hold off on the grenade launcher until they've closed with us.' She didn't bother waiting for a reply. She knew they'd follow orders. As they turned, Mass's driving station swivelling with the Wader so he could face the direction they were moving in, she heard Hogg open up with the Heavy Machine Gun. Miska traversed the huge 20mm cannon as far to the right as she could, looking through the rudimentary optical sight built into the slit in the weapon's ballistic shield. Water was lapping over the cupola as Mass awkwardly manoeuvred the Wader round. He was trying to step to the side as well but the water resistance was making that difficult.

More tracers now but the tracers were only one in every three of the inbound rounds. Hogg called out a position. Miska followed his tracers and saw movement about a quarter of a mile from them to the south. She magnified her vision and started firing, aiming high and leading the movement, giving the Triple S Waders time to walk into the falling cannon rounds.

Miska saw cannon rounds splash down in front of the Wader. Saw their wake in the water and heard them thump against the armour having been slowed down enough to be harmless. The Wader was mostly facing south now. It was at just enough of an angle for both Miska and Hogg to fire. She was aware of Corenbloom firing the 20mm cannon and Kasmeyer firing the HMG in the other Wader.

'Raff, you're rear security!' she shouted over the dull bass boom of the cannons and the higher and faster shots from the HMGs, hoping that the CIA agent's noise filters would enable him to hear it. She was very conscious that they could be backing into an ambush. 'Mass, use the trees for cover! Nyukuti, tell Hemi to do the same! Then I want you on local security, watch the water and the trees around us!' She fired again, and then used the pedals, which were now underwater, to move the cannon around and fire at one of the other Triple S Waders. Mass moved the Wader behind a tree and Miska had to stop firing.

'Boss!' Hogg practically screamed in her ear. 'In the trees we can spot and snipe!' Miska glanced at him. She wanted Hogg where she could keep an eye on him but she knew she was being selfish.

Hemi's Wader was making a huge bow wave as it splashed through the water trying to move behind cover. Incoming cannon and HMG fire tore up the bark of the enormous tree they were making for. She saw rounds splashing into the water, others sparked off the Wader's armour. She assumed the latter were HMG rounds and not cannon rounds. When they'd made it behind the relative and temporary safety of the trees Miska stood up and signalled for Kaneda to spot from the trees. The sniper pulled his sodden ghillie suit over himself and leapt off the Wader. Tiny molecular sized hooks on his gloves, kneepads and boots helped him scale the tree like a spider. Hogg did the same. They looked like large, wet, moving patches of moss scaling the huge trees. The firing had stopped but Miska knew that the Triple S Waders would use the lull to close with them. Just for a moment she thought of how much easier this would all be with modern weapons. *I mean we might be dead by now, but at least it would've been over quickly*. The Bastards hadn't had much in the way of decent weapons when they'd assaulted Faigroe Station. On Barney Prime they'd had to make do with modified civilian weapons. Just once she'd like to be able to bring all the toys to bear on a problem.

'What's the plan, boss?' Mass asked from the driver's seat.

'Let Hogg and Kaneda spot for us while these Triple S assholes close. Then, when we know where they are and they're in close enough range, we make a run for dry land laying down as much ordnance as we can,' she told them. High-noon-style gunfights like this were mostly a zero sum game and three on two lessened their odds considerably. All they had going for them was Hogg and Kaneda acting as spotters.

'Raff, anything behind us?' she asked.

'Not that I can see,' he replied. It wasn't the most reassuring reply.

'Nyukuti?'

'No fish,' the stand-over man replied. She knew he was smiling by the sound of his voice.

The face in the water! Just for a moment she convinced herself that she had imagined it but she knew she hadn't. If she hadn't seen the face, ordered the Waders hull down in the water, then Triple S would have had them dead to rights. *Was it a warning?* she wondered. She tried to remember what it had looked like but she had only caught a glimpse of it, just a sense of the inhuman.

She heard a whistle from above her. She looked up to see Hogg free his hands from his ghillie suit to signal the position and distance of the three incoming Waders.

'Mass, you're going to back us straight back to the land, this is about speed not finesse, but stay hull-down,' she told the button man. He nodded. 'Nyukuti, I want you on the GMG, Raff you're on the HMG, everyone shoots, we destroy one move onto the other. Nyukuti, signal the others.'

Nyukuti stood up to signal the other Wader.

Miska knew Hemi's Wader had one less shooter than them.

'What about rear security?' Raff asked.

'What're you, Delta Force? Just do as you're fucking told,' Mass told him. 'I'll watch our backs.'

'Mass sees anything,' Miska added, 'Raff switches back to the SAWs.'

Another whistle. Miska glanced up and Hogg let them know how much closer the Triple S Waders were, their change in position. Kaneda would be doing the same for Hemi's Wader.

'We go now,' she told them. They would be able to keep the

tree between themselves and the third Wader at least for a time, or until the enemy Wader changed position.

Both the Waders made a slow motion sprint through the water towards the muddy bank and the fungal forest. They were taking fire almost immediately. The water exploded all around them as the Triple S Wader's GMGs opened up. Miska's wired reflexes slowed everything down. She saw the tracers bursting through the slow motion explosions of water. The dimples in the ballistic shield from the enemy's HMGs. She pumped the trigger again and again. The 20mm cannon made the whole Wader shake. She heard the rhythmic thump of Nyukuti firing his GMG. In what was left of her periphery she was aware of the flickering muzzle flash of Raff's HMG. There was so much water in the air she had no idea if she was hitting or not. Cannon round and bullets shot past them. She felt them, slowed down by the water resistance, hitting the armour. As soon as she saw movement through the water and the incoming fire she rapidly adjusted the cannon and fired again and again until she lost the target. Raff and Nyukuti both slowed their rate of fire, searching more carefully for targets.

Then they really started taking hits as the third Wader manoeuvred itself into position. She heard Raff swear as incoming HMG rounds dimpled his weapon's ballistic shield. He changed target and started firing longer bursts, trying to suppress the third Triple S Wader.

'Nyukuti, suppress this one!' Miska shouted, meaning the second Wader, the one they were already engaged with. She heard the rate of fire from the GMG pick up again as the stand-over man fired as many 30mm HEAP grenades as he could in the general direction of the second Triple S Wader. Miska switched target and started pumping rounds towards the third Triple S

Wader. Their Wader lurched to the side as an incoming grenade exploded right next to them. Almost tipping over, one side went under the water. Mass, somehow, managed to wrestle the machine upright. They were sitting in water up to their waists now.

'Reloading!' Nyukuti shouted. It was the last thing they needed to hear. She switched target. A 20mm round punctured the Wader's armour. She heard Raff curse. Nobody seemed to be hurt but the third Wader had their range now. Miska ducked as HMG fire ate away at the cannon's ballistic shield. The third Triple S Wader's cannon went silent when it should have been killing them. The tree that Kaneda had hidden in started exploding as grenade after grenade from the third Wader's GMG hit it. Miska guessed Kaneda had shot the cannon operator. It would have been a great time to attack the third Triple S Wader with her own cannon but while Nyukuti was reloading the GMG she couldn't risk letting up on the second Wader.

She felt the bump as the Wader hit land. The 'mech' lurched forward as its rear legs clawed their way up onto the bank. Miska knew they were sitting ducks on dry land. She wanted their firepower but she knew they would get torn apart trying to get deep enough into the fungal forest to conceal themselves. Already grenades, cannon rounds and bullets were tearing into the forest, cutting down tree-sized mushrooms, sending clouds of spores into the wet air. Sparks flew as a cannon round flew through the front armour of the Wader, destroyed Nyukuti's seat, and continued through the rear armour. Another near miss from a grenade rocked them and covered them in the greyish swamp water.

'Everyone out!' Miska shouted. 'Fall back into the woods, find cover!'

Raff was straight out the back of the Wader, sprinting for the fungal trees, Mass close behind him. Nyukuti was waiting for her. 'Go!' she shouted. More cannon rounds were penetrating the primitive mech's armour. Nyukuti leapt over the back of the Wader, his boots landing in the mud. Miska was out of her seat grabbing her AK-47/flamer combo when the grenade hit. The Wader's armour saved her but the mech tumbled over, sending her sprawling into the mud, her gun going flying.

Nyukuti was lying face-down in the mud as well. She saw sparks from the Wader as cannon round after cannon round tore into it. More fire. Tracers flying through the air from the west, through the fungal forest. She saw Mass go down. There were people waiting for them on land. They were caught in an L-shaped crossfire between the concealed enemy on land and the Waders behind them, a classic ambush. Miska knew she was about to die.

Doesn't matter, you fight. It was her dad's voice she heard in her head. She scrambled for her weapon. It was covered in mud. It didn't matter. It was an AK-47. She glanced back at Mass. He was on his feet, being helped into the treeline by Raff. She looked at Nyukuti. He was still moving.

'Nye! Get on your fucking feet, lay down some fire!' she screamed at him and he was pushing himself onto one knee. Bringing his SAW up. Firing at their ambushers.

Miska was aware of Hemi, Corenbloom and Kasmeyer jumping from their Wader and running. Moments later the Wader blew. The force of the explosion knocked all three of them off their feet. It bounced Miska into the slimy bottom of her capsized Wader and sent Nyukuti sprawling as well.

'Fuck's sake!' Miska spat. In the fungal wood Mass and Raff were trying to return fire but they were horribly outgunned.

Miska was sure that there was at least a squad of the Triple S ambushers.

Hemi was on one knee firing at the ambushers as Corenbloom and Kasmeyer half ran, half crawled towards the fungal trees even as the huge mushroom-like growths were being torn apart by incoming ordnance.

'Nye! Unless you are fucking dead, move!' Miska shouted, as much because she didn't want Nyukuti to be dead. *Where did that come from?* Nyukuti was moving again. Up on one knee firing into the ambushers. Miska turned her attention to the three incoming Triple S Waders. She had no idea why she hadn't been torn apart by their cannon fire yet. Her best idea was to use her grenade launcher as a mortar. Try and drop a grenade into their open cupola.

One of the trees breathed fire all over the first Triple S Wader. Miska heard screaming and watched burning figures jump off the Wader. She could see the glow of the still-burning Triple S contractors as they sank into the water. Then the Wader exploded. It took a moment for Miska to realise that the tree they had been passing was the one that Kaneda had been hiding in.

Miska turned her attention to the second Triple S Wader. She saw something fall into its cupola. As the driver stood up a crossbow bolt sprouted from his face. Moments later his head exploded. There was frantic movement inside the Wader and then the grenade exploded. Bodies tumbled into the water. They were passing the tree that Hogg had been hiding in.

Miska looked around for the third Wader but couldn't see it, and it didn't seem to be attacking them. She could hear the sound of a vicious firefight behind her. Bullets sparking off their Wader. Nyukuti returning fire.

She started to turn as something hit her hard in the back.

Then again, and again, forcing the air from her diaphragm. Her ceramic backplate split with the third shot, her inertial armour undersuit hardening. But something made its way through, lodging in her subcutaneous armour close to her spine. She was slammed into the slimy underside of the Wader again. She went down on her knees and started to turn. Nyukuti was moving. He put himself between her and the incoming rounds. She saw his body shake as he got hit again. He fell backwards. His face had been replaced by a red cavity. Miska brought her AK-47 up. She saw Kasmeyer turning away from her and towards Hemi. Hemi was charging the Sneaky Bastard, an empty M19 carbine in one hand, his *māripi* in the other. Kasmeyer tried to bring his SAW up but Hemi hit him like a truck. The *māripi* bit into Kasmeyer's arm. He bounced off the huge fungus he had been hiding behind and Hemi ripped the *māripi* down his arm. Kasmeyer dropped the SAW, but it still hung from its sling. Kasmeyer tried to bring his left arm up defensively. Hemi hit it repeatedly with the toothed weapon until that was useless as well. Then he swung the *māripi* at Kasmeyer's neck.

'No!' Miska shouted but the *māripi's* teeth bit into Kasmeyer's neck. Hemi looked her way. 'Alive!' she shouted. Kasmeyer sank to his knees, blood spurting from the wound. Hemi pushed the *māripi* back into a loop on his load-carrying plate. He grabbed Kasmeyer's neck wound, trying to stem the bleeding. It put them another gun down.

Their ambushers were up. They had split into three four-man fire teams and were conducting fire and manoeuvre. Two fire teams would provide withering covering fire while the third moved. The most northern fire team was trying to get into position to flank them. Catch them in another L-shaped crossfire. Miska slung the AK-47/flamer combination across her back. She hit the quick-release on Nyukuti's SAW and lifted it up. With the underslung grenade launcher it had a real heft to it. The collapsible stock nestled in her shoulder and she started laying down fire. This brought her attention, and withering return fire caused her to take cover behind the capsized Wader. Among the fungus trees she could see Mass, Raff and Corenbloom taking the occasional opportunistic shots but then having to take cover due to the sheer volume of return fire. The air was full of spores from the bullet-punctured fungi. Miska peeked out and fired a long burst from the SAW and then ducked back around the Wader.

Then the Triple S ambushers were taking fire from their flank. There was the pop of grenade launchers. Explosions followed by screams as shrapnel from 30mm grenades tore the contractors apart. The fire was coming from the water. Miska moved quickly to the water's edge, using the capsized Wader as cover. Her remaining eye went wide as she saw the swamp creatures rising from the water firing slugthrowers. Absurdly, Miska thought they had chimneys for a moment. It was only because one of the swamp creatures was so fat that Miska realised what they were, or rather who they were. Grig, Gunhir, Bean and Kaczmar, the Nightmare Squad. Their sodden ghillie suits were thrown over their backs, their faces covered in waterproof camo-paint. The 'chimneys' were simple printed snorkels and periscopes that had allowed them to remain hidden. Now the Bastards had the Triple S mercenaries in a crossfire.

'Mass!' Miska practically screamed. The Mafia button man didn't hear her. He was using the distraction of the Nightmare Squad to lay some fire down himself. 'Mass!' Raff tapped Mass on the shoulder and pointed at Miska. 'Reload your 19! Sling it! Get Kasmeyer's SAW, reload it! We all move when I say!'

Mass nodded, reloaded his M19 and, keeping low, he ran to where a clearly frustrated Hemi was trying to keep Kasmeyer alive. Miska risked a few short bursts with Nyukuti's SAW but it was the Nightmare Squad doing all the work. The fungal forest was full of tracers tearing up the undergrowth. Tree-sized mushrooms fell to the earth. Of course they couldn't keep up such sustained fire forever. Miska glanced around the corner as Grig, Gunhir and Bean, as one, fired grenades from their M19's under-barrel launchers and then, along with Kaczmar, took cover behind the thickest fungal tree they could find and knelt down to reload their weapons.

'Now!' Miska shouted at Mass as the remaining Triple S contractors concentrated their fire on the Nightmare Squad. Miska came around the Wader. She moved quickly towards their ambushers. She fired the SAW's grenade launcher first. Sent four HEAP grenades flying towards the contractors. She switched to the SAW, marching forward firing long burst after long burst at any movement, suppressing fire. On her right Mass was doing the same. Corenbloom and Raff were moving forward firing their M19s as well. Miska kept firing until the SAW ran dry. She tossed it. A tracer opened up her cheek. She barely felt the phosphorous burn. The Nightmare Squad were firing and moving forward again. It didn't matter who you were, what your combat experience was, sticking your head up in this kind of firestorm was pretty much a death sentence. Miska swung her AK-47 up and started firing three-round bursts at the ambushers, the weapon twitching and firing anytime she saw movement in her limited periphery, cursing the primitive optical sight. She sent a HEAP grenade towards any really persistent return fire. The AK-47 ran dry. Miska took shelter behind a tree. She was breathing heavily. She could feel the spores as she inhaled them. Return fire ate away at her soft fungal cover. Someone charged her. She had no idea why they didn't have a gun. They looked wild-eyed. Miska triggered the flamer still bolted to the side of the AK-47. But she hadn't lit the pilot light. The flamer squirted liquid fuel all over the crazed contractor. He kept coming. Miska let the AK-47/flamer drop on its sling and fast drew her Glock, shooting him as he was almost on her. The muzzle flash ignited the fuel. She kicked him away from her and put two more bursts into his face. He fell to the ground and burned.

There was movement behind her. She swung around and fired. Missed. Adjusted for her one eye. She took a hit to the chest, staggering back. She fired wild, using the Glock to suppress on full automatic. It wasn't ideal. The contractor went down. She had no idea if she'd shot him or not. The slide was back on the empty Glock. She stuffed it back into the drop holster and drew the cut-down Winchester from its back sheath. She saw one of the contractors ahead of her. She fired the shotgun, knocking the woman into one of the fungal trees. She fired again and again, emptying the shotgun's box magazine, then its tubular magazine as she closed. The rounds battered the woman's armour. Miska transferred the empty shotgun to her left hand and drew her knife. She rammed it upwards into the woman's throat. It was only then Miska realised that she was the one doing the screaming.

It was as though she'd just come to. Miska pulled her knife out of the contractor's head and let her slide down into the mud. She still felt a little dazed as she looked around. Kaczmar was finishing off one of the contractors with a hatchet. Bean was scalping another before starting to saw off an ear. Miska stared at them for a moment. She knew she should establish order here. Then she remembered Nyukuti. Nyukuti was dead. Kasmeyer had tried to kill her. He had killed Nyukuti.

Miska turned and ran back through the spore-filled forest air towards where Hemi knelt over Kasmeyer's fallen form. Miska skidded into the mud next to him.

'I'm s-s-sorry,' Kasmeyer managed, blood bubbling out of his mouth, 'they knew about my family.'

'Who!' Miska screamed but of course he had gone. Hemi took his red hands away from Kasmeyer's neck.

'Sorry boss.'

Miska just stared at Kasmeyer's corpse.

CHAPTER 19

Miska stared at Kasmeyer's body.

It had stopped raining.

'Boss?' Mass asked. 'Miska!' Her head shot around to look at the button man. He looked angry. 'You all right with this?' Deeper in the fungal woods she could hear Kaczmar and Bean butchering the dead and dying. Taking their trophies. She looked at Mass, trying to make sense of his words through the fury that threatened to engulf her. She glanced back at Nyukuti's body.

'Wrap him in his poncho,' she told him, 'we'll come back for it later.'

She could read the challenge in Mass's eyes but instead he nodded curtly and turned to make his way towards the riverside where Nyukuti's body lay next to their capsized Wader.

Hogg and Kaneda were neck-deep in the water as they waded towards dry land. She could see the third Triple S Wader now. It was on its side bobbing up and down in the water. It looked like its legs had been blown off. There were no signs of the Wader's crew but Miska could make out bloodstains.

'You need to let me look at that,' Hemi said. She had almost forgotten he was there. His hands were still stained with Kasmeyer's blood. It took a moment for Miska to work out what she was talking about. As she did she became aware of just how much pain she was in. One of Kasmeyer's rounds had caught her in the back and lodged in her subcutaneous armour much closer to her spine than she was happy with.

'Gel it and attach a medpak to drive it,' she told him as she winced, unstrapping her hard ceramic armour plates. The back plate was useless now anyway. She actually cried out as she shrugged out of her inertial armour top. Hemi had gloved up and knelt down behind her. She winced again as she felt the cold medgel against the wound. Driven by the medpak the gel would slowly suck the bullet out, repairing the damage behind itself, but while that was going on Miska knew that she only needed to take one good blow to that part of her back and the bullet would bisect her spine.

'Jesus Christ!' she heard Mass shout from the riverside. Hemi had dropped the medpak and was reaching for his M19 carbine. Miska was reaching for her Glock. Then she remembered that it was empty.

Sloppy, she thought as she rapidly reloaded the pistol.

Mass had drawn his sidearm and was covering the Ultra as he rose out of the water. Hemi lowered his weapon but Miska didn't think he entirely relaxed. The Ultra was blessedly dressed. He wore inertial armour in jungle pattern camouflage. His face was painted with waterproof camo-paint that made him look in-human. Only then did Miska realise that it had been the Ultra's painted face she had seen in the water. She guessed that he had been what had happened to the third Triple S Wader as well.

'Goddamned freak,' Mass muttered as the Ultra walked by.

Miska watched him approach as Hemi knelt down behind her again to adhere the medpak and wire it to the medgel.

'You just used us for bait didn't you?' she asked the Ultra as he reached them. She felt Hemi pause for a moment as he attended to her wound.

'We had to draw the ambushers out. Surprise was the only advantage we had, so heavily outnumbered as we were,' he told her. His voice was music over the sound of Bean and Kaczmar's butchery.

'You going to control your men?' she asked.

He looked into the fungal forest where the two serial killers were hard at work.

'They are controlled,' he said. 'In order for this to work their ... our ... appetites must be indulged. We're unleashed at your will but once released we're not taps that can be turned off and on.' It wasn't quite a challenge to her authority. She had, at the end of the day, given him autonomy to run the unit the way he saw fit as long as he didn't hurt non-combatants. They weren't really meant to operate with the Legion's more conventional elements.

Miska was aware of Hemi tensing behind her. So, it seemed, was the Ultra, as he glanced the Maori's way.

'Done,' Hemi told her as he stood up, peeling off the gloves.

'Join the others,' she told him. 'Get everybody back on the clock, I want three-sixty security.' Hemi nodded and started towards the rest of the squad. 'I dropped Nyukuti's SAW somewhere in the woods, retrieve that, get the spare ammo from Nye's body, and see if the Triple S have got any ammo or grenades we can use.'

Hemi listened and then went on his way, making towards Nyukuti's body first. Miska turned back to the Ultra.

'Have your guys do the same with the ammo and get them ready to move,' she told him.

'I can't come with you,' he told her.

Miska gaped at him. She didn't have time for this kind of bullshit. Then just for a moment, she had a horrible thought. Would the N-bomb work on someone so clearly augmented with Small Gods' tech? *But then why would he have gone along with this as long as he had?* He had little to gain, after all. Besides, maybe a Small God could walk away from an N-bomb going off in their head, or even just have their body reject the device.

'What do you mean you can't come with me?' she demanded.

'You kill Resnick then you can probably prove that he's augmented with illegal Martian tech, or possibly even connect him to the Spartans. If I go then perhaps our own secrets are exposed.'

It was a fair point.

'And your pet monsters?' she asked.

'Grig and Gunhir are quite disciplined. Bean and Kaczmar will do as they're told once I have spoken with them.'

'No more mutilations,' she told him. The Ultra frowned for a moment.

'I've always wondered at the difference. They were dead before it happened. Mostly.'

'What about your signs?' Miska asked. 'Were they all dead already?'

'People must know fear.'

'We were the only ones who saw it,' Miska pointed out but the Ultra was walking away. She looked down at Kasmeyer's body. Fungus was already starting to grow out of the wounds. All of them were going to be having anti-fungal baths when they got back to the *Hangman's Daughter*.

If we get back, she thought. Though the odds were starting to even a little.

Mass had just finished wrapping Nyukuti's body in his poncho and was heading back to rejoin the others.

'Mass,' she called. He turned to face her. It was clear that he was still angry. She suspected it was the need to differentiate himself from the Nightmare Squad and perhaps the fear that he wasn't as different as he might wish. 'Kasmeyer's body as well,' she told him.

'Fuck that guy!' he snapped. 'Kasmeyer turned on us.'

'Somebody forced him, somebody with influence and reach,' she told him. Mass didn't answer, he just made his way over to the body. Miska wasn't sure she liked the guarded expression on his face, but she left him to it and started making her way towards the Nightmare Squad. A sodden Kaneda and Hogg had made it to not-so-dry land.

'Good work,' she told them as she passed and it was true. Without them the heavy weapons on the Waders would have torn them apart. Kaneda nodded, Hogg just watched her pass. She could practically feel the judgement in his eyes.

'That ain't right,' Raff said as she passed the mushroom tree he was leaning against. She knew he meant the mutilations.

'Yeah? Well you get what you pay for,' she muttered. What had he expected when they'd embarked on this path? She'd known serving soldiers who'd done as bad. Hell, Resnick had recruited his own band of war criminals in so-called legitimate mercenary, sorry, 'military contractor' circles.

'Miska?'

She looked up to see Hemi sat on the stem of a fallen mushroom tree, wiping mud off his inherited SAW. Nyukuti's

312

switchblade sword-boomerang was leaning against the tree. Hemi picked it up.

'You want this?' he asked.

Miska moved towards him, looking down at Nyukuti's strange weapon.

'I guess you'll never get the chance to find out if you're tougher,' Miska said as she took the boomer-sword and tucked it into some of the straps on the back of her load-carrying plate.

Hemi shrugged. With the rain gone the first of the pollen started to fall from the canopy far above.

'That is weird,' Miska muttered.

'That's just all kinds of trap,' Mass said next to her. He sounded spooked.

They were lying in a waterlogged ditch looking at a clearing within a small, low wood that existed far below the dense canopy of the huge trees. It had stopped raining but intermittent waterfalls still fell from the leaves far above, the water broken up by the secondary canopy. The much smaller, Earth-like trees were the least surprising thing. There were a number of overgrown Corinthian columns in the clearing. Only a few were standing. They looked as though they had been scattered around by some giant's hand: a failed project, signs of intent to build a temple. And then there were the heads. They were impaled on poles just in the treeline surrounding the clearing, all in various states of decomposition. Dead eyes and hollow sockets staring at nothing, clusters of fungal growth sprouting from their wounds, moss crawling across their faces like a virulent skin disease. But even the mass of severed heads weren't as surprising as the crashed spaceship.

'I'm a little disappointed that we're not dealing with aliens,'

Bean said on the other side of her. Miska didn't like being this close to the repellent Scottish cannibal but she had to admit he was right. More and more this nonsense had the hallmarks of Small Gods involvement.

'What do you think?' Miska asked Bean. 'Long-range strike craft? Maybe a hundred years old?' Which would date it round about the time of the War in Heaven, when the Small Gods had grown themselves bodies from the Grey Goo Wastelands.

Bean turned to look at her.

'I used to live in a cave,' he told her.

'I really believe that.'

The long-range strike craft had come down hard but it looked mostly intact. Half buried in the soft mud, the craft was part of a hillock that led to higher ground on the other side of the clearing. Much of the higher ground was obscured by the pollen fall and rising, humid mists that were starting to creep in. The airlock was open. It looked strangely inviting.

'I know the trees, though,' the cannibal told her, pointing at a tree.

'Don't point,' Miska told him. Movement was what would give them away.

'They've got to have eyes on us,' Grig said from where he was covering their right flank. Gunhir was on the left, Kaczmar, Kaneda and Hogg were providing rear security. Corenbloom, Hemi and Raff had eyes forward with Miska, Bean and Mass. The Ultra was, in theory, waiting for them back in the fungal wood, some two klicks south.

Grig was, of course, right. They were in a reasonably obvious place as well. If she were Resnick then she'd try and get behind them. Except she didn't think Resnick was here for her. She and her Bastards were just a pain in the ass to him.

It might have stopped raining but the pollen fall was so heavy it might as well have been snow. After the battle at Camp Badajoz, Miska had assumed that the pollen affected electronic systems that it could gain access to. Hence sealed goggles and ear covers protecting cyberware. Their inertial armour undersuits might have been sophisticated tech but they had little in the way of moving parts, and that was sealed inside the clothing itself. She had assumed that mechanical devices like slugthrowers would be impervious to the pollen but she didn't like the way the pollen seemed to be gathering on the weapons, despite their attempts to wipe it off.

'Mass, you're in charge, Grig's second, listen to him, he knows what he's talking about,' Miska told them. In a situation like this she would have far preferred to put Grig in charge but if she didn't respect the chain of command then she couldn't expect them to. She just hoped that Mass had his ego in check to know enough to listen to Grig. 'Kaneda, Hogg, I want you hunting. Find Resnick's people and kill them quietly.'

Neither of them responded. She just heard them slither out of the ditch.

'The rest of us?' Grig asked.

'Find firing positions,' Miska told them. They knew what to look for. 'Keep the defoliant squirters and the flamers handy but don't switch on the pilot lights unless you see the tree people. Understand?' She glanced at them, saw nods, heard muttered affirmatives. Grig was explaining it to Kaczmar in sign language.

'The enemy of my enemy is my friend?' Mass asked.

'You know me, Mass, I'm all about the diplomacy.' She turned to Bean. 'What are the trees?' she asked.

'Apples, walnut, oaks and ash, the death tree,' he told her and then grinned at her with a mouth full of canines.

'The moss-lain dryads shall be lull'd to sleep,' Mass muttered.

'Huh?' Bean grunted.

'It's Keats,' Hemi supplied.

Miska hoped the dryads were asleep.

'Where you going?' Grig asked.

'Into the ship,' she said, and grinned.

'You'll get cut down the moment you put your head up,' he told her. It was clear that he didn't approve. She didn't think he was right, though. Resnick had some expendable assets he could afford to waste on them but if Mars had risked sending a Spartan then he was here for something a lot more important. She was starting to think that he was hunting a Small God in his master's name.

You can be as sneaky as you like but sooner or later, you're just going to have to cover a lot of open ground, Miska decided, as she sprinted across the clearing. She practically dived through the open external airlock door.

Down on one knee, she switched on the AK-47's aim-light. She wasn't even remotely surprised when the light flickered and died almost immediately. It had momentarily illuminated an open internal airlock and a fungus-overgrown, debris-strewn corridor. She swung around behind her, half expecting to see more of the tree women rising from the mud, but all she saw was mist, trees and decapitated heads on poles. It looked like a picture from old Earth.

She moved into the corridor so she could get the hull between herself and the outside. Her one remaining eye was amplifying what little murky light was managing to make it in from the outside. She would be in pitch darkness if she went much further into the ship. Ignoring her own advice, she tried to light the pilot light on the flamer. The blue light wouldn't provide much illumination but it would be enough for her remaining eye to do the rest. The pilot light wouldn't light. That was bad news. She cleared the nozzle as best she could and tried again. Nothing.

One more time and then I'm giving this up as a bad idea, she decided as her thumb worked the nozzle. The ignition switch sounded deafening to her ears in this confined space but the pilot light flickered into life and illuminated the damp, fungal-infected mess with a cold blue light.

She moved through the ship with much more purpose than she felt. Every step sent up spores from the fungal growths underfoot. She had pulled her gas mask down but she could still feel the spores making her exposed skin itch. She had assumed if there was a Small God then this would be where she would find them, but she was starting to suspect that this had been little more than a one-way transport from Earth. She was about to turn back when she saw the open door to the bridge just ahead. She stopped and listened. All she heard was the steady drip-drip of condensation. Nothing moved inside the ship and she couldn't hear anything outside, certainly no mass gunfight. Satisfied that she was alone, Miska moved carefully and quietly into the bridge. The view screen had shattered and earth had half filled the bridge. Miska wasn't sure that roots should be able to grow into and through armoured hull the way they had here.

She was about to back out when something occurred to her. Miska ran a search for net access, expecting to find nothing. She was reasonably sure that a hundred years ago they had relied on hardwired connections, due to the war. She was more than a little surprised when she found the faintest trace of a connection.

She stood motionless in the half-buried bridge for a moment.

'This is a stupid idea on so many levels,' she told herself. That was underselling the idiocy of what she was contemplating. There were so many reasons not to trance in to a Small-Gods-connected hundred-year-old net. Not least because of some of the horrible net infections that were chucked around during the War in Heaven. With all their tech down she wouldn't even have a window into the real world. To make matters worse they were in the middle of enemy territory and she had nobody to provide trance-watch for her.

Just for a moment she thought about Nyukuti.

But she had to know.

She found the least fungal piece of damp earth she could and sat down. Then she closed her eyes and reached for the faint connection.

If anything it was a disappointment. It was a fragment of the ship's net, presumably being run off some still-functioning backup power source, which was impressive in its own way. This wasn't net architecture. It was net archaeology. The disappointment was that the system had been cleansed. It was a flat black plain of ashes interspersed with the odd data fire and the husks of black obelisks that had presumably once housed systems and information.

Cartoon-net-Miska sighed and prepared to trance out when the owl landed on the closest obelisk husk. Miska stared at it. Then she shouldered her club full of attack software and made her way towards the owl.

'But you're just an owl, right?' she said as she looked up at it. She had seen the bird before when she had been forced to trance in to the net back on Barney Prime. When she had met the net icon of the woman in the ancient dress, in a VR construct of a cliff top that overlooked an equally ancient coastal town. The owl had been there perched on the ruins of what Miska had suspected was some kind of temple.

'I am, indeed, an owl,' the owl confirmed. She spoke with the accented voice of a woman. Miska struggled to guess the age of the woman. Either quite young or very old, as though the voice had a dichotomous nature to it.

'You know that talking owls are reasonably rare,' Miska explained, though she supposed anything went on the net, even way out here. 'You got a name?'

'Yes,' the owl told her.

The bird wasn't moving her beak. Miska was just hearing the voice.

'I've often thought that people who take language completely literally don't really understand communication. I don't have time for games. I'm guessing this is some weird Small Gods circle jerk. You'll feed me some cryptic shit and then expect us mere mortals to dance on the end of your strings.'

'But you have time for obnoxious speeches?' the owl asked. There was no rancour in the bird's old woman/young girl's voice. It had sounded like a genuine enquiry.

'Shall we get to the point?' Miska asked.

'If we hold back anything it is either for the sake of security, or because we do not know,' the owl told her. 'We are most certainly acting in our own best interests, but yours as well.'

'Who is we?' Miska asked.

'That would be security.'

'You know, you could just hire us,' Miska suggested.

'If we had discovered what was going on quickly enough, we probably would have,' the owl told her.

319

'Well, exposition me,' Miska told the bird. She had to admit she was intrigued. 'Who is the Small God?'

'Artemis,' the owl told her. Miska shook her head. 'Goddess of the woods and the hunt.'

'Yeah?' Miska asked. 'African? Native American? Scandinavian?'

She was impressed, and quietly pleased, when the owl appeared to have a pained expression on her raptor features.

'Greek,' the owl told her. It made sense. The Small Gods who claimed to be manifestations of Greek and Roman mythology tended to be the main players back in the Sol System. They seemed to feel that they had the right to their namesakes. The most aggressive being Mars/Ares, of course.

'So some AI, alien or otherwise, grows herself a body out of nanotech from the Grey Goo Wastelands after the bombing, steals herself a long-range strike craft and flies here to set up her own kingdom of shrubbery? Then, I guess, things get tricky when the colonists arrive. But why does New Sun care? Is it just Small Gods family squabbles? Because I get that.'

'You're missing a few pieces,' the owl told her. 'Artemis grows from the Grey Goo, as you say. Data-raids Earth's net and finds the inconsistencies in the planetary survey that was made before the war with Them—'

'The plant life that's too evolved, the strange heat transfer between Eridani B and Ephesus ...' Then something occurred to Miska as she thought back to the artefact on Barney Prime. Raff had told her that it was just one of a number of incredibly rare artefacts that were as old as the universe itself, and seemed to make a mockery of the laws of physics when they turned up. 'Wait a minute. Is there a Cheat here, is that what Mars is after?'

The owl spent a suspiciously long time considering the answer.

'We think so,' the owl finally said, 'but we don't think it's what New Sun is after.'

'Why?'

'Because we believe it is somewhere deep within Epsilon Eridani B, beyond even the crush limit of Martian technology. We would also appreciate it if you would keep this information to yourself.'

Miska shrugged. She didn't really care one way or another.

'All right, so Artemis comes out here to form the ultimate horticultural society, do the god thing and create her own life, the tree ladies.'

'We believe that Artemis's dryads are little more than what you would consider drones,' the owl told her. 'But there was one other step that Artemis took. She found reference to a Project Crom, a biotech programme that utilised Themtech ...'

'Naturally occurring bio-nanites,' Miska said, thinking back to her conversation on the boat with Hemi. 'She used this Project Crom to stimulate the plant life here even further on its evolutionary path. So what, her own vegetable queendom?'

'We don't think so. We think it's part research project, part hiding from her abusive family.'

'She only started killing when the war started. She was happy to live in peace with the Maasai colonists, wasn't she?' Miska asked. She had just been trying to defend herself. Admittedly, in the Bastards' case, perhaps a little too proactively.

'Just so.'

'Let me guess. New Sun want to weaponise her work?' Miska asked.

'They think they can turn the planet into one huge military

biotech manufacturing facility. They could quite literally grow their weapons of war. The possibilities are boundless.'

And terrifying, Miska decided. She tried to avoid big picture thinking for the most part but the idea caused cold dread to creep through her very being. It was a very unusual feeling and she didn't like it. The pollen alone, the ability to turn off your enemies' most sophisticated weapon systems, was a game-changer. At best it would lead to warring swarms of nanites, itself an end-of-civilisation scenario.

'The UN would never grant them a colonial charter,' Miska said but she didn't believe it herself as she said it. She suspected that Martian intelligence had enough money and enough dirt on the UN Colonial Committee to push something like this through. The owl just looked at her. The flames of the data fires around them reflected in its round eyes. Miska had long known that short-sighted greed and fear tended to win out over long-termism and enlightened self-interest every time.

'So they need to kill Artemis and push the colonists off-world?' Miska asked. The small-scale proxy war made sense as well, just another colonial brushfire war, not big enough to draw any real attention. *Until the infamous Bastard Legion turns up*, Miska thought. It explained the all-out smear campaign.

'I expect they would rather take Artemis alive,' the owl told her. 'But yes, they certainly need to neutralise her.'

'So where is Artemis?' Miska asked.

The owl spread her wings.

'We don't know,' the owl told her. 'At a guess, watching.'

'Waiting for the mortals to amuse her?' Miska asked. The owl didn't say anything. It just flew away. Miska watched it go and then tranced out.

*

She opened her eyes. She was lying on the wet earth. She was somehow managing to feel cold, clammy and sweaty from the rising humidity at the same time. She was in darkness. The pilot light on the flamer had gone out and she couldn't get it to light again.

'Shit,' she muttered.

She had almost found herself feeling sorry for Artemis. *But somehow the Small Gods always find ways to behave like assholes*, Miska thought as she sat up.

'Miska! Come out and face me!' Torricone screamed from outside the ship.

CHAPTER 20

Without the flamer's pilot light Miska couldn't see a thing. Fortunately she was able to follow the sound of Torricone's voice as she felt her way along the long-range strike craft's overgrown bulkheads. Whoever was controlling Torricone had overplayed their hand. The kind of horrible things that Torricone was shouting at her were so unlike him as to be absurd. The content of his graphic threats and insults were easy to ignore. She did, however, wonder at the control mechanism as she groped her way through the ship back towards the open airlock. The sequestered couldn't have been controlled remotely because of the pollen. That meant they must have been receiving orders verbally before they went into battle. Verbal orders could only be so sophisticated. You couldn't plan for every contingency in advance, after all. That was the problem when you tried to turn people into machines.

She could see the grey light from the open airlock now. See the corridor that led to the outside. See the figure that was crossing back and forth in front of the airlock, casting his shadow down the corridor as he ranted about all the improbable things he would do to her when he caught her. Miska knelt down by the corner and aimed up the corridor, the pad of her finger on the AK-47's trigger. It would be so easy. One shot to put him down while she couldn't see his face. While his shouted words made him a stranger. Problem over. Except she knew she'd have to close and make sure that he was dead. That would be no fun at all.

She knew this was a trap. He was there to draw her out. She relaxed her finger on the trigger and slipped it back over the trigger guard.

You have to stop walking into traps, she told herself. Even as she moved up the corridor Miska had no real plan as to what she was going to do when she reached the outside.

It was weird. Seven of the sequestered were faces she sort of recognised from the *Hangman's Daughter*. They were all on their knees, stripped to the waist, many of them with prison tattoos on display. They looked like they were at prayer, except they had knives held to their own throats, as if they were about to fall on them. It was clear that it was a pose. Among the trees, the head-poles and the mist it was almost artful. *And*, Miska decided, *not meant for me*. This had been staged for someone else.

She was hunkered down by the strike craft's interior airlock. She could see Torricone pacing backward and forward in front of the airlock as he ranted, his voice going hoarse. He was stripped to the waist as well. He had his back to her at the moment. A crucified Christ stared at her from his skin. He looked beautiful until he turned. The programmed madness was evident in his contorted, twitching facial features. His eyes were all Torricone, however. He looked trapped in his own eyes. After what he'd seen, the acts that his body had been forced to do, Miska was pretty sure that killing him would be a mercy.

Coward! her inner voice snapped. That was the easy way out. She stepped through the airlock anyway and levelled her weapon at Torricone.

'Michael,' she said quietly. He swung towards her. It was easy to believe that it wasn't him any more. As long as she didn't look in his eyes. He tensed, ready to charge. The pad of her finger started to depress the rifle's trigger.

Then strange things happened in the air behind Torricone, as though she was looking at a distorted image of the undergrowth. Suddenly he was yanked backwards. She could see branches on the transplanted Earth foliage moving where Torricone had just been dragged through them.

It doesn't make sense ... Miska just about had time to think when the first of the sequestered deserters charged her. She swung round to face the screaming man. She squeezed the trigger and nothing happened. She just about had time to hit the sling's quick-release. The AK-47/flamer combo dropped into the mud and he was on her. He stabbed at her with his blade. She guided the knife hand away from her and hit him in the throat hard enough to take him off his feet, crushing his windpipe. He hit the floor and she moved quickly away from him, expecting the rest of them to be all over her but as soon as the first hit the ground, the second was on his feet charging her. Miska fast drew the Winchester, levelled it, squeezed the trigger, wasn't terribly surprised when it didn't fire. She sidestepped the second sequestered deserter's charge and used the shotgun as a club to take out his knee. He went sliding face-down in the mud and Miska stamped on his head until he stopped moving. Now the third was charging her. She threw the shotgun at him, distracting him momentarily as she drew the Glock. Tried to fire it. Nothing. She used it to break the sequestered deserter's nose, free hand on the back of his head as she kicked out his knee and took him to the ground. He tried to get back up, blood all over his mouth. That was when Miska's knife found his throat.

'Enough of this, this Thirty-Six Chambers bullshit!' Miska screamed into the apparently empty clearing. She had left bodies in the mud. That was entertainment enough, she decided. She was breathing a little heavy. Her squad hadn't interfered because they were waiting for Resnick. Though she was pretty sure that nobody had a functional weapon at the moment, bar knives, hatchets and other exotic weapons. *And Hogg's crossbow*, she thought. Miska hadn't heard any violence in the trees which meant that her people hadn't found Resnick's so-called Double Veterans either. 'Come out and play.'

Resnick was using her as bait for Artemis. Everyone likes gladiatorial combat after all, and Miska needed Artemis as bait for Resnick. The sad thing was that one of the reasons this job had appealed to her was because it had seemed so simple: fight in a war. Between Martian special forces, Small Gods, sequestered deserters and P-fucking-R, somehow it had become very complicated.

They came through the mist looking exactly like the mythological figures they so desperately wanted to be. Up close, in their 'natural' environment, Miska could see that there were four different types of the dryad drones. Each type shared characteristics with one of the four types of Earth trees present, the oak, apple, walnut and ash.

Artemis, however. Artemis was something else. She had a

more obviously statuesque woman's figure. A skin of smooth, sectional bark covered a powerful looking musculature, leafy twigs for hair, thicker branches formed a spine across her upper back and shoulders. She wore a loincloth of moss that became a skirt at the back and carried a long bow and arrows in her left hand. Both the bow and the arrows looked as though they had been grown rather than made. Her eyes were two glowing ovals the colour of amber resin. She had no mouth that Miska could see but the bottom part of her face curved down into a sharp point. She was stood with four of her handmaidens, among the overgrown Corinthian columns on top of the mound formed by the crashed ship. Miska had to force herself not to step back. Artemis was terrifying through sheer physicality alone. Miska was struck by the seeming futility of Resnick's impending assassination attempt. Frightening or not, Miska felt drawn to the 'goddess' but she had heard that was always the case with the Small Gods. Their sheer force of personality was hardwired.

'This is just entertainment, right?' Miska asked. She had to force herself to look away from the so-called goddess. She was looking for Resnick to make his move now. She was pretty sure that a lot of his so-called Double Veterans had just tried to use their weapons out in the woods somewhere. Resnick would be close though, he'd have a contingency, he'd want to be sure.

'How is it different to you watching wars on vizzes?' the goddess asked. Her voice sounded like wind blowing through the trees. Her 'mouth' trisected the triangular bark below her eyes. She sounded odd using a word like 'vizzes'. Miska was almost disappointed.

Concentrate! Where the fuck was he?

'Mars is trying to kill you,' Miska told her as she searched the surrounding area. *It's movement that gives you away,* she told herself.

'My half brother wants me dead.' It wasn't a question, just a simple statement of fact.

Miska had meant the planet, or rather the government of the planet, but it was pretty much the same thing.

'I think it's more he wants the planet for himself,' Miska said. She had no idea what Artemis was going to do, though it must have been obvious to her that some drama was unfolding here. She seemed content to let it play out.

'There is nothing he won't try and turn into a weapon,' Artemis said.

'Yeah, well one of his assassins is here now and he may just have the tools for the job,' Miska told the goddess. She was sure that there was movement in the woods now but it was too far away for Resnick. Even if he had a bow or a crossbow like Hogg's he couldn't be sure it would hit. 'If you've got any intel you could offer, like his whereabouts, well that ...' Just the slightest movement. 'Move now!' she ordered the goddess, as Resnick seemed to explode out of the earth at Artemis's feet. Miska was moving but it was futile. He had some kind of hypodermic dagger in his hand and it was stabbing down towards Artemis's leg. Miska watched as the blade pierced the bark of an empty husk that looked like Artemis. One of the handmaidens stepped forward. Root-like tendrils wrapped themselves around Resnick, stilling his struggling form, the tips of the roots growing into his nostrils, holding his mouth open, his eyelids.

'Don't kill him!' Miska shouted. Resnick had used an old-fashioned ghillie suit and the even older technique of being really sneaky, mostly from being quiet and still. He must have either observed or guessed the rough area where Artemis would reveal herself and then moved towards her very slowly. It was as much luck as observation skills and knowing what she was looking for that had allowed Miska to see the movement. *God, he's good though.*

'Why?' Artemis asked as she grew out of the earth next to Miska.

'Ah!' Miska cried, almost stabbing the goddess. 'I want to do it,' Miska told her after she had composed herself. Only up close did she realise just how big Artemis was. She had to be at least ten feet tall.

'Well, your warning saved my life,' Artemis admitted. Somehow Miska doubted that, but she wasn't about to argue.

'He's got some more people around,' Miska said.

'So have you,' Artemis pointed out.

'They want to kill them as well,' Miska admitted.

'You're quite bloodthirsty, aren't you?'

'They did some bad things. What are you going to do now?' Miska asked. It wasn't as if Mars was going to stop because Resnick had failed.

'I had hoped to live in peace with the modern world. We observed the colonists. I like them well enough, their ways, but now ...'

'The pollen?' Miska asked. Artemis nodded. 'The colonists?'

'They can stay or leave as they wish. If they stay then things will become simpler for them.'

'Why did you attack my people?' Miska asked.

Artemis looked down at her. 'Same weapons, same equipment. It was only when you came here that we realised you were different from these others,' Artemis said and gestured to Resnick's struggling form.

'So you get that we're on your side?' Miska asked hopefully. 'Because we could really do with getting a shuttle in here to evac.'

'Don't you have some unfinished business to deal with?' Artemis asked. Figures were emerging from the woods on the high ground at the northern end of the clearing. Resnick's so-called Double Veterans. The dryad drones were moving back into the trees. The handmaiden holding Resnick plucked the hypodermic dagger from his grip and then she too backed into the woods, her tendrils drawing back from the Spartan's strug-gling form until he was free. Miska looked around and Artemis had gone.

'It was nothing personal,' Resnick called. He was on his feet now, moving down the mound created by the crashed ship. 'Just a job.'

'I'm still going to kill you,' Miska told him. Though she had been hoping that the handmaiden could hold him down while she stabbed him to death because he would be filled with Martian nanotech. He would be faster and stronger than her. His Double Veterans formed a staggered line either side of him. There were ten of them. She recognised some faces from the aerostat. Doubtless they had already tried to shoot her and found their weapons not working. Doubtless her Bastards had done the same as soon as Resnick and the Double Veterans had appeared.

'I think we both know that's not how this is going to go down,' Resnick said. Miska was aware of her people walking out of the woods behind her. Knives, hatchets, *māripi* already drawn. She noticed that neither Hogg nor Kaneda were with them. This, she hoped, was a good thing. *Either that or they're both already dead.*

Mass came to stand one side of her, Grig the other.

'Come a long way from sitting in a nice warm mech,' Mass muttered.

'It's just war, fam, just war,' Grig told him and then turned and grinned at her.

Miska used her thumbs to gesture at the legionnaires on either side of her.

'The real deal.' She pointed at Resnick's Double Veterans. 'Copycats.'

Resnick just strode towards her.

'Get 'em!' Miska told her people. The Bastards charged.

Bean died first, of his own stupidity. For reasons best known to himself he charged Resnick. Resnick batted the hatchet out of Bean's right hand. Miska heard the bones in the cannibal's hand breaking. The Spartan locked up and then broke Bean's left arm and now he had a knife. He hamstrung Bean because he could. The cannibal hit the mud and Resnick stamped on his head so hard he got grey matter on the sole of his boot.

Corenbloom went down next. He was backing away from one of the Double Veterans, knife in hand, looking for an opening, obviously outclassed, when he got too close to Resnick as the Spartan strode towards Miska. Resnick punched Corenbloom in the side. It looked like a casual blow from his left hand. Miska heard the audible crack of Corenbloom's hard armour plate breaking as the force of the blow spun him into the air. He hit the mud hard and didn't move.

Miska was struggling to hold her ground as he closed with her. This wasn't some Martian-tech augmented Triple S contractor like Major Sheldon had been on Faigroe Station. This was a full-blood Martian Spartan and, unlike her, he didn't have a bullet lodged close to his spine.

Resnick threw a lazy sidekick at her. He was clearly feeling overconfident. She didn't step back enough to avoid the blow, just enough to take some of the force out of it. Her inertial armour helped too. It still knocked the wind out of her. He may have been fast but he wasn't fast enough to draw his leg back before she'd rammed the diamond-edged blade of her knife into his leg, hard enough to go through his inertial armour and whatever bullshit subcutaneous armour his nanotech-filled body provided. She tore the blade down his leg and was rewarded with a grunt of pain. It would probably be the last lesson she taught him.

His attacks were a little more careful after that. Not that he had to be. Miska concentrated on keeping the knife he had taken from Bean out of her flesh. Which was a good tactic as far as it went, but it meant she got hit, kneed, and head-butted a lot. Still, at least he wasn't kicking her now. She was trying to bide time, look for any opening, any advantage, the slightest edge, but he wasn't making any more mistakes.

Miska almost managed to get out of the way of a punch to her face. Had it contacted fully it probably would have powdered her jaw despite the reinforcement. Her head whipped round as she spat blood out. Her lack of depth perception wasn't helping and he knew that, he'd snuck the blow in on her blind side. He hit her in the chest hard enough to turn it into one large bruise. She felt her hard armour breastplate crack. She stumbled back and decided to sit down and try and breathe again.

'You know you can't win this, right?' Resnick asked as he closed with her. He wasn't playing with his food. It was simple psych warfare one-oh-one. He would look for any advantage. Humiliating his opponent didn't come into it. Besides, he was right.

His boot flew at her head. Miska managed to move out of the way so that it only caught her a glancing blow. It still cracked her half-helm, made her IVD jump, and left her with the strong urge to vomit as she went sprawling in the mud. Where she lay she could see his muddy boots getting closer. She was absurdly pleased that she had managed to hold onto her knife. It wasn't difficult to play dead. She plunged the knife into his boot. He started to move but wasn't quick enough. She stabbed again, biting in just under his kneecap. This time he actually cried out in pain. Then she aimed the diamond-edged tip straight for his groin. She felt his fingers grab her wrist. She looked up into dark eyes. It was over.

He snapped her wrist. It felt like a compound fracture. She only had a moment to experience the pain before his fist hit her in the top of the head. Her helmet split but it saved her life. She still lost consciousness just for a moment.

She was lying in the mud. She opened her eyes. Everything slowed down. She had known she was going to lose. She felt Resnick pull her up into a sitting position. Her right arm flopped around, her undersuit staining from the inside as blood filled her glove, the knife still held loosely in her right hand. Resnick made a triangle with his arms around her neck and started to squeeze. She clawed at him with her left. Fought as hard as she could as he sought to cut off the blood supply to her head.

As she fought, as everything slowed down, as she died, she caught a snapshot of the rest of the fight. Maybe Artemis had told herself this was like two groups of ancient warriors battling. Maybe she had convinced herself this was another gladiatorial tribute. It wasn't. It was a sordid little gang fight. A prison yard brawl.

There were already bodies on the ground turning the grey

mud crimson. It took her a moment to differentiate who people were. Everyone was caked in mud from head to foot. She could tell which one was Kaczmar, however, by his bulk. He was sat atop one of the Double Veterans, simultaneously biting his cheek while trying to tear open the man's mouth. Miska imagined she could hear the sound of the flesh ripping over the noise of the battle.

Raff had locked up the arm of another Double Veteran as he repeatedly stabbed her in the armpit. Grig had another round the neck as he tried to push the tip of his knife into the contractor's skull. Mass held his victim against a tree; he had somehow managed to get his hooked fisherman's knife through their inertial armour and was dragging it upwards. Both Gunhir and Hemi were sat upon struggling Double Veterans, knees pinning their arms. Gunhir was repeatedly clawing at his victim's face, while the diamond-edged titanium teeth of Hemi's *māripi* pounded another Double Veteran's face into so much ground beef.

She hoped Artemis was enjoying the show.

Miska was becoming weaker, losing consciousness. Then a crossbow bolt landed in the mud in front of her. The crossbow bolt exploded. The force of the explosion battered into Miska and she lost consciousness.

Miska came to again, reawakened by struggling medical implants. Immediately the panic hit her as Resnick's strangulation threatened to cut off the oxygen supply to her brain. She could feel her subcutaneous armour cracking under his incredible strength. Her knife was useless in her right hand. Then she saw the rock. The fingers on her left hand closed around it. The pinnacle of Martian military training and nanotechnology was killing her and she had a rock.

It was an awkward blow with her left hand, back into where she hoped his eye was. All she had to do, however, was think about what Resnick, this Martian drone, had tried to do to her Legion, the things that New Sun and Triple S had said about her, about her father, and she found the rage to power the blow. The jagged end of the stone caught him in the eye. There was a satisfying scream of pain. The grip on her neck loosened. Miska pushed with her legs and they both went sprawling into the mud. Then it was her turn to howl with pain as she elbowed him in the nose with her right arm. It jarred her compound fracture, but he let go of her. She rolled off him. Managed to push herself up onto her knees. Resnick's eye was a bloody mess. Now he looked angry. *Good.* She smashed the stone into his face, turning the expression of incredulous rage red. She did it again. And again but this time he caught her left arm. He kicked out from the ground, catching her in the stomach and sending her flying with the force of the blow. Resnick was up on his feet again.

'Why won't you just die?' Miska asked as he stalked towards her. It seemed like a reasonable question. Then Resnick was stood over her. He moved as though to stamp on her. Then his hand came up and he caught another crossbow bolt. He quickly threw it away from himself. Even as the crossbow bolt blew up in mid-air another thumped into his buttock and exploded. His leg blown from under him, he flopped into a messy somersault, his head battering into the earth on the way down.

Miska didn't waste any time. She screamed again as her left hand wrestled her knife, which she had somehow managed to hold on to, out of her useless right hand. She threw herself into the air as Resnick tried to push himself up, a chunk missing from his buttock and the top of his left leg. She screamed out again as she landed on him, jarring her broken right arm, forcing him into the mud. She plunged the knife into his neck, pushing it upwards. She felt resistance from whatever armour he had under the skin, some subcutaneous inertial armour-like nanotech application, then resistance from his spine. She kept pushing as he bucked under her. She kept pushing until he was still. Then she twisted the knife and tore it out but she hadn't finished. She pushed herself unsteadily to her feet, awkwardly clawing at the straps on her back before finally managing to pull out Nyukuti's boomer-sword. The angular blade clicked open. She swung the blade again and again. She kept swinging it even as the others gathered around her. She kept swinging the blade even though every jarring movement sent agony coursing through her from her compound fracture. She kept swinging until Resnick's head came off. Then she passed out from the pain.

'This is for the pain,' the Ultra's beautiful voice told her. She opened her eyes and looked up at his face, made alien by the camo-paint. She opened her mouth and accepted the painkiller that would supplement her body's own, seriously strained, medical implants. She needed them at the moment. At the very best she was horribly concussed.

'Why did your reactive camouflage work back there?' she asked him. They were down by the water again. She could see Torricone, hog-tied, lying face-down in the mud. Still sequestered, still following his last instructions as he struggled against the Ultra's bonds. There was something pathetic about it.

'I don't know,' he told her. 'Perhaps because it was part of me, perhaps Artemis allowed it.'

She noticed that her arm had been bound. She wondered when the medpak that had been driving the medgel on her back had stopped working. She was lucky that Resnick hadn't hit her there.

She turned back to the Ultra.

'You came back for Torricone?' she asked. He just nodded. 'Why risk discovery?'

The Ultra gave this some thought.

'I think Artemis knew I was there anyway,' he told her.

'Why?'

'Just a feeling.'

'You didn't answer my question,' she pointed out.

Silver eyes spent some time looking into her own.

'Because if he died, if you killed him, it would hurt you, perhaps irrevocably,' he told her.

Miska didn't know what to do with that. Eventually she had to look away. There were four bodies wrapped in their ponchos down by the water. She looked around and saw Kaneda lifting Hogg's crossbow.

'What happened?' she demanded.

'My rifle stopped working. When Hogg didn't shoot I went looking for him. It took a moment to work out how to work this thing,' he said holding up the crossbow. 'It was my last shot that got him as well. I'd used two bolts on one of Resnick's people in the wood.'

'What happened to Hogg?' Miska asked.

'He was dead when I got there,' Kaneda told her.

'One of Resnick's men?' Miska asked.

'I guess,' Kaneda said as though no other possibility had occurred to him.

Miska looked around at the others. Most of them were sat in the mud, their backs against the fungal trees. Corenbloom was conscious. She was relieved that he had lived, at least. Hemi and

Mass were sound asleep. The rest of them were watching her with weary, wary eyes.

'We've called for an evac,' Grig told her. She knew that the Nightmare Squad had been carrying a tight-beam uplink. It appeared that Artemis had chosen to let them leave, allowed their tech to work.

Miska pushed herself to her feet despite protestations from the Ultra.

'Grig, Mass ... Mass!' she shouted. Mass started awake. 'With me!' she snapped. She staggered over to the bodies. She spent a moment or two searching the ponchos until she found Hogg's. He'd been killed with a knife. It'd been done professionally as well, and, she suspected, very quietly.

'What's up?' Mass asked as he and Grig joined her. He sounded groggy.

'Did you guys have eyes on each other when you were in the woods?' she asked.

'You think one of us did this?' Mass asked. He sounded more surprised than offended. Chances were it had been one of Resnick's men, that was the most logical answer. Except something was bugging her. Just as Hogg was about to tell her something about her father, something he didn't want to say on the boat in case it was overheard, he got killed.

You're paranoid, she told herself, *this was a war.*

'Just answer the question,' she told them.

'No,' Grig answered, 'we were too strung out, too much ground to cover. We kept it simple. If either Mass or myself opened fire then the rest would join in. When we tried—'

'Your weapons didn't work,' Miska finished for him. Grig just nodded and suddenly all three of them were in shadow as Kaczmar loomed over them.

'Jesus Christ!' Mass snapped as Kaczmar held up Resnick's severed head.

'I thought you would want this,' he shouted.

They really did need to do something about his hearing.

'Yes, yes I do,' Miska said, 'Thank you!'

The huge serial killer just nodded.

'Bean was my friend,' he told her loudly.

'I'm sorry for your loss,' Miska ventured.

'I want to eat his corpse. Something of him will live on in my colon. It's what he would have wanted.'

CHAPTER 21

The Ultra had managed to talk Kaczmar out of eating Bean's corpse. *Just another day in the Legion*, Miska thought.

'Are you actually going to drink blood out of his skull?' Corenbloom asked. All of them were sat, exhausted, in Pegasus 1's cargo hold, heading back to Waterloo Station.

'It's evidence,' Miska told him. The disgraced FBI agent nodded.

'Is that why you're keeping that prick alive?' Mass asked. He nodded to where a gagged Torricone had been strapped into one of the fold-down bucket seats. He was still trying to follow his last verbal instructions. Still trying to kill Miska with hate on his face and panic in his eyes.

'Yes,' Miska lied. She was too tired and in too much pain to argue with Mass at the moment.

'Fine,' Mass said. He groaned as he pushed himself out of his seat. Like everyone else bar Grig, Raff and, of course, the Ultra, Mass was a mass of bruises, minor cuts and some not so minor cuts. Most of them in the back of the ship were a patchwork of medgel, swellpatches and mud. Mass had been one of the legionnaires who'd required attention from a fleshknitter. Miska was pleased to be back in an environment where technology worked again.

'Hey!' Miska shouted as Mass punched the bound Torricone in the face. The Ultra was on his feet, interposing himself between Mass and the struggling sequestered Torricone. Mass had his hands up and was backing way.

'Simple reciprocity,' he told the prolific serial killer. 'It's done now.' He went and sat down again.

'Fuck's sake, Mass,' Miska muttered, shaking her head. Her arm was wrapped in a medpak-driven medgel cast, applied by the Ultra after the shuttle had picked them up. Artemis had remained true to her word and had let them leave. The Ultra had also reapplied medgel and a pak to the bullet lodged in her back.

Corenbloom was sat on the other side of the cargo bay, slowly drifting off to sleep. He'd been hit pretty hard and had spent most of the fight in the mud.

'Corenbloom,' Miska subvocalised over a direct comms link. He jerked awake and looked around for a moment as though trying to work out where the voice was coming from. 'When we get back I want you and the Doc to look over Hogg's body.'

'Why?' Corenbloom asked. 'You don't think it was one of Resnick's guys?'

'I think it was one of Resnick's guys. I'm just being thorough.'

'Let me get some rest, but then sure.'

She opened a comms link to the *Hangman's Daughter* and spoke with her father. It seemed that the ship was under siege.

Miska, four of her mud-covered mercenaries and Raff made

their way down the Central Concourse, weapons at the ready. Except Miska couldn't hold her AK-47 because of her broken arm, so she just had the ageing Glock in her left hand. Her right hand worked just well enough for her to hold onto Resnick's head.

She had sent the Ultra and the rest of the Nightmare Squad back to the *Daughter*. She could have done with their firepower if things turned nasty but any way she cut it they were bad press. Kaczmar would get his ear fixed and his (non-human-flesh) meal when they docked somewhere they weren't going to get lynched. There had been some groaning when she'd ordered them to clean their weapons. She had been worried about the pollen that had adhered to and jammed up their weapons down on Ephesus, but now it was just yellow dust. There was still a lot of mud to clean off, however. The Ultra had offered to clean her guns. Stubbornly she'd insisted on cleaning the Glock herself. She would do the rest later when her right arm worked again. The Nightmare Squad had passed on any spare ammunition to Mass, Corenbloom, Hemi and Kaneda.

Kaneda was ahead of her, Corenbloom behind, pushing the bound and still-struggling sequestered Torricone ahead of him. Mass and Hemi were on the other side of the street. Raff was moving more casually, coming along for the ride but trying to make it clear, through distance, that he wasn't one of the Bastards.

There weren't a lot of people on the street but even hardened mercenaries decided to give the five mud-covered, heavily-if-anachronistically armed Bastards a wide berth. Especially when their leader was carrying the commander of Triple S (elite)'s decapitated head.

Miska magnified her vision when the concourse's curve

brought Salik's nineteenth century townhouse into view. There were four guards that she could see. They looked like Triple S (conventional). She guessed they'd run out of special forces operators. She called the targets for the rest of the fire team.

'They try and bring their weapons up, nail them,' she subvocalised. The electromagnetically-driven rounds the carbine-configured Kopis gauss rifles fired would move a lot faster than their own chemical explosion-driven rounds would. She should have had McWilliams bring down some gauss weapons with him. *And a platoon of Offensive Bastards*, she thought, but they had been too intent on evaccing. They had no idea when Artemis was going to trigger the planet-wide pollen bloom.

Lomas Hinton had been shot to death in the stall of a toilet. There had been at least three shooters according to the news reports. Somebody had put the head of a decapitated rat in his mouth and, to really drive the message home, the words 'rat motherfucker' had been painted on the stalls in the victim's blood.

Someone had fire-bombed the Waterloo Station offices of New Sun's PR company. The words 'tell the truth' had been painted on the walls.

A number of 'reporters', those who had toed the New Sun/ Triple S line, had their tongues cut out. The words 'tell the truth' had been tattooed on their foreheads. Again they had claimed that three masked assailants had done this.

Needless to say, the Bastard Legion were being blamed. Given how Mass had chuckled when he'd seen the news report, there was a chance that the Legion was actually responsible this time. There was certainly something Mafiaesque about the attacks, Miska decided. What worried her a little was that the attacks must have had hacker support so that the 'assailants' hadn't been caught on security viz. If it had been the Legion, then she was less than pleased about the use of a hacker. They were dangerous to her. On the other hand, she hadn't been there so it wouldn't be fair to criticise their call. All of this had, of course, caused outrage on the station. As a result the *Hangman's Daughter* was currently clamped to the station with Salik's security force, the elements of Triple S that had been up on the station, and a few other mercenary groups including the Dogs of Love camped outside.

Salik had, however, reluctantly agreed to allow Pegasus 1 to dock at the lower ring after Miska had explained some of what had happened down on the planet. Nor had there been a security force waiting for them. It seemed that the CEO of Waterloo Station hadn't informed Colonel Duellona of Miska's return. They had become aware of the *U.S.S.S Teten* when they had approached Waterloo Station to dock. The FBI destroyer had lit them up with radar and lidar but they still didn't have the jurisdiction to move on them, it seemed. Still, their close proximity to the station suggested that the powers-that-be were giving some thought to granting the FBI some kind of authority.

One of the Triple S mercs outside of Salik's house noticed them.

'Don't—' Miska started. Kaneda's suppressed marksman-configured M19 whispered. A red smear appeared on the wall behind the observant mercenary.

'Don't!' Mass shouted, M19 carbine up, backed by Hemi's SAW as they closed with the guards. 'We will kill you!' Mass warned them. The other three mercenaries decided that they didn't want to die today.

*

The liveried servitor droid seemed almost as upset as Salik's security detail when Salik let Miska, Raff, Corenbloom and the still-struggling Torricone into the house. She had thought that Mass was going to complain about Miska taking Corenbloom with her instead of him, but Mass was a combat officer. Corenbloom was intel. He would be more useful upstairs.

They had tracked mud all over the antique rugs and carpets. Corenbloom pushed Torricone into the drawing room ahead of him. Miska followed. Raff tried to make himself as unobtrusive as possible. She was a little disappointed that nobody gasped when they saw what she was carrying.

Salik was sat on his chair like the troubled monarch he was. Chin on his thumb, index finger pointing up past his nose. Duellona, face like thunder, was sat on an antique two-seat sofa next to a very nervous looking Campbell. There were two other people in the room. A grey-faced woman, her hair in a bun so severe it seemed to stretch her features, sat in one of the antique chairs. She wore an understated skirt suit the same colour as her face. The other woman was at least six and half feet tall. Her head was shaved, both her ears were pierced and stretched, and she wore a red power suit. Miska recognised her as Kiserian Omiata, a Maasai elder and head of the Colonial Council.

'Ah, Miska,' an unhappy-looking Salik said as she entered the room. 'I spoke with your sister this morning.'

'How was that?' Miska said, looking around. Corenbloom moved the struggling Torricone to one corner.

'Bracing,' Salik told her.

'She always was the difficult one,' Miska said, though still looking around the room.

'UN?' she asked the grey-faced women. Miska was guessing

that she was the UN's conflict inspector. The woman nodded, a profound look of distaste on her face. 'Catch.'

Miska tossed her Resnick's head. The woman caught it instinctively, realised what she'd done and flung it from her. Miska watched it roll around on the already-soiled carpet.

'Miss Corbin.' Anger warred with disgust in her voice, but there was no fear there. 'You have been accused—'

'That's evidence,' Miska said pointing at the head. 'Major Resnick, head of Triple S elite in the Ephesus system, is a Spartan. Martian special forces, you'll find traces of all sort of illegal Martian nanotech in that head.'

'How much longer are we going to have to—' Duellona started. Miska shot her once, dead centre forehead. All sorts of automated security systems unfolded from discreet places and armed humans and drones appeared as if by magic. Miska held her hands up and allowed them to take her Glock. Corenbloom seemed relieved to be disarmed right up until he was wrestled to the carpet.

'Look!' Miska shouted as they tried to wrestle her to the carpet as well. Salik held a hand up to forestall them. Duellona was staring at Miska, the bullet hole in the centre of her forehead slowly closing.

'You're a Small God!' the UN conflict inspector gasped.

'Which I think is a breach of the articles of conflict, not to mention Interstellar Law and numerous treaties,' Miska said, much more brightly than she felt.

'Let her go,' Salik told his security people, and they released Miska.

'And now I have to kill everyone in the room,' Duellona told them. 'And there's not a single thing you can do about it.'

Miska whistled for Duellona's attention. The Small God

turned to look at her. Miska held up the hypodermic dagger that Resnick had been armed with. Gunhir had given it to her. It turned out that Artemis's handmaid had simply discarded it. Apparently it was of no interest to drone and master.

'Maybe, maybe not,' Miska said. Duellona stared at her. Miska could almost see the calculations. Odds were that Miska, particularly in this state, wouldn't be able to do much against an actual Small God, but there was always that slightest chance, and you couldn't play the games the Small Gods play when you were dead. Miska barely saw Colonel Duellona move. One minute she was there, the next gone. Her ears caught up with the sound of broken glass. There was a roughly Duellona-shaped hole in one of the drawing room's windows. Miska moved quickly to the window. She could see Duellona sprinting down the main concourse. The curve was such, and she was moving so quickly, that it looked like she was running up hill.

'Boss?' Kaneda subvocalised over the comms. She knew he was asking if she wanted him to take a shot.

'Leave her, you've got nothing that'll touch her,' Miska subvocalised back. *More's the pity*, she thought. Then she turned to Salik and pointed at the broken window. 'Not armoured?'

'This is the original building ...' he started and then changed tack. 'There's no point. They'd just shoot through the brickwork.'

'Okay, obviously New Sun—' Campbell started.

'Shut up,' Miska told him. The executive did as he was told. 'I think you'll find that New Sun no longer exists. Mars will already be shutting that company down to hide any links between this failed operation and themselves.'

'Look, I don't have to listen to this conspiracy theory nonsense from a proven war criminal.' Campbell tried to stand up.

Miska pushed him back down into the antique sofa. Campbell turned towards Salik. 'I need some assurances for my safety here!' he insisted.

Salik opened his hands questioningly and looked up at Miska.

'You tell the truth and I promise you can leave this room alive, but then I suggest you start running,' Miska told him.

'Are you threatening me?' Campbell demanded. He turned to Salik. 'Do something!'

'She's not threatening you,' Salik explained. 'If New Sun is a Martian front, then I suspect you're about to get your contract cancelled.'

Miska gestured towards Torricone with her thumb.

'The head of my so-called "punishment squad". He has been sequestered. That shouldn't be difficult to prove. Again, New Sun and Triple S using highly illegal tech. As well as what's in his head I've got eye witnesses, including one independent journalist—' she pointed at Raff, who waved '—who can vouch for Torricone and the other members of his squad attacking me. And this is all your problem now,' she told the room. She saw the grey-faced lady from the UN, Salik and Councillor Omiata exchange looks. Campbell was looking more and more frightened.

'And this latest round of atrocities?' the woman from the UN asked.

'The same,' Miska said. 'False flag operations conducted by sequestered ex-legionnaires tricked into defecting by New Sun's lies.'

'That's not true!' Campbell protested.

Miska turned to him, smiling. More and more she was sure that it was Vido who'd had Hinton killed, the PR agency fire-bombed and the 'journalists'' tongues cut out. There was, however, only so much Campbell could say about this without incriminating New Sun for the things they had actually done.

'Something to add?' she asked. Campbell's face was covered in sweat. His eyes were darting around as though looking for an escape route.

'Why are we even talking about this?' Campbell demanded, 'She's a slaver!'

'Never denied it,' Miska said. 'Makes you wonder why I'd lie about other things, doesn't it?' This time Campbell chose, wisely, to remain quiet. 'Have you got the facilities to check for sequestration on the station?' she asked Salik. He nodded. Miska pointed at the UN conflict inspector. 'Check the results, see if it looks like Martian tech to you.' The grey-faced woman nodded. She still looked a little stunned. Catching Mars in the act was as bad, if not worse, than them getting away with it, diplomatically speaking. Nobody wanted a confrontation with Mars.

'Then what do you want me to do with him?' Salik asked over a private comms link. She hadn't even seen him subvocalise. It was a question she'd been dreading. He had deserted. She had to kill him to maintain discipline. She had already tried to do it. It was suddenly very quiet in the room. Miska could feel eyes on her. Raff and Corenbloom were both watching her intently. This was another reason that she hadn't brought Mass with her. It was in Corenbloom and Raff's best interests to be discreet about this matter. Besides all they would know was that she had, rather rudely, subvocalised a private message to Salik.

'Let him go,' Miska told Salik over the private comms link. 'Make it clear that he needs to be discreet and he never crosses our paths again.'

Salik nodded.

'I shall make it clear that it's my decision to let him live contra to your instructions,' Salik told her over the private link.

'Thank you,' Miska said. It would help if it ever came out. Though somehow she wasn't comfortable with lying to her Bastards any more.

Two drones and a human member of Salik's security detail appeared. They escorted the struggling Torricone out of the room. Miska caught her last ever glimpse of him and immediately looked away. It felt like actual physical pain, like something breaking inside her. She did her very best not to acknowledge it, to ignore it.

'Well, if Salik and Colonel Corbin are finished with their private conversation,' Councillor Omiata said, 'can I assume that New Sun and Triple S forces will offer a full and unconditional surrender?'

'And submit to a full UN investigation?' Corenbloom suggested. The UN conflict inspector nodded. She still seemed a little stunned. The severed head probably hadn't helped.

Campbell didn't say anything. He knew who was behind New Sun. He must know what they were going to do to someone who had screwed up this big.

'What was it all about?' the councillor asked. 'I still don't see what you had to gain from these actions. You must have realised that you were going to be found out.'

Again Campbell ignored her, locked up in a prison of his own fear.

'They were hoping that by the time they were found out it would have been too late,' Miska told her, shaking herself out of her thoughts. 'You would have lost, they would have what they wanted. The problem was we kept on pushing their hand. Camp Badajoz effectively gave us strategic control of the north, even though we didn't realise the importance. They had to get us out of the mix, which would in turn weaken your hand.'

'What was so important in the north?' the woman from the UN asked.

'Artemis,' Miska told them. She gave them a moment to let that settle in. Watched the dawning realisation on their faces.

'So this was just another Small Gods family squabble?' the UN conflict inspector asked.

'Not quite,' Miska said, and then turned to Councillor Omiata. 'We won the war, so we get the combat pay and expenses due us.'

Omiata regarded her coolly and then looked to Salik.

'Fair is fair,' he told the councillor.

'Why do I get the feeling that our victory is coming with something of a caveat?' Omiata asked.

Miska explained what New Sun had been up to, their plans to turn Ephesus into one huge manufacturing facility for weaponised biotech. She also told them about Artemis's plan to destroy all technology on the moon, and effectively cut it off from the rest of humanity.

'And you call this winning the war?' Omiata asked. Oddly she sounded more amused than angry or upset.

'Better than the alternative,' Raff suggested.

'Artemis is happy to live with those of your people who wish to stay,' Miska said.

'Technology can be as much a curse as a boon sometimes,' Omiata said. 'I'm sure many will stay.'

'I suspect she'll allow some of the older tech to work. You may also find that she introduces her own kind of tech. Be careful. Whatever she is, she believes she's a goddess. She may only want to bestow her bounty on those who worship her.'

Omiata pursed her lips. 'Thank you for the warning, Colonel.

Frankly we have enough gods of our own. We don't need another one.' Then she looked at the shaking, sweat-covered Campbell and just shook her head sadly. She stood up, nodded to Salik and turned to look at Miska. Miska couldn't shake the feeling that there was just a hint of sympathy in her otherwise inscrutable expression.

Campbell stood up as well. 'Well, as you can imagine I need to return to the—' he started.

'Stay where you are,' Salik demanded. He turned to the woman from the UN.

'I think the best thing to do is to call the *Teten* in,' the UN conflict inspector said. 'I have the authority to give them jurisdiction as peacekeepers. They can take the New Sun staff and the Triple S command ...'

It hurt so much because of her broken arm that she actually screamed in pain but Miska grabbed Campbell and threw him out of a window. It was a different one to the window that Duellona had jumped out of.

'Miska!' Salik complained. The woman from the UN was staring at her. Miska gestured towards the newly broken window with her thumb.

'You all saw that, right?' she asked. 'He was alive when he left the room.'

Outside, Campbell was trying to crawl away on two broken legs, the result of his four-storey fall. Kaneda, Mass and Hemi fell in with her and Corenbloom as they left Salik's house. Raff went his own way.

Miska shot Campbell twice in the back of his head as she walked past him. One more murder hardly seemed to matter, after all. She heard Mass laugh.

CHAPTER 22

They had actually cheered when Miska and the others walked out onto the *Hangman's Daughter*'s hangar deck. She'd put bombs inside their heads, forced them to train like marines and then put them in harm's way, and yet they'd cheered when she walked on board. She felt pressure behind her artificial eyes. Nothing brought people together like an external enemy that they really hated.

Most of the Offensive, Sneaky, and Heavy Bastards were there in full combat gear, as were a great deal of the support staff and a few new faces. The Armoured Bastards were there in the remaining, still-functioning Machimoi. Cargo exoskeletons had only just started clearing away the makeshift barricades they had been using as defensive positions. It seemed that the Bastard Legion, or at least about two companies' worth of them, had been ready to repel boarders. She could see the surviving members of the Nightmare Squad milling around as well.

Her dad was wearing the remaining stolen Cyclops war droid. He was busy organising the step-down now that the besieging forces were no longer outside the *Daughter*. She made for Vido first. She guessed that Golda was still tranced in to the CP at Camp Reisman. Vido was talking to the three Mafia old boys he liked to hang around with. She noticed that they were all in full combat gear as well. As she approached they walked away, throwing casual salutes her way. Vido saluted more smartly as she reached him. She returned the salute.

'What did you do, Major?' she asked by way of hello, glancing at the three wiseguys walking away.

'Ask me no questions ...' he said. Miska suspected it was force of habit.

'Just tell me this. You had to have net support. Who did you use?'

'Hypothetically, if I was to do the kind of thing that you're suggesting, I'd use Zaple,' he told her.

It could have been worse. Zaple himself was chickenshit. His annoying net icon alter-ego, however, was much less chickenshit.

'You did good,' she told him. 'We got paid, there's some rewards on the way. We'll make sure people get to sample the pleasures of Waterloo Station before we move on.'

'The war's over?' he asked.

'The war is over.'

Miska made her way across the busy hangar deck towards the Nightmare Squad. As she approached she could smell the acrid stench of the same anti-fungal chemical shower she'd had in the airlock before entering. Miska was gratified to see they were all stripping down and cleaning the kit they'd used on Ephesus. A shadow fell across her.

'Still leading from the front, Colonel?' her dad asked. She

wasn't sure if she detected disapproval emanating from the Cyclops or not. Miska looked up at him. He used the hand on one of the war droid's limbs to salute her. She still wasn't sure she liked that. She opened her mouth to explain it was circumstantial. In the end it required someone with her experience to lead what was, effectively, a special forces op.

'She has to.' It was Rufus Grig who'd spoken.

Miska was suddenly very much aware of Mass standing a little way off, watching them.

'Something to say, Sergeant?' her dad asked, the Cyclops head swivelling to look at the ex-SAS vigilante.

'With the best will in the world, we're not a military force. We're a well-armed, adequately trained prison gang. Doesn't matter what rank she needs to present herself to outsiders. If she can't lead from the front, if she isn't strong enough, then they won't respect her,' Grig continued. Miska was interested to note he said 'they' rather than 'we'. 'Most of us would kill her as soon as look at her if we got the chance.' Grig glanced at the Ultra but the prolific serial killer seemed busy spraying fungicide on his equipment. 'But we like her because she's always in the shit with the rest of us. Because she's the most fearless, the craziest of us, and she doesn't like people fucking with the Legion.'

It wasn't what her dad wanted to hear. It wasn't how military command worked, for a good reason. She glanced over at Mass. She remembered what he had said about Red. She might have been in command because of the N-bombs, but she wasn't the *Hangman's Daughter*'s 'daddy'.

'Something to add, Captain?' she asked. Mass took this as invitation to join them.

'Torricone?' he asked. That was exactly the conversation she didn't want to have publicly.

'What about him?' she asked.

'What's going to happen to him?'

'What gives you the right to ...' her dad started.

Miska held up her hand and her dad went quiet.

What gives him the right? she thought. *Everything that Grig had just said.* 'The UN is going to cut his head open. He's evidence of sequestration.'

'And then what?' Mass demanded.

'What do you want me to say, Mass? He does us the most use in the hands of the UN. New Sun removed his N-bomb when they sequestered him. The UN will probably give him over to the Barney Prime authorities where he'll either serve out the rest of his bid, or more likely get freed on appeal.'

'He needs to die,' Mass said. Miska wasn't sure whether Mass was actually angry with Torricone for defecting and for the fight they'd had, or not. Either way this was a power play. He was trying to weaken her position.

'I'm not declaring war on the UN,' she told him.

'Send him,' Mass said nodding at the Ultra. The Ultra looked up but didn't say anything.

'Don't tell me what to do,' Miska warned.

'Sorry, boss, all I'm saying is that there's a solution if you want it,' he told her. She could see that a number of the nearby legionnaires had stopped what they were doing to listen. 'I mean, if Torricone is subject to the same rules as the rest of us.' Mass was clearly playing to the audience now. She almost told him to learn how to make a quieter power play. Like Vido. But then it struck her that they were probably playing good *Mafiosi*, bad *Mafiosi*.

'Why wouldn't he be?' Miska asked, narrowing her eyes. She knew what was coming.

'Because you're in love with him,' Mass told her.

'You're way out of line,' her dad growled.

'We all know it,' Mass said.

'Even if I was, it's none of your fucking business,' Miska told him, trying not to think too much about watching Torricone get marched away by Salik's security, and the accompanying ache that memory brought. 'But I'll be honest, I don't think you're quite the observer of human behaviour you think you are.'

The Ultra stood up as Miska approached. She felt strong arms wrap around her as her own slid around his corded neck.

She kissed him because she was angry at Mass. She kissed him because nobody would try and shank the Ultra in the showers. She kissed him because he was pretty. Most importantly she kissed him because she wanted to. Despite the stench of chemicals he somehow tasted of spearmint. It started as a performance but she felt herself responding.

She broke the clinch to the sound of catcalls. There was something comedic about a Cyclops war droid not knowing quite where to look.

She couldn't help but smile. It was less than subtle but she knew it would take some of the wind out of Mass's argument. Then she saw the hurt expression on the Ultra's face.

She had stimmed herself to stay awake long enough to strip down and clean all her kit. Then another, more thorough, shower in fungicide. It made her skin stop itching. It burned instead. Finally she made it to a real shower. Then the exhaustion engulfed her and she started to really feel the pain from her various injuries, the ache from her muscles. Finally she allowed herself to think about Torricone and she slid down the wall to the floor in the shower room.

Miska awoke some sixteen hours later. She had managed to make it as far as her bunk aboard the *Little Jimmy* before she'd crashed. She was awoken by a blinking comms message in her IVD.

'What is it, Dad?' she asked across the comms link. She knew she couldn't go back to sleep. She had to follow up payment, authorise shore leave, see about getting the battle damage to the mechs fixed and the numerous other things that were involved in running your own private penal legion.

'Salik wants to see you,' her dad told her.

'Okay, tell him I'll come and see him when I get the chance.'

'He's outside.'

The airlock slid open. Miska frowned. Salik was there with one of his security detail and four of his ridiculous liveried servitor droids. Two were carrying ornate chairs, the third a similarly ornate table, and the fourth a picnic hamper.

'I initially thought canapés and champagne, but decided that a submarine sandwich and fine beer might be more appropriate,' Salik announced. They were sat in the middle of the otherwise empty hangar deck.

'You were right,' Miska said through a mouthful of sandwich, though she did like champagne. She hadn't realised how hungry she was. Salik was drinking tea and eating more refined sandwiches. They even had the crusts cut off. 'Would have thought you'd be pleased to see the back of me?'

Salik gave her question some thought.

'Well you have been ... difficult ... but I spend most of my working life trying to hide my revulsion of people like

Campbell ... I'm not sure I like what you do here but I also know that I profit from the misery of conflict so I am in no position to judge you, and you are refreshingly honest and straight forward.'

'Wow,' she said, and took a swig of her beer and then another mouthful of the sandwich. 'Thanks for the testimonial, but so?'

'I have a proposition for you,' he told her. 'Let me represent you as an agent. I can find you work. Find free ports that will accept the *Daughter*, run interference for you with the colonies, and find employers that otherwise wouldn't touch you. I can open up whole new markets for you, get you on preferred suppliers' lists.'

Miska stopped chewing, swallowed and took another swig of the beer. It was really good beer. It was certainly an attractive offer. It would take some of the worry out of wondering where the next job was coming from.

'Despite the ship, despite the number of inmates, I don't think we could muster more than two companies. We've got a few mechs and a few combat exoskeletons but we're short on vehicles, air support and shuttles. There are better equipped, and if I'm honest, more professional units out there. Why us?'

'Because you had considerably less than this when you started, because you play fair, because you scare people, and because I see a great deal of potential. With me as a mentor ...'

'You know I have an overabundance of paternalistic advisers here?' she asked.

'A poor choice of words,' he admitted with a degree of chagrin.

'Wouldn't it be a conflict of interest?'

'You would simply be a preferred supplier for conflicts I'm running, nothing unusual about that.'

'We get the final say on who we work for? I'm becoming asshole-averse.'

Salik looked a little pained. 'Ideally I will act as buffer between you and the assholes,' he told her, 'but yes, you would have final say.'

'Jobs we find ourselves?' she asked, thinking about Raff.

'I get no cut.'

'How much for the ones you get us?' she asked, narrowing her eyes as she took another bite of her sandwich.

'Twenty-five per cent,' he told her.

'Fuck off!' she said with a mouthful of bread, meat, cheese and peppers. 'Twenty-five for a series of conversations while we risk getting our asses blown off? Ten per cent.'

'Twenty.'

'Fifteen.'

Salik didn't look entirely happy.

'Agreed,' he finally said. 'I'm not sure how profitable this will be, but if nothing else it'll be interesting.'

They had talked about the evacuation of Ephesus for a little while. As Councillor Omiata had suspected, quite a few people had chosen to stay, including the councillor herself. Salik suspected that the Maasai colonists were already in contact with Artemis but nobody else was, so there was a panic, particularly from the various mercenary units, to get off-world before the lights were switched off.

After Salik had left, Miska had found herself sat on the deck leaning against the bulkhead close to one of the airlocks. She could make out the letters E and C scratched into the metal. She was sipping one of the beers that Salik had left behind.

She was aware of the guard droid's approach but she only

looked up when it crouched down next to her. It had a viz screen mounted on its head. It was one of the droids her dad used for PT, exhorting the legionnaires to greater effort through the medium of creative verbal abuse. At the moment, however, the image on the screen was that of a concerned father.

'Breakfast beer?' he asked. It was her third but she didn't feel like telling him that. 'You need to get that eye replaced.' The guard droid pointed at the eye patch dressing she wore over her left eye.

'I'll add it to my list of things to do.'

'You okay?'

'It was a rough one, Dad. I don't mind being shot at, stabbed, punched, kicked and strangled, but I didn't like the way they came after us on this one.'

'It's something you may have to get used to,' he told her.

'As long as people realise the consequences,' she said. Neither of them spoke for a few moments. Then she looked up at the screen. 'Come to tell me I handled this wrong?'

The image on the viz screen just shrugged. 'You're commanding unconventionally, but Grig has a point. I'm uncomfortable with the Nightmare Squad but you know that. Frankly, you were up against some pretty heavy odds and you lost a reasonably small amount of people.'

'If you don't include the sequestered,' she muttered.

'They made their choice. I heard you lost Nyukuti to friendly fire.'

'Someone sent Kasmeyer after me. And Hogg knew something. He knew you from the Occupation.'

'Me?' her dad asked.

'He was part of the resistance.'

'I never ...' he started. 'Edited memory.'

362

Miska just nodded

'You think someone killed Hogg?' he asked

'I had the Doc check his wounds,' Miska told her dad.

'Is that why Corenbloom pulled all the blades from the guys you went after Resnick with from the armoury?'

'Yes. Hogg was killed with a printed USMC pattern fighting knife—'

'Just like the kind we give to the legionnaires,' her dad finished.

'Kaneda, Grig, Kasmeyer, Hogg, Bean and Corenbloom all carried one. Everyone else had their own blade. Doc checked each of their blades against the wounds, no match.'

'Raff?' her dad asked.

'Nobody was paying that much attention but—'

'It's not a difficult knife for anyone in the Legion to get hold of, and you couldn't surveil them in Artemis's no-tech zone. I take it that Triple S didn't carry the same kind of blades?' he asked. Miska just shook her head. 'So an inside job?'

'Yeah, and one of the guys I've got investigating it is one of the suspects.' Though she was pretty sure that it hadn't been Corenbloom.

'And you think this is to do with me?' her dad asked. He sounded uneasy.

'I think all of it is, somehow. I mean it makes sense. Think of the circles we move in, the things we do and we ... I don't know ... we seem to keep bumping up against Mars, against the Small Gods.'

'When's this over?' her dad asked.

Miska looked up at the screen in surprise.

'You know when this is over. When I find the people who killed you.'

'And what about the people who ordered it, and their bosses, and their bosses. You going to kill everybody, Miska?'

Was she? Right now she just wanted to rest.

She had lain on top of one of the Centaur APCs and tranced in. She had done the bare minimum she had to get done on that particular day in the CP at Camp Reiman. It had mostly been admin stuff. She had made an appointment with a 'ware clinic that Salik had recommended, to get her eye replaced. Even doing the bare minimum, it had seemed like a long day. Having tranced out, looking up at the hangar deck's ceiling, she knew she needed some downtime, some time to heal and get back into a solid PT routine.

She sighed when she saw the blinking comms link. She opened it.

'You've got be fucking kidding me!' she snapped. She rolled off the top of the APC and landed on the deck, crouched like a cat. She howled in pain. In her anger she had forgotten just how bashed up she was. She managed to recover enough to storm across the hangar deck, relieved that she was armed.

The exterior airlock door hissed open.

'Seriously, have you got a death wish?' Miska demanded.

'We need to talk,' Torricone told her.

Shit, shit, shit, shit, shit, shit! Miska thought. *Such a bad idea!*

Torricone was curled up against her back, asleep, his arm draped over hers in her cramped bunk on the *Little Jimmy*.